P9-DIH-070

She released her
dreams into the wind...
and they found their
way into his heart.

continued . . .

Indigo Blue

"A marvelous, moving, poignant, and sensual love story. . . .
Ms. Anderson holds her readers spellbound."
— *Romantic Times*

Early Dawn

"Never stinting on the harsh reality inherent in the setting,
the author tempers the roughness with a powerful love story
and remarkable characters. She draws out every emotion and
leaves readers with a true understanding of life and love."
— *Romantic Times*

Comanche Heart

"Highly sensual and very compelling . . . a truly spectacular
read." — Linda Lael Miller

Star Bright

"Catherine Anderson brilliantly grabbed my attention right
away with a brainy tale of intrigue . . . an emotionally moving and romantic treat that you're sure to enjoy."
— Night Owl Romance (Top Pick)

Morning Light

"This is a story not to be missed. *Morning Light* delivers on
all levels and is a fantastic read that will touch readers at
the very core of their being."
— The Romance Readers Connection

Sun Kissed

"This smart, wholesome tale should appeal to any fan of
traditional romance." — *Publishers Weekly*

Summer Breeze

"The kind of book that will snare you so completely, you'll
not want to put it down. It engages the intellect and emotions; it'll make you care. It will also make you smile . . . a
lot. And that's a guarantee." — Romance Reviews Today

My Sunshine

"With the author's signature nurturing warmth and emotional depth, this beautifully written romance is a richly rewarding experience for any reader." —*Booklist*

Bright Eyes

"Offbeat family members and genuine familial love give a special lift to this marvelous story. An Anderson book is a guaranteed great read!" —*Romantic Times* (Top Pick)

Blue Skies

"Readers may need to wipe away tears . . . since few will be able to resist the power of this beautifully emotional, wonderfully romantic love story." —*Booklist*

Only by Your Touch

"Ben Longtree is a marvelous hero whose extraordinary gifts bring a unique and special magic to this warmhearted novel. No one can tug your heartstrings better than Catherine Anderson." —*Romantic Times* (Top Pick)

Always in My Heart

"Emotionally involving, family-centered, and relationship oriented, this story is a rewarding read." —*Library Journal*

Sweet Nothings

"Pure reading magic." —*Booklist*

Phantom Waltz

"Anderson departs from traditional romantic stereotypes in this poignant, contemporary tale of a love that transcends all boundaries . . . romantic through and through."
—*Publishers Weekly*

SILVER THAW

A MYSTIC CREEK NOVEL

Catherine Anderson

A SIGNET BOOK

SIGNET
Published by the Penguin Group
Penguin Group (USA) LLC, 375 Hudson Street,
New York, New York 10014

USA | Canada | UK | Ireland | Australia | New Zealand | India | South Africa | China
penguin.com
A Penguin Random House Company

First published by Signet, an imprint of New American Library,
a division of Penguin Group (USA) LLC

First Printing, January 2015

ISBN 978-0-451-41834-0

Printed in the United States of America
10 9 8 7 6 5 4 3 2 1

This book is dedicated to my great-niece, Nichole Meyerott, her daughter, Rowan, and her wonderful husband, Bryan. When I think of you, I'm always reminded of the wonderful Fourth of July that we shared as a family before Rowan made her debut. What a delight it was later to see Nichole rock her daughter in Grandma Mary's chair. Through so many generations, the love has endured.

I would also like to thank Rosie Blake for sharing so much information about her Lincoln ewe, Marble, whose wool froze to the ice and was jerked out when she stood up. From Rosie I learned about sheep jackets and about the lifelong mating of mourning doves. The doves you will meet in this story actually frequented Cinnamon Ridge for several years.

Much appreciation also goes to Kate Allen, my helper, who researched heavy plastic knives sturdy enough to be used as lethal weapons, watched police pat-down procedures with me online, and knew how people can use credit cards to make cash withdrawals from ATM locations. No matter how crazy it gets at our house, Kate always greets a challenge with good cheer.

I will also be forever grateful to Julia Ashton, my adoptive sister and personal assistant, who is always there for me, through thick and thin. I don't know what I'd do without her.

Last but not least, I want to thank Father James Radloff, who, by example, taught me and so many others how to keep our faith even when it may seem that all hope is lost. He is a phoenix who rose from the ashes to triumph over adversity at Holy Communion Catholic Church in Bend, Oregon.

Prologue

A brisk November night breeze lashed the pines and bushes that surrounded Amanda Banning's front yard. It caught at the strip of pink paper between her upraised fingers and whipped it away, tumbling it into the darkness. Amanda likened releasing the strip to sending messages in a bottle, only hers were sent on the wind, a practice born a month earlier out of isolation and the relentless silence after her six-year-old daughter, Chloe, had gone to bed. Amanda couldn't afford a television, and the clock radio she'd purchased at Good As New on West Main had lousy reception. Amanda doubted the problem was with the device; rather, she suspected it was that her home was surrounded by too many trees. Occasionally, when atmospheric conditions were just right, she could find a station and enjoy some music that didn't crackle, but mostly she picked up white noise.

The nightly silence had grown oppressive, driving home to Amanda just how alone in the world she was. Sending messages on the wind gave her a sense of connection with others, and a way to express her thoughts and yearnings instead of keeping them pent up inside.

She smiled and pulled her flimsy jacket close to hold the cold at bay. She didn't really care if anyone read her notes. No one would ever know who wrote them, after all, and that was liberating. She could write anything she wanted, no matter how silly or serious. It helped, writing them. She wasn't sure why, but it did.

Tonight her messages had been goofy. She'd recently walked with Chloe into the town of Mystic Creek and gotten a library card, which allowed her to borrow storybooks for her daughter and romance novels for herself. Why she felt drawn to love stories, Amanda didn't know. She hung on the words written by authors such as Jodi Thomas, Susan Wiggs, Emilie Richards, and countless others. Nearly eight years in a nightmarish marriage should have forever banished romantic notions from her head. Maybe, she reflected, it was true that hope springs eternal in the human breast, because there remained within her a deep, aching need to be loved and cherished.

So tonight she'd written, *I wish I could meet a man as kind and wonderful as the hero in one of the romances I love to read, someone who'd be a fabulous father to my little girl and make both of us feel safe.* Normally Amanda wished for far more practical things, like enough money to pay her electric bill, but she was halfway through a story, and she was falling madly in love with a character named Jake. Amanda's only question was, do men like that really exist? Her rational side always answered that question with an unequivocal no, but she couldn't deny her yearning to think otherwise. *Dumb, dumb, dumb.* She'd be better off to believe in Santa Claus and strike the word *man* from her vocabulary. In her experience, *man* usually became *manhandle.*

Sighing, Amanda looked at the sky, hoping to see stars,

but it was too overcast. *Probably snow clouds.* So far, she hadn't found a snow shovel at any of the three second-hand shops she'd searched. She and Chloe would have to wade through the white stuff until she found an afford-able scoop. Problem: Chloe had no waterproof boots. Why hadn't she checked out the winter weather in Mystic Creek before she picked this town as their hiding place?

She shrugged and said aloud, "Because you couldn't afford bus fare for two to anywhere else, and Mystic Creek defines the term *out in the middle of nowhere.* Mark will look for you in Olympia, Washington, not cen-tral Oregon."

Blinking at the sound of her own voice, Amanda went back inside, locked the door, and fastened the chain guard. She didn't believe the chain would keep out an anemic sparrow, but it might buy her enough time to grab the cast-iron skillet that she kept handy on the kitchen table. She made her rounds of the house, checking to be sure the back entrance and all the windows were locked. In Chloe's room, she lingered to smooth her sleeping daughter's dark hair, so very like her own, back from her forehead and bent to press a kiss to her upturned nose.

Chloe stirred in her sleep and cried, "No, Daddy, no! Leave Mommy alone! Don't hurt her! Stop!"

Amanda's heart twisted. Since she'd left her husband, Mark, Chloe's nightmares had mostly abated, but every once in a while the child woke up screaming. Amanda sat on the bed and gathered Chloe in her arms. "It's only a dream, sweetness. Daddy isn't with us anymore. We're far, *far* away from him. He can't hurt us anymore."

Chloe shuddered and hugged Amanda's neck. "You were on the kitchen floor, and he was kicking you with his boots."

Amanda recalled that night, and it troubled her that Chloe was reliving it in her sleep. "It's okay. I'm fine. We ran away, remember?"

Chloe pressed close to Amanda's body. Minutes passed before she drifted off to sleep again. As Amanda tucked Chloe back under the covers, she whispered, "Have sweet dreams, darling. Only beautiful, wonderful dreams."

Beautiful dreams. That had become Amanda's mantra to herself each night before she fell asleep, for she often jerked awake from nightmares, too, her heart pounding and her body drenched with sweat. She was coming to accept that no matter how far she ran, she might never feel safe.

Moments later, Amanda, still wearing her jacket, huddled on the worn old sofa near the single lamp to read more of her library book. *Jake.* She grinned as she drew a blanket around her for extra warmth. No man on earth would pick wildflowers and leave little bouquets on a woman's porch as he had. *Get real.* But Amanda enjoyed losing herself in the fantasy anyway. It sure beat what she knew about reality.

Chapter One

Jeb Sterling swore under his breath as he trudged across his steer pasture, snatching up litter. Small pieces of pink paper decorated the grass, looking like overblown clover blossoms. They were everywhere. Why had someone chosen to toss trash from a car window in front of *his* place? Jeb took pride in his property and spent hours each summer at the business end of a Weedwacker. His fencing, made of metal pipe that he'd welded together, always sported immaculate white paint. The landscaping he'd done around his house could be featured in *Better Homes and Gardens*. He did *not* appreciate some jerk using his land as a garbage dump.

Stalking around the enclosure, Jeb grumbled aloud as he picked up the pink slips and crushed them in one hand. As he captured the sixth before it fluttered away, his anger changed to bewilderment. *What the hell?* Somebody had written a note on this one. Smoothing the damp, wrinkled strip, Jeb read aloud, "'I wonder how much money I need to buy a decent used car. I don't care if it looks awful as long as it runs. Walking back and forth to work in this cold weather is the pits.'"

Frowning, Jeb collected more pink strips from the pasture, then found a few more on his front lawn, and another in his driveway. He took the lot inside and sat at his custom-made dining room table, which he'd designed to seat twelve, twenty with inserts, similar to tables once common among large farm families.

Pushing a hank of blondish brown hair off his forehead, he smoothed the notes flat. *I wish I could find secondhand winter boots for my little girl. I can't afford new ones, and my boss says we'll soon have deep snow.* Jeb shook his head. Winter boots for a kid didn't cost all that much. Or did they? Thirty years old and determined to stop counting birthdays, Jeb remained a bachelor and had no kids. He was not an expert on the cost of children's apparel. Maybe one of his younger brothers or sisters would get married and start reproducing soon. Then Jeb's parents might stop bugging him about settling down and providing them with a grandchild.

Judging by the handwriting, delicate and flowing, Jeb decided the notes had to be from a woman. Most guys he knew did a print-write thing.

The next note made him grin. *I wish I could meet a man as kind and wonderful as the hero in one of the romances I love to read, someone who'd be a fabulous father to my little girl and make both of us feel safe.* Jeb guessed this lady liked to read sappy love stories. His smile faded. Why did this woman and her child feel unsafe? And, hello, was he being targeted? He found it difficult to believe these messages had landed on his property by accident. Maybe this gal had seen him working outside and decided he looked like promising husband material.

No way, sister. Jeb wasn't that desperate. His mother kept telling him the lady of his dreams would cross paths with him right when he least expected it. But so far that hadn't happened, and Jeb was coming to accept that it probably never would.

Just then his dog farted. Jeb groaned and glanced over his shoulder. "Damn, Bozo, turn the air blue, why don't you?"

A brindle Fila Brasileiro mastiff, Bozo had a dark brown muzzle and ears, with a gold body that looked as if it had been splattered with different shades of mud. The dog woke from his nap, yawned, and then shook his head, sending strings of drool flying from his flapping jowls to decorate everything within a three-foot radius. When Bozo was younger, Jeb had raced around to clean up the drool immediately, but then he'd read online that once dried, it could be wiped easily from surfaces or vacuumed up.

"If I ever meet the right woman, she'll take one look at you and run screaming in the other direction. You know that, right?"

Bozo growled—his way of talking. Grinning, Jeb resumed reading the notes. *My only weapons are a cast-iron skillet and a butcher knife hidden under my mattress so my daughter won't find it. If my husband tracks us down, I pray that God will give me the strength to knock him out with the frying pan. I will die before I let him hurt my baby again.*

Bozo let loose with another fart. Flatulence was a trait of the mastiff that Jeb had overlooked when deciding on a breed. Waving a hand in front of his face, he wished he could lend this poor lady his dog, not to torture her with the less-than-aromatic delights, but for security. With Bozo on guard, she wouldn't need a heavy skillet for protection.

Jeb turned his attention to the next note. *Damn,* he thought. *This could become addictive.* He felt as if he were peering into someone's heart. This lady clearly had an abusive bastard for a husband, was as close to flat broke as a person could get, and, to top it all off, had a little girl she could barely support.

Jeb wondered once again if she was targeting his land with her notes. He thought of his cantankerous old neighbor across the road. Tony Bradley, who farmed full-time for a living, had a heart of gold that he tried hard to hide. *Time to take a stroll.* If Tony had found pink slips of paper on his land, then Jeb could relax. Jeb didn't like the idea that some desperate female had set her sights on him. Even if she had no car, she could walk by his land if she lived nearby.

Bozo went with Jeb to Tony's place. Mastiffs needed plenty of exercise, at least a thirty-minute walk each day, which Bozo got by following Jeb around as he tended to his livestock. Extra walking never hurt—although he tried to make sure his mastiff seldom ran. That was bad for the joints and hips of a dog that weighed two hundred and thirty pounds; also, mastiffs could easily become overheated, even in cold weather.

With the crops all harvested, old Tony was in "winter" mode, when he repaired his equipment, fed his animals, watched TV, and worked crossword puzzles. Jeb found him tinkering with his tractor, an ancient John Deere that had lost nearly all its identifying green and yellow paint and was probably worth more as an antique than Tony's whole farm was.

"Hey, Tony!" Jeb called out. "Got tractor problems?"

The old man resembled a stout stump with a two-day growth of whiskers and was dressed in tan Carhartt outerwear smudged with grease. He cast a cranky glare at Jeb. "Betsy never has problems. Kind of like a woman, son. All she needs is a little lovin' to keep her motor tuned."

Jeb drew to a stop near a front tire that was taller than his hip. Bozo chose that moment to shake his head and send drool flying. Just then, Mike, Tony's red tri Australian shepherd, bounded out from under the tractor. The two canines sauntered off to take turns pissing on every bush in sight.

"What brings you over?" Tony wiped his hands on a rag so greasy that it only smeared more oil onto his fingers. "If you haven't found a new cleaning lady and you're wantin' to hire my wife, you're out of luck. Mike sheds like a son bitch and I'm sloppy, so we keep Myrna pretty busy."

Jeb hadn't started looking for a new cleaning person since his last one had quit. "I'm between jobs right now." Jeb saw no need to elaborate. He and Tony had been neighbors long enough that the old man understood his on-and-off-again work schedule. Jeb had just finished a furniture order from a man who'd wanted a special Christmas gift for his wife, but otherwise it had been a slow season. "I figure I can muck out the house myself for a while. When the building market picks back up in February or March, I'll send out some feelers." He winked. "And I promise not to steal Myrna."

Tony, a tobacco chewer, leaned sideways to spit. "Good thing. She's got a hip goin' out on her, I'm afraid. Hurtin' her off and on."

Jeb hated to hear that. Myrna was a sweet gal and only sixty-three, a bit young to need a hip replacement. "I hope she gets to feeling better soon. A couple of months back, my mom hobbled around from pain in her hip." Kate Sterling's version of hobbling was to limp at a fast pace. "She was about to see Doc Hamilton when the discomfort went away."

"I see his partner, Dr. Payne." Tony chuckled. "Signed on with him out of curiosity. If I was a young doctor with a last name that sounds like *pain*, I'd get it changed."

"He may be young, but I've heard he's good," Jeb observed. "Maybe you should take Myrna to see him."

"Damned woman won't go. She's too stubborn by half, my Myrna."

Not sure what to say, Jeb whacked the frozen ground with the heel of his boot. Tony worshiped his wife and didn't share personal stuff unless he was truly troubled.

"So what brings you over?" Tony asked.

Jeb fished a handful of pink strips from his coat pocket and extended the crinkled lump. "Just wondering if you've found any of these on your land."

Tony squinted. "Son bitch. You gettin' those, too? Got my Myrna in a tailspin, I'll tell ya. She drives me half nuts tryin' to figure out who's writin' 'em. Has me lickin' my finger to test the wind direction."

Jeb stuffed the notes back in his pocket. "I didn't consider the possibility that they floated into my place on the wind. How many have you and Myrna found?"

"A good twenty." Tony spat again, narrowly missing Bozo, who'd come to lie at Jeb's feet. "I got my theories on it, if you don't mind me sharin'. The writer is a female, and she's lonely. Has no friends. Works as a cook somewhere and makes barely enough to scrape by. Also yearnin' to find herself a man. In one message, she wished for Prince Charming to carry her and her child away on a white steed to live happily ever after."

"Really." Jeb recalled the note about the woman's wish to find a hero. "She must be having a hard time of it."

"And she's probably uglier than a fence post if she's that desperate."

Jeb thought about it and decided Tony might be right. A beautiful woman didn't normally have to search for a man to rescue her. Men stood in line to apply for the job. Not that Jeb cared if this gal was homely. She clearly needed a friend. He tried and failed to imagine having nobody to talk to. He'd grown up in Mystic Creek and couldn't go into town without seeing someone he knew. He also had heaps of family here.

"Well," he said, "I'm glad to hear the notes aren't landing only on my property."

Tony laughed. "You're safe. I haven't asked our neighbors if they've found any, but you can rest assured, as many as we've gotten, you aren't bein' singled out."

Jeb studied the clouds. "Looks like snow tonight."

Tony nodded. "Myrna says there's a bastard storm front moving toward us."

Jeb ended the conversation the way he and Tony always did, by walking away. He and Tony said only what needed to be said. Polite farewells weren't part of their repertoire.

Bozo lumbered alongside Jeb's left flank. Three rounds of obedience training had paid off. Well, mostly. Sometimes Jeb got the impression that Bozo believed the obedience classes had been for Jeb. Nevertheless, the dog had good manners and mostly did as he was told. That was a good thing. Mastiffs could be difficult if not properly raised.

When you owned a mastiff, being in control was important. Bozo was gentle and well socialized, so his protective nature rarely showed itself. Early on, Jeb had made the mistake of leaving Bozo at home while he was out on a job, and the dog had eaten his sheep shed. Jeb had come home to half-consumed planks and a collapsed roof lying willy-nilly on the ground. Marble, his Lincoln ewe, had stood in her pen *baa*ing because her shelter was gone. Now Jeb rarely left Bozo alone. He was afraid his house might be targeted next. Bozo wasn't a bad dog, but he could be destructive when he got lonesome.

Lonesome. Jeb stopped in front of his log-and-timber ranch home and gazed off in all directions. Somewhere out there, probably within pitching distance, a very lonely woman was writing messages and tossing them into the wind. The thought bothered Jeb. He didn't care if she was the homeliest female who'd ever breathed—if she needed a friend, he'd happily apply for the job. Nobody deserved to be so unhappy.

As he climbed the inlaid paver steps leading to the front door, he glimpsed yet another pink slip tangled in a holly bush. Curiosity got the better of him. What did she have to say this time? He pricked his thumb retrieving the note. Sucking on the injured digit, he read the damp missive. *I wish I had a friend. I'd make chocolate chip cookies, my favorite, and hot chocolate, and we'd sit at my table to talk. I need to talk. Nobody special required. I just need to have a conversation with another adult. I see people at work, but that isn't the same.*

Jeb turned to gaze into the distance once again. *Where are you, lady?* The wind in this country gusted in all directions, coming in from the south during the late afternoon and evening. The sudden shifts made message tracking an inexact science. Huckleberry Road, where he lived, ran parallel to Bearberry Loop and Elderberry Lane, where most of the residences sat on one-acre parcels. Why Elderberry was called a lane, Jeb didn't know. It was nothing more than a dirt road that never got plowed or graded unless a neighbor took the initiative.

Once inside, Jeb sent his baseball cap sailing toward his handcrafted juniper coat tree. *Missed by a foot.* Tomorrow he'd have to dust the hat off because it'd be covered with dog hair. Contrary to what he had implied to Tony, he wasn't keeping up with the cleaning as well as he'd like. He was fussy about his house. *Thanks, Mom.* Kate Sterling was a meticulous housekeeper, and she'd passed on at least some of her obsessions to every kid. Jeb had inherited the kitchen and bathroom manias; he had to have a sterile place to cook and to brush his teeth. Now the rest of the house was going to hell, and that was starting to bug him, too. Cleaning spree tomorrow, he decided. He'd knock it out in about four hours and be good for another couple of weeks, if he could teach Bozo to stop shedding.

"Fat chance of that." He reached down to pat his dog's head. "That lady needs a dog to talk to. You're all the company I need."

But as Jeb prepared dinner—he loved to cook—he had to admit that as great a listener as Bozo was, Jeb rarely went a day without talking to other adults. His mom called daily. His two sisters, real chatterboxes, bugged him about three times a week. His three brothers called fairly often— even Jonas, who was away at college. And, of course, his dad, Jeremiah, rang him occasionally.

Guy conversations were simple, no chitchat required. *How you doing*? Good. *Just calling to check in.* All's fine on my front. How about you? *I'm fine.* After that, the call usually ended with, "Love ya." Jeb appreciated the brevity. That wasn't the case with his mother and sisters, who had to fill him in on friends, gossip about a neighbor, or a great sale at Macy's in Bend. He hadn't minded the time Sarah had called him crying because her hair was striped with green. Jeb had found that interesting, a dye job and weave gone bad. What the hell was a *weave*, anyway? And why did Sarah, who had perfectly nice hair the same toffee color as his, feel a need to streak it with different shades of blond or red that could come out the wrong color? Jeb preferred to go with what God had given him.

Jeb began chopping vegetables for a stir-fry. He tossed chunks of raw carrot, celery, broccoli, and cauliflower over his shoulder to Bozo, keeping the onions and garlic for himself. Bad stuff for dogs. Something about causing their bone marrow to stop producing red blood cells.

Behind him, he heard Bozo gnawing on the safe stuff. Dinner preparation was *their* time. He'd been feeding the dog vegetables since he was a pup, and he'd become a greenie gobble gut. Not a bad thing, according to the vet. Jeb made a quick pot of rice in his electric pressure cooker, whipped up some broth gravy, and took a seat at the round kitchen table to devour his meal while Bozo crunched on his evening kibble.

Afterward, Jeb tidied up the kitchen and sat back down at the table with a measure of brandy to have a long discourse with Bozo about the mysterious writer of the pink slips. In between Jeb's sentences, Bozo growled, his way of replying. Jeb followed the rules of polite exchange and didn't speak until Bozo had had his say.

Their conversation ended when Jeb finished his

brandy. As he and Bozo sauntered toward the down-stairs master suite, Jeb said, "That poor woman needs a mastiff like you, one who talks. We've had a perfectly fine conversation."

I'm dreaming. It's just a dream, Amanda told herself, only no matter how she tried to wake up, she couldn't. *Mark.* He'd locked his arm around her throat and held a partially loaded revolver to her temple as he described how her brains would look splattered all over the wall. The pressure against her larynx prevented her from speaking. All she could do was moan, quiver with terror, and pray the chamber would be empty when he pulled the trigger.

Click. The sound snapped Amanda to a sitting position in bed. The sheet was tangled around her legs. Her breath came in wheezy jerks. Perspiration ran in rivulets over her ribs. Even awake, she could still feel the strangling sensation in her throat. *Oh, God, oh, God.* She jerked at the bedding to free herself and staggered to the bathroom to empty her bladder. *Not real. Only a dream.* But telling herself that didn't help her to stop shaking. Too weak to stand, she remained on the commode until the nightmare released its hold on her.

The house seemed oddly bright as she left the bathroom. She went to a living room window, drew back the curtain, and saw at least a foot of snow outside. Though her heart sank, she had to admit it was beautiful. The never-used mailbox, mounted on a post at the edge of the front yard, looked like a loaf cake topped with fluffy white icing. Because she lived at the end of Elderberry Lane, a dead-end road, no cars had passed, leaving the carpet of snow undisturbed. In places it lay in powdery drifts. The boughs of the pine trees drooped under the weight. It was a winter wonderland.

If only she could stay inside and admire it. She turned up the thermostat to take the chill off before she woke Chloe for school. Half of the old baseboard heaters didn't work, and twenty minutes later, the house still felt cold. Chloe was tiny and thin. Amanda hated to expose her to icy drafts. Somehow she would keep the child wrapped in a blanket while she got her dressed. Otherwise Chloe's teeth would chatter as she ate her oatmeal and a roll that Amanda had brought home yesterday from Chloe's school cafeteria, where she worked. *Job perk*. At the end of each shift, Delores, the head cook, allowed her helpers to divide the leftovers. According to her, some law made it illegal to feed the kids day-old food. The portions Amanda received weren't haute cuisine, but they reduced her grocery bill each month, enabling her to make ends meet. Well, almost. The cost of electricity this month might break her.

As grim as their situation was, Amanda shoved away her memories of the nightmare and felt peace settle into her heart. At least Mark wasn't a part of this snowy picture. No angry outbursts, no blows, no furniture being thrown, no holes in the walls. As icky as the weather might be, Chloe would feel safe while they ate breakfast.

Amanda walked to her daughter's tiny bedroom, which she'd painted avocado, using what Landon Ramsey, the young owner of Sticks and Stones Building Supply, called a "residual" color. In regular-speak, that meant he'd mixed it for a customer who'd changed her mind and refused to purchase it. Amanda had figured she couldn't go wrong at five dollars a gallon—at least Chloe's room got clean walls. Amanda had decorated the room with thrift-store chic, buying curtains, a cute bedspread, and old throw rugs to cover the worn linoleum.

It wasn't a little girl's dream, but Chloe loved having her own bookshelf, purchased for a song at Second Time Around. The proprietor, a cute brunette with green eyes named Tally Tancy, didn't look old enough to operate a business, but her store, which offered large and small used appliances, plus furniture, seemed to be thriving. Tally delivered anywhere in town for twenty dollars, always accompanied by her Rottweiler mix, Nita, who went everywhere with a fresh knucklebone clamped between her teeth. Though rickety and banged up, Chloe's bookshelf had been dropped off for free, and it was now filled with books that had cost only a quarter apiece.

Flipping on the clown lamp on her daughter's bedside table, Amanda leaned over to say, "Surprise, surprise, sweetheart. It snowed last night!"

Chloe blinked open her chocolate brown eyes, so very like Amanda's own. With a squeal of delight, she scrambled from bed to peer out her ice-encrusted window. Amanda grabbed a blanket and draped it around the child's shoulders.

"Isn't it pretty?" she asked.

Chloe nodded. Then she frowned. "We still don't have snow boots, Mommy. Our feet will get wet walking to the bus stop."

"Nope! Remember those bread sacks I've been saving? They'll keep your feet dry."

Chloe shoved a hank of curly hair out of her eyes. "But, Mommy, nobody at school wears bread sacks for boots. My friends will laugh at me."

"Got it covered." Amanda gave the child a hug. "When we get to the bus stop, I'll walk around to flatten the snow, and you can take the sacks off before the bus comes."

Chloe reached up to touch Amanda's cheek. "Are you going to wear bread sacks while you walk to work?"

Amanda suspected that she'd slip and fall if she tried, but she would wear them as far as the bus stop so Chloe wouldn't worry all day about her mother wearing wet running shoes. "Absolutely! Maybe I'll start a new fashion fad."

Chloe giggled. Amanda left her to admire the snow while she gathered her daughter's clothing. Then, working as quickly as possible, she helped her get dressed. Thanks to Mystic's Good as New and the Vintage Boutique, the child had nice, warm outfits, and this coming Saturday, Amanda would walk with Chloe to town and buy her some snow boots at Charlie's Sporting Goods, whether she could afford them or not.

Jeb was feeding his stock when he found two more slips of pink paper. *Damn.* This gal didn't need a phone to be a chatterbox; she managed just fine with a pen. *My little girl still has no boots, and it's going to snow. I'll keep her feet dry somehow. She'll take sick if she sits in class all day tomorrow with wet feet.* The next note read, *Our heaters are awful. Half of them don't work, and the house is like an ice cube.* Jeb wondered what kind of heaters she had. Probably malfunctioning baseboard or wall mounts, neither of which would produce heat efficiently. *Shit.* Just what this lady needed—an electric bill the size of Bozo.

Jeb trudged through the snow with his meandering dog, who had to mark every shrub and fence post he encountered. More pieces of paper had caught on bushes and become frozen stiff. They'd drifted in last night, probably on the south wind. Jeb turned in that direction. A few other houses were located farther south on Huckleberry. Maybe she lived right on his road. *Nope.* He'd never seen a woman walking to work along Huckleberry.

While he forked hay, he pictured the surrounding terrain and the thoroughfares that ran parallel to one another. Trying to pinpoint where the woman might live, he voted for Elderberry. It curved toward the end, putting some of those houses directly south of his and Tony's land. She apparently worked the day shift somewhere. Maybe he'd get in his truck tomorrow morning and cruise Elderberry until nine, keeping his eye out for a woman afoot. Was it beyond all possibility that she was a knockout?

Well, hell, I'm really losing it. His only consolation was that his neighbors were also curious about the message writer. He chuckled as he pictured Tony, at Myrna's urging, licking his finger to test the wind. Jeb was tempted to do it himself. *That isn't happening.* As curious as Jeb was about the woman's identity, he wasn't about to declare the pink slips of paper "finger-lickin' good."

Chapter Two

The next two weeks passed quickly for Amanda. On Saturday after receiving her bimonthly paycheck and tallying her cash to make sure she could pay the electric bill, she took money out of her car fund and walked with Chloe into Mystic Creek to buy the child a pair of snow boots, pink if possible. After crossing Elderberry Bridge to the town center, which featured a fountain and was surrounded by shops, Amanda gave Chloe a penny to make a wish. As the child tossed the coin, Amanda sent up a silent prayer for a windfall, or even just a bit of good luck. *Two wishes for the price of one.*

Because of the cold, Amanda allowed Chloe to admire the natural pedestrian bridge only from afar; it was a gorgeous arch of moss-covered rock that over the centuries the rushing water had worn into a tunnel. Chloe loved the legend about the bridge, that when a man and woman met on its path, they would find true love. The girl wanted to visit the bridge every time they walked to town, hoping that her mother might meet the man of her dreams.

Not today. Amanda hustled the child along the south

side of East Main, appreciating, as always, the antiquated two-story storefronts with either living quarters or extra storage on the upper levels. Most of the shops had unique names: Simply Sensational Fragrances and Beyond, owned by a lovely older lady, Mary Alice Thomas; the Shady Lady, which Amanda surmised offered sexy apparel and bedroom toys; and the Silver Beach Salon, operated by a young woman in her late twenties named Crystal Malloy, who changed her hair color nearly as often as Amanda did her socks. There were also the Pill Minder, recently purchased by Drake Mullin, who Amanda guessed was in his early thirties; Healthful Possibilities, run by Taffeta Brown, who looked about twenty-five; A Cut Above, another hair place; and catty-corner across the street from Charlie's, Chopstick Suey Chinese Eatery and the Jake 'n' Bake.

The slogan under Charlie's store sign read, "If we don't have it, we'll order it," and the interior of the building bore out that promise; the narrow aisles were crammed with everything imaginable. Amanda had to ask a young lady with sandy brown hair where the children's snow boots were located. Once she found them, she zeroed in on the cheapest brand.

When they unearthed a pink pair in the right size, Chloe cried, "Molly has pink boots, too! Now we can be twins!"

Amanda was pleased. Even these less expensive boots would set her back, but at least they wouldn't demolish her car fund.

Before leaving the store, Amanda insisted that Chloe don her new footwear, and she stowed the child's school shoes in her ever-present backpack. Without a car, Amanda had learned that grocery shopping—or any other on-foot activity—required more carrying capacity than her arms alone could provide.

After leaving Charlie's, Chloe pleaded with Amanda for a visit to the Mystic Creek Menagerie, a gigantic circular structure, once a sawmill but now converted into a mall. The center focal point was a slowly revolving round-table restaurant. Chloe yearned to eat on what she called "the merry-go-round."

"Not today, sweetie." The prices at Dizzy's Roundtable Restaurant, run by Tony Chavez, made Amanda dizzy just looking at them. "But buying snow boots does call for a celebration! How about lunch at Taco Joe's?"

Chloe clapped her hands. "I love Taco Joe's!"

So did Amanda. Eating there didn't cost an arm and a leg.

As they once again crossed the town center, Amanda caught the delicious aromas drifting from Pecks' Red Rooster Restaurant, Mystic Creek's one fine-dining establishment. The owners, Chris and Kimberly Peck, had built the restaurant to optimize views of the creek and natural bridge, and though Amanda had heard from her boss that the Pecks were generous people, she doubted their menu prices reflected their largesse.

After a fun lunch at the taco place, with the owner, handsome young Joe Paisley, capping off the meal with complimentary root beer floats, they began the long walk home. As Chloe chattered, Amanda's mind drifted. She was jerked from her mental meandering when Chloe said, "Taco Joe is really cute. Maybe someday you'll meet him on the bridge!"

Amanda smothered a startled laugh. "Maybe so," she said. But a man wasn't really the answer to her problems.

She was still married, a concept Chloe didn't yet comprehend.

On the way home, Chloe's new boots leaked. *You get what you pay for*. Still, the poor quality irked Amanda. Not that she could blame Charlie Ramsey. At least he carried items for those who couldn't afford better.

On Monday morning, she stowed Chloe's regular shoes in her school backpack and slipped bread sacks over the child's feet before putting on the boots, hoping that the plastic would help keep Chloe's socks dry as they trudged to the bus stop. She thanked God for small blessings when it worked.

A little over a week before Thanksgiving, on a Monday afternoon, Amanda was surprised when, just after lunch cleanup, a time set aside for the cafeteria team to do next-day prep, Delores announced that she was letting everyone off early.

"School is closing early, too," she explained.

Amanda's heart sank. Normally her shift ended well before Chloe, attending first grade in the same building, hopped on a bus, giving Amanda time to reach the drop-off point before Chloe did.

"The forecast says an ice storm will hit sometime tonight, with temperatures as low as minus thirty," Delores continued. "Right now, freezing rain is falling on top of the accumulated snow, which is turning it to solid ice. It'll be dangerous getting home, and I'm guessing if the storm actually hits, school will be canceled tomorrow."

Again, Amanda's heart took a plunge. She got paid only for the hours she worked, and received no health benefits. She couldn't survive if the school stayed closed for long.

Mary Lou Hansen, another assistant, with kinky red hair and merry blue eyes, said, "I don't think I've ever seen it that cold in Mystic, and I've lived here all my life!"

The gray in Delores's brown hair, twisted into a French roll, gave testimony to the twenty years she had on her helpers. Wiping her hands on a chef's apron that barely covered her belly, she fixed a solemn blue gaze on them and said, "Back in the eighties it got that cold, or at least close. Living in Mystic Creek ain't for sissies." She took her apron off and tossed it in the laundry basket. "Andy finished up early and has our car heating." Delores's husband was the school janitor. "Anyone interested can divide the leftovers. If the power goes off, you'll have no way to heat them without a gas stove, but if you're low on groceries, cold food beats nothing."

Amanda wasn't one of those lucky few who had a propane range, and she was always low on groceries. As she and Mary Lou began divvying up the food into containers that they washed and brought back each morning, she prayed the power wouldn't fail. She and Chloe would freeze without electricity to heat their ramshackle rental.

As Amanda left the cafeteria with farewells and be-safe wishes, she dreaded her mile-plus journey home. *My own fault, having to walk.* She'd never told Delores or her coworkers that she had no car because she didn't want them to feel obligated to give her rides. Amanda had also feared that she wouldn't get the job if the school board learned she had no vehicle, so she'd lied on her application. It wasn't really a falsehood; she had two legs that provided her with reliable transportation.

Freezing rain. Not only would it hurt when the bits of

ice hit her face and bare hands, but it would also be cold. And slick. She absolutely could not slip and fall. Her tight budget left no room for an injury that would make her miss work.

Outside, Amanda hid in an alcove and waited until she heard Mary Lou's vehicle leave the parking lot. A sense of urgency bubbled at the base of her throat, a need to connect up with Chloe, but she couldn't risk being seen on foot.

When the sound of Mary Lou's engine died away, Amanda stepped carefully out of her hiding place. The concrete walkway and the recently plowed asphalt, now covered in a sheet of ice, were so slick that she could barely stay standing. *Oh, God.*

Amanda picked up her pace as much as she could. Chloe would be frightened if Amanda wasn't at the corner to meet her.

Thirty minutes later, Amanda crossed the East Sugar Pine Bridge. In the distance, she saw Chloe standing like a forlorn waif at the end of Elderberry, where the school bus had dropped her off. She waved and called out what she hoped was a reassuring hello.

"Stay right where you are, baby. I'll be there in just a minute!"

Amanda was shuddering with cold by the time she reached her daughter, whose teeth were clacking like castanets. Grabbing Chloe's hand, she guided the child over the slick ground toward the house, fairly certain that she looked like an inebriated ice skater to the many neighbors along Elderberry Lane.

After a long soak together in the ancient claw-foot tub filled with piping-hot water, Amanda dressed Chloe in double layers before putting on her own clothes. Then she grabbed blankets from her bed and led the way to the kitchen, where she wrapped the girl in worn fleece and deposited her on a chair.

Standing at the sink, Amanda gazed out at the frozen world beyond the frosty glass. Her heart squeezed with dread. She considered going to a motel, but that would cost money she couldn't spare, and the conditions outside were too dangerous for pedestrians. If a vehicle spun out of control, she and Chloe might be hurt. The safest option was to stay put and pray that the power stayed on.

Just then, the small house filled with the deafening sound of sleet hitting the roof. Startled, Chloe jumped up, tripped on her blanket, and would have fallen if Amanda hadn't caught her.

"Whoa, whoa, whoa," Amanda said as she sat down on an old dinette chair and drew her daughter onto her lap. "It's only frozen rain."

Chloe stared at the ceiling as if she expected it to collapse on top of them. "It sounds like marbles hitting."

"Yes, it does." Amanda raised her voice to be heard over the din. "I'd say it's turned to hail. Hail can be as big as marbles, and it makes a very loud sound on roofs. Let's have a snack and then we'll sing songs so the noise doesn't bother us."

During the summer, when he had a vegetable garden to shield from frost, Jeb checked the Weather Channel on his cell phone daily, but he seldom looked at a forecast during the winter. He preferred to take whatever came and be surprised. His mother, on the other hand, lived by the reports and called him at about eight that evening.

"That was one heck of a hailstorm we got earlier," Jeb said as a conversational starting point.

"That was only an appetizer," Kate warned him. "Before the night is over, it's going to get really bad. Is the heat lamp in your chicken coop wired to your backup generator? They're saying it could drop to thirty below."

Jeb couldn't remember Mystic Creek ever having temps that low. "Mom, only a fool or a weatherman tries to predict Oregon weather. For an accurate forecast, look out a window."

Kate Sterling made a disgruntled sound. "I mean it, Jeb. You need to get your livestock inside shelters, and if your coop isn't hooked up to your generator, you should bring all the chickens indoors."

Jeb gulped back a laugh. Only his mom would think to rescue his poultry. "No worries. I bought a generator that supplies all the outbuildings with emergency electricity. The animals and chickens should be fine."

After Jeb told his mom good-bye, he considered calling Tony to make sure he was locked down for a storm, but then he decided that the old man had been farming too many years to appreciate advice from some young fart across the road. So instead of dialing his neighbor, Jeb thought of his message writer. *His* message writer? When had he started to think of her that way? He looked out his kitchen window, once again wondering if she lived on Elderberry. She might be in for a cold night if the electricity went off. Jeb could only pray that didn't happen—and that she had a strong roof. His had taken a real beating earlier.

Nothing on television interested him, so he coaxed Bozo from his hiding place under the dining room table and turned in early to finish the espionage novel he'd been plowing through. Hail resumed thrumming on his second-story roof, which, as loud as it was, created a soothing drone downstairs. After reading the last page, he judged the book to be so-so. Yawning, he tossed the paperback onto his nightstand and turned off the light. He smiled when he felt the mattress sink beside him under Bozo's weight. The dog seemed to think Jeb wouldn't notice that he had a sleeping partner if he waited for darkness before jumping up.

At a little after ten, the hail stopped, giving Amanda's ears a rest. To stay warmer, she'd bedded down with Chloe on the sofa where the high-back cushions and padded arms offered more insulation than the beds. Nervy and restless because of the weather, she was driven from their warm nest to pace from room to room. At a window, she looked out at the silent, frozen landscape. There it was again, the feeling of being cut off from meaningful human contact. She slipped into the kitchen to write a few notes on pink paper, then braved the blasts of freezing wind on her porch to release her messages.

Afterward, she snuggled with Chloe on the couch to get warm again and retrieved her love story, drawing solace from Chloe's small, toasty body. A few minutes later, the house went suddenly dark. From the kitchen, she heard the old refrigerator's motor chug to a stop. *Thank goodness Chloe is asleep. The pitch-blackness might frighten her.* Groping her way to the kitchen, Amanda fetched the candle and matches she'd left on the table. She nearly lighted the taper but changed her mind. She had only this one, and she needed to use it sparingly. Careful not to trip in the dark, she pulled the blankets and comforters off both beds, and added them to the pile on the couch. With the power out, blankets and body heat were all they had to keep from freezing.

Within ten minutes, the drafty house became unbearably cold. Amanda collected more pillows, bath towels, and sheets from the linen closet to provide them with extra warmth. That helped, and clutching Chloe close against her, she finally fell asleep.

She had no idea how many hours passed before she was jerked awake by a loud popping noise in the kitchen, followed by the sound of gushing water. *Oh, no. The pipes!*

Shuddering, Amanda hurried to the other room. With trembling hands, she lighted the candle and squatted to open the cupboards beneath the sink, hoping she could stop the flood by turning off the valve. Her heart sank when she saw that the water was surging through a crack in the wall behind the curved PVC tubing. There was no way to turn off *that* gusher unless she ventured outside to the water main in the pump house. *Problem.* Her flashlight batteries were dead, and she had forgotten to get new ones. That left her with only the candle, which would be extinguished the instant she stepped outside. She'd be unable to find the water main in the darkness, and she might fall and injure herself if she tried.

Her first responsibility was to protect her child, which she would be unable to do if she went down on the ice and froze to death. After returning to the sofa, she concluded that the owner of this dump needed to address the problem. Fishing her cell phone from her pocket, she was relieved to see the screen light up and indicate a full charge. She dialed her landlord. All she got was a message machine. It was the middle of the night, after all. Then an awful thought struck her. *Maybe he's away to visit relatives over the holiday.* Hopefully not. Thanksgiving was more than a week away.

She slipped under the covers and held her daughter close, praying that her landlord would call her back before the entire house flooded.

A loud pounding on the front door jerked Jeb erect in bed. Wearing only sweatpants, he cursed as he hurried to the entry hall. Tony stood on his porch, and typical of him, he bothered with no greeting when Jeb answered his knock.

"Power went out last night. We need to form a team and go check on our neighbors. Not everyone has generators or a backup source of heat."

Jeb's generator had kicked on automatically, and being located at the back of his house outside the laundry room, it hadn't made enough noise to wake him. He rubbed the sleep from his eyes and blinked. Judging by the pale hint of light on the horizon, the full break of dawn was an hour away.

"What time is it, anyway?"

"Five thirty and time to get rollin'," Tony replied. "I've already called Pete. He's got a woodstove for heat, so his wife won't freeze to death while he's out helpin' others. And seein' you without a shirt is bad for my self-esteem. I must've been in the back row when muscles were handed out."

Jeb knew Pete, a fledgling farmer in his thirties. Chafing his hands, he invited his neighbor inside. "Can't help how my upper half looks. What's the temp out there?"

"Twenty below, and Myrna says it'll be even colder tonight."

Jeb shut the door. He was all for helping neighbors, but if he, Tony, and Pete meant to be effective, they'd need to divide the area into sections, gather emergency supplies, and keep in touch by cell phone in case one of them came up against a situation he couldn't handle alone.

Over coffee that Jeb made quickly at his built-in coffee center, the two men discussed a plan of action. When Jeb was asked which road he wanted to take, he said he'd cover Elderberry Lane. Bad of him, he guessed, but if his message writer lived on that road, maybe she'd get her wish and find a hero standing on her porch.

Jeb found himself thinking of the woman often. She sounded so isolated. He had wished a dozen times that he could figure out which house she lived in and knock on her door to ask if she would make those chocolate chip cookies for him. He'd driven Elderberry a few times early of a morning, and he'd only ever seen a dark-haired woman walking her little girl to the bus stop. In the glare of his headlights, she'd looked too pretty to be the message writer, and her child had been wearing pink snow boots, which the composer of the notes said she couldn't afford to buy. Nope. If a woman that pretty were in the market for a rescuer, she'd have no problem finding one.

Interrupting Jeb's thoughts, Tony said, "Even though I had my diesel truck hooked up to a block heater all night, I had a hell of a time startin' it this mornin'. Way I figure, even if we have only a team of three, we can drive some of our neighbors to relatives or friends who have backup heat."

Jeb took a swig of coffee. "How long do you think this outage will last?"

"Could be days if another storm hits. Pete knows a guy who works at Mystic's Lightning Bug Electric, and he says lines are down all over the area. They get one fixed, and another tree falls, and just the weight of the ice is snappin' the wires in two." Tony shook his head. "I've never seen it this cold. Myrna forgot a plate of brownies in our microwave. It's mounted above our cookin' range on an outside wall. Our house felt warm as could be, but when she found those brownies this mornin', they were froze solid with frost on top. Without heat, some folks could freeze to death."

The thought gave Jeb the shivers. "What's our plan if we run across a neighbor who has no friend or relative in town with a woodstove or generator?"

"If we got room, which I don't, we can put 'em up in our homes. Or we can drive 'em to a motel or B and B that has a backup generator. A last resort would be to call the cops. The churches will provide shelter, and the cops will know where to take people."

Jeb could count the churches in Mystic Creek on the fingers of one hand. He guessed that when they ran out of room, the fire station, the sheriff's department, and other public places would take people in.

The mention of shelters reminded Jeb of his livestock and chickens. "Before I can go shopping for emergency supplies, I have to tend to my animals. My truck will be overloaded, so I'll leave Bozo in the laundry room. Not much in there he can eat."

"Long as you'll be gone, the doors might start lookin' tasty to him," Tony said with a chuckle. "Good thing you're a woodworker. You can replace anything he chews up."

Jeb donned shoe chains and thick outerwear before taking care of his animals. He knew that Charlie Ramsey would open up the sporting goods store early so people could get supplies. Jeb just prayed Charlie had plenty in stock.

Marble, Jeb's frosted gray Lincoln ewe, met him at the gate of her pen. For a moment, Jeb thought his eyesight had gone haywire. The sheep looked lopsided. After entering the enclosure, he saw that Marble was as bald as an onion on one side from her flank to her shoulder. *Say what?* He walked her pasture and found where her mottled wool had frozen to the ice and been jerked out by the roots when she stood up. *Ouch!* Jeb led the ewe into her shed and put a sheep jacket on her, threw in fresh straw, and made sure the electric ring in her trough had kept her water from freezing.

En route to the barn, he nearly stepped on a gray mourning dove roosting in the snow. For weeks now, he'd seen a pair of doves on his land. Circling the bird, Jeb realized it had frozen to death. He wondered where its partner was. Mourning doves were monogamous, and he knew this bird's mate would die of grief. Recalling how Marble's wool had frozen to the ground, Jeb concluded that the dove may have gotten stuck in the snow. It saddened him to think of its mate left alone to face certain death.

With a hand gone jerky from the freezing air, Amanda tried calling her landlord again and still got his answering machine. At this point, she was inclined to believe he just wasn't answering the phone. If so, he had a great game going, collecting the rent and spending nothing on repairs. She couldn't afford to fix anything. When this was all over, she'd have to start looking for another place to live.

Above them, a loud cracking sound cut through the air. Chloe gave a start and stared at the ceiling. "Mommy, is our roof breaking?"

"No, of course not." Amanda injected more certainty into her voice than she actually felt. She and Mark had lived in a few dumps, but the roofs had always held fast. "You know how this house creaks at night? I think this is the same thing." *Only much louder.*

It took Jeb nearly an hour in town to buy emergency supplies. The backseat of his crew-cab pickup was packed with survival blankets, fuel and wicks for paraffin and kerosene lanterns, D batteries for flashlights, a few actual flashlights in case some people didn't have one, hand warmers, candles, matches, miniature propane tanks for gas camp stoves, about three dozen energy bars, two of which he'd reserved for himself and tossed on the dash, and several cases of bottled water.

Only then could he begin checking on residents. Though he'd chosen Elderberry Lane as his primary route, he knew several older women who lived alone on Ponderosa. His mother hung out with them at the senior center, and she would expect Jeb to check on them since he lived so close.

He decided to start near the town center on Ponderosa, so his first stop was at Kay Brickle's. The postmistress of Mystic Creek, she was short and stout with permed gray hair and a mouth that always seemed to be in high gear, mostly to spread gossip.

Trying to be polite, Jeb cut her off. "I've got no time to chat, Kay. It appears to me that you're set up to weather the storm." Jeb heard the hum of a generator outside. "Does that motor produce enough power to run your furnace?"

"Well . . ." Kay began most sentences with that word, drawing it out until it grated on Jeb's nerves. "Of course it runs my furnace, and I've got a woodstove as backup. I'm not stupid like some folks I could name in this town."

Jeb grew worried as he drove farther along Ponderosa. He got no answers when he knocked on the doors where he knew his mom's friends lived. As he progressed from house to house, he saw bright illumination gleaming through the windows of Mary Melissa Dilling's place. He thanked God for his shoe chains as he walked to her front porch. From inside he heard a chorus of voices and laughter. When he knocked, Donna Harris, who lived on the adjacent acre, opened the door. Her blond-streaked hair was feathered around her face to set off her merry green eyes.

"Hi, Jeb. Welcome to our ice storm party!"

Jeb peered over her shoulder to see Donna's sister, Lisa Meekins, Ellie Kay Hathaway, Nancy Hayes, Michelle Nelson, and Thipin Jarlego gathered around a large round table. It looked as if they were playing cards.

"I just wanted to check on all of you," Jeb explained. "I was getting pretty worried when no one answered my knocks."

"Mary Melissa has a backup generator!" Thipin Jarlego, a petite blonde with blue eyes who looked younger than her sixty-five years, flashed a ready grin at him over her fanned cards. "When we heard this storm was coming, Judy Burr lent us her husband, Ralph. He blew out our pipes, filled them with safe antifreeze, and we moved in here, dogs and cats included. We're snug as bugs in a rug."

Jeb thought he counted five dogs and six cats, but there was so much activity going on that he might have missed a critter or two. He noted that Mary Melissa's woodstove emitted a blast of heat. "You have plenty of wood within easy reach?"

"We put on shoe chains yesterday and loaded my back veranda with enough logs to last a week," Mary Melissa assured him as she crossed the living room to give him a hug. Mary Melissa, whose friends called her M&M, was a short sixty-year-old woman with dark brown hair and eyes, and an attractive oval face. "Can't believe you drove on those icy roads to check on us. Your mama and daddy raised you right."

Donna patted Jeb's arm. "No need for you to worry. The Burrs are fine, too, with their backup power, and Sheryl Moses, our young lady fireman—who's available, by the way—winterized her house and is staying at the station in case of emergencies."

Jeb ignored the matchmaking attempt. "How about Father John at the Catholic church?"

"The congregation put in a backup generator a couple of years ago that supplies power to the church and the rectory, so he's fine. Probably calling around to offer other folks shelter. If people bring food and bedding, that church will hold a lot of families, and the church kitchen was designed to cook for crowds."

"That's good to know. I've only just started my rounds." Jeb refused food, even though he was starving. "I need to get back out there. Tony Bradley is covering Huckleberry. I need to hit Elderberry. I think a lot of older folks live along that lane."

Donna laughed. "Have fun with Lucy and Ethel Patrick."

"Who?" Jeb had never met the women.

Donna's smile broadened. "You'll know who they are soon enough."

As Jeb left the house, he heard one of the women say, "He is so stinkin' cute. If I were thirty years younger, I'd snatch him up in a heartbeat. What's the matter with the younger gals in this town?"

Jeb chuckled, forgot to watch his step, and almost did a butt plant on the ice.

Elderberry turned out to be the geriatric center of Mystic Creek. Jeb started at the more populated end where the road intersected with West Sugar Pine. He helped so many old people that only a few stuck in his mind. One memorable character was Christopher Doyle, a hunched old fellow who claimed he was ninety years young. At his next stop, Jeb found a sweetheart named Esther McGraw, eighty-one and still going strong. She had no heat, and her phone wouldn't work because it ran off electricity.

"Newfangled gadgets!" she complained. Wobbly on her feet, possibly because she was weighted down with blankets, she led the way to her living room. "I'm worried about why my daughter hasn't come to check on me. It isn't like her."

Jeb secured her house and drove her to her daughter's. By two that afternoon, his day had become a blur. At some point, hunger forced him to grab a frozen energy bar, break off chunks, and hold them in his mouth until they thawed enough to chew.

He kept in touch with Tony and Pete by cell phone. They sounded as exhausted as he felt, and he was more than thirty years younger than Tony. During his rounds, he met many old people and a couple of younger women,

Deb Kistler and Arlene Harmon, thirty-two and forty-one, respectively, who both had backup generators and looked after each other.

The gray gloom of dusk had descended by the time Jeb reached the end of Elderberry. A clapboard house sat back from the gravel thoroughfare, now overlaid with thick ice. He saw no tire tracks outside the garage and decided it must be a vacant rental. As he turned his truck around to head home, he noticed disturbed spots of snow in the front yard. *Footprints*. On the off chance that someone lived there, Jeb parked on the road and trudged through the white drifts to gain the rickety porch. He heard footsteps inside, and a moment later, a woman cracked open the door to peer out at him over a flimsy chain guard. All he could see clearly of her face was one brown eye, which regarded him with suspicion.

By then, Jeb had his introductory speech memorized. "Hi, I'm Jeb Sterling from over on Huckleberry Road."

When he'd finished his spiel, she drew the door open a bit wider but didn't disengage the chain. With a clearer view of her, Jeb realized she was the woman he'd seen walking her daughter to the bus stop. Saying she was pretty didn't do her justice. She had a lovely oval face, a wealth of long dark hair, and beautiful coffee brown eyes. She wore a jacket with a blanket draped over her shoulders.

"My kitchen pipe broke last night and gushed water everywhere. I had no light to turn off the water main. Now the leak has stopped by itself. I think the line froze solid."

Jeb guessed she had no source of heat with the power out. She looked halfway frozen, and her eyes conveyed a panic she was barely holding at bay. With temperatures predicted to plummet to thirty below that night, he doubted she and her child would survive. He didn't want to inquire after her husband or ask if she had one. Those seemed like rude questions to hit her with.

"I can come in and have a look if you'd like," he offered.

She made a gallant effort to conceal the fact that she was shivering. If the house was in as awful condition as the front porch, it probably had little if any insulation.

"I guess," she replied, sounding none too certain that it was wise to let him inside.

"Great. I'll go get my tools."

When Jeb returned to the porch, the woman didn't unlatch the chain to allow him entry. "How can I know for sure that you're truly a neighbor?" she asked. "My little girl and I live alone. I may not be the brightest person alive, but I'm not so dense that I'll let a strange man into my house without verifying his identity first."

Jeb nearly retorted that he guessed she and her kid could freeze to death if she thought that was a safer option. But he wanted to be inside before he told her that she and the child would need to stay elsewhere for a few days. He saw fear in her eyes, the kind that ran so deep it obliterated a person's good sense.

"Smart thinking," he said instead. Drawing his phone from his pocket, he called the Bradley place, and Myrna picked up. He explained the situation and asked the older woman if she'd be kind enough to vouch for him. Then he slipped the phone through the crack of the door. "Here, talk to Mrs. Bradley. She lives across the road from me and has known me for years. Her husband is out helping neighbors, too."

With quivering fingers, the woman grasped the cell

phone. Apparently Myrna sang Jeb's praises, because after returning the device to him, the young woman unfastened the chain guard and let him inside.

When Jeb stepped over the threshold into a small living room, he felt no rise in temperature. *Shit.* He scanned the living area and saw no woodstove, only electric baseboard heaters. A little girl with tousled dark hair was huddled on an old sofa with blankets and pillows piled over her. Her eyes, brown like her mother's, grew as round as dimes when Jeb smiled at her. *Hmm. A woman and girl, living alone, with lousy heaters. No tire tracks in the driveway, either, to indicate that this gal owned a car. Could she be my message writer?*

His brows snapped together in a frown when he saw the thick sheet of ice that had formed on the kitchen floor. "You stay here, if you don't mind," he said to the woman. "I'm wearing shoe chains and won't be as likely to slip." He glanced down and saw that she wore only socks, one with a hole in the toe. "Chains really help."

Upon entering the kitchen, Jeb saw that a wall pipe under the sink had frozen and burst. There wasn't a whole lot he could do except find the water main and turn it off, which would prevent further flooding when things thawed.

He scanned the kitchen. His livestock had better digs. Even so, this woman had tried to make it into a home, with ruffled curtains at the window, red apple canisters on the countertop, a teapot clock on one wall, and cute magnets on the refrigerator. His gaze jerked to the table, where a pink tablet—a very familiar pink—lay next to a vase of fake flowers and an empty cast-iron skillet. Focusing on the stationery, he saw a stack of slender strips resting on top. *No question; she's my message writer.*

This was no time to think about that. He had more urgent matters to focus on. "Ma'am, where is your pump house? I need to turn your water main off."

She gestured with a hand that was faintly blue from the cold. "Out behind the garage, but if you do that, we won't have anything to drink or be able to use the bathroom."

Jeb knew that there was no way she would get a drop of water out of those frozen pipes. If it fell to below thirty tonight, this woman and her child could freeze to death. Her wary posture warned him not to say anything about that yet. He'd deal with relocating them when he returned to the house.

Chapter Three

Amanda yearned to dive back under the covers with Chloe, but she couldn't until the man left. *No drinking water. No toilets.* She studied her daughter, who had gone quiet. That worried Amanda. Chloe always chattered non-stop, falling silent only when she was asleep. Was the child getting hypothermic even as Amanda studied her? Panic rolled over Amanda. She couldn't think what to do. Her brain felt as frozen as the water on the kitchen floor. Eyes dull, Chloe stared at Amanda. *Present physically but disconnected mentally.* Amanda felt the same way.

She flinched when the front door opened behind her. Her feet had gone numb in the damp socks, and she couldn't trust her balance as she turned to face the man. He stood well over six feet tall and looked huge in a tan jacket almost the same tawny color as his hair, cut short and lying in lazy waves over his forehead. Chiseled features, a strong jaw, and hazel eyes. Standing with his feet spread and his knees locked, he exuded strength. She'd been on the receiving end of male strength often enough to be wary, no matter what his neighbor lady said.

"I don't want to be rude and ask personal questions,"

he began, "but this is a situation that leaves me no choice. Do you have a relative or friend in the area who has a nonelectric source of heat that you can bunk with until the power is restored?"

Amanda's mind got stuck on "nonelectric." She stared up at him, trying to think, but her gray matter seemed to be misfiring. "Pardon?"

His gaze sharpened on her face as he repeated himself. This time Amanda heard his question, but it took her a moment to answer. "No, I'm new to Mystic Creek, and I have no family here."

He sighed. "Well, ma'am—" He frowned. "I'm sorry. I don't recall your name."

"Amanda Banning." *At least I remember that.*

"Well, Ms. Banning, I've got to get you out of here to someplace with heat. You and your little girl can't stay here." He planted his fists on his hips, letting her know that he didn't plan to take no for an answer. "If you have no friends or family in town, your only option is to stay at a motel or B and B with a backup generator."

Amanda couldn't afford a motel room, not even for one night. She and Chloe would have to find another rental unless her landlord responded to her calls and paid for repairs. This house was no longer livable.

"I don't have the money for a motel." Amanda's voice sounded hollow even to her.

"I'm sure some shelters have been set up. A lot of people have no heat, and churches with backup power have probably opened their doors. I can call the local authorities to find out where you might go."

Amanda's heart skipped a beat. "Authorities?"

"The sheriff's department," he explained.

Amanda wanted nothing to do with cops. What if the

shelter made the television news and Mark saw her or Chloe's face? *No, no, no.*

"I don't think that's a good plan," was all she could think to say.

Jeb studied Amanda Banning in bewilderment. She'd referred to herself as being stupid in some of the notes, and right then, he couldn't argue the point. She didn't seem to be tracking. He shifted his gaze to her hands, which were blue with cold. Maybe her body temp had dropped too low. He glanced at the little girl and noted that her expression had gone blank. No way could he leave them here, absolutely no way.

"You can't stay here tonight. If you can't afford a motel, I'll lend you some money."

She shook her head. "I can't accept a loan. I may not be able to pay it back."

Jeb hesitated, then decided to jump in with both feet. "My home is large, and I have a backup generator, so you and your daughter will be warm there." When her eyes widened, he added, "And you'll be safe as well. In Mystic Creek, neighbors help each other out. Myrna, the lady you spoke to on the phone, lives right across the road. Her husband, Tony, is a nice fellow. It would be good for you to get to know them. Then you'd have at least three friends in town, including me. What do you say?"

She shook her head again. "You may be my neighbor, but you're also a total stranger. I can't even remember your name."

"Sterling, Jeb Sterling." He considered putting her and the child up in a motel despite her objections. He could leave her with enough cash to eat out. But that was problematic because only one of Mystic Creek's motels had an eatery next door, and that was a pizza parlor called Wood Fyre Delights, open for only lunch and dinner. He couldn't let them walk any distance in this weather. "Do you have a car?" he asked, as if he didn't already know the answer. Right now wasn't the moment to tell her he'd received at least fifty of her messages, which had revealed things about her that she wouldn't wish him to know. She was giving him enough trouble as it was.

"No. I'm saving for one, though."

"Well, saving for one isn't the same as owning one. The conditions outside are treacherous. Even if I put you in a motel, you could slip and get hurt trying to reach a café. You'll be safest at my place. My cupboards are well stocked and so is my freezer. There'll be no shortage of food or heat."

"I explained why that isn't—"

Jeb cut her off. "Your only other option is to find a shelter." He pulled his cell phone from his pants pocket and looked in his contacts for the nonemergency number to the sheriff's office. He dialed it often to talk with his brother Barney, who was a deputy and often got desk duty. "I'll just call and find out where I can take you."

"No, please, don't!"

Jeb knew why Amanda Banning wanted no contact with the authorities. She was hiding from a maniacal husband. He doubted she would be risking exposure if she went to a shelter, but he couldn't discount the possibility entirely.

"Then you have to collect a little clothing for you and your daughter," Jeb said, injecting firmness into his tone. "I'll take you to my place. Yours was the last house on my route, so I can build a fire to get you both warm and throw a hot meal together." He kept his finger poised over the nonemergency number. "This is an either-or situation, and in any case, you can't stay here. I won't allow it."

Her chin came up. "We're not your responsibility."

"You became my responsibility the instant I walked into this freezing house."

"I'm a full-grown woman, and I—"

"Then behave like one." Jeb knew that was harsh, but he was past caring. "Think of your child. Look at her. Do you honestly believe she'll survive another night here?"

Jeb broke off. As he watched her struggle to make a decision, he recalled Tony's comment that she must be as ugly as a fence post if she had to throw messages into the wind in search of a man. Tony had guessed wrong. Jeb couldn't see a single homely thing about her. She had beautiful brown eyes, large, expressive, and edged with thick, dark lashes. A dainty nose, straight-bridged and just right for her oval face, thrust from between her arched brows. Her mouth, soft and full, sported an upper lip defined in a perfect bow. She'd drawn her long mahogany hair back into a ponytail. With the blanket draped over her shoulders, he could see little of her figure, but he suspected her body was as lovely as her face. She wore no wedding ring, but because of her notes, he knew that she was married and trying to save money to get a divorce.

A smile twitched at the corners of Jeb's mouth. She'd wished for a hero to keep her and her daughter safe, and she'd just hit the jackpot. She made him think of that dove he'd found frozen to death in the ice just before dawn. He'd been too late to save the bird, but he was here in the nick of time to help this woman.

* * *

Amanda remembered how the old lady on the phone, Myrna somebody, had raved about what a trustworthy man Jeb Sterling was. She had gone beyond feeling cold to a strange apathy. Sterling was right; Chloe might die tonight if Amanda insisted on staying in this house. Still, he was a big, broad-shouldered man. Being close to him frightened her. But then, after living with Mark, she'd probably be afraid of Peter Pan.

"All right," he said. "Let me make this simple for you. You're coming to my place for the night. I'll cook supper while you and your daughter sit in front of the fire. If you're worried that I'll get out of line, I'll invite my mom or one of my sisters over to spend the night. Then you should feel safe. This is a bad situation, and I don't blame you for feeling wary. It's only smart. But these conditions are deadly. Which is riskier, gambling on me or the weather?" He fiddled with his phone and then turned the face toward her. "You see that forecast? Right now, it's twenty below, but another storm is moving in. This is going to feel warm compared to what we're going to see later."

"The power may come back on," she reminded him.

"Lines are breaking everywhere. The power crews are working around the clock to restore electricity. People's lives are at risk. But they can repair lines and transformers only so fast. Are you really willing to bet that your electricity is going to come back on?"

"All right," she heard herself say. "I'll get us a change of clothing." *And my money.*

"Get more than one change of outfits," he said. "Enough to last you for a few days, just in case this next storm does even more damage."

Amanda went over to hug Chloe close. "Mommy is going to pack us an overnight bag. This nice man is taking us over to his house where we'll be warm and safe."

Chloe pressed her face against Amanda's shoulder. In a whisper, she asked, "What if he's mean like Daddy?"

Amanda's heart panged. "Oh, sweetie, I don't think he is."

"You didn't think Daddy was, either."

"That's true." Amanda saw no point in denying it. She'd made a horrible mistake by marrying Mark. "But even if this man isn't nice, we won't be cold or hungry at his house. Mommy thinks we'll be much safer there than we will be here."

"Okay." Chloe wiggled away to huddle under the covers again.

Amanda saw that Jeb Sterling stood with his tawny head bent as if he found the worn rug fascinating. She knew he'd overheard their conversation. Oh, well. Now he'd ask her dozens of questions. The thought gave her a dull headache. She stopped to fetch her still-frozen shoes, considered donning dry socks, and then decided the effort would be pointless. Once in the truck, her shoes would thaw and make her socks wet again. She didn't have enough pairs to waste on a few minutes of comfort.

She stopped dead outside the bathroom, where a layer of ice reached into the hallway. *Another broken pipe.* A wave of anger at her landlord swept through her, but she was too cold to sustain it. When the storm passed and the power came back on, she'd have no choice but to move. *There goes my car fund, my divorce fund, and Chloe's first real Christmas.*

Poised at the edge of the ice, she heard the chinks of Jeb's shoe chains as he approached behind her. "I can get toiletries for you," he offered. "If you try to walk on that, you'll fall and bust your ass."

Amanda shot him a startled look. He rubbed the bridge of his nose. "Sorry. I could have said that in a nicer way."

Under Mark's tutelage, Amanda had learned every filthy word known to mankind, and never once had Mark apologized. "It's okay." She told him where to find their toothbrushes, toothpaste, and her deodorant. When he asked where she kept her cosmetics, she replied, "I don't wear makeup."

He glanced sideways at her. "It's a good thing you don't need any, then."

Amanda wanted to ask what he meant but decided she didn't want to know. If he meant she was pretty, she knew better, and her question would throw up more warning flags. If he meant she was so ugly that cosmetics wouldn't help, she'd heard it before and didn't wish to hear it again.

While he gathered bathroom stuff, Amanda hurried through the bedrooms to collect clothing, which she stuffed in pillowcases. In short order, she met Jeb in the hallway, ready to leave with him. Hands down, it was one of the craziest things she'd ever done. She'd reclaimed her butcher knife, which she'd kept hidden under her mattress. If he tried to harm Chloe, Amanda would stab him. She would never allow anyone to hurt her baby again—never.

She heard him talking as she returned to the living room to collect her daughter. For a moment, she thought he was speaking to himself, but then she realized he had called someone on his cell phone.

"I'm wrapping it up," he said. "I'm taking a lady and her little girl to my place for the night. How are things going for you guys?" A brief silence. Then, "Good. If you're as tired as I am, it's time to call it a day."

Jeb's truck heater had barely coughed to life when he pulled up in front of a huge post-and-timber home. Chloe, perched in the middle of the back bench seat, stared at the house as if it were a mansion.

"You live here all alone?" Amanda couldn't resist asking.

Jeb grinned. "I had plans to get married and have a family when I built it."

"Did your fiancée break your engagement?"

"Never engaged," he replied. "Never even came close. The right lady hasn't come along." In the deepening dusk, his gaze held hers. "Now that I've answered a personal question, you owe me one."

Amanda didn't want to lie, but she also didn't wish to appear secretive and arouse his suspicions. "What would you like to ask?"

He turned off the truck engine, opened his door to get out, which illuminated the cab, and replied, "I'm not sure yet, and I don't want to waste my question." He smiled back at Chloe, who was engulfed in a red parka. "I know your mom put bread sacks on your feet to keep them dry, but how would you feel about me carrying you to the house? It's really slick out here, and I don't want you to fall."

Chloe sent Amanda a questioning look. In that moment, meeting her daughter's gaze, Amanda, whose brain seemed to be working better now that she was breathing warmer air, remembered something that she'd left behind at the rental, an SD card filled with pictures of Chloe. *Important, so very important.* Without those photographs, she'd be powerless to protect her child from Mark when she filed for divorce. How could she have walked away without them? *Calm down.* Even if they couldn't live in that awful old house again, she'd be able to get the SD card later.

Amanda was so lost in her own thoughts that it took her a moment to reassure her child. "It's all right, sweetie. It's very slick."

Unbuckling her seat belt, Chloe looked at Jeb. "Okay, I guess."

Jeb nodded. To Amanda, he said, "Sit tight. I'll come back to help you to the porch. I don't want you to fall, either."

"I don't need help."

He arched a brow that was the same tawny color as his hair. He was a handsome man. Amanda found it amazing that he'd managed to remain single. Judging by the grandness of his house, he had money as well as good looks.

"I'm the only one wearing traction chains, so please, humor me," he said.

Amanda watched as he carried Chloe up onto his front porch, opened the massive door, and deposited the child inside what she presumed was an entry hall. Seconds later, he returned to the truck and opened the front passenger door. Amanda unfastened her seat belt, exited the vehicle, and promptly slipped. Jeb caught her around the waist.

"Lean against me. I'll keep us both standing."

He took short strides so she could keep pace. Amanda didn't like being held against his big, hard body, but she knew she'd fall if he turned her loose. It seemed to her that time went into slow motion. When she was safe on the less icy porch pavers, he finally released her.

He opened the door, revealing a frightened-looking

Chloe just inside. "In you go. I'll get your things and then build a roaring fire."

Amanda heard the latch engage behind her. She rubbed her arms through her thin jacket as she inched from the huge hallway to peer at the home's interior. To the right was a gigantic living room with a rock fireplace that took up most of one wall. Beyond was a large dining room with one of the widest tables she'd ever seen. *This isn't a house; it's a palace.*

Just then Jeb returned, his shoe chains clanking on both the outside pavers and the interior slate floor. In the warmer air, Amanda's sense of smell sharpened, and she caught a whiff of piney cologne as he strode past her to deposit her bulging pillowcases on the gold carpet at one end of a large, dark-chocolate sofa. As promised, he immediately opened a hand-carved box and took out logs and kindling for a fire. He crouched to lay crumpled newspaper in the grate.

"Come on in. I don't bite."

Holding Chloe's hand, Amanda moved into the room, feeling out of place and as nervous as a witch in Salem. She studied him as he worked, wondering how it must feel to live alone in such a big house. He moved with easy grace for a tall and muscular man, his shoulders bunching beneath the jacket, his legs taut under his denim jeans as he shifted his weight. When he lighted the paper and flames licked up through the logs, firelight danced across his face, making his hair shimmer like gold.

He pushed himself to his feet and slid a brown otto-man in front of the hearth. Then he lifted the top to with-draw a fleece blanket from an interior storage area. "You two can snuggle up and get warm while I throw a meal together. Anything special you'd like?"

Amanda drew a blank. "Anything hot."

He laughed and shrugged out of his jacket. As he walked to a gorgeous juniper coat tree, Amanda took measure of his build, which was deceptively slender, belying the strength she'd felt when he'd stopped her from falling. He wore a blue work shirt tucked in at the waist.

Over his shoulder, he said, "You should probably put those wet shoes on the hearth to dry and put on another pair."

Amanda realized he was speaking to her. Embarrassed to admit it, she said, "I don't have another pair."

He threw her a startled look. Then he disappeared, returning a moment later to hand her a pair of thick wool socks.

"Thank you."

He only nodded before disappearing again.

Amanda removed her shoes and wet socks, then helped Chloe remove her boots. The woolen footwear felt heavenly on her feet. After setting their shoes near the fire, she drew her daughter onto her lap and draped the blanket over them both. "I don't know if I'll ever feel warm again," she whispered.

"Me, either." Chloe shivered. "Hold me close, Mommy."

Amanda tightened her embrace. Glancing around the room, she saw photos on the mantel. An older man who looked a lot like Jeb and a dark-haired woman smiled down at her from one frame. In another, Jeb stood flanked by two younger guys who also resembled him. Jeb had his arms curled over their shoulders. All three were grinning, showing off teeth so white they could have been models in a toothpaste commercial.

Oh, God, I hope I haven't made a horrible mistake by coming here. Pressing her cheek against her daughter's hair, she detected the faint smell of food. Her stomach snarled with hunger, calling to mind the frozen leftovers she'd forgotten at home. Coming here hadn't been a mistake.

The delicious aroma of what she guessed was braised chicken grew stronger. A man who cooks? Amanda was surprised. Mark wouldn't even help wash dishes, and he had often slapped Amanda for putting "shit" on his plate.

The tension slipped from her shoulders as the heat from the fire surrounded her. It felt so good that she could have gone to sleep. Just then a monstrous dog lumbered into the room. She didn't need to look to be sure it was a male. He had the most massive head she'd ever seen on a canine. He also looked vicious and capable of devouring people before using their bones to pick his teeth.

He let loose with a low, rumbling growl. Amanda couldn't think what to do. If she moved, he might leap. Chloe screamed and burrowed against Amanda to hide her head under the blanket. Amanda was tempted to join her.

When Jeb heard Chloe's scream, he had just set the digital timer on the pressure cooker, so he rushed to the living room. When Chloe peeked out at him from her mother's arms, he couldn't help but think she was the cutest little thing he'd ever seen.

Resting a hand on his dog's shoulder, Jeb said, "This is Bozo. I named him that because he's such a clown." Chloe peered out at him again. "I know he looks scary, but the truth is, he wouldn't bite a flea to get it off his back."

"He growled at us," Amanda said.

"I don't doubt it, only it wasn't really a growl. That's just how he talks."

"Are you one of those people who says his dog is smiling when it snarls?"

Jeb chuckled. "Trust me, I don't wear blinders when it comes to Bozo. He's a mastiff. At his last vet check, he tipped the scales at two hundred and thirty pounds. He once ate my sheep's shelter because I'd left him alone. But people are safe. He's a very social animal. The only reason I didn't have him with me today is because I didn't have room in the truck with all the emergency supplies."

The beast growled again. Chloe squeaked and shrank against Amanda. Jeb walked over to crouch in front of them. The mastiff came with him. "Don't be afraid, honey. That's just how Bozo says hello. If you don't say hi back, you're going to hurt his feelings."

Chloe poked her head up from under the blanket to stare at the giant dog. Bozo pressed forward, whining and rumbling at once. Jeb decided he'd better take a stab at translating dog language into English. "He's saying that he's never been around a little girl and would really like to make friends with you. Though Bozo is very big, he has a gentle heart. He's always careful not to knock people over, and I'm guessing that he'll be even more cautious around you because you're so small."

Chloe studied the dog. "What melted his lips?"

Jeb saw Amanda stifle a smile, and he almost grinned himself. "Mastiffs just have droopy jowls." He winked at the child. "When he starts to shake his head, be sure to duck. He throws drool everywhere."

*   *   *

Amanda gathered the courage to stretch out her hand to pat the dog on the head. Looking beyond his sagging lids, she searched his red-rimmed brown eyes. She saw no viciousness, only an appeal to be friends. She didn't want Chloe to be afraid of dogs. Her daughter was already fearful of far too many things.

Upon seeing her mother touch the mastiff, Chloe dived back under the blanket. Bozo licked Amanda's fingers and then rested his wet, drool-laced chops on her knee. He frowned as he studied the trembling lump under the fleece.

Still hunkered down in front of them, Jeb said, "He's nothing but a big old love, Chloe. He's only ever seen little girls at a distance, and he'd probably like to get a better look at you."

Chloe finally peeked at the dog again. Bozo growled, sending her back into hiding. As if the dog sensed the child's terror of him, he rolled over onto his back, rumbled again in a friendly way, and paddled his front paws in the air. The huge animal looked so silly that Chloe, who'd bared her head again, giggled. At the sound, Bozo leaped to his feet with surprising agility. Chloe didn't dive for cover quickly enough and received "doggy" kisses. The child sputtered and tried to push the dog's head away. Bozo contented himself with licking her tiny hands.

"Don't be afraid," Amanda said. "As scary as he looks, I don't think he's mean."

Soon, with Jeb narrating an explanation of Bozo's behavior, Chloe slipped off the ottoman and sat on the floor. It was apparently love at first meet, because the child quickly went from timidly petting Bozo to hugging his thick neck. The dog growled happily.

Jeb returned to the kitchen to check on their meal, and before Amanda knew it, Chloe was curled against Bozo for warmth, the light of the fire bathing them with its heat, both of them fast asleep.

Jeb rounded the corner into the living room. "Dinner's done." He glanced down at the sleeping pair and grinned, shaking his head. "Dumb dog. He's supposed to be a watchdog. Instead he's never met a stranger." He lifted his gaze to Amanda's. She found herself thinking that he had beautiful eyes, their hazel depths shimmering like topaz in the flickering light. Even so, the spacious room didn't seem big enough to hold him. "I can put Chloe's dinner in the warmer. When she wakes up, she'll be hungry, but for now, maybe we'd better let her sleep. It's been a long, cold, scary day for her."

Amanda hated to leave her warm nest, but hunger drove her to discard the blanket and stand. Jeb led the way to the kitchen—if it could even be called that. Amanda took in double ovens and so many built-in appliances that she didn't know what half of them were. Jeb Sterling believed in living large. The kitchen was huge. His dog was gigantic. His pickup had a full and comfortable-looking backseat. And his house was a sprawling place, sparsely decorated but pleasant and homey despite that.

"I've never seen so much counter space," she said. "Five individuals could cook in here at once. I think this is even larger than the school cafeteria kitchen." She ran her fingertips over the dark marbled granite of the work island. "This is gorgeous."

Oversize oven mitts on his hands, Jeb circled her, carrying serving dishes. "I'm one of six kids. When my family visits, the kitchen doesn't seem quite so big. And

everyone is elbow to elbow, cooking, chopping, or stir-
ring."

Once again, Amanda found herself wondering how
this handsome, tawny-haired man with twinkling eyes
and a smile that could light up a room had managed to
stay single for so long. She guessed he was about thirty.

When he had all the food on the round kitchen table,
he motioned for her to take a seat across from him. Once
she'd lowered herself onto a chair, he bent his head to
bless the meal. Mark had never allowed prayer in his
house. Over time, Amanda had learned to say the blessing in silence, never letting her expression give her away.
Though Jeb didn't say the words aloud, she appreciated
that he observed the tradition, one with which she'd
grown up. Her dad had always done the honors. The
memory made Amanda miss him.

"If you'll dish Chloe a plate, I have the warmer ready."

He had roasted a whole chicken with potatoes and
carrots and had made a tossed salad. "How on earth did
you get this done so fast?" she asked.

"Digital pressure cooker. Everything is cooked in a
third of the usual time."

Amanda gave Chloe a chicken leg and a small serving
of vegetables, afraid to dish up too much for fear the
child wouldn't eat it all. She didn't want Chloe to be
made to sit at the table until she finished swallowing bits
of food she didn't want. Glancing at Jeb, she wondered if
he would get as angry as Mark had if Chloe's appetite
didn't meet his expectations.

"What?" he asked softly.

Amanda shook her head. "It's nothing." Excusing herself, she stood and collected the plate. "Where is the
warmer?"

"Just around the end of the peninsula bar," he replied. "Second bottom drawer, stainless-steel front."

Amanda found the appliance and tucked Chloe's meal inside. When she resumed her seat at the table, she saw that Jeb had carved the remainder of the hen into pieces. She placed a folded paper towel on her lap and then chose a breast before filling the remainder of her plate with vegetables and salad, which had been tossed with a berry vinaigrette. The poultry was melt-off-the-bone tender and delicious. Jeb filled their glasses with water from a pitcher. Until she took a drink, Amanda hadn't realized how thirsty she was.

"This is wonderful," she told him. "Thank you for inviting us here."

"I'm happy to have you."

They ate in silence for a minute, but it wasn't uncomfortable. Jeb seemed to be as hungry as she was. He apparently realized that he was gobbling. After swallowing a mouthful, he smiled and said, "Sorry. I've been flat-out all day, and the energy bars I tossed on the dash were frozen solid before I found a moment to try eating one."

Amanda shared her experience with the frozen leftovers. "We held pieces of pizza in our mouths until they thawed enough to chew them."

"I didn't have time for much mouth thawing. It was a crazy day." He wiped the corners of his lips with his napkin. "Tony, across the road, pounded on my door well before dawn. I felt grumpy at first, but now I'm really glad he recruited me to help. I didn't realize how many oldsters live on Elderberry. Most of them were in desperate straits."

He told her about a lady who'd become offended when he poured RV antifreeze down her drains, inferring that he felt her house was small enough to be on wheels. Then about an old man who'd proclaimed himself to be ninety years young and had fallen and bruised his hip while trying to bring in wood. "And I can't forget my mom's friends on Ponderosa Lane," he told her. "I knew Mom would skin me alive if I didn't check on them, so I went to their houses first. Nobody answered their doors. I was getting really worried that they were inside, frozen stiff, when I saw Mary Melissa Dilling's house lit up like a Christmas tree."

Amanda listened intently as he described the "ice storm party." He had a gift with words and helped her envision each lady. It impressed her that he knew not only their names but also approximately how old each was. She'd never lived in a town where people were acquainted with practically everyone. It gave her a warm feeling.

"Then I ran into Lucy and Ethel," he continued, grinning. "Twins who are seventy-five, never married. I think they've lived their whole lives on a little stage of their own making. Lucy has bright red hair and wears even brighter red lipstick. Ethel is a little plump and hasn't bothered to cover the gray. Honest to God, I felt as if I'd just entered an old *I Love Lucy* rerun. I kept expecting Ricky to walk in and swear at Lucy in his mother tongue."

Amanda couldn't resist inserting, "I've never watched a *Lucy* rerun."

"Then you are in for a treat. Every once in a while, when I'm feeling down, I'll watch an episode on Netflix. Some humor never loses its appeal." He took a bite of chicken and then swallowed. "Anyway, they both called me sonny and followed me around, spouting off like retired female drill sergeants. I almost cleaned my ears to make sure I was hearing them right. I left my 'sonny' days behind years ago."

"You can't be that old."

"Thirty as of last July. I've quit counting birthdays. Makes me feel ancient."

"Thirty isn't old."

"Spoken like a person who hasn't gotten close yet. When you arrive, it's a shock. You wonder where all the years went since you turned twenty-one."

"I turned twenty-five in September, so I'll be there before I know it."

"Don't be in any rush. Once you hit that landmark day, your friends will wear black armbands to your party, and your cake will read, 'Over the Hill.'"

Amanda was too nervous about bedtime to muster another smile. As for a party to celebrate her birthday, she hadn't had one in years.

When they finished eating, she cut circles around Jeb as she helped to tidy the kitchen. They touched hands once, the contact sending a jolt up her arm. Then they bumped into each other, which set her off balance and prompted him to grab her arm to steady her. Again, she felt an electrical tingle dart over her skin. *Not good.* But she was stuck here, at least for tonight. The only positive things about it were that she finally felt warm and her brain was working again. Now she understood why she'd forgotten the SD card, which she guarded with almost as much diligence as she did her daughter. She'd been too cold to think.

After they finished cleaning up from dinner, Jeb brought in a leather sling of wood and started a fire in the adjoining family room. "This woodstove will keep the whole house toasty overnight. The heat rises and makes all the upstairs bedrooms cozy, no matter how cold it is outside."

He went to the living room to grab Amanda's pillowcases and led the way upstairs. Though there were four large, unoccupied bedrooms, Amanda decided to use only one. She'd sleep better with her daughter next to her and the butcher knife under the mattress. The queen bed, already made up in case one of his family members came to stay, would be large enough for both of them. There was also an adjoining bath, so Amanda could barricade the door without worrying that Chloe might need to relieve herself during the night.

Jeb put their things on a dressing bench. Then, placing his hands on his hips, he turned to face her. "Amanda—I hope you don't mind me using your first name, but calling you Ms. Banning seems over the top at this point."

"No, I don't mind." She just wished he'd stop looking at her as if she were a tasty morsel that he might enjoy for dessert.

"Anyway," he said with a wave of his hand, "I couldn't help but notice how nervous you were of me in the kitchen. And while carrying the pillowcases, I also noticed that you packed a butcher knife."

Amanda glanced at the bags, trying to think how she could explain. "I sleep with it for protection," she admitted.

He nodded. "I figured as much, but under my roof, you aren't going to need it. I present no threat. I give you my word on that. And no one else can get in this house at night without waking Bozo. He sleeps with his ears pricked."

"And what will Bozo do, lick an intruder to death?"

He smiled. "Bozo is very friendly but not dumb. He knows the difference between friend and foe. If anyone enters this house uninvited, he'll wish to God he hadn't."

Amanda's skin prickled under Jeb's sharp gaze. "What will Bozo do?"

Jeb winked at her. "I'm not sure because no one has ever broken in, but I've been told that a lot of mastiffs will grab a man by his gonads, back him into a corner, and bite down a little harder each time he dares to move."

"That's comforting to know."

He laughed and moved past her. "The thought gives me the heebie-jeebies." He paused in the open doorway and turned to look at her again. "I know I'm a stranger to you. If you're still uneasy about spending the night here, I can invite my mother over. I keep all the beds made up for unexpected guests and have fresh towels in all the baths. It would pose no inconvenience for me."

"The road conditions are nasty."

"My father would drive her. He's got a big four-wheel-drive truck with studded tires like I do. So don't worry about that. Just say the word, and I'll call her."

Amanda didn't want to trouble his mother. Besides, the very fact that he'd offered to invite his mom made her feel safer. If he had nefarious intentions, he wouldn't do that.

"I'll be fine for one night."

"You may be here longer. Another ice storm is supposed to hit before morning."

She drew in a quick breath, hoping he was wrong about the coming weather. Staying here for a night was doable, but she wasn't sure her nerves could handle more than that. With his large, muscular frame, he blocked the doorway, her only avenue of escape. Being in this room with him made her feel as if all the oxygen had been sucked from the air. He exuded strength. The directness of his gaze made her skin burn. If he made a quick move toward her, she might fall over in a dead faint.

Only his sense of honor might keep him from getting out of line, and Amanda didn't know him well enough to be sure he even had one.

Chapter Four

Amanda prayed it wouldn't be necessary to stay in this man's house for more than one night. She was about to say as much when something slammed against the metal roof. She gave a violent start before she realized it was hail.

"Speak of the devil," Jeb said. "We'd better get back downstairs in case it wakes Chloe. Last night even Bozo got scared and crawled under the dining room table."

Amanda trailed behind him as they descended the stairs. As Jeb suspected, the storm had awakened Chloe and the dog. But neither of them seemed frightened.

Crouching beside her daughter, Amanda said, "You slept through dinner, sweetie. Do you think you can eat now?"

Chloe nodded, so Amanda picked her up and carried her to the kitchen, Bozo following on her heels. Jeb got the child's meal from the warmer and placed it on the table. Then he said, "Do I have any comers for hot chocolate?"

"Me!" Chloe cried. Then, remembering her manners, she added, "Yes, please."

"Yes, please," Amanda echoed.

She gave Chloe a paper towel and sat beside her while she ate. Jeb filled mugs with hot water from the coffee center. Then he mixed in packets of Swiss Miss, another thing she'd mentally consigned to the unaffordable bin. "Who wants marshmallows?"

"Me!" Chloe crowed with delight. "I love marshmallows."

"Me, too!" Jeb replied. "But I hate the dehydrated kind."

Seconds later, Chloe grinned at Jeb from beneath a chocolate mustache. "This is so yummy! Thank you, Mr. —" Chloe broke off. "Um, I can't remember your name."

"Sterling." Jeb took a sip of his drink. "Aw. Just the thing to chase away the chill on a winter night, and you're welcome. And 'Mr. Sterling' is a mouthful. You can call me Jeb if you like."

The little girl dimpled a cheek at him. "My mommy says it's impolite to call adults by their first names."

He nodded. "Mr. Jeb will work, then."

"Okay, Mr. Jeb." Chloe glanced into her mug. "You've got miniature marshmallows. They're my favorite."

Amanda warmed her hands on her mug, wishing the cold feeling inside her would dissipate. Unlike her daughter, she couldn't quite relax. How had she and Chloe ended up here, about to spend the night in a stranger's home?

Chloe seemed to be as hungry as Amanda had been, because she cleaned her plate. Jeb said, "You were a hungry girl. I can warm up some more for you."

Chloe looked tempted, but then a wary expression settled on her face. "No, thank you."

Jeb shot Amanda a questioning look, but he didn't

pursue the matter. After Chloe finished her hot drink, Amanda took the child upstairs for a bath.

While Amanda ministered to Chloe, Jeb bundled up to brave the storm, strapped chains back on his shoes—which was a pain in the ass—and decided as he ventured outside that he'd dig out a second pair of boots to wear only outdoors. The hail felt like rocks hitting his head, which hurt like hell, but he didn't dare run to reach an outbuilding for fear he'd slip and fall. Thank God he'd left Bozo behind and had locked his other animals inside shelters this morning.

As he reached the first pen, he dug in his jacket pocket for his gloves. *Damn*. He'd laid them out to dry inside the house. No way was he going to walk all the way back. He'd just tough it out. With that thought still rolling through his mind, he grasped the door handle of the ewe's shed, and his hand froze to the metal. When he jerked it loose, he parted company with some skin, which also hurt like hell.

The sheep bleated a hello that he barely heard over the din. Jeb checked to make sure the animal's jacket remained fastened. With so much wool missing, she needed the extra protection. After feeding her and refreshing her water, he pulled his jacket up over his head and braved the hail again to reach the barn. All okay there. Next he hurried to the chicken coop. His mother was sure to ask after the flock.

When he returned to the house, he heard the murmur of Amanda's and Chloe's voices upstairs. Tender of foot on the uneven slate, Jeb sometimes wore Romeo slippers inside the house, but since he had guests, he donned another pair of boots and stood close to the woodstove to warm himself, listening to their voices. For some reason, their soft chatter made him feel melancholy. He'd always believed that he would be married by now, with a couple of kids. Instead he rattled around in this huge house all alone. That was disappointing. But he guessed everyone experienced disappointments in life.

Amanda's laugh, a musical sound, drifted down like the notes of a song. He hadn't seen her smile without restraint, but he was willing to bet her face was aglow right now. She was a beautiful woman, petite and fine-featured, with a wealth of dark hair and a trim, small-breasted build. He enjoyed watching her move. Just by looking, he could tell that she was active and a hard worker. When he thought of how he'd nearly driven past her house, thinking it was vacant, he sent up a heartfelt prayer of thanks.

Jeb thought of his mother's prediction, that when he least expected it he would cross paths with the right woman. Maybe, just maybe, he'd finally hit pay dirt. *Get real, Sterling. The woman is still married.* Even so, Jeb allowed himself to dream a little.

Lost in the possibilities, he was startled when Amanda walked into the kitchen. "If you don't mind," she said in a soft, shy voice, "I think I'll turn in now."

Jeb wished she'd chat for a while so they could get better acquainted. But she was probably tired. "I don't mind at all. I'm dead on my feet, so I'll be hitting the sack, too."

She grasped the banister, staring at him as if she had something more to say and couldn't quite get it out. "Um, thank you for helping us today." She glanced at the ceiling. "That's a horrible ice storm. I'm so glad we aren't still trapped in that old house, trying to stay warm. I think you saved our lives."

Jeb felt a flush crawl up his neck. "You saved your own by deciding to trust me."

She pushed at her hair. "Dinner was wonderful, too. You're great with Chloe. Normally she's very reserved around men, but she seems to like you."

"I'll take that as a compliment. She's a sweet kid. I'm sorry if she's had bad experiences with men." Because he'd read so many of Amanda's notes, Jeb knew far more than he wanted to reveal. She'd be embarrassed if she learned that the wind had brought him daily special deliveries. "It's good that she's starting to relax with me."

"Well," she said, "I guess I'll say good night."

"G'night. Sleep tight. The master suite is down here, so I won't be coming up."

He watched her climb the stairs. When she disappeared, he turned off the lights, leaving on only one in the kitchen in case his guests wanted something before morning.

With a snap of his fingers, he got Bozo to follow him. The silly dog gazed at the stairs as if he'd lost his best friend. "Traitor," Jeb whispered. "Show you a pretty face, and you're ready to jump ship."

Jeb lay in bed on his back with his head resting on his folded arms. As always, Bozo jumped up on the mattress the moment the lamp went out. Jeb stared into the darkness above him, listening to hail strike metal. He hoped the sound didn't disturb Amanda's or Chloe's rest. On the second floor, they were a lot closer to the roof than he was. Thinking of the butcher knife, he wondered where Amanda had stashed it. Probably under her mattress, handle right at the edge so she could grab it and skewer him if he tried to touch her. If having it gave her comfort, he was glad. He had a feeling she had endured some pretty bad stuff during her marriage.

Just then, a loud rumble vibrated through the house, adding to the din of the hail. Jeb shot upright in bed. *Sweet Jesus.* Was his roof collapsing? He'd made sure that the support beams could withstand more than twenty pounds of weight per square foot.

Jeb leaped from bed, pulled on jeans, and ran upstairs, flipping on light switches as he went. His heart pounded. He stopped in the hallway, stared at the alder-plank ceiling, and was about to call out for Amanda and Chloe to evacuate when he realized the rumbles and thumps were coming from their room. Bewildered, he stepped to their door and pressed an ear to the wood. It sounded as if something heavy was being pushed or pulled across the uneven slate. What the hell? Then it hit him that Amanda was barricading the doorway, probably with the dresser.

Pulse returning to normal, Jeb turned to leave and nearly fell over Bozo. Sighing, he patted the dog's head and led the way back to his bedroom. Off with the jeans. Head pillowed again on his folded arms, he stared into the darkness.

When Bozo jumped up on the bed and circled before lying down, Jeb whispered, "Let's hope that makes her feel safe enough to get some rest."

Bozo growled a response. Jeb fell asleep on that thought.

When Jeb awakened the next morning and looked out his bedroom window, he saw a world encrusted with thick ice. It was beautiful—but also treacherous. He showered, shaved, and scrubbed his teeth. Then he threw on clothing warmer than he'd worn yesterday. Thermal underwear. Up top, he pulled on a sweatshirt and then doubled the layer with a sweater. He had no idea how much damage the storm had done during the night, but he suspected it was extensive. Amanda and Chloe would be going nowhere today and probably not tomorrow. The thought eased his mind. If Amanda even acted as if she meant to go back to that awful rental, he would pitch a fit.

When Jeb got downstairs, he took a page from his mother's book and listened to a weather update. He learned of widespread power outages, downed trees, blocked roads, half-frozen people being taken to Mystic Urgent Care or to St. Matthews in Crystal Falls, and another day of school closures. He decided that he'd better take a chain saw with him as he made his rounds on Elderberry.

He was about to put on his jacket to tend his outdoor animals when he heard the rumbling sound again. He winced, picturing Amanda struggling to move that dresser. She could pull a shoulder muscle or hurt her back. A few moments later, she came downstairs. Tousled dark hair lay over her shoulders. Her eyelids looked heavy with sleepiness. Using the newel post to swing down to the first floor, she stopped, lifted a delicate, arched brow, and asked, "How bad is it?"

He gestured toward a window. "Really bad, I'm afraid. No school today. Power's out in places all across town. People are being taken to urgent care or the hospital in Crystal Falls. It dropped to thirty-five below. In Mystic, that's unheard-of."

She splayed a hand over her heart. She wore an old, oversize T-shirt and holey sweatpants and still managed to look beautiful. "I p-p-pray all our neighbors—that everyone—is all right."

After watching her struggle to utter the word *pray*,

Jeb decided it was something she didn't often say. He figured the reasons behind that were ugly. "I'll be heading out as soon as I've taken care of my animals."

"Animals? You have others besides Bozo?"

That shot to hell his theory that she'd ever walked past his place and seen him working outside. "Horses, some steers, a pig, and a Lincoln ewe, plus chickens."

"Oh, Chloe will love seeing them."

"Not this morning," he said as he pulled on chained boots and donned his Carhartt jacket. "It'll be slicker than greased owl shit out there. Maybe tomorrow."

She nodded. Then she frowned. "How slick is greased owl shit?"

Jeb felt heat prickle on the nape of his neck. He needed to clean up his mouth. "Pretty damned slick." He winced, deciding he was a lost cause. "Sorry—it's a Southern saying I picked up from Dad, and my mom's not here to threaten me with a bar of soap."

"Your mother threatens to wash your mouth out with soap?"

Jeb pictured his spry mother. Amanda reminded him of her in many ways, something he needed to think about. He'd heard of women falling for men who resembled their fathers and men who went for gals who reminded them of their mothers. He kept his heart on a much shorter leash. "Not only does she threaten, but she'll also grab a handful of my hair, even though she's short and it's a stretch, to shove my head over a sink."

"And you allow that?"

Jeb tried to picture himself using his strength against the woman who'd raised him. He shrugged. "She never follows through. She's just bent on getting grandkids and keeping our mouths clean so they don't embarrass her when they go to kindergarten." Jeb's sisters sometimes talked even worse than he did, and he'd heard them being threatened with bars of soap, too. "Mom is the matriarch. She tries to keep all of us in line. The soap thing—it's more a joke than serious. When we were kids, we actually got soap scrubbed against our clenched teeth, but that never happens now."

Amanda inclined her head. "My mother insisted on clean language as well."

Jeb started for the door and then did a U-turn. "I almost forgot. I'm going to wear gloves this morning. Last night I grabbed hold of the door handle to my ewe's shed, and my hand froze to the metal. I lost a little hide."

He fetched his dirty old leather gloves from the closet shelf where he'd left them yesterday to dry.

"Let me see," she said, walking toward him.

Jeb felt silly. He wasn't a kid who needed his scrapes kissed. But she looked so concerned that he showed her anyway.

"Oh, no." She gave him an accusing look. "Why didn't you say something? That needs to be bandaged!"

He couldn't help but grin. "It's just a raw patch, Amanda, nothing serious."

"But it must hurt. Where is your first-aid kit?"

Jeb didn't want to be fussed over, but if he protested, he might seem grumpy. He told her where the kit was kept, sat at the table, and braced himself for some pampering. He hadn't had a woman nurse him since he'd left home.

With gentle care, Amanda cleaned the raw patch. He'd given it a good wash last night, and it was already glazing over with a hard crust. It would be sore for a few days, but he'd live through it. While she dabbed on antibiotic ointment and wrapped his hand in gauze, he distracted himself by trying to breathe in her scent. No perfume. She smelled of bath soap, shampoo, and woman, an essence all her own. He wished he could press his face to her hair.

"Do you have any idea how beautiful you are?"

She jerked as if he'd poked her with a pin and gave him a startled look that soon morphed into suspicion. *Great move, Sterling. You sure blew that all to hell.*

"I know how beautiful I'm not." Her words were clipped. "I do own a mirror."

Jeb wished he could call back the words. She'd begun to let down her guard, and his big mouth had shot it back ten feet in the air. "Uh, can you cook?"

"Cook?" Her tone told him she hadn't been expecting this. "Well . . . yes, it's the only thing I do halfway well."

"Would you mind fixing me some hot food? It'll be a long day, and after I'm done tending to animals, I won't have time to fix anything." He thought of the man who'd fallen yesterday. "I hauled in enough wood to last the night for the old guy who bruised his hip, but by now, he might be running low."

"You must hurry then." She wound tape over the gauze. As she returned the first-aid supplies to the case, she asked, "What would you like for breakfast?"

A taste of your mouth. Aloud Jeb said, "Some bacon, eggs over easy, and a couple of pieces of toast will do me. Lots of bacon, four eggs."

She moved toward the bathroom to put the kit away. "I'll have it ready."

Jeb put Bozo's boots on him, and together they went out to care for the critters. *The only thing she does halfway well?* The lady needed a large dose of self-confidence.

When she looked in a mirror, she didn't see the same woman he did.

When Jeb returned to the house, he sat down to perfect eggs. A lot of people broke the yolks of eggs over easy. She'd added fried potatoes and gravy to his order.

When he glanced up, she shrugged. "They'll stick to your ribs better than only toast."

She seemed tense as he took a bite. Flavor burst over his tongue, and he closed his eyes in appreciation. "This is fabulous, Amanda. Thank you."

"It's just plain fare." She walked to the sink to begin cleaning up. "I can't stay here without earning our keep. I need to pay my own way."

Jeb understood that. "If I could come home for a hot lunch, I'd be a happy man."

She turned with a dishcloth in her slender hand. "What would you like?"

"Think freezing cold and weak with hunger. By noon, I'll be starving."

She looked at him with a plea in her eyes. "Can you give me some hints?"

He thought fast. "I'd love a hearty beef stew, lots of spuds, celery, onion, and carrots with tender meat in a thick tomato and broth sauce."

She nodded, looking relieved to have some direction. "If you have all the ingredients, the stew will be waiting for you."

Jeb finished his breakfast and stuck his plate and utensils in the dishwasher. Then he gave Amanda a tour of his larder, cupboards, and chest freezer. She flinched when he gestured with his hands. She said that she and Chloe shouldn't impose on him another night. Jeb prayed he wouldn't come home to find lunch ready but her and the child gone. The very thought nearly gave him a heart attack.

"When bad weather hits, neighbors help neighbors," he said. "If you feel like you're running up a debt, you're right. When the next storm strikes, I'll be glad if you show up to lend me a hand. That's what we call paybacks. It's about helping out, and being there for each other. That's one advantage of living in a small town."

She nodded, but Jeb wasn't sure she really got it. Glancing at his watch, he knew he couldn't waste more time trying to reassure her. "Okay, I'm off to the races."

Standing by the table, she knotted her hands together and held them at her waist. "Take care."

"I will." Jeb wished he could ease her mind. He regretted asking her to fix lunch. She clearly feared that he might dislike what she made. *Shit*. He'd hoped to make her feel welcome, not give her more to worry about. He remembered that he needed to get his chain saw and chose to exit by the back door. As he pulled the door closed behind him, heading Bozo off at the pass with the angle of his leg, he yelled, "The downstairs bathroom could use a good cleaning." *Why the hell did I say that?* He poked his head back inside. "Only if you have the time. No big deal if you can't get to it. And Bozo is a beggar while I cook. He can't have garlic or onions, but other vegetables are fine."

After a shower, Amanda threw on clothes and the wool socks, and hurried back downstairs, intent on preparing Jeb a lunch that would keep him going until dusk. She hoped he liked what she fixed. Mark had sneered at her meals so often that she couldn't help worrying. She considered using the microwave thaw cycle, but in the past, she'd ended up with rubbery meat. So she decided to put the beef chunks in a Baggie floating in hot water while she threw together a batch of homemade bread. Not the proper way to thaw meat, she knew, but she'd never heard of anyone getting sick from it. She was elbow-deep in dough when Chloe appeared. Amanda washed up, served the child the extra breakfast she'd made, and resumed work. If lunch wasn't ready when Jeb got back, she had no idea how he might react.

After eating, Chloe went back upstairs to dress, and then wanted to help. Since leaving Mark, Amanda had been allowing Chloe to assist in the kitchen. That meant it took twice as long to prepare a meal, but Amanda enjoyed the one-on-one time. That wasn't the case now. Chloe's *help* would slow her down.

Thinking fast, she said, "Would you like to clean the bathroom?"

Chloe clapped her hands. She'd never been allowed to clean the bathroom before. Amanda found squirt bottles of antiseptic and glass cleaner, which she felt the girl could do no harm using, gave Chloe a roll of paper towels, and lined her up for an hour of squeezing the trigger and polishing. While giving Chloe instructions, she fretted over the bread dough. What if it started to rise and fell flat while it baked? All she'd be able to do was hide the evidence. Jeb hadn't asked for homemade bread. She needn't reveal that she'd wasted some of his flour and yeast, a criminal offense in Mark's household.

Amanda had just checked on Chloe's progress, covered the loaves to let them rise, and was about to start the stew when she noticed Bozo pacing by the back door. She called to tell Chloe she'd be on the rear porch while the dog did his business. But then the canine looked up at her as if he expected something more.

"What?" She felt silly for asking the question.

Bozo loped to the laundry room, waited for her to catch up, and then bumped a cupboard with his muzzle.

"Okay." Amanda opened the door. "And just what will I find in here?"

A set of red canine boots lay on one shelf. She'd seen pictures of the things but had no clue how they went on. Bozo lifted a front paw. The boots were all shaped the same, so she tugged one of them onto his foot and fastened it. The others were a snap.

"You are one lucky boy," she told him.

After bundling up, she stood on the porch, teeth chattering, while the mastiff toured the backyard. *Please, God, don't let him wander off.* Jeb would not be pleased if he came home to find Bozo gone.

The mastiff behaved well, going only a little way from the steps and then returning. She wondered if he always displayed such eagerness to end his potty runs, or if it was just too cold for him. Her flimsy jacket provided little protection, and back inside, she was shaking as she removed Bozo's boots.

The stew. If she didn't get it started soon, the meat wouldn't be tender by the time Jeb got back. Amanda was at the sink, peeling potatoes and carrots and tossing Bozo treats over her shoulder, when she heard Chloe sniffling behind her. She turned to see that the child's face was puffy and red from crying.

"I'm sorry, Mommy," Chloe said, wringing her small hands. "It said on the can that the bubbles would do all the work."

Amanda glanced toward the bathroom. "What bubbles, sweetie?"

"I found them under the sink. I wanted the bubbles to do the work so I could hurry back to help you cook."

With mounting dread, Amanda hurried to the bathroom. Her heart skipped a beat when she saw the mess Chloe had made. It looked as if a snowstorm had swept through. The large mirror was sprayed with foam and then had been smeared at one lower corner, presumably by Chloe in an attempt to clean up. The granite countertops, slate shower, toilet, and even the vanity cupboards now wore a layer of drippy white. It would take Amanda ages to undo the damage, and that was time she couldn't spare if she meant to have a noon meal waiting for Jeb.

"It's all right," she assured her daughter, hugging her close. *This is my fault. I should have supervised her cleaning efforts.* "I don't think any permanent damage is done. When lunch is over, I'll come in and clean it up."

"But then Mr. Jeb will be here. He'll be mad at me when he sees what I did."

Amanda couldn't argue the point. Jeb had no children and didn't understand how interesting life could sometimes be as a parent.

Amanda closed the bathroom door. "Let's just hope he doesn't see it."

"He'll want to go potty and wash his hands." Chloe's lower lip quivered.

Thinking quickly, Amanda said, "I'll encourage him to wash at the kitchen sink!"

She just prayed the foamy spray hadn't damaged the walnut finish on the vanity. The rest she felt sure she could restore to its original condition, leaving no sign that the "working bubbles" incident had ever happened.

By nine, Jeb had run low on emergency supplies and was back at the sporting goods store, filling a cart. Charlie was nearly sold out of some things. When Jeb entered the outerwear department and saw fine-quality stuff for both adults and children, he got an idea. Grabbing his cell phone, he dialed Myrna Bradley's home number. She answered on the second ring. Jeb said hello and asked how she was doing, then got to the point. "Do you believe it's okay to tell a little white lie if someone needs help and won't accept it?"

"Absolutely. That's why they're called little white lies."

Jeb grinned. "Remember that lady you talked with yesterday? She and her little girl need some decent outerwear. They don't even have gloves, mufflers, or caps, so far as I've seen. The little girl's parka is okay, but her snow boots leak. The mother has one pair of shoes, a thin jacket, and nothing else. I'd like to buy them some stuff, but if I call home to ask for their sizes, I'm afraid her pride will get in the way. She doesn't like being indebted to me."

"Hmm. Are you at a store right now?" Myrna asked. When Jeb affirmed that he was, she said, "Stick tight. She'll hear me on the answering machine. Right?"

"I'd think so."

"I'll get back to you in five."

Jeb started to ask about her plan, but she hung up. He pocketed his phone and continued shopping. True to her word, Myrna called him back in about three minutes.

"You got a pen and paper?"

Jeb grinned, went to the end of the aisle, put Myrna

on speaker, and opened a cell-phone notes application. "I'm ready. Shoot."

After Myrna had given him the sizes, she said, "Okay, here's the white lie. My kids come to visit with their young'uns, and they always forget to bring snow clothes, so they buy more and leave it with us. Now that the kids have outgrown everything, Tony's been bitching at me to clean out our closet, and with the bad weather, I tackled that chore. I meant to take everything to Good as New, but as I was tossing stuff in a bag, I thought of her and her little girl and decided to ask if they needed anything. She took a minute to say yes, but then she volunteered their sizes."

"You're an angel, Myrna."

"I'm a good liar when I need to be. So here's what you do. I told her I'd have you stop by here to pick up the clothes. Since she may watch from a window, you'll leave here with a garbage bag stuffed with newspaper. Act like it's heavy. Once back in your truck, do the switch, replacing the newspaper with the clothes. And for God's sake, don't forget to remove the tags and stickers. Tony doesn't when he gives me gifts."

"Got it," Jeb said, grinning so broadly his cheeks ached. "And God love you, Myrna. You've got a heart of gold."

Still smiling after he broke the connection, Jeb finished shopping and returned to the clothing section. For Amanda, he found a blue down-filled parka with a hood trimmed in fake fur. He also got her some matching snow pants and boots, plus a pair of pull-on, low-cut shoes that were waterproof. For Chloe, he chose pink all the way. He forgot gloves, hats, and mufflers, causing him to make a U-turn. *Tags and stickers*. He had to remove those. They'd be a dead giveaway.

The older lady running one of the registers had dyed black hair swirled up into a stiff cone atop her head. Face slathered with makeup, she looked like an alien. When she saw Jeb using his knife to remove the tags from his purchases, she said, "Oh, darling, let me help."

Darling? Jeb gave her a study and realized, with a lurch of his stomach, that she was coming on to him. *Shit.* She was older than his mother. She went to work with a small pair of scissors, her long scarlet nails flashing.

Kate Rush, a twentysomething blonde whose sister, Misty Baker, owned the Cherokee Rose florist shop on Seven Curves Road, caught Jeb's gaze and winked at him, a telltale sign that he wasn't the only man this older gal had victimized.

"Are these gifts?"

Jeb jerked his attention back to the man hunter. When she smiled, her caked cheeks creased with more lines than a road map. "Yes, ma'am."

She flapped a hand. "Don't call me ma'am, you handsome thing. My name is Bernice Kaley, Bernie to my friends, and I'd love to count you as one."

Jeb was afraid she'd give him her phone number next. She studied his credit card before swiping it.

"Jebediah Sterling. Now *that* is a masculine name if ever I've heard one."

Jeb made his escape as fast as possible. Circling the store to the parking lot, he threw all his purchases onto the truck's backseat and then walked across the icy asphalt to Flagg's Market, where he could buy cases of bottled water.

Amanda felt as nervous as a kitten in an overpopulated dog kennel. Because of the fabulous meal Jeb had thrown together last night, she felt less than confident about preparing his lunch. *Ridiculous.* That voice in her brain whispering how stupid and ineffective she was at everything was Mark's, not her own. She was a good cook. Mark had demanded tasty meals, forcing her to create great dishes on a limited budget. She could surely make Jeb Sterling a hot dish that would please him.

Her shoes had dried, so she put them on. When she looked out a window, she shivered even though the house was toasty. *Power lines thick with ice. Trees that looked frozen solid.* If she were out in that weather, she'd want a hot meal, too.

Chloe sat at the table drawing on paper filched from Jeb's office trash as Amanda removed loaves of bread from the oven. Bozo, snoozing beside the girl, suddenly lifted his gigantic head and released a happy "Woof!" Amanda suspected Jeb had pulled up in his truck. Chloe cast her a panicked look.

"He's going to see the bathroom, Mommy. I just know it."

Amanda had laid out a towel and soap by the kitchen sink, hoping to keep Jeb out of there. She heard the front door open, followed by the clank of chains on the slate.

"I'm home!" he called, his deep voice reaching them in the kitchen.

Followed by Bozo and Chloe, Amanda went to meet him. Standing in the entry hall with a bulging black trash bag at his feet, he pulled a wet stocking cap off his head. His burnished face was red from the cold, and his tawny hair stood up in spikes. Amanda had never seen so handsome a man, not because he was *GQ* perfect, but because he looked good without trying. "Man, this house smells divine!" Indicating the garbage sack with a dip of his head, he added, "That's from Myrna across the road. She called me on my cell and asked me to drop by her place to pick it up."

"Her kids left a bunch of outerwear at her house, and Tony asked her to get rid of it. She called to see if Chloe and I might want some of it, asked our sizes, and said she'd set aside whatever would fit us. The rest is going to Good as New."

Jeb stripped off his soiled leather gloves and smoothed his hair. "I've still got houses to visit, so I'm short on time. Let me shed a few layers, wash up, and I'll be ready to eat."

Chloe, leaning against Amanda's leg, stiffened. "I, um, laid out soap and a towel for you by the kitchen sink," Amanda said, her voice wobbly with nervousness.

He laughed. "My hands are too filthy for that. Frozen traps, sewer lines, you name it. I don't want all those germs in the kitchen. Be right in."

Chloe made a soft bleating sound that made Amanda's heart twist. "I can disinfect the kitchen sink," she tried. "I have a towel and a bar of soap all laid out for you in there." *Please, God, don't let him go in that bathroom.* "It'll be nicer. That way, you can fill us in on your day while you wash up."

"I'll fill you in over lunch," he replied.

Jeb divested himself of his jacket, kicked off the chained boots, gave the growling Bozo a pat on the head, and then walked in stocking feet around Amanda and Chloe toward the bathroom. Chloe spun to follow him.

"I'm sorry, Mr. Jeb. I didn't mean to do it!"

Jeb froze with his hand on the door handle. "Do what, honey?"

Amanda could see Chloe trembling and wished she

had a weapon. Her insides clenched tight, she took a step toward her daughter.

Jeb opened the bathroom door, stared at the disaster for a second, and then said, "Holy Toledo, what happened here?"

Chloe started to sob.

Chapter Five

Jeb stared in amazement at his once-beautiful bathroom. The foam Chloe had sprayed on everything but the walls had gone watery and dripped, leaving pools of liquid white on the countertops and the slate floor. He'd dealt with some pretty awful messes in his day, which went with the territory when you raised livestock, but he had never witnessed a bathroom attack.

It wasn't really funny, especially considering Chloe's distress, but Jeb felt an urge to laugh swelling at the base of his throat. He kept a spray can of bubble cleaner in one of the vanity cupboards, which he used to clean the porcelain sinks, and he chose to use it for precisely the same reason that Chloe had, so the bubbles could do most of the work.

"This is a quite a disaster," he found the presence of mind to say.

"I'm sorry," Chloe said in a tiny, choked voice.

Jeb turned to look at the child and saw that she was trembling with apprehension. He swept her up in his arms. She shrieked with fear and pushed against Jeb's chest, trying to escape his embrace. "Hey, hey, hey," he crooned. "Don't be scared, sweetie. I'm not mad."

Chloe fixed a swimming brown gaze on his and stilled in his embrace. "You aren't?"

Jeb noticed that Amanda stood as stiff as a board and had knotted her slender fists. *Fair enough*. She'd said in one of her breeze-delivered notes that she'd die before she ever let him—meaning her nameless husband—hurt this child again. So now she expected the worst from Jeb.

Ignoring the mother, Jeb focused on the little girl, whose body quivered against his chest. He stepped into the bathroom, talking as he bent to fetch the spray can of bubbly bathroom cleaner, which felt half empty. "Of course I'm not mad," he assured Chloe. "It's clear that you made a mistake, but I'm betting it was only because you've never cleaned a bathroom before."

"Nope," Chloe agreed, still shaking.

Jeb finally allowed his laughter to erupt. Giving the can a brisk shake, he commenced with spraying the mirror again with snowy white and then turned on a trickle of cold water. "Well, sometimes, the only thing to do when you mess up is to make the best of it. So I think we should have a little fun."

"Fun?" Chloe squeaked, but Jeb felt the tension ease slightly from her frame.

"Fun," he assured her. "Let's draw pictures!" He started by drawing a small heart in the foam. Then he rinsed his fingertip in the water. "Your turn."

Chloe stared up at him, her eyes still shadowy with fear. It occurred to Jeb that her father might have sometimes lulled her into believing he wasn't angry, only to turn on her when she relaxed. The thought nearly broke his heart.

"It's okay," he said in a low voice. "Take your turn. I promise nothing bad will happen."

With a still-shaky hand, Chloe drew an arrow through the heart.

"Cupid's bow? Very good," Jeb said. Next he drew a fair replica of his dog's head, floppy ears included.

"Bozo!" Chloe giggled. "You forgot his melting lips!"

"You add them," he encouraged. "But rinse off first or you'll smear our picture."

The little girl drew what Jeb could recognize as jowls by using his imagination, and then she added zigzag lines dripping from Bozo's bottom lip.

"Drool!" Jeb said with a chuckle. "That tells me you've been treated to one of his string-slinging moments."

Chloe nodded, looking up at Jeb with large, innocent brown eyes. Searching her expression, he saw wonder and incredulity that he wasn't mad at her. In that moment, Jeb knew he was a goner. It was far too easy to lose one's heart to a child, any child, but a little girl like Chloe, who'd been mistreated, didn't merely worm her way into a man's affections. She crashed right through all his defenses.

Amanda turned her back and walked away so Jeb and Chloe wouldn't see her tears. She wasn't sure what kind of reaction she'd been expecting from this man, but she'd never in her wildest dreams thought that he'd turn the bathroom debacle into a game to make her daughter laugh. In the kitchen, after grabbing a paper towel to wipe her face and blow her nose, Amanda washed and dried her hands, and then began slicing the still-warm bread. From the other room, she could hear Chloe giggling and Jeb laughing. Amanda knew Jeb had worked hard all morning, and she found it extraordinary that he could muster the energy during his only break before dark to make a child feel better.

When man and girl entered the kitchen, Amanda had a platter of warm bread, plates, and a saucer of butter on the table. She was filling bowls with stew when Jeb nearly startled her out of her shoes with, "Holy smokes, home-made bread? Oh, man! That smells so good I could almost swallow my tongue. My machine-made stuff isn't the same."

"Mommy's bread is the best!" Chloe exclaimed.

Amanda heard chairs scrape as they seated themselves. Then Jeb said, "Let's pretend this is our appetizer. We can say the blessing before we eat our stew."

"I like the heel," Chloe said.

"No," Jeb said with an exaggerated note of complaint, "I have dibs on *all* the heels."

Amanda suspected that Jeb hoped for some verbal sparring from Chloe, but cowed as she'd been for most of her life, she quietly said, "Okay, you can have them."

Jeb chuckled. "I was teasing, Chloe. We'll share the heels." Silence. "Amanda, are you a heel lover, too? Chloe and I can divide them up into thirds."

Amanda found herself smiling. Glancing over her shoulder, she said, "I prefer a center slice slathered with butter."

"You've got it." Jeb pulled a center slice from the plat-ter and put it on Amanda's bread plate. "The smell of that stew has my mouth watering. Ladle it up faster."

Amanda almost switched gears to super speed, but then she realized Jeb hadn't issued an order. He was teasing again. She released a breath she hadn't realized she'd been holding. Her muscles began to relax.

After she had set bowls of stew on the table, she took a chair across from Jeb, with Chloe sitting to her right.

"Chloe," Jeb said softly, "would you like to say the blessing today?"

Chloe shot him a startled look. "I don't know how. Daddy never let us pray."

Jeb switched his gaze from Chloe to Amanda. "Are you against praying over food?"

Amanda said, "Heavens, no. I grew up in a household that prayed before every meal, only we held hands and my dad always did the honors."

"Well," Jeb replied, "in my family we take turns." He extended his hand across the table to Amanda, and then each of them grasped one of Chloe's. Feeling the warmth and strength of Jeb's long, thick fingers around hers sent a shiver up Amanda's spine. Jeb said, "You can say the blessing, Chloe. It doesn't have to be a memorized prayer. You can just tell Jesus that our lunch looks good, and that we're thankful for the gifts."

Chloe stammered at first, but she finally got the words out, finishing with, "I'm so hungry my stomach is growling!"

Jeb laughed and said, "Amen."

Amanda realized that she'd forgotten napkins and excused herself to fetch sections from the roll of paper towels.

"Don't bother folding them," Jeb told her. "We'll only unfold them again."

Amanda handed each of them a towel and kept one for herself. Her stomach knotted again as she watched Jeb take a huge bite of fresh bread. He murmured his pleasure as he chewed. One down. Now, if only he liked the stew.

After spooning some into his mouth, he said, "Fabulous. This is even better than Mom's. Don't tell her I said that. She'd never get over it."

Amanda bent her head to hide a smile of sheer relief. As she tucked into her meal, she enjoyed the wondrous experience of dining with a man without feeling as if her stomach were tied in knots. Jeb excused himself and got up to serve himself a second helping. To Amanda's surprise, Chloe said, "'Scuse me," grabbed her own empty bowl, and raced after him. "May I have more, too?"

"Absolutely," Jeb assured the child. "One ladle or two?"

The child's smile wavered. "One. I get in bad trouble if I don't eat all my food."

"Hmm. Well, you won't get in bad trouble around here," Jeb told her. "So you get two ladles, and if you can't eat all of it, we'll pick out the chunks of meat and vegetables as treats for Bozo. The rest can go in the laundry room slop bucket."

"How come Bozo can't eat all of it?"

"Because onions and garlic make dogs sick. He can eat all the rest, though. My pig, Babe, will devour what's left."

When they got back to the table and resumed eating, Amanda couldn't resist saying, "I had dogs growing up, and we fed them cooked onions and garlic all the time."

Jeb shrugged. "Everyone in my family used to, too. But in recent years, they've discovered that onions and garlic, along with chocolate, grapes, and raisins, are very toxic to canines." He cocked an eyebrow. "Maybe cooked onions and garlic aren't as harmful as raw. I've never researched it online."

"What do onions and garlic do to them?" Amanda asked.

"It stops them from producing red blood cells, or something like that. It's been a while since I read about it, so I can't recall the particulars."

Amanda picked a piece of tender beef from her bowl, cleaned the sauce away with her spoon, and fed it to the eager mastiff, who sat with his dripping jowls nearly touching her elbow. Since she'd tossed him bits of raw vegetables while she cooked, she'd apparently become his go-to person for the day's treats.

After giving the dog a bite, she shot Jeb a questioning look. "I hope it's all right to feed him at the table. I should have asked first."

Jeb grinned. "He's tall enough to rest his chin on the table, with a long enough tongue to wash all the dishes for me before I can get them to the sink. So I don't allow him to touch the table, but I do toss him treats. You can give him more if you like." He studied the dog, frowning slightly, and Amanda could have sworn she heard him whisper, "Traitor."

Lunch was so enjoyable that Amanda hated for it to end. When Jeb returned to the entry to pull on his storm gear, she followed. He was bent at the waist to put on his chained boots when she said, "Thank you for not getting angry about the bathroom. If the cleaner damaged the wood finishes, I'll repair them."

He glanced up. "I finish wood for a living. I doubt the cleaner hurt it any, but if it did, I'll take care of it. Don't worry about it. Okay?" He straightened. As he drew on his coat, he added, "I'm not given to frequent outbursts of temper, Amanda. That isn't to say that I don't get angry. I do. But it takes a lot to rile me."

Gesturing toward the bathroom, Amanda said, "That was a lot."

He flashed his sunny grin, warm enough to make a crocus bloom in the dead of winter. "That was an accident. Chloe just hoped to save time by letting the bubbles do the work. I like the way she's thinking. I bought the damned stuff for the very same reason." He winked. "I'm just old enough to read the fine print."

"For a man with no children, you're very understanding."

"I was a kid once. When you meet my dad, ask him about the time my brother and I decided we wanted a yellow lab instead of a black one and spray-painted the dog."

Amanda couldn't stifle a giggle. "You didn't!"

"Oh, yeah, and it wasn't water-soluble paint. My dad had to call the vet to see what he could use to get it off. The vet said the usual solvents would burn the dog's skin. They discussed shaving him, but it was the middle of summer, and the dog spent a lot of time outside with my father. The vet said the risk of a sunburn was more dangerous than any toxins in the dried paint. So Blackie went around wearing yellow patches for a while. Labs shed a lot, and Blackie's fur, held together by the paint, hung off him like leaves about to fall from a tree limb."

Amanda laughed again.

"And every time a chunk finally fell off, my dad made us pick it up and reminded us that we'd better never paint the dog again."

"You didn't get a spanking?"

Jeb shook his head. "My dad would give us a knuckle rub on our heads sometimes, but he didn't believe in spanking." He glanced at his watch. "I gotta go. There are a lot of old people on Elderberry."

Amanda hugged her waist. "I know. We moved there

in August, and Chloe hoped to find kids to play with on our road. Instead she sat on the porch and watched ants crawl for the remainder of the summer." She swallowed hard. She hated to ask him for a favor. "Um—will you be going near the end of Elderberry today?"

"Yeah. Why?"

"I forgot a little SD card in my top bureau drawer. It's extremely important to me."

"No worry. I'll grab it for you." Turning toward the door, Jeb nearly tripped over the bag of clothing that Myrna had sent over. He handed it to Amanda. "I hope some of this stuff will come in handy." He paused to glance back at her before exiting. "By any chance do you like chocolate chip cookies?"

Startled by the question, Amanda took a moment to reply. "They're my favorite."

He winked. "No special order, but it sure would be nice to come back home to some."

"How do you like them, crisp or chewy?" she asked.

"Chewy, but then, I've never met a chocolate chip cookie I didn't like, so either will make me happy."

After the door closed behind him, Amanda carried the bag into the family room adjoining the kitchen. "Maybe you can see what Mrs. Bradley sent over to us while I do dishes," she told her daughter.

Chloe was soon squealing with delight, which drew Amanda back to her.

"Look, Mommy," she cried. "I got a brand-new pink jacket with white fur and snow pants to match." She peered into the bag again. "And new pink boots!" Her face fell. "What if nothing fits?"

"Everything should," Amanda assured her. "I gave Mrs. Bradley our sizes."

Amanda picked up the pink parka. It looked and smelled brand-new—too new for a garment left inside a coat closet since last winter. Suspicious, she sat down on the brown love seat and started riffling through the bag with her daughter. Gloves, mufflers, a woman's down-filled blue parka with a fur-lined hood. Women's snow boots and ski pants. And most suspicious of all, a sturdy pair of low-rise winter shoes, made more like boots. An expert on secondhand clothing, Amanda searched the innersoles for an impression of someone else's foot. These things weren't secondhand. She sniffed the shoe, and all she smelled was fresh-from-the-box newness.

Amanda couldn't resist trying on the blue parka. Oh, how delicious it felt, the down instantly holding in her body heat. How many times, as she'd walked to work, had she yearned for a better jacket? This one reached to below her hips and had a drawstring waist. And there were pants, gloves, a muffler, a stocking cap, and boots to match! Not a single item showed any wear.

She sank back down on the love seat. Jeb Sterling could be very sneaky when he chose to be. He'd known that Amanda wouldn't accept these things as gifts. She almost told Chloe they couldn't wear them, but when she looked at the child, she couldn't force the words out. Chloe had donned her snow pants and pink boots—expensive ones this time, that would never leak—and she pranced around like Cinderella trying out her pretty glass slippers.

Suddenly Chloe froze and peered at her mother. "Mommy, are you sure these things came from Mrs. Myrna? They don't smell like thrift-store stuff."

Amanda's throat tightened. *Now or never.* She needed to tell the child that these were gifts from Mr. Jeb that they couldn't keep. Only—oh, how the thought of doing that sliced at her heart. She'd prayed for good snow boots for Chloe. She'd even asked for a warm jacket for herself. Now her prayers had been answered. Wouldn't it be wrong, somehow, to refuse these things simply because they'd come from a man to whom she didn't wish to be indebted?

"I think Mr. Jeb played a trick on us," Amanda settled for saying. "He saw that we needed warmer clothing, but he knew I wouldn't allow him to buy any for us."

Chloe hung her head. "That means we can't keep it, doesn't it?"

Amanda took a deep breath and released it. "No. I prayed for us to have all these things. God does answer prayers, Chloe. We needed them very badly. I think what we must do is graciously accept the presents and tell Mr. Jeb thank you."

Chloe's eyes sparkled when she lifted her chin. "He's nice. Isn't he, Mommy? Not mean like my daddy."

Amanda's guard went up. "We haven't known Mr. Jeb long enough to be certain that he's nice, sweetie. But I must agree that he seems to be."

Chloe shook her head, sending her dark hair in a silky flow over her shoulders. "I know he's nice."

Amanda didn't want her child to be hurt by putting her trust in a man who didn't deserve it. "Sweetie, you can't possibly know that for sure, not yet."

"Yes, I can. Bozo told me."

"Bozo?" Amanda recalled how the mastiff had told her about his boots.

Chloe nodded. "It was in dog talk, Mommy, but he said it loud and clear. Mr. Jeb is nice. He never hits dogs or little girls. He doesn't do that to mommies, either. And he don't kick dogs or people in the tummy."

"Doesn't," Amanda corrected, feeling as if she'd just stepped into water way over her head. She knew that Chloe and Bozo had formed a friendship, and she didn't wish to make light of that. Besides, Amanda couldn't deny that the dog seemed to adore Jeb; he never cowered from him, and even had quality doggy boots to put on his feet before he went outside. All the signs confirmed that Jeb was a kind and caring man. "Maybe Bozo has it right," she conceded. "But let's be cautious before we trust Mr. Jeb too much. Okay?"

Chloe nodded. "He didn't get mad about the working bubbles."

"No, he didn't." The declaration reminded Amanda that she still hadn't done the dishes, had lots of work waiting in the bathroom, and then would need to start supper. She pushed herself up from the love seat and shrugged out of the parka. "Don't leave any of your new things lying on the floor. Fold them neatly and put them back in the bag. We'll decide where to put them later."

"Why not in the closet where Mr. Jeb puts some of his stuff?"

Amanda, moving toward the kitchen, paused in midstride. "Because that is Mr. Jeb's closet. We are only his guests. The moment this ice melts, we have to go home."

"Our house is icky and has leaks."

Amanda still hadn't gotten a call from her landlord, so she wasn't sure what to say. "Broken pipes can be fixed. Don't start thinking that this will last; it's only temporary."

"I sure do like it here. I wish we could stay."

"I'm sorry, sweetness. That can't happen."

"Why not?" Chloe frowned; then her expression brightened. "I know! We can go to town, and you can meet Mr.

Jeb on the natural bridge! Then you'll fall in love, and we can stay here for always!"

"I don't think Mr. Jeb is interested in meeting me on the bridge and falling in love."

Chloe put her hands on her hips. "I see how he looks at you when you aren't watching him."

Amanda froze in midstride again. "What do you mean? How does he look at me?"

Chloe pursed her lips. "I don't know. Sort of like you're chocolate ice cream and he doesn't have a spoon."

Amanda's stomach knotted. She finally collected her composure, ignored the comment, and went to work. A few minutes later, as she polished the granite countertops and the stainless-steel appliance fronts, she decided this was the most beautiful kitchen she'd ever seen. Auxiliary power hadn't been run to a few of the less crucial appliances, but necessary things ran fine. No need for flashlights, blankets, bottled water, or anything else. Amanda recognized perfect when she saw it.

The bathroom required less time to clean than Amanda had anticipated, so she took a break with Chloe at the kitchen table, drawing pictures on the paper she'd found in Jeb's office trash. *What an office.* It had built-in cabinets and bookshelves. She'd felt sad as she studied the two desks with cubbyholes and cupboards above them and file cabinet drawers on either side. Jeb truly had built this home for a family and had even thought to make sure his future wife would have her own workstation.

Chloe didn't mind the typing on the reverse side of her drawing paper, and Amanda felt guilt-free about using the sheets because Jeb had already thrown them away. Amanda created pictures of the ice-encrusted world outside, failing to duplicate its magical beauty. Chloe drew pictures of Bozo, some of them so true to life that Amanda wondered if her daughter might become a skilled artist.

After baking chocolate chip cookies, Amanda decided to make steak Diane sans the tableside fire show for dinner. Flambéed dishes were fun, but considering the way her luck ran with men, she'd probably set Jeb's hair aflame. Chloe insisted on helping, so Amanda tied a dish towel around her neck to serve as an apron, stood her on a chair, and assigned her the task of washing the red potatoes, a head of broccoli, and some green beans. Bozo, who had attached himself to Chloe with invisible strings, became their cleanup helper, devouring every tidbit that hit the floor. Amanda had adored her dogs as a kid, and she found herself falling in love with Bozo, too. He was a gentle giant. She made sure to put his snow boots on often to go outside, only now she wore her new parka as she waited on the porch, and she barely felt the cold.

Gazing out over the frosty landscape, she hoped that she and Chloe could go home tomorrow, but a thaw didn't appear to be imminent. They might be stuck here for far longer than she'd planned. At least it was a pleasant place to pass the time. She needed to be grateful for that, and for the duration of their stay, she would cook and clean for Jeb, the only ways she knew to repay his kindness.

Jeb had put in a lot of long days, but today beat them all. He drove from house to house, helping elderly people and getting a break only when he sat behind the steering wheel. As he skated to and from his truck, he began to think evening would never come.

His last stop was at Amanda's place. No people in dire need here, at least not now. He'd find Amanda's SD card and check the house. He was pretty sure he had flipped off all the switches in her breaker box. Sometimes the power went off while people were cooking, and if they weren't home when the juice came back on, fires could start.

As Jeb pulled into the driveway area, dusk had settled over Mystic Creek. He grabbed a flashlight, aware that some of the rooms might be dark, and were probably still coated with ice. With a sigh, he cut the truck's engine, opened the driver's-side door, and braced himself for another skating session. As he walked toward the ram- shackle rental, something about its silhouette against the darkening sky seemed off-kilter. Jeb stopped, stared, and felt a jolt of alarm when he determined that the front section of the roof had collapsed. *Shit.* Without any heat inside the dwelling, the snow and ice hadn't thawed enough to slide off. The storm last night had added to the weight.

Making his way to the porch, Jeb shone his flashlight beam through the front windows. He saw three support beams lying in a tangle, like pickup-sticks, over the old sofa where Chloe and Amanda had huddled together for warmth just yesterday. *Thank God I insisted that they go home with me. If I hadn't, they'd both possibly be dead right now.* No way would Jeb allow Amanda to reenter this dump to get her personal things. The rest of the roof could cave in at any moment. Jeb didn't like the idea of going inside himself.

Amanda was stubborn, though. And, from what Jeb had seen, she had precious little by way of possessions. He couldn't stay in there long enough to get all of her knickknacks, but he could make a quick sweep to collect pictures, important paperwork, and whatever else might be irreplaceable.

Because the front of the house was impassable, Jeb made his way out back and scaled the two steps of the stoop. The door was locked. He rammed the panel with his shoulder and nearly fell into the ice-covered kitchen. *Son of a bitch.* He caught his balance, shone his light on the locking mechanism, and saw that the metal had been mounted on rotten, crumbling wood. *What the hell?* Who in his right mind would rent out a hovel like this?

Feeling like a moose walking on window glass, he stepped into the kitchen. The ice had crusted over, making it less slick than yesterday. He crept through the house, carefully avoiding debris in the dining area and living room to reach the short hall, where the two bedrooms and bathroom were accessible.

Following Amanda's example from yesterday, he took pillowcases from the linen closet and began filling them with anything Amanda might consider invaluable. In her bedroom, he found a framed photo of Chloe, a worn Bible, three novels from the local library, and clothes in her wobbly old bureau that were one step up from being rags. As he stuffed them into a case, he found the SD card and tossed that in, too.

In Chloe's room, he gathered more clothing, all of better quality than her mother's, a clown lamp, a picture of her mom, and about thirty children's books. As Jeb swept the books from the shelves into the bag, he heard a loud groan and then a crack that resounded throughout the house like a rifle shot. He froze and listened, his heart pounding with fear. He was a big man, his body well padded with muscle, but he would be just as vulnerable to injury as Amanda and Chloe if roof beams rained down on his head.

That's it. I'm out of here. If he'd missed anything else important, that was too damned bad. No possession on earth was worth dying for. Collecting the stuffed pillowcases, Jeb moved through the house, trying to be light of foot. As he passed through the kitchen, he thrust Amanda's pink tablet in one bag. He didn't breathe easy until he'd reach the backyard. Turning, he stared at the house, his eyes burning from the extreme cold. His entire body jerked when, with loud snaps and a huge *boom*, the rest of the roof fell in. *Sweet Jesus.* Jeb had never seen anything like it. Amanda's landlord ought to be sued for allowing people to live in such a rattrap. He should at least be forced to reimburse his tenant for all her furnishings — not that there was anything inside worth a hoot, anyway.

As he walked to his truck, Jeb realized he was shaking. If he'd taken even a minute longer to get out, he would be caught under a pile of rubble right now. What frightened him even more was that it could have been Amanda and Chloe in there.

As he drove home, ever conscious that his studded tires had become as ineffectual as his shoe chains on the slick ice, he pondered how to tell Amanda that her home would never be habitable again. She'd be devastated. She clung hard to her independence. How could she afford to furnish another rental?

He imagined the shadows that would haunt her brown eyes when she realized she had nowhere to go.

Chapter Six

Jeb was no expert on kids, but he decided he shouldn't tell Amanda about the roof cave-in when Chloe was present. He would leave the pillowcases filled with their things in his truck until the child was asleep. Then he'd sit Amanda down at the kitchen table and tell her as gently as possible that she'd just joined the ranks of the homeless.

As he pulled up in front of his house, it hit him that those two pillowcases on his backseat contained almost the entirety of Amanda's and Chloe's personal effects. *I will never allow them to live in a dump like that again.* As the thought settled into his brain, he realized that he had no say-so about what Amanda did. *The hell I don't.* He could help her find another rental. As for furniture, he had plenty to spare that she could borrow until she could afford to buy her own. Before she got another house, he'd do a walk-through to make sure it was structurally sound.

Feeling as tired emotionally as he was physically, Jeb entered his home wishing he had a pocketful of magic. Only he didn't. Bozo came racing to the door at such a high speed that he slipped when he braked and would have fallen if Jeb hadn't grabbed his shoulders to steady him. Not an easy feat when the dog weighed more than he did. Jeb guessed Bozo had separation anxiety. He was seldom left at home.

"Whoa, boy! I put in slate to prevent slipping. Don't burst my bubble."

Jeb received a wet slurp from Bozo's tongue that got him on the mouth. He resisted the urge to wipe the kiss away. He felt, way down deep, that doing so would hurt Bozo's feelings.

Apparently Bozo's sharp hearing had paid off, because tonight no one else came to greet him. Jeb set a sack of surprises for Chloe near the closet door. Then he peeled off layers of heavy outer clothing, hanging it on the coat tree, knobs, mantel corners, and the top of the open closet door to dry overnight. He found his second pair of work boots inside the closet, stripped off the chained ones, and sat on the sofa to pull on footwear that wouldn't make him sound like a ghost rattling through a haunted house.

By then, Bozo had vanished, telling Jeb that the dog's eager greeting had been out of habit more than true mourning over his absence. He went into the downstairs bathroom to scrub and disinfect his hands, noting that Amanda had cleaned up the "working bubbles" mess and made everything shine like new.

When he crossed the hallway and stepped into the kitchen area, he saw his dog sitting beside Chloe, who knelt on a chair at the table. The mastiff gazed at the child with absolute adoration. Jeb no longer resented the dog's shift of affection. He felt the same way about the little girl and, with mounting concern, realized that he was becoming just as attached to her mother.

Am I losing my mind? She was just another pretty

lady, only she was put together like a small, perfect gift, wrapped in shabby paper with a tattered bow. But, oh, man, he wanted to strip that away and see what was hidden underneath.

I need to go on a date, no strings attached, and score. Jeb dragged in a deep, bracing lungful of air. Amanda was beautiful, no question about it, and he was coming to believe that she was just as lovely on the inside. But that was no reason for him to hurtle clear over the edge. That was a good way to get his heart broken.

Busy at the work island, Amanda moved in the fast, efficient way that had become eye candy for him. The kitchen television was on, the volume turned low. While chopping a tomato, she paused to listen to the weather forecast with a darling wrinkle of her nose. Clearly, she did not like what she'd just heard. Jeb allowed his gaze to drift over her and linger in places it shouldn't. Chocolate chip cookies, a sweet little girl, a dinner that smelled like heaven—and a woman who was swiftly laying claim to his heart. He needed to snap out of it. Just because his mom believed in fated lovers who hadn't found each other yet didn't mean that he had to plunge into the insanity with her.

Amanda saw Jeb standing there, jerked, and cut her forefinger. As she grabbed her hand, he saw blood pooling. She turned her back on him to run cold water over her injury. He hurried past Chloe and his besotted mastiff to enter the work area. Stepping close behind Amanda, he peered over her shoulder, watching her try to stop the bleeding with a viselike squeeze of her fingers just below the cut as the icy flow worked its magic.

"How bad is it?" he asked, sensing that his nearness made her uneasy.

"Oh, it's nothing." She moved to put a slight distance between them. "I just need to stop the bleeding."

Jeb determined that the cut ran deep. It wasn't long, though. A butterfly bandage would pull the edges together and do the trick without his having to take her in for stitches. Even so, she had to be relieved of KP duty for the rest of the evening. Oddly, his earlier exhaustion vanished. Being near her revitalized him. How nuts was that?

"My turn to play nurse." He grabbed a kitchen towel and stepped over to the freezer side of his Sub-Zero. When he'd filled the towel with ice to create a pack, he moved back to the sink. Amanda tried to protest, but he wouldn't allow her to finish the meal when she was hurt. *Screw that.* "Here. Get it on ice, squeeze it hard, and go sit with Chloe. I'll finish up."

She sent him a flash of those gorgeous eyes, which were beginning to make him feel as if he might lose his balance, fall in, and drown. "You've worked hard all day," she said. "You must be exhausted."

Jeb made sure nothing required his immediate attention in the kitchen. The oven timer read ten minutes, allowing him plenty of leeway to bandage her finger and then take over the meal prep. He went for the first-aid kit, saying over his shoulder, "Keep pressure on it. I'll have you fixed up in no time."

When he returned, he found her sitting near Chloe, icing and squeezing the finger. "I've ruined the towel. You'll never get the stains out."

Jeb figured she might be right. "It's pure cotton. I'll be able to use it in my shop." He dragged a chair around to sit beside her and went to work. She'd whacked the blade deep, which told him that the mere sight of him, when unexpected, frightened her into a mindless zone. He wished he knew the full name of the jerk who'd made her so afraid of men. He'd be online later tonight to locate him. *Ten minutes*. That was all Jeb figured he'd need to teach the bastard a lesson he'd never forget. "It doesn't need stitches," he pronounced, still so angry from thinking about her husband that his molars ached from clenching his teeth. He willed himself to relax, not wanting Amanda to think he was angry with her. "I think you'll live."

"Well, of course. I've lived through far worse."

Jeb glanced up. The memories of far worse injuries were etched upon her face. How could any man lift a hand to her? Jeb knew from Amanda's notes that she slept restlessly, terrified that her husband might find her. That saddened him. Even armed with a knife or a skillet, Amanda stood no chance against such a man. She undoubtedly realized that and felt afraid much of the time. Despite the fabulous smell of chocolate chip cookies and a mysterious dinner that filled the room with a mouthwatering aroma, he felt his stomach turn.

"Okay," he said as he sat back on the chair. How could a lady's forefinger be so little? On his finger the same cut would have been a nick. It drove home to him just how much larger he was, and the realization made him want to shrink and slump his shoulders. "Got you all fixed up. So where are we with dinner? I'll finish up."

"You have latex gloves under the sink. I'll just put on one of those and finish everything. I was almost done, anyway." She looked over her shoulder. "The instant the oven timer goes off, everything will be ready. I made steak. I've got vegetables in the warmer, and all the salad needs is diced tomato. I'll be fine."

Jeb's kitchen gloves were extra-extra-large, and her

small hands could easily fit inside to protect the bandage. *Shit.* He'd created a balloon at the end of her finger, using enough gauze to cover a bullet wound. He guessed it was a subconscious reaction to how protective he felt. If that no-account, abusive jerk found her here, Jeb would kick the snot out of him.

"You're not lifting a finger," he insisted.

He went to the kitchen and finished chopping the tomato, jumped to remove the baking pan from the oven when the timer went off, and fetched the vegetables from the warmer. He walked back and forth, bringing the food to the table. As he grabbed plates, flatware, and paper towels for place settings, he asked, "Is this steak Diane?"

Interrupted while telling Chloe to put her drawing materials on the extra chair, Amanda sent him a wary look. "Yes, but I did it my own way. I'm not good at flambéed dishes. Well, I don't know for sure, but I'm thinking that fire and I don't mix."

Jeb figured Amanda and an abusive husband didn't mix, either, which was fine with him. She was ready to move on—had, in fact, already moved on—and she'd landed in his lap. He couldn't help but believe that divine orchestration might be at work. He'd never put much stock in the legend of Mystic Creek, that any lonely stranger who stood along its banks was destined to find true love, but now, with Amanda in his home, he wondered if there wasn't some truth to it.

He set the table. He flapped paper towels as if they were made of fine linen and settled them over his guests' laps, not surprised when Amanda flinched. Then he played server. He considered flambéing the entrée, but as much as Chloe might love it, he didn't want to upstage Amanda's efforts to prepare a fine meal.

And it *was* fine. Jeb liked to play chef and gave himself high marks, but this lady was phenomenal. After asking Chloe to say the blessing, which she delivered with more confidence than she had earlier, Jeb dug into the meal.

"School is canceled again tomorrow," Amanda said after swallowing a bite of salad. "It sounds as if Mystic Creek has been hit horribly hard."

She was clearly trying to hide her worry. Jeb figured she was concerned because she couldn't afford so many days off, and he regretted that he'd be adding to her stress when he told her that the roof of her rental had collapsed.

"It's definitely the worst weather I've ever seen," he agreed. He took a bite of the steak, chewed, and then swallowed. "Oh, man, you're kidding me!"

Amanda's face drained of color. "Is it awful?" She jumped up from her chair and circled the table. Jeb noticed that she stood between him and Chloe. "I'll fix you something else really fast."

His heart hurt for her, but he had no time to dwell on that. "Awful?" He gestured with his fork. "You take this plate, and I'll pout for a week."

He saw her shoulders relax. "So you like it?"

"Like it? It's delicious." Jeb watched as she resumed her seat, then added, "Just for the record, not everything anyone prepares is always going to be fabulous. When you don't hit your goal, the food will most likely still be edible, and in this house, edible gets high marks. I'm never going to get mad because something isn't quite to my taste."

"My daddy did," Chloe chimed in.

"Hush, Chloe," Amanda whispered.

Chloe flashed her mother an apologetic look and filled her mouth with food.

Jeb pretended he hadn't noticed the exchange, wondering just what kind of hell Amanda had lived through if even her meals had been cause for mistreatment.

"This salad is a gourmet delight," he commented, and meant it. Except for the tomatoes, which he had added, all the other ingredients had been chopped into tiny pieces, allowing a blend of flavors that made dressing unnecessary. "I'm doing good if I throw wedges of tomato over iceberg lettuce."

Some of the color seeped back into Amanda's cheeks, but Jeb noticed that her hands trembled as she resumed eating. "It's minced salad. My grandma always made it for holidays, and I became addicted."

He decided ordinary conversation was needed to dispel the tension. Turning to Chloe, he asked, "So, how did your day go, princess?"

"How come you're calling me princess?"

Jeb shrugged. "You're as pretty as a princess, so why not? And because you look like a princess, today I got you some shampoo and bath bubbles that every princess should have. I left the bag by the entry closet."

Chloe started to wiggle from her chair, but Amanda stopped her. "Not right now, sweetie. We're still eating. It's impolite to leave the table unless it's necessary."

To assuage the child's disappointment, Jeb asked again about her day.

Chloe smiled, revealing missing front teeth. "I helped Mommy cook, and then I made the chocolate chip cookies all by myself with hardly any help."

"Wow! You did?" Jeb glanced at Amanda, who blushed and dipped her head. He determined that although Chloe was taking all the credit for dessert, her mother had more than supervised. "I've got ice cream in the laundry room freezer. After dinner, we'll have a dessert party!"

All during the meal, Jeb tried to think how he should tell Amanda about her house. He insisted on cleaning the kitchen while she got Chloe bathed and off to bed. He handed her a latex glove to protect her injured finger. Chloe grabbed her sack of surprises from the hallway, and then the pair trailed upstairs, Bozo at their heels. Jeb wondered if the dog hoped for more treats or if he was just head over heels in love with the little girl. He suspected it was the latter.

When the kitchen was tidy, Jeb bundled up to do his outdoor chores. Bozo, otherwise occupied, didn't accompany him. When Jeb returned to the house, the sounds of Chloe giggling, Amanda laughing, and Bozo doing his growly thing drifted down to him from upstairs. He doffed his outerwear, pulled on no-clank boots, drew two snifters from the liquor cabinet, and grabbed a bottle of fine brandy, which he carried to the table. He didn't know if Amanda imbibed, but tonight he had a hunch she would need two fingers of false courage.

When Amanda reappeared downstairs, she was alone. Gesturing behind her with the gloved hand, she said, "Bozo climbed in bed with Chloe. I wasn't sure if you allow him on your furniture, but he wouldn't get down, and I couldn't lift him."

"He isn't allowed on the furniture, but after I turn my light off, he *sneaks* onto my bed. I let it go. He likes to cuddle. He's big, but he's careful. He won't roll on her."

With extra caution, Amanda removed the glove so as not to disturb the absurdly large bandage. "You got

Chloe no-tears shampoo *and* bath bubbles. How did you know to do that, not having kids yourself?"

"Mary Alice Thomas," Jeb replied. "I call her Ma. She adores kids and knows everything little girls Chloe's age like."

"Oh, Mary Alice! I know her. Well, only in the most casual way. When Chloe and I walk to town, I often go into her shop to browse. Chloe loves the play corner. I can't afford most of the stuff, but Mary Alice always has things marked down in a basket by the register, and sometimes I can get something special for Chloe."

For Chloe. That told him all he needed to know about this woman. No marked-down perfume for herself, only special things for her little girl. Jeb knew the shop owner well—had known her all his life, in fact—and he suspected that Mary Alice grabbed items off the shelf and quickly marked them down when she saw Amanda coming.

"Why do you call her Ma?" Amanda asked.

"Everyone does," Jeb replied. "For years, she's signed everything with only her first initials, M and A. At some point, someone called her Ma, and it stuck."

After putting the glove back under the sink, Amanda resumed her seat across from him. "I have a feeling my bed will be a little crowded tonight. I got the impression that Bozo has no intention of moving."

"I'll call him." He gave her a grin. "At times, obedience classes do pay off."

She rested her elbows on the table. "I'm accustomed to sleeping in a small space. Chloe nearly cuddles me off the bed. He looks so happy, being with her. I really don't mind if you let him stay." A dimple flashed in her cheek. "I'm glad you bought nontoxic bubbles. Bozo ate them."

Chuckling, Jeb poured each of them two fingers of cognac. He saw shadows slip into her eyes. "Uh-oh. You a teetotaler?"

"No," she said softly. "It's just that my husband got mean when he drank."

"I don't, but we can have decaf coffee if you like."

"It's fine. I haven't tasted fine brandy in a long, long time."

Jeb slid a snifter over to her. "One thing about Bozo moving into your bed is that you won't need to shove the dresser in front of the door. He'll stand guard. He loves that child so much, he'd kill anyone who entered that room intending to do her harm."

Amanda's cheeks went rosy. *Oops*. She had been hoping he hadn't heard her moving the dresser.

"Even you?" she asked.

It took Jeb a moment to recall where they'd been in the conversation. "Bozo loves me, too. I don't think he'd ever bite me, but he might to protect you and your daughter. And if I were trying to hurt you, I'd have it coming, so I wouldn't blame him."

Jeb tried to think of a gentle way to tell her about the roof cave-in. A copy of the *Mystic Creek Daily* lay near her elbow. He tapped it. "This is a couple of days old. I haven't been getting a newspaper delivered since the storm hit. But with this weather, I'm guessing that few people responded to the classifieds. Now might be a good time to check out the available homes for rent."

"Do you think the pipes at my place are beyond repair? I keep hoping my landlord will call." She shrugged. "Chloe and I can make do for a few days with bottled water. I can't afford to move unless I have to."

"You have to, Amanda. I stopped by there this evening to get your SD card. Busted pipes are the least of the problems now."

She gave him a questioning look.

"With all the snow and freezing rain, the weight was too much for the roof. When I got there, I found that a section over the front room had collapsed."

Her face drained of color. Jeb hated that he had no choice but to tell her the rest. "I knew the house would never be habitable again, so I broke in the back door to get your SD card and personal effects. While I was in Chloe's room, the house groaned and then a cracking sound went through the rooms. I skedaddled as fast as I could. I was barely off the back stoop when the rest of the roof caved in."

"Oh, my God." She cupped her hands over her face. "You could have been killed."

"What bothered me more was that you and Chloe could have been inside. When the front section went down, support beams fell on the sofa where you two were snuggling yesterday to stay warm."

She lowered her hands and, if it were possible, grew even paler. "We heard a loud cracking sound, and Chloe asked me if the roof was breaking."

Jeb's stomach clenched.

"I told her it was nothing."

Jeb could imagine the awful pictures spiraling through her mind. "On a bright note, I think I got everything out of there that's important." He listed the things he could recall, including her pink writing tablet. "I put everything in two pillowcases, but I left them in the truck. I didn't want to break this news until after Chloe was asleep."

"Did you find the SD card?" A trill of panic slipped

into her voice. "I absolutely can't do without that, no matter how dangerous it'll be for me to go back. It's—"

Jeb cut her off. "I got the SD card. I couldn't get your bedding on the sofa. It was covered with debris."

The tension eased from her shoulders. "The SD card is the most important thing. And the photographs, of course. I don't have many of Chloe. My husband wouldn't pay for professional ones, and I could use his fancy camera only while he was at work. I saved the pictures onto a card so he wouldn't know I'd touched his equipment."

Jeb could only wonder what her husband would have done if he'd caught her.

"Thankfully, when he noticed an SD card was missing, he thought he'd lost it."

Jeb forced a smile. "I'm glad you have pictures of Chloe. That's great."

"It's a nice camera. You can put it on a timer to take pictures of yourself." As she spoke, her cheeks lost color again, but she visibly collected herself and smiled. "Thank you *so* much for getting our stuff. It was a dangerous thing to do."

"All's well that ends well."

"All hasn't ended well yet. I need to find a place to live."

Jeb pushed the newspaper toward her. "Before you start worrying yourself sick about buying all new furniture, I can lend you plenty. When I built this place, I tore down the original dwelling, and most of that furniture is stored in my shop. I've even got a cookstove and an old washer and dryer. I keep meaning to sell all that stuff but haven't gotten around to it. You can borrow it for a while and get it out of my way."

"You've done too much for us already," she protested.

"It's old stuff, Amanda. I'll be glad to get rid of it. When you're done with it, maybe you can save me the headache and sell it for me. My shop is huge, but it's taking up space I can use for my work."

Without indicating whether she would accept his offer, she studied the classified ads. When she saw a house of interest—which Jeb suspected appealed to her only because of the low rent—she asked about its location. Because she walked to work every day, she wanted a place within a mile of the school.

Sweet Lord. She couldn't walk a mile each way to work throughout the winter. She'd be on unpaved roads that hadn't been plowed. She would freeze, even wearing the coat he'd gotten her, and she might slip on the ice.

He tried to think of ways he might help her. He couldn't imagine being so poor. Even at university, he'd had a car, medical insurance, decent clothes, and spending money. How did someone as nice as Amanda get dealt such a rotten hand of cards? It made him angry— no, not only angry, but so pissed off his hands shook. Where were her parents? Her brothers and sisters? Her aunts and uncles and cousins? And to have no friends? Surely she'd had friends during her lifetime.

Early on, she'd mentioned being twenty-five. Chloe was six, possibly almost seven, which meant Amanda had gotten pregnant at seventeen or eighteen. Had her husband cut her off from all her relatives and acquaintances?

Maybe one day Amanda would tell him about it. For now, he didn't want to reveal that he'd been reading notes she'd tossed into the wind, or that he knew she'd written them. It was enough to know what little he did.

He sensed that she would almost rather slit a wrist

than accept charity, so he couldn't offer her money. If he meant to help her, he had to convince her she was paying her own way.

Jeb took the problem to bed with him, barely slept, and awakened in the morning with a crazy plan. Okay, so he'd cooked her and Chloe a meal the first night. She had no way of knowing if he could fix anything else. Maybe pressure-cooked chicken, vegetables, and salad were all he'd mastered.

Jeb slipped into the kitchen before Amanda woke up, put bacon into a skillet, turned the flame on high, and then set about making oatmeal, which he deliberately scorched. Drawn by the awful smells, Amanda appeared in the old T-shirt and sweats, her eyes going wide when she saw the bacon on fire and smoke billowing from a pot. She smothered the grease with baking soda and slapped a lid over the works to put out the rest of the flames. Then she set the ruined oatmeal under a stream of water.

As she turned to face Jeb, she said, "I thought you were a good cook. You said you even made homemade bread."

He winced at the misstep. "I got rid of the bread machine." *Telling white lies is becoming a habit.* "The loaves came out gooey inside."

Bozo, who'd followed Amanda downstairs to lie near her feet, let loose with a fart that turned the air blue. As Jeb fetched a clean skillet, he glanced at the huge dog and wondered if that was canine-speak for *What a bunch of bullshit.*

Amanda took the second pan from him. "I'll cook. It's the least I can do."

"What about your finger?"

She held up the digit in question, which now sported a butterfly bandage. "It's fine. I'll just wear the glove. It worked great to bathe Chloe."

Jeb studied the small bandage. "When did you put that on?"

"Last night." She donned the glove and began laying strips of bacon in the clean pan. "I came back down after you were in bed. I couldn't sleep with that huge glob catching on the covers." She smiled at him over her shoulder. "It's a cut, Jeb, not a mortal injury. I knew where to find the first-aid kit."

As she turned on a burner, she asked, "Have you listened to a weather report yet?"

"No, I looked outside. It's a holy mess out there."

She glanced at the kitchen television. "Do you mind if I tune in for an update, just in case the authorities changed their minds and school is open today? I need to work every shift I can."

Jeb shook his head. "I don't mind, but buses won't be out on those roads. If you're okay with making breakfast, I'll check on my livestock. It's twenty-five below. If my water rings crapped out, I'll be busting through ice."

Chloe appeared just then, wearing her new snowsuit, boots, cap, and parka. With gloves and a muffler clutched in her hands, she asked, "Mr. Jeb, can I go with you to see your cows?"

Jeb figured he could explain later that he had only steers, both destined for dinner plates. He'd wait until Chloe was, like, maybe, sixteen to tell her. If he still knew her then. The thought of not knowing her at that age made him sad. Against all his better judgment, he was coming to care too much about Amanda and her daughter. *Not smart.* Jeb was starting to worry that he'd left "smart" behind when Amanda had peered out at him over a chain guard with one expressive brown eye.

Amanda seemed nervous about letting Chloe go outside with him. Jeb wasn't sure if she was worried that one of the animals would harm her daughter, or if she thought the danger might come from him. He couldn't think how to reassure her, so he pretended not to notice her uneasiness.

Once Bozo was booted up like the humans, he accompanied Chloe and Jeb as they braved the outdoors. As always, the dog wandered away to mark his territory, leaving splatters of yellow on the ice. As Jeb let Chloe *help* him care for the animals, he decided that he'd lived his life "smart" for thirty years, and where had it gotten him? Alone, that was where. He liked having Chloe around to ask rapid-fire questions. *Why does the sheep wear a jacket, and nobody else has one? How come the cows blow smoke from their noses? Why do your horses sleep standing up?* Jeb explained that Marble had lost some of her wool and needed the protection even inside her shelter. The other animals could go back to their stalls if they got too cold. And it was steam coming from the cows' nostrils, not smoke.

The horse question stumped him. "I'm not sure why horses sleep standing up. Sometimes they lie down in their stalls, but they don't do it often."

Chloe fell in love with Babe, the pig, who was also destined for dinner plates. Every couple of years, Jeb got a new shoat and named it Babe. The child looked adorable with the pink muffler bunched around her neck and her cap pulled down to meet her dainty eyebrows. She crowed as loudly as the rooster when she met the hens.

"They are so pretty! Why do they all look different?"

"Well, I like to raise different breeds. Some are great for laying and some are—" He broke off. With her big brown eyes fixed on his face, how could he tell her that some breeds were better for eating? "And some lay Easter eggs, already colored pretty blue and green." He had no idea from what hat he'd pulled *that* rabbit.

"Nuh-uh," Chloe said, wrinkling her nose. "Eggs only come in white or brown."

Jeb laughed and tugged her cap down over her eyes. "Wanna bet? In a minute, you'll see for yourself that my hens lay colored eggs."

She pushed the wool back up and fixed an incredulous gaze on him. "Really?"

"Yep. I'll show you."

Chloe twined her gloved fingers over the holes in the pen wire and stared at the birds as they made gluttons of themselves over spinach and grain. With an appalled expression, she asked, "I didn't eat one of them, did I? Our first night here, when we ate chicken, it wasn't one of these chickens, was it?"

Jeb did a mental windmill motion with his arms to keep from stepping off into that hole. He'd lived most of his adult life trying never to utter falsehoods. Now, he was either lying or skirting the truth with alarming frequency. "Oh, no," he assured Chloe. "You didn't eat one of *these* chickens." That wasn't a lie. They were still clucking and devouring spinach. "I occasionally buy a fryer at the grocery store." That, too, was a fact. When Jeb had no fryers ready for harvest, he did buy some. "*These* hens are my little friends." *Why did I add that? I'm just digging myself in deeper.*

"What are their names?" Chloe asked, okay with eating chicken from a Styrofoam tray, but *not* okay with eating a feathery critter she'd actually met.

Jeb was thrown by her question. *Names?* Thinking quickly, he pointed through the wire. "That one's Sweetheart." His mind raced for more handles. "The rooster is Bogie, named after Humphrey Bogart, because he was so"—he almost said *sexy* but changed gears to say—"handsome. And that one's Fuzzy, and the ornery one"—*I'm truly brilliant under pressure*—"is Ornrietta."

"What are the other ones named?"

Jeb feared that he'd trip over his own lies if he named any more hens. He needed time to create and memorize a list. "You know, princess, it's twenty-five below, no time for me to tell you the names of over twenty hens. Your mommy will get upset."

Foremost in Jeb's mind was the thought that if he got lucky enough to keep this child and her mother with him, none of his chickens would ever see a dinner plate.

"You stay here, okay? Hold on to the wire so you don't slip while I collect the eggs."

"Oh, I hope you find some blue ones!" she exclaimed.

At the back of the coop, Jeb had pocketed only four eggs when he heard a ruckus, hens clucking, Bogie crowing, and Chloe shrieking. He hurried around the structure and saw Chloe inside the run. Jeb had heard of chickens flying the coop, but he'd never actually seen it occur. Wings lifted, hens were running in all directions outside of the pen. He made his way to the open door and reached for Chloe, his intention being to get her out of there and shut the escape route before any more feathered inmates skedaddled.

But the fast motion of his hand sent Chloe diving for the ground to avoid the blow she clearly expected. Jeb was so horrified that he forgot all about the fleeing fowl. He dropped to his knees to gather the little girl into his arms, thankful for once that everything was frozen solid. On a warm day, they'd both have been covered with chicken shit.

"Oh, baby," he said. "It's okay. Don't be afraid."

"I just wanted to pet one!" Chloe wailed, trying to dodge his hands. "But all of them ran! I didn't mean to let them loose!"

Jeb drew her against his chest. She trembled in his embrace like a spring aspen leaf in a high wind. "It's all right. Of *course* you wanted to pet one. It's my fault, not yours. I should have helped you go inside." His experience at soothing a hysterical child could have fit inside a cold-remedy cup, but he instinctively began to rock back and forth, doing a butt plant on the heels of his boots and then shifting forward. "It's okay. I won't *ever* hit you, Chloe, I promise. Not ever."

He felt her shuddering subside a bit, and then she shifted in his arms to brush at his cheeks with her glove. "Don't cry, Mr. Jeb. I know you won't ever hit me. Bozo told me so. But I still get scared and *think* I might get hit."

Until that moment, Jeb hadn't realized that tears were streaming down his cheeks. *Damn.* He never wept, not because he didn't feel like it sometimes, but because his dad had raised him to keep a stiff upper lip. But seeing this child prostrate on the ground with her arms folded over her head to deflect blows had opened his flood-gates.

Chloe caught more tears with her fingers. "Don't cry. Sometimes I even do it if Mommy swings her arm toward me, and she *never* hits. I just duck. I can't help it."

Jeb gathered her closer, embarrassed that she was trying to comfort him when it should be the other way around. "You're just hand-shy, sweetheart." He loosened one arm from around her to wipe her cheeks. *Tears born of terror.* What had that son of a bitch done to her? Jeb suspected he had whacked her a lot, much as he might a pesky housefly. "It just makes me sad, is all. Little girls shouldn't be afraid that an adult is going to hit them."

"I know." She brushed her glove over his cheek again. "But my mean daddy didn't care." She squirmed to sit erect on the downward slope of his thighs and gazed out at his backyard. "I'm sorry, Mr. Jeb. All your chickens are loose. How are we going to catch them?"

That was a damned good question. Collecting himself, Jeb followed her gaze. Hens streaked one way and then another. Bogie, the caretaker of his flock, had gone into rooster panic mode, taking flight to check on first one cluster of females and then another. Bozo, distracted from his pissing tour, had turned to stare at them, his expression a mixture of alarm and eager anticipation. *Something to chase!*

"Bozo, no!" Jeb yelled.

But he was too late. Bozo surged forward, his boots slipping under him, to approach a cluster of hens. Kicking up his speed, the dog was almost upon them when he lost traction and went into a slide, all two hundred and thirty pounds of him cannoning into the birds. Feathers flew, and so did Bozo, bypassing the chickens to plow into the front of Jeb's shop. Jeb's feathered *friends* took off in all directions.

"Well, shit," he said.

Chloe got off his lap. "My mommy says that people

who say that word have filthy tongues. After we catch the chickens, you need to scrub yours really hard."

Jeb almost laughed, but it wasn't funny. He couldn't cuss like a sailor around a little girl. His mother would scalp him. "You're right. I'll scrub my tongue really good with a toothbrush when we get back inside."

As he pushed to his feet and helped Chloe up, Jeb was thankful for the chicken shit that his birds deposited on the bottom of the run with amazing frequency. Frozen solid, it provided plenty of traction.

Only that wouldn't be true once they left the pen. He knew how treacherously slick it was out there, and Chloe wore no shoe chains. "Sweetheart, I think you need to go back in the house. I'll catch all the chickens, okay?" Just then, Bozo regained his feet and lunged at another hen, only to do another belly flop. *This isn't looking good,* Jeb thought. "I don't want you falling and getting hurt."

Chloe jerked her hand from his. "I'll be okay, Mr. Jeb. I don't fall as far as you do."

Jeb started to protest, but with amazing dexterity Chloe had already shot out of the pen. "Sweetheart, chickens peck!" he yelled. "They might hurt you!"

She took a spill and quickly regained her feet. "They can't peck me through my clothes!" And off she went. Bozo saw a partner in crime and did a slip-slide approach, falling just as he reached Chloe. The collision knocked Chloe down again. She giggled and sprang back up, clearly delighted that they had to chase chickens in below-zero temperatures. Watching her fall and regain her feet with so little effort made Jeb feel old.

What followed was a comedy of errors. At one point, Jeb went down on his back and slid toward Babe's pen, his head going under the fence rails. With his butt shooting shards of pain up his spine and his head swimmy from hitting the ice, he blinked and looked up at a pig snout and beady eyes. Babe gifted him with a snotty snort, which splattered his face. *Yuck*. When he'd collected his senses enough to wipe his cheeks, he found that the drippings had frozen to his skin. With far less agility than Chloe, he struggled to his feet, took a deep breath to dredge up some macho, and took off after the chickens, who seemed to have multiplied in minutes from twenty-seven to well over a hundred. And, stupid bastard that he was, he'd never clipped their wings. The little bitches huddled and clucked until he got near them, and then they flew away, leaving him with nothing to grab but drifting feathers.

Chloe loved it. She caught Bogie first, and then, losing her footing en route to the run, fell several times, always keeping the rooster above her so she wouldn't injure him under the crush of her slight weight. She made Jeb feel like an overmuscled bumpkin. *What the hell?* She was so tiny. How come he was blowing this?

At some point, Amanda appeared in her blue parka and snow boots. Jeb guessed she'd seen what was happening from the kitchen window. So far as Jeb could tell, she wasn't any more graceful on the ice than he and Bozo were. When she did an ass plant, he worried that she might have hurt herself, but he didn't have time to dwell on it. He doubted she'd ever met a chicken. Now she was trying to catch the damned things.

Slowly but surely, they collected all the hens and returned them to the run. By then, Chloe had learned the hard way to shoo the fowl away from the door before she opened it to return another chicken to the flock. The cold wind had made Amanda's eyes water, and the tears had frozen to her cheeks. Jeb felt older than Methuselah. Panting, Bozo lay sprawled on the ice, his jowls spread over the crusty snow, making Jeb worry that his lips might have frozen to the ground. But, no, he drooled so much that sticking was impossible.

Jeb still needed to collect the rest of the eggs, and Chloe begged to go with him. Amanda nodded to let Jeb know it was okay, so he held the child's hand as they walked behind the coop. It wasn't until Jeb collected two more eggs and started to stuff them in his pocket that he realized the four he'd gathered earlier had been crushed.

"Well, shit," he said. "What a slimy mess."

Chloe was clinging to the shed to stay upright. "You definitely have to scrub your tongue, Mr. Jeb. It's filthy."

Jeb couldn't help but laugh, and Chloe grinned up at him. As their gazes locked, something intangible yet magical passed between them.

Amanda picked her way toward the house. "I'd better go back inside to finish breakfast," she called. "We've all worked up an appetite."

"We'll be right there," Jeb yelled back.

After gathering more offerings from his flock and wiping his egg-smeared fingers clean on his jacket, Jeb grabbed Chloe's hand so she wouldn't slip on the ice. Why he bothered, he didn't know. She'd fallen at least a dozen times already, and as far as he could tell, no damage had been done.

"Will you tell me more of the hens' names tomorrow?" Chloe asked.

Jeb glanced down into her innocent eyes. He could come up with more names today while he checked on neighbors. He'd keep a running list on his center console when he got short breaks between houses. Maybe he could call two of the hens Lucy and Ethel. Tomorrow when Chloe helped to do chores, he just hoped he wouldn't need a cheat sheet. "Sure. I can do that."

"I heard you call one of them Bitch. Only I can't remember which one she is."

He winced. "Um, that isn't really a name, Chloe. It's another not-very-nice word."

"Oh."

As they walked with caution across the yard, Job gave her fingers a quick squeeze. "So Bozo is talking to you, is he?"

She nodded. "In dog language. He told me you never hit people or pull their hair, and you never, *ever* kick mommies in the stomach."

Jeb felt as if a shod horse hoof had nailed him in the solar plexus. He yearned to assure her that he would never allow anyone to be mean to her or her mother again. But that was a promise he wasn't sure he could keep. At least he could tell her that she was right about him ... or, rather, that Bozo was.

"Uh ... no, I don't. Never. Now, we both know Bozo can't really talk, not with words, anyway. So how did he tell you all that stuff about me?"

Chloe gave him a gap-toothed grin that dimpled her rosy cheeks. "Bozo loves you. When he's snoring on the floor, he doesn't wake up when you walk around his legs. And when you wave your hand after he toots, he isn't afraid you'll hit him. You don't even get mad when he slings drool. Mommy says I should wait to be sure you're *really* nice before I let myself like you too much, but I think that's because my daddy tricked her. He made her think he was nice when he was really very mean."

"Ah." Jeb rolled that revelation through his mind. "So your mommy doesn't really like me very much yet."

"She's starting to. She says you *seem* nice." The child's eyes grew round. "Oops! I forgot to say thank you for my snow clothes! Mommy told me I should."

Jeb stopped just short of his back steps. "You need to thank Myrna for the clothes. She's the nice lady who lives across the road."

Chloe shook her head. "Mommy said you bought it all. She knows. Clothes in a closet for a long time don't smell like these do. I thought she was going to give it all back, but she said it didn't seem right to say no to answered prayers."

Jeb's heart caught. He had to fess up. Nothing else would do with those big eyes trained on his face. "Well, she's right about the clothes. I bought them. No wonder your mother doesn't trust me yet. She knows I told her an out-and-out lie."

Chloe squeezed his hand. "Mommy says you did it for a good reason. I don't think she's mad at you."

"I sure hope not."

Jeb whistled for Bozo before they went inside. Still grasping Chloe's hand as they scaled the steps, he realized that even with two pairs of gloves separating their fingers, he could feel the child's trust in him seeping through the layers. It was a precious gift.

Chapter Seven

Sans the parka and snow boots, Amanda still wore her sleeping outfit when they reentered the kitchen. To Jeb, she looked beautiful with a crease on her cheek from the pillow and her long hair tousled from the chicken-chasing escapade. The soft curve of her unfettered breasts drew his gaze. He had to force himself to look away. *Easier thought than done.*

After Jeb doffed his outerwear, Chloe tugged on his hand. "It's time for you to go wash your filthy tongue," she informed him.

Amanda sent Jeb a questioning look. He ignored her and, accompanied by Chloe, went to the master bath. As Jeb bent over the sink to scrub his tongue with a toothbrush, Chloe said, "All the way back. You need to get *all* the dirt off."

Jeb had always gagged easily, and now was no exception. What he didn't expect was for Chloe to gag from watching him. She ran to the toilet, hunched her shoulders, and coughed up clear stuff. Alarmed, Jeb dropped the toothbrush in the sink.

"Are you okay, princess?"

Straightening, Chloe gulped and nodded. "Hearing sick sounds makes me get sick, too."

Remembering that he'd had the same problem as a kid, Jeb lifted her onto his hip. "Well, I think I did a good job." He poked his tongue out. "Is it clean enough?"

Chloe peered into his mouth. "You've still got blue bumps at the back."

"Toothpaste." Jeb swallowed and opened up again.

"Say aw for me."

"Aw."

Chloe sighed. "It could stand more scrubbing, but then we'll both upchuck again, and I don't want to."

"Me, either."

Amanda had made bacon, fried potatoes, and oven-browned slices of homemade bread. Chloe's egg was already scrambled.

"How do you want yours this morning?" she asked Jeb when they returned to the kitchen.

Jeb asked for over easy and got perfect eggs. During the meal, Chloe fretted that breakfast was too high in fat, which to Jeb was a bewildering observation from a six-year-old. But then, Chloe seemed mature for her age in many ways, especially when she spoke.

Amanda caught Jeb's gaze. "Mark detested high-fat meals."

Mark. Jeb finally had a name for the son of a bitch. He wondered what Mark had done to Amanda when her cooking hadn't suited his dietary preferences. *Mark Banning.* Now he could use his people-tracking app to find the jerk and pay him an unexpected visit someday. Oh, how Jeb looked forward to that. He might end up in jail, but it would be worth it. His father had zero tolerance for abuse of women or children, and he'd raised his sons to rectify matters if they ever got wind of an infraction.

Late to make his rounds on Elderberry, Jeb had just taken a bite of potatoes when his phone chirped. He fished the device from his hip pocket, saw that the text was from Tony, and slid his finger across his iPhone screen to read the message. "Praise the Lord!" he exclaimed.

Amanda and Chloe gave him startled looks.

"The west side of town has power again," he explained. "The people on my route have electricity!"

"Yay!" Chloe clapped her hands. She glanced at her mother. "May I say 'praise the Lord,' too, Mommy?"

Amanda smiled. "In Mr. Jeb's house, yes, you may."

"Praise the Lord!" the child shouted.

"This means I can wrap it up early today," Jeb told them. "I've hauled up enough wood to last most folks for days. Since it's a no-school day, how about if we look at some rentals this afternoon? Maybe we can find you a new place to live."

"Does that mean our leaky pipes can't be fixed?" Chloe asked her mother.

Amanda replied, "The pipes aren't the problem now. The snow and ice grew too heavy for our roof. Remember when we heard the loud crack, and you thought our roof was breaking? Well, you're a very smart girl, because you were right."

"You mean it broke?"

Amanda nodded. "We are fortunate that Mr. Jeb wouldn't leave us there. Some roof beams fell on our sofa, and we could have been injured."

Chloe looked at Jeb, her eyes wide. "Could it have squished us? Could we be dead?"

Jeb didn't want this kid to grow up terrified of storms. He reached over to tweak her nose. "That is an old house and not built very well. Normally roofs don't break."

Chloe nodded as if his answer satisfied her. Then that too-old-for-her-years expression flitted across her face. "Mr. Jeb, do good houses cost a lot of money?"

"Not all of them. We'll see what we can find." Jeb had a plan. But for now, he needed to humor Amanda and let her believe she'd soon be living on her own again.

When Jeb finished checking on the neighbors, he dropped back by the house to pick up his guests to go rental shopping. Amanda appreciated his offer. She and Chloe couldn't remain here for weeks. On her budget, a rental would be stark compared to this luxury, and the longer Chloe was here, the harder it would be for her to readjust.

Once Jeb got Amanda, Chloe, and Bozo into his truck and they were out on the road, Chloe squealed in delight. "It's so pretty! Everything sparkles."

Jeb studied the terrain. "I've been so busy working, I haven't taken the time to notice. You're right; it's spectacular. A lot of folks call it a silver thaw because the ice makes everything look sort of silver."

Amanda turned the phrase over in her mind. *A silver thaw*. For a long time, her heart had felt nearly as frozen as the world around them. She'd felt no warmth toward anyone but Chloe. Now, being around Jeb, she was starting to see the world in a different light. She'd grown fond of his silly dog, who occupied the backseat with her daughter. The pillowcases that held Amanda's worldly goods had been stowed under the bench seat because Jeb had forgotten to bring them inside last night. *Jeb*. When he smiled, he made Amanda's heart feel as if it were melting. She found that frightening. It troubled her to even think about trusting a man again. She didn't care how nice he seemed or how handsome he was. He was still a man.

"I can't afford anything that rents for over five hundred a month," she told him. "And if possible, I need to pay less. My budget is pretty tight."

"Gotcha," Jeb replied.

Their first stop was at an efficiency apartment in a large older home converted into flats. "This could work," Amanda pronounced. "Small, but within a mile of the school."

The landlady, a brunette of about thirty, frowned at Chloe. "No children allowed," she said. "My parents live here, and they don't like noise."

Amanda's heart sank. "But she's a very good little girl, ma'am, and you didn't say in your ad that no children are allowed."

"I'm saying it now," the woman replied.

Next Jeb took them to an old house that rented for four hundred a month. It reminded Amanda a lot of her last rental. Still, it was close enough to Chloe's school for her to walk to work. The owner, an old man, was hard of hearing, and they had to shout for him to catch what they said.

Under his breath, Jeb told Amanda, "This place isn't suitable as a doghouse."

"But it's in my price range and close to the school."

"Weak roof, no foundation, and the floors are rotten. You and Chloe could fall through. I vote no. You have a place to stay for now. You aren't that desperate."

Amanda felt pretty darned desperate. She studied the ceiling. "How can you tell that the roof is weak?"

*   *   *

Jeb sighed and took another walk through the house. He pointed out to Amanda signs of a stovepipe fire on the ceiling. He discovered that only one burner on the range worked. The kitchen exhaust fan sounded like a jet engine taking off. The one toilet rocked back and forth when he nudged it, telling him the floor was so rotten that the commode could fall through at any moment.

"I cannot—" Jeb stopped and rephrased what he meant to say. "You and Chloe can't live in a dump like this." Jeb was glad the man couldn't hear a word he said. He stood near them, acting as if they might steal anything not anchored down. "It's unacceptable."

"You're not in charge of our lives. I make my own decisions, and I don't need your blessing to do *anything*. Are you reading me loud and clear?"

Jeb nearly grinned. Amanda's small chin had come up, and she looked ready to take him on. As browbeaten as he suspected she had been, she still had the mettle to stand up for herself. He felt both frustrated and proud of her.

"Let me put it differently. *Please*, with *sugar* on top, don't rent this house. I'm not picking it apart to be difficult. It's not safe. I won't be able to rest at night knowing that you and Chloe are asleep in here with a fire going in that woodstove."

Even under her down parka, he saw her shoulders slump. "Foul play. You're trying to put a guilt trip on me."

Jeb wished he could plant a kiss on her forehead instead. He settled for winking at her. "Is it working?"

She threw up her hands. "For rent this low, everything we look at may be a dump. You need to understand my financial situation. I can't afford a palace."

"Be patient. We'll find something that is at least *safe*. Something, maybe, that I can work on to make better."

"I can't allow you to do that. You've done too much for us already."

"You, Ms. Banning, are not in charge of my life. I make my own decisions. Are you reading me loud and clear?"

She burst out laughing, and it was a glorious sight to behold. Her eyes danced. Her face flushed and seemed to glow. *Shit*. He was falling head over heels for a woman who didn't even *like* him much yet.

After they returned to the truck, Amanda said in a flat, toneless voice, "There aren't any more I can afford."

"Tomorrow always comes!" Jeb grinned at her. "Am I really so bad you can't wait to get away from me?"

Chloe chimed in from the backseat. "I don't want to get away from you, Mr. Jeb. I don't think Mommy means it that way."

Amanda's lips quivered as she struggled to suppress a smile. "You are exactly right, Chloe. And Mr. Jeb knows that isn't what I meant." To Jeb, she said, "It isn't about *you*. It's about *me*. I need to make it on my own. Mark constantly told me I'd *never* survive if I left him, and believe me, I had a thousand good reasons to do so. Now I've done it, and I need to prove him wrong. Can you understand that?"

"Yep, I get it, honey." He wished he could bite off his tongue. "Amanda, I mean. I get it, but is it necessary for you to manage with absolutely *no* help?"

"Yes."

Thinking fast, Jeb said, "Over the last few days, I've spent a small fortune on supplies for my neighbors. Most of them offered to reimburse me, but I wouldn't take their money. In years past, they helped others, expecting nothing in return. The men cut and chopped wood, then delivered it to people who could no longer do it themselves. The women baked and then delivered the goods to those in need. They cleaned homes for free. If a toilet plugged, the women showed up with plungers, and if that didn't fix it, they called their husbands. Now, those who are ill or elderly are calling in their chips. They once did it for someone else, and now someone else is doing it for them. In Mystic Creek, that's how things work."

"You're describing a town where everyone loves each other. That isn't reality."

"It isn't the reality here, either," Jeb confessed. "Do you think I *like* Lucy and Ethel?" Remembering his decision to create a list of hen names, Jeb almost said *shit* out loud. He'd forgotten to work on it this morning. "They're bossy. They follow me around like supervisors. They *do* say thank you, but they haven't offered to reimburse me for a dime. And they call me *sonny*. I keep expecting one of them to grab me by the ear."

Amanda was clearly struggling not to laugh, and Jeb deliberately pushed her over the edge so he could see her face light up again. "The only *nice* thing about them is that they have Herman's ashes on a shelf with candles lighted all around his urn."

That did it. And this time when she laughed, she was so taken by surprise that she snorted. "Who was Herman? Not a husband. You said they never married."

Jeb returned his attention to the road. "Herman is a long-since-deceased cat. They have pictures of him everywhere. He was a fat tuxedo with long white eyebrow hairs and whiskers. Their devotion to a pet is about all I can find to like about them."

From the corner of his eye, he glimpsed Amanda closing her eyes. "Do you think they ever made rounds during a storm to help their neighbors?"

"I doubt it," Jeb replied. "But I helped them anyway, because in Mystic Creek that's how things are done. Help with no paybacks." He paused. "I work with saws. If I cut off all the fingers on my right hand and I need help, who will I call?"

"Your mother."

He grinned. "Okay, you've got that right. The *point* is that I'm hoping I could call you instead, and that you'd show up to take care of me."

Now he saw a tear slipping down her cheek. *Damn.* He almost drove into the ditch.

"I will," she murmured. "If you ever need me and Chloe, we'll be there. I promise."

Jeb hadn't intended to make her cry. "Bargain, sealed without a handshake. We all need help sometimes. I admire someone who's proud. I think all of us need at least *some* pride. That said, too much pride can be a bad thing. I count you as a friend now." *That was good, another rabbit out of his hat.* "I hope you count me as one of yours. Bottom line is, you're in a mess right now. You were doing great until this storm struck, but now you do need a little help. It's not like the storm was your fault, but it's left you without a home. I care about you two. Are you reading me loud and clear?"

She nodded. "Like bold print."

When they got home—and it worried Amanda that she'd fleetingly thought of it as *home*—they made their way over the treacherous ice to the front porch, with Jeb, wearing shoe chains, holding Chloe's hand, and Amanda carrying the pillowcases filled with their belongings. She couldn't *wait* to check the SD card to make sure that it had survived the storm. Without it she would have no proof of what Mark had done to her little girl.

But despite her concern about the pictures she'd taken of Chloe's injuries, what loomed at the front of her mind was that Jeb, who would normally carry the bags, considered her daughter's safety more important. He was even putting Amanda's safety second.

Watching him hold Chloe steady on the ice, Amanda felt a lump lodge at the base of her throat. And it *hurt*. They had escaped Mark, who had inflicted harm on those he should have loved, and landed with Jeb, a man who had no reason to give a fig about either of them. And yet he *did*. Her thawing heart was in serious danger, but how could she steel it against him when all she sensed from him was goodness?

Jeb invited Chloe to go with him to tend to his animals. Amanda was left to prepare dinner. Her thoughts were so tangled that she couldn't think what to fix. She definitely had to do a fast thaw of meat. She grabbed hamburger, found Jeb's instruction book for his digital pressure cooker, and decided to give it a try. After browning the meat, she added rice, canned broth, cream of mushroom soup, spices, grated cheddar, and some diced veggies. She could think of no way to describe how nervous she felt about fixing a meal using an unfamiliar appliance. She only knew Jeb and Chloe would return soon and all of them were hungry.

Mark had detested one-pot meals, but when Jeb and Chloe arrived and they all sat down and ate, Jeb said he'd never tasted a better one. Amanda relaxed about the food, but other concerns kept her as tense as a freshly tuned guitar string.

Over the meal, Jeb could tell that Amanda was upset. He couldn't blame her. She had little money and hadn't earned a dime since Monday. She had a little girl to care for and needed to find a house to rent that she could afford. She would probably have to spend every cent she'd saved to get settled in a new place. Jeb planned to do a reverse search on the address of her former rental to get the name of the owner, who, in Jeb's opinion, should at least reimburse her for the loss of her furniture.

"Mr. Jeb has a red hen named Lucy," Chloe announced. "And a gray one named Ethel. We didn't have time for him to tell me the names of the rest. He said it was too cold to stay outside."

Amanda nodded. "Mr. Jeb is right."

After eating, Jeb helped clean the kitchen, which went quickly because the pressure cooker made very little mess. While Amanda stowed the latex glove under the sink, Jeb put Bozo's snow boots on him, grabbed his jacket, and took the dog out back for a final evening run. He had a hunch that Bozo would sleep with Chloe again.

Later, right after Chloe fell asleep, Jeb heard over the news that the predicted morning temperatures would still be so low that there would be no school again. Jeb suspected that the bus drivers were having trouble getting the engines to start. The roads were also still dangerous, and the classrooms might be too chilly to be safe for the children.

When Amanda came back downstairs, Jeb gave her the latest report. She shook her head. She wore a green sweatshirt, which looked almost as old as she was, over faded jeans. With her hair twisted up and caught with a clip, and her face bare of makeup, she still managed to look gorgeous.

"I can't afford to miss this much work."

"I guessed as much," Jeb replied as he drew two snifters and a bottle of fine brandy from his liquor cabinet. Bozo had gone upstairs with Chloe, and Jeb missed the sound of his snoring, but he couldn't fault the dog for falling in love when he was guilty, too. "I hope you'll join me," he said as he sat at the table. He had briefly considered adjourning to the living room where they'd be more comfortable, but he suspected Amanda felt more at ease with the table as a barrier between them. "Two fingers of good cheer and conversation after a wonderful dinner seems like a great way to end the evening."

Amanda took a seat across from him. "It's nice to enjoy the ritual of a nighttime brandy again. Mark got so mean when he imbibed that I came to detest spirits of any kind."

"It sounds to me as if Mark got mean no matter what."

"True," she replied in a thin voice. "But he was especially vicious when he was drunk."

Jeb measured out liquor into the two glasses. "I don't get drunk. Mostly I enjoy one measure of brandy, sometimes two."

She smiled. "In that way, you remind me of my dad. He loved his evening brandy."

"You miss him," Jeb observed, hoping she'd talk about her family. "Where is he now? Your father, I mean."

Shadows darkened her eyes. "He passed away after a battle with cancer." She cupped the snifter in her palms. "I still feel guilty because I couldn't be there afterward to support my poor mom. She was an only child, just like

me, and Dad grew up in foster homes. I was all she had."
She took a sip of the brandy, and at the taste, she closed
her eyes and smiled. Lifting her dark, lush lashes, she
added, "Mark allowed no phones in the house. Dad died
right before Christmas. Mom sent me a letter, but with
the backlog in post offices at that time of year, I didn't
get it until New Year's Eve."

"And I'm guessing Mark wouldn't let you go to see
your mom."

"You're a good guesser." She toyed with a saltshaker.
"I don't contact Mom anymore. It's safer for her not to
know where I am. She's a lousy liar, and if Mark thought
she knew, he wouldn't hesitate to beat it out of her."

"It seems to me that it ought to be safe enough to call
her on your cell—or mine. You could refuse to tell her
where you are."

Her gaze clung to his. "I worry about the cell phone
call being traced."

Jeb couldn't argue the point. He wasn't sure how all
that worked. However, he did know that if his phone was
lost or stolen, he could pinpoint its location easily with
Find My iPhone. He had an iPad in his office, and the
location app worked within seconds.

"Maybe for now it's better to be safe than sorry," he
conceded. "So let's change the subject. I lost my cleaning
person a few weeks ago, and though I've managed to
keep on top of it so far, this is a big house. I'm not busy
now, but I will be soon, and any time I spend working
indoors is time away from my shop, where I earn my in-
come. I've also noticed that you're beyond excellent as a
cook."

"Are you offering me a job?" she asked, her tone incredulous.

"I am. I'm not much of a cook. I'd really enjoy hot breakfasts and dinners. You could keep your cafeteria job as backup in case it doesn't work well for you here. When your shift ends, you can do the household shopping in my truck or the older one out in my shop."

She searched his expression as if she were waiting for him to say one of her duties would be to service him in bed. He bit back a smile. "On weekdays when you work at the cafeteria, you wouldn't need to do housework. You could do that on weekends. I'm pretty easy to please. A weekly pass is good enough for me. I'm offering room and board, plus a thousand a month. With no electricity, water, propane, or garbage collection services to pay for, you should be able to save enough for an older-model vehicle in only a few months. I know my way around cars, so I'll be happy to help you find something dependable."

Amanda shook her head. "I think you're dreaming up a job because it's the only way you can think of to help me."

Guilty as charged. But Jeb wasn't about to admit it. "I've been looking for a housekeeper and cook for what seems like forever. You can ask Tony across the road. It's easy for me to find someone to clean, but finding someone to work split shifts during the week to cook me breakfast and dinner is another matter."

She nodded, which eased the squeezing sensation in Jeb's chest. "That would be difficult. The cost of gas alone to drive each way would make someone think twice."

"And there's the wear and tear on the vehicle. I understand that it isn't ideal for most people, but if you lived here, it wouldn't be so bad. You could work at the school and be back here in plenty of time to spend the afternoons with Chloe."

She joined him in taking another sip of brandy. "What would the neighbors think?"

Jeb couldn't stop himself; he barked with laughter. Then he sobered because he saw that Amanda was serious. "I guess it won't be the most conventional arrangement, but in this day of people living together without getting married, why would we bother to lie about it?" He shook his head. "Hell, we could just say we're living together, and no eyebrows would be raised."

"I'm still married. Not because I want to be. I haven't wanted to be for a long time. So a car isn't all I'm saving for. I need money for a divorce, enough to hire an excellent attorney who can make sure Mark never gets unsupervised visitation with Chloe." She broke off and swallowed. And then, in a whisper, she continued. "Mark can be *difficult*. I'm afraid he'll hurt her." Her face flushed. "You'll think I'm a horrible mom when I tell you this, but he's hurt her before. I can't let that happen ever again."

Jeb realized that he needed to tread cautiously. Amanda had just opened a door, and he wanted to keep it open. "I don't, for a second, think you're a horrible mother. I've seen how much you love Chloe. It may have taken you longer to get her away from him than you wanted, but you managed it. And I know it hasn't been easy for you. But you're doing it. And you're doing it without any help."

"I won't be if I take this job!"

"Sure you will. You'll be getting fair wages for the work you do for me. That isn't *help*; it's earning a living." He reached to replenish their snifters, noting that his was nearly gone. "Proof's in the pudding. Am I acting mean yet?" He lifted his glass. "I say we need to make a toast to success at your new job."

"I haven't agreed to work for you yet."

"True, but it's an offer I don't think you should refuse. You can save for an attorney to keep Chloe safe after the divorce *and* save for a car." He toasted to the agreement. "Tell me, did your dad get mean when he drank his brandy at night?"

A soft, glowing smile curved her lips. "Dad never got mean. He was so sweet and such a hard worker. He treated my mother like a queen."

Jeb had grown up in the same sort of atmosphere, one of the reasons he'd never been able to settle for a second-rate woman. He'd wanted what his parents had—true love. "So you grew up believing that *all* marriages are like that."

She shrugged. "I was young when I got in trouble."

"How young, exactly?"

"Seventeen, almost eighteen. Chloe will be seven right before Christmas, and I'll turn twenty-six next spring."

"So you were way too young to understand that all guys weren't good of heart like your dad, that there are a lot of rotten apples in the barrel."

"I've never really analyzed it. I only know I got one of the rottenest apples."

She took another sip of brandy and murmured with pleasure. Jeb realized that she had tasted her share of fine brandy and missed it. "I'm thinking that your dad sometimes poured you a nip or two."

She grinned, dimpling both cheeks. Oh, how he loved those dimples. "He even got Momma to join us. And I drank brandy with him long before I was of age. Dad believed that kids need to experience the effects of alcohol in a supervised environment so they won't go out and get stupid somewhere, followed by getting hurt."

He nodded. "My dad—his name is Jeremiah, by the way—felt the same way. He was always careful about how much he let us kids taste when we were young, but when we got to be teenagers, he allowed us to have enough to understand the effects."

Amanda's gaze, which Jeb could have gotten lost in, clung to his. "He sounds like a really great dad."

"He is." Jeb thought about his father. "He could be stern, but only when one of us was really messing up. And even then, we knew we had it coming."

"I think I'd really like your dad."

Jeb thought, *Yes, you will.* He fully intended to take *this* lady home to meet his parents, and in all his thirty years, he'd *never* done that.

"So," he ventured, "what do you think about my job offer?"

"I have reservations."

"Are you nervous about living with me?"

She studied him for a long moment and then smiled slightly. "I have every reason to distrust you, but Bozo is telling me and Chloe, with canine eloquence, that you are a kind man. It's just that I *need* to make it on my own. Even if I can't raise Chloe in grand style, just managing to do it will make me feel better, like a whole person."

Jeb understood that. She was one of the sweetest people he'd ever met. A wonderful mom, kind to animals, a hard worker. Mark Banning didn't deserve to breathe the same air she did, and so far as Jeb was concerned, the marriage had been nothing more than writing on a form, the words never recorded in heaven.

"I expect you to work for your wages and for the use of my home," he said. "And just because I've made the offer doesn't mean you have to accept it. I'll be glad to take you out again tomorrow to look at more rentals."

Amanda gazed into her brandy. "I've already done some figuring in my head. If I keep the cafeteria job, the most I can give you during the week is four hours a day. I make twelve dollars an hour at the school and work only five-hour shifts. That is a grand total of three hundred a week, twelve hundred a month. And out of that, I must pay for taxes, rent, electricity, garbage collection, and food. Even if I work long hours for you on weekends, I can't put in enough time to be worth what you're offering to pay me." She gestured at the house. "No charge for living here? I'm sorry, Jeb, but your offer means I won't be doing it on my own."

"Okay." Jeb moved forward with as much caution as he would have on cracking ice. "What do you think is a fair wage?"

Her eyes went soft, like chocolate melting in a pot. "Five hundred a month is more reasonable."

Jeb wondered where she'd come up with that number, but he wasn't going to make it easy for her. "Seven hundred a month then. You'll be working weekends, remember. So I'm figuring in time and a half for overtime."

He knew that his offer of free room and board, plus the seven hundred, was worth far more than she could make for cooking and cleaning anywhere else, but he hoped that since she'd had limited work experience, she didn't realize that.

He did well with his business. He was by no means

wealthy, but he had a nice cushion in the bank, and he really wanted to help this lady and her child. Amanda took another sip of brandy.

"Cleaning people charge me fifteen an hour," he elaborated. "Some want twenty, and they don't cook for me."

"Just for cleaning?" Her eyes widened. "If I had a car, I'd go into business!"

She finished her brandy, pushed up from the table, and said, "I'd like to sleep on it. Once I've done some figuring, I'll know a fair wage. And I need to decide if I'm even interested."

Jeb had hoped they could come to an agreement tonight. But since he was asking her to live with a man she barely knew, he figured "maybe" was all he could expect. He'd give her time to mull it over and, he hoped, conclude that he was harmless.

Except that where emotions were concerned, he wasn't sure he was harmless at all.

Chapter Eight

Bedding twisted around Amanda's legs as she tossed and turned, trying to find a comfortable position. Nothing could switch off her racing thoughts. What was happening here? Jeb Sterling seemed like such a kind man. His home was warm, snug, and attractive. Chloe loved the animals, Bozo especially. As Amanda rolled over and punched her pillow for at least the twelfth time, she couldn't help but smile at the sight of the child and dog, curled up together like two puppies in the womb. Except, of course, that the mastiff in no way resembled a puppy, and the beautiful little girl, cast in shadow yet gilded by the glow of the night-light, didn't either.

Mentally circling the job offer, Amanda tried to sort out the pros and cons. She wouldn't necessarily have to accept Jeb's loan of his older truck. She could still walk back and forth to her other job until she bought her own vehicle. And if Jeb was as kind and stable as he appeared, Amanda and Chloe would be safer here than they would be living alone.

Mark could find them at any time. And he wouldn't give up. He would *never* give up, not even if he entered into a relationship with another woman. The moment Amanda had married him, she'd become one of his possessions. How many times had he told her that he'd see her dead if she ever tried to leave him? Fear turned Mark on, and so did violence. She knew that now.

What options did she have, if she looked at the situation dispassionately? Every rental within her price range would be a dump. She and Chloe could survive, but Jeb had offered Amanda an opportunity to give her child far more than the bare necessities. She had to think of Chloe's welfare. And if Jeb turned out to be a wolf in sheep's clothing, she could leave in a blink. She had so few possessions that packing and running wouldn't take long.

Possessions. Amanda remembered the two pillowcases she'd left downstairs. *The SD card.* What if it had been damaged, either during the storm or from being tossed around in a bag with shoes and picture frames? The very thought made her pulse skitter. Far worse, what if it had fallen out of the pillowcase during transport?

Taking care not to wake her daughter, she slipped out of bed. Bozo opened one eye, regarded her sleepily, closed it again, and stretched. Amanda sneaked downstairs to dig through the pillowcases and find the photo storage device.

With shaking fingers, she finally located the SD card and sneaked into Jeb's office. Not wishing to wake him by turning on a light, she felt her way to his chair and computer. Once she'd booted up the system, light from the screen was all she needed in order to see. To open Windows, she needed his password. *Hmm.* She pursed her lips and typed in *Bozo. Bingo.* He loved that silly dog so much that of course he'd use that name.

After plugging the card into the SD slot, she selected

that drive and sighed with relief when a box flashed on the monitor screen. There was an option to save the photos to Jeb's hard drive. She didn't want to do that. Instead she selected "View files on this device."

In a blink, there they were, dozens of photographs, a sad and terrible testimony to Amanda and Chloe's past. Toward the end of their time with Mark, Amanda had been diligent about documenting the abuse done to her and to her daughter. The dated pictures would show how Mark had escalated the violence, using only his fists on Chloe at first until more vicious acts were required to satisfy him. Amanda hoped the scars on Chloe's body would vanish over time. They were already fading. But even if they were barely visible by the time Amanda could file for divorce, the photo documentation would provide proof to a judge that the child's father was dangerous.

A new screen popped up, asking Amanda if she wished to view the photos in a program called Chandelier. Amanda had never heard of it and guessed that Jeb had bypassed free online downloads in favor of purchasing a fancy photo app. *So do I want to view them in there?* She considered the risks—and the possible benefits. An expensive application might allow her to organize and tag the pictures, noting Mark's absurd reasons for inflicting each injury. Viewing the pictures wasn't the same as saving them onto Jeb's hard drive. How would it be different from viewing them on an external storage device like an SD card?

Gathering her courage, she selected "Yes," and in an instant the images popped up in frames with the time and date when each picture had been taken displayed beneath it. *Perfect.* As Amanda had hoped, Chandelier also offered her the option to underscore each image with notes.

As she typed, memories flashed through her mind. Each image drove home to her how maniacal Mark could be, and her skin felt as if it might turn inside out. What if Jeb awakened and caught her on his system? She should probably wait to do this when he was gone from the house. But if she did that, Chloe might see the photographs. Since coming here, the child hadn't awakened screaming from nightmares, and Amanda wanted to keep it that way.

No, this opportunity, while Jeb slept, was too good to pass up. She might not be able to afford a computer for months, and to do this elsewhere before she filed for divorce would be difficult. She could possibly use a library computer, but she doubted it would have a fancy album program similar to Chandelier. And in a public place Amanda would have little privacy. In most of the pictures, she and Chloe were either nude or wore little clothing. Amanda didn't want passing strangers to see these images.

She spent three hours tagging photos. Then she saved all the pictures back onto the SD card. Chandelier offered her several closing options. No, no, *no*. She didn't want to save the files on the Web! Couldn't anyone see them then?

Just then, Amanda heard footsteps. Her heart felt as if it had leaped clear into her throat. In a split second, she jerked the SD card from the computer, shoved it into the pocket of her sweats, and minimized the program screen.

Jeb appeared in the office doorway. By the dim, flickering light from the screensaver, she could see that his tawny hair was tousled from sleep. He, too, wore sweatpants, but he hadn't bothered with a shirt. Amanda had known at first sight that Jeb was muscular and superbly fit, but nothing in her imagination had prepared her for the reality. Every bulge in his arms and shoulders was defined, his belly was ripped, and his golden chest hair shimmered in the shifting illumination. He leaned around to flip on an overhead light. His skin, she noted, was the color of caramel. Second to chocolate, caramel was her favorite sweet.

Amanda's stomach felt as if dozens of butterflies had taken flight inside her and were flapping their wings against her ribs. *No, no, no!* She would not allow herself to feel attracted to Jeb Sterling.

"What on earth are you doing up at his hour?" he asked, his voice gruff with sleepiness.

"I—um—couldn't sleep." She vacated the chair as if it might send jolts of electrical current through her at any moment. "I thought some computer time might relax me."

He passed a hand over his eyes and stifled a yawn. "You don't need to come down in the middle of the night. I don't mind if you use my system. Even if you accidentally erase my hard drive, all my business data is backed up on storage devices and kept in a fireproof lockbox, so no harm will be done."

Amanda pressed a palm over her pocket, where her own vital information was safely stowed. The card seemed to burn her skin through her worn knit pants. If only she could trust Jeb enough to respect her privacy, she'd ask to keep her own all-important records in his lockbox. During that roof cave-in, she could easily have lost the pictures that would protect Chloe from Mark in the future.

Only she didn't know Jeb well enough to trust him

that much yet. She *almost* had that much faith in him, but even if she told him the SD card held very confidential information, he might get curious and look. The thought of him viewing dozens of nude photos of her made her cringe. She would just have to find a safe hiding place for her SD card, and in the event of an emergency, it would be the second thing she grabbed, after her daughter.

Jeb turned from the doorway. "Don't let me interrupt you."

Amanda was afraid to stay in the office, which, given the hour, might look suspicious because he knew she had to get up with Chloe in the morning. She followed him through the dining room to the kitchen, where he stood at the sink getting a drink. Amanda still needed to close Chandelier, but she couldn't do it now. If she went back into his office, he might wonder why. Still, she didn't want him to see those pictures. Bleeding, bruised, and swollen, her body hadn't been anything close to attractive, and for reasons she couldn't bring herself to analyze, if and when she chose to let him see her naked, she wanted to look as good as possible.

He turned the tap back on to refill the glass. "You want some? I think thirst is what woke me up."

"Um, no, thank you."

Beginning to feel like a stick of displaced furniture, she decided to head upstairs before he deemed her behavior peculiar. She could sit on the top riser and listen until he returned to bed. Then she could sneak back into his office to figure out how to get those horrible pictures off his monitor without saving them anywhere.

"I think I'll head back up," she said. "Now that you've quenched your thirst, I hope you sleep well."

He lifted his glass to her. "G'night. Sleep tight."

Amanda ascended the stairs. At the landing, she sat on the top riser and waited. She waited, and *waited*.

Forehead creased in a frown, Jeb gazed after Amanda. She hadn't shut down his computer or turned off the light, and he didn't like to leave his Dell on when it wasn't in use. That left his system vulnerable to unwanted updates that sometimes messed up Windows. Taking the fresh glass of water with him, he went to his bedroom to grab a shirt, then returned to his office and started to shut down the computer. A pop-up window warned him that the Chandelier program hadn't been closed, and that he risked losing his data if he continued without saving. Jeb wasn't sure what Amanda had been doing with Chandelier—possibly looking at his albums, which was harmless enough. But just in case she'd been doing something else and had created a file, he didn't want to close down without saving her information.

When he brought the exit screen back up, he was asked if he wanted to save his photos to the Web or to a file. He knew the program and could have selected not to save Amanda's pictures at all, but he figured they must be important to her if she'd come downstairs in the dead of night to view or tag them. He decided to save her stuff into a picture file named Amanda. The file saved automatically to Chandelier and My Pictures on his system. And then the photos popped back up on the screen with another prompt to close.

Jeb wasn't ready for what he saw. He'd expected the kinds of pictures people normally took. Snaps of Chloe blowing out birthday cake candles. The two of them on vacation. Stuff like that. These images brought bile to his throat. Stupefied, he stared at an entire page of frames that displayed Amanda's nude body, marked horribly with bruises, cuts, and abrasions. *Sweet Christ.* Jeb scrolled down, seeing more images that made his stomach roll. *Abuse?* The term didn't come close to describing what he saw. *Torture* was more like it. Anger turned his blood hot. In the back of his mind, he knew that Amanda had never intended for him to see all this shit. And maybe his invasion of her privacy was unforgivable. But, damn, Jeb was glad she'd unintentionally left her pictures up. He could have talked with the woman for hours and never learned just how bad it had been during her marriage. *Mark can be difficult? Mark was especially vicious when he was drunk?* Those were understatements.

Why, Jeb wondered, had she documented Mark's abuse of her? If Jeb had gone through something so horrific, he'd want no reminders. Evidence? He tossed out that reason. He had several friends who'd gotten divorced, and it was pretty much a no-brainer. Even if Mark contested, Amanda would have no problem dissolving the union, although it might be more costly. But it rarely got too complicated unless the custody of a child or children became an issue.

Chloe. Amanda had said she needed a good lawyer to make sure Mark wasn't granted unsupervised visitation. *Of course.* His brain, foggy with sleep, wasn't tracking well. Using his mouse, Jeb bypassed the sections that featured only Amanda. Being beaten because she'd burned the toast? Or because she'd been a penny short when she returned what remained of the grocery money Mark had given her? As horrible as that was, he knew there had to be more, a lot more, or she wouldn't have been so worried about the SD card.

Then, bang. *Pictures of Chloe.*

Jeb wasn't a man to whom tears came easily, but as he perused photos of the child with nasty bruises, one on her cheek, another on her shoulder, a large one on her ribs, followed by pictures of her skinny, bruised thighs, his whole body snapped taut, and his eyes swam. Thank God for Bozo's doggy eloquence about Jeb's character. If not for the silly dog's adoration of Jeb, the child might be hiding in a cupboard every time he entered a room. *I'll never let him hurt my baby again.* He'd read that on one of Amanda's strips of pink paper. He'd known that Mark had harmed Chloe, but never in his wildest imaginings had he thought of anything this bad or this frequent. He'd envisioned spankings that got out of hand or swats on the head that were uncalled for. If only Jeb could get ten minutes alone with Mark Banning, he'd teach the bastard to *never* lift a violent hand to a woman or child again.

Now Jeb understood why Amanda had kept pictorial evidence. The dates under the photographs showed an escalation of Mark's violent attacks. Normally, after a divorce, each parent was granted reasonable visitation with their children. With this proof, dated and tagged with explanations, no judge would ever grant Mark Banning visitation with his child unless the visits were supervised, and maybe not even then.

For a woman who thought of herself as less than bright, Amanda was one smart cookie. At great risk to herself, she had stolen one of Mark's SD cards and taken these photos while he was gone. *Jesus.* What if she'd slipped up—just once—and left one of these images on the bastard's camera storage? Mark might have killed her.

Jeb nearly jumped out of his skin when Amanda's voice cut through the room. He hadn't heard her approach, yet she stood in the doorway, her hands knotted at her sides, her face blanched with anger.

"How *dare* you!" she cried, her voice throbbing with outrage. "Those are *mine*. You had no right to look at them."

Jeb opened his mouth to frame a response but he didn't get a chance. Amanda stomped toward him. Her whole attitude radiated fury. "They're for the eyes of only a judge!"

Jeb noted that even in anger, Amanda kept her voice pitched low so as not to awaken Chloe. Unlike Mark, even in a rage, she was mindful of her daughter's well-being.

Jeb sank back in the chair, keeping his body limp so he wouldn't appear aggressive, and let her rant at him until she finally ran out of steam. He got it now. *Oh, sweet Jesus, do I ever get it.* What pierced his heart most was when she cried, "I was starting to *trust* you! What in God's name was I *thinking*?"

Keeping his own voice low, he said, "I didn't intend to invade your privacy. You didn't shut down my system, and I always turn it off when I'm not using it. I only came in to close it down. Then Chandelier asked what to do with your files. I figured they might be important, so I didn't want to close without saving them. I created a file in My Pictures, named it Amanda, and meant to shut down afterward. But the pictures popped back up on the screen."

She covered her face with shaking hands. "When you saw me naked, you should have shut down! Instead you kept looking! I saw Chloe! Her photos are at the bottom!"

Jeb had no defense. Maybe he should have closed down after seeing the first photo. He could blame it on shock or half a dozen other things, but all he really wanted to do was stand and draw her into his arms. "I'm glad it happened." *Not the most brilliant comeback.* "Otherwise I would never have known what that animal did to you and your child."

She dropped her arms. "Well, I hope you enjoyed your little porn session!"

Jeb didn't take that jab into his heart because he understood how vulnerable she felt.

"I took those pictures for a very good reason!" she cried. "They weren't for you to ogle."

"I know why you took them, Amanda, and it was a very smart move. You must have been scared to death he'd catch you every time you used his camera."

She stopped breathing. In the overhead light, he saw her eyes bulge and her face go red. Then, with a whoosh of released air, she started to sob. Horrible, tearing sobs that racked her entire body. Having two sisters and a mom he loved, Jeb knew this was his cue. She'd completely lost it, and a hug from him now, if not welcomed, would at least hold her up. He rose from the chair and gathered her close, resisting the urge to squeeze her tight.

Leaning against him, she pressed her face to his chest. Her body still jerked with sobs as she mumbled, "If you think—my accepting your—charity gives you the right to invade my privacy—you can take your damned charity—and shove it up your ass."

Jeb couldn't recall ever having heard Amanda use a cussword. Her language told him how very upset she was. And he didn't blame her. But he was still glad he'd seen the photos. Amanda, and by extension Chloe, might be in more trouble than Amanda imagined.

"Come with me to the kitchen."

"We'll wake up Chloe," she objected.

"No," he insisted. "We'll keep our voices down and just talk. We *need* to discuss this, honey. Sometimes, when we're in the thick of a mess, it isn't always easy to stand back and look at the whole picture." *Bad choice of words*. "The whole situation," he amended. Jeb knew she needed to calm down to absorb what he needed to tell her. "If you love Chloe and want to keep her safe, you'll come with me to the kitchen. We'll have another snifter of brandy, and we'll just talk. Okay?"

Halfway down the hall, he kept an arm around her waist, afraid she might collapse. Then, when he felt that she'd regained her composure, if only just a little, he released her to lead the way.

Despite her outrage, Amanda sat at the table and didn't object when he poured each of them some brandy. Right then, she *needed* a stiff one. She wanted out of this house so fast it would make his head spin, but she couldn't drag her daughter out of bed in the middle of the night, out into these frigid temperatures. Besides, where would they go? There probably wasn't a vacant motel room for miles around. Maybe a drink would take the edge off her fury. Maybe.

Jeb, seated across from her, wasted no time in trying to excuse his behavior or regain her goodwill. Instead he said, "From this moment forward, you have to trust me, Amanda—not only a little, not only halfway, but with your whole heart. No secrets, no more holding back."

"You just broke my trust. Don't you dare ask for it back."

He raked a hand through his hair. "I went in to shut down my system. When the pictures popped up, what

should I have done, cover my eyes? And after seeing—"
He lifted his palms. "I was horrified. No, *stupefied*. And I
couldn't figure out why you had kept such horrible reminders until I recalled your saying that you had to
make sure Mark was never alone with Chloe. Then it
dawned on me. I was still groggy, but my brain finally
started to work."

"And that's your explanation for looking at pictures
that are so very *private*?"

He made no effort to improve his apology. "Has it
occurred to you that Mark may have already filed for
divorce and been granted one? And what if he was also
granted visitation with, or sole custody of, Chloe?"

The blood drained from Amanda's face. In fact, she
felt as if all the blood in her body might be leaking out
the bottoms of her feet. "He can't do that! I never did a
thing to give him reason to divorce me."

Jeb shrugged. "Take a sip of brandy, honey."

She wondered fleetingly when he'd decided that he
had any right to address her with terms of endearment.
Needing a gulp of brandy to calm down, she did as he
said.

"I'm not an attorney," he went on, "and the laws vary
from state to state. I do know, however, that it's pretty
easy to get a divorce almost anywhere. People decide
they want out, and in no time, they're free of the marriage. I had a buddy whose wife divorced him online." He
waved his hand. "A lot of my friends have gone through
divorces. It's a piece of cake, except for the division of
marital assets or a quarrel over custody of the kids."

Amanda wanted to scream that his friends' divorces
had nothing to do with her.

"It's also possible to get a divorce by claiming desertion. In most states a judgment of desertion requires that the spouse at fault must be gone for a certain period of time, and I have no idea what time frame we're looking at. In what state did you reside with Mark?"

"California," she whispered. "Eureka, California."

"I'm not familiar with California law, but in most states, the abandoning spouse is considered to be at fault unless he or she appears in court to give valid reasons for leaving. Most of the time, notices to inform you that you must appear in court are served to you at your last known address. If the court can't locate you—and in this case, you've made every attempt to ensure that you can't be found—the divorce proceedings can continue without you. You would be considered a 'no-show.' And, to add another layer of trouble, you left with Mark's child. You've been in Mystic Creek since early August, if I remember right."

Amanda's anger vanished like a fire doused with a five-gallon bucket of water, and was replaced by fear. She knew where Jeb was going with this, and her heart went out of rhythm, making her afraid she might faint.

"So you've been gone for months." He cradled the snifter in his palms. "I'm not sure how courts work, but looking at the facts, you've left Mark, taken his child, and kept her hidden from him."

"I *had* to leave him," Amanda cried, even as the logic of his words slithered into her brain. "You must know that!"

"I do know that. But no Eureka judge has seen those pictures or heard your side of the story. With only Mark present to testify, how do you think he handled it? With the truth or with a passel of lies?"

It went without saying that Mark would lie. Amanda

felt terror stretch the muscles of her face tight. "So you think there's a possibility that Mark has already filed for divorce and gotten one?"

Jeb made a slow figure eight with his glass. "Yes, I think it's possible, and considering his desire to hurt you in any way he can, I think he would request sole custody of Chloe as well." He lifted a hand. "There *is* another possibility, so try not to panic. Judging by what I've read, men like Mark are insanely possessive of their wives and kids, so he may see filing for divorce as a last resort. To him, that may be admitting defeat."

"He's said a hundred times that he'll never let me leave him."

"And that's in your favor. A divorce may be the last thing on his mind. But that doesn't mean it isn't one of his options, and you can't just hide on the tracks, waiting for the train to hit you."

Amanda closed her eyes. "What should I do?"

"We're going to hire the best family law attorney that we can find. *You* are going to file for divorce and make every attempt to deny Mark visitation of any kind."

"I can't afford that yet."

"I can."

She lifted her lashes to stare at him. "A really good attorney costs thousands."

"Yes. I've never hired anyone in family law, but I did hire a lawyer to litigate a job injury case once. It was expensive, but in the end, I didn't lose everything I owned because some drunk dipshit failed to tie off his safety gear to a roof truss."

Amanda could hardly breathe. But she had to breathe. Passing out on the floor wouldn't save her daughter. "It's not your responsibility to protect Chloe."

"It became my responsibility the moment I walked into that rattrap rental and met you. Don't you get that?"

"You barely know us."

He held her gaze, offering no quarter. "Fine. Hide on the track. Wait for the train. Let him get his hands on your child. He may kill her, you know."

Amanda wobbled on the chair. Black spots danced before her eyes. Jeb leaped up, circled the table, and locked her against him with an arm around her shoulders. "Amanda, please, let me help you. I've had no family to support. I make damned good money. My savings can take a huge hit, and I'll never feel it."

She had no choice but to lean against him. It was that or fall off the chair. "It'll be a lot of money. I may never be able to pay you back."

"If you can't, I'm fine with it. Money isn't that important to me. It's a bank statement, and half the time, I throw them into a file, unopened until I do tax preparation. If I don't step in and help you protect Chloe, I won't be able to live with myself."

He jerked a chair around to sit beside her, maintaining a firm hold on her arm to keep her upright. "I'm sorry for dumping all this on you tonight. I knew you'd left Mark. I knew you were saving for a divorce. But I never dreamed the abuse was so bad, so I didn't focus on the legal ramifications until I saw those pictures. You can't remain in hiding. You need to see a lawyer and start building an ironclad case against Mark, a case that will blow his arguments clear out of the water. If he's already obtained a dissolution of the marriage with custody or visitation privileges, you'll throw a huge wrench in his fan blades with those pictures."

"I need to pay you back," she whispered.

"Then we'll figure something out."

"Like what, sex on demand for the next ten years of my life?"

He ran his hand up her arm, igniting her skin. "I'm not that kind of man. If you don't know that by now, both our boats are sunk."

Amanda couldn't allow her boat to sink; Chloe was in it with her. "I do know—or at least hope—that you aren't that kind of man. But after Mark, it's hard to trust again."

"We'll figure that out, too. But going with the worst-case scenario, what if I did demand sex as a way for you to pay me back? Are you willing to go that far?"

Amanda's vision had cleared. She pictured Chloe's sweet face, and love for her child welled up within her until her chest ached. "I'll do anything, even die, to keep Mark from getting his hands on her."

Jeb pecked her on the cheek, his warm, silken lips leaving a tingling spot on her skin. She found herself wishing he'd kiss her on the lips and suspected that he was thinking the same thing. *Madness*. She had to think only of Chloe.

"Then we're good to go," he said. "I'll call around in the morning. Through my brother Ben, who raises rodeo stock, I know some people with deep pockets. Maybe they can steer me toward a phenomenal lawyer. We have to get all our ducks in a row."

Amanda nodded.

"You feeling better? For a minute, I thought you might faint on me."

"I'm still shaky, but the dizziness is gone."

"Good." He let go of her arm and stood. "Maybe now we can both get some sleep."

Amanda gave him a pleading look. "Just like that?"

"Finish your brandy while I shut down my computer. Then we can talk some more, if you like."

She watched him walk away, too frightened and nauseated to appreciate the loose yet powerful swing of his stride as he returned a moment later.

"I saved your photos on my hard drive and to a USB flash drive." He sat down across from her and shoved the device toward her. "And, no, I didn't ogle your body again. Keep that in a safe place. If we lose those photos, we're in trouble."

Amanda curled her fingers around the slender piece of plastic. "What if Mark has custody, he finds us, and demands that I hand Chloe over?"

Jeb's jaw muscle started to tic. "Then I'll run with her. I probably can't get her out of the country, but I can keep her in hiding until your attorney gets this mess turned around."

Incredulous, Amanda said, "You could be charged with kidnapping. Serve prison time. Why would you risk that for a child you barely know?"

"Because I love that little girl, and I'm thinking like you. I'll die before I let Mark touch her again."

Chapter Nine

Lying in bed later, Jeb felt as uncertain about this situation as Amanda probably did. He had no idea why he felt so compelled to help this woman. She had nailed it when she said that she and her daughter weren't his responsibility. Any sane man would boot them out the door and wish them luck. But Jeb couldn't do that. He'd felt drawn to Amanda from the start. Maybe, if he were honest with himself, she was also right about his motives. Way down deep, was he hoping that if he helped her, she would reward him with her love and all the physical privileges that came with it?

When he searched his heart, he knew his motives were selfless. If Amanda came to love him, he would count himself a lucky man, but he would never try to force her into it.

He could only pray that he didn't awaken in the morning to find Amanda and Chloe gone. Though he felt he'd done a good job of reassuring Amanda, he had to be realistic. Asking her to accept that much money from him, and believe there would be no strings attached, was expecting a lot.

*   *   *

Amanda entertained the same line of thinking as she slipped into bed and gathered Chloe close in her arms. Jeb was, after all, a man, and she'd caught him looking at her body a few times—in Chloe's words, as if Amanda were a bowl of chocolate ice cream and he didn't have a spoon. There wasn't a doubt in her mind that he was physically attracted to her. Amanda had never considered herself particularly desirable to the opposite sex, and before meeting Jeb, she would have bet her whole car fund that a guy so handsome and virile would never give her a second look. Yet he had. That bewildered her. How many times had Mark told her that she was ugly? He'd called her Fat Butt or Tiny Tits far more often than he'd used her actual name.

Maybe a woman didn't need to be pretty in order for a man to want her. Mark had certainly helped himself to the goods plenty of times, ejaculating even as he told her how ugly she was.

Pressing her face to Chloe's hair, Amanda breathed deep and wondered if trusting Jeb, even in small measure, wasn't one of the worst mistakes of her life. Oh, well. As long as Chloe remained safe, Amanda didn't care what Jeb might do to her. He'd have to get very inventive to outclass Mark. Chloe was all that mattered.

Just then, almost as if he sensed her distress, Bozo licked the back of her wrist. Amanda turned her hand, intending to pet the animal, but before she could make contact, he began to bathe her palm. She recalled Chloe saying that Bozo *talked* to her about what a nice man Jeb was. Maybe, Amanda decided, Chloe had it right about the mastiff's sentiments. She smiled and evaded the canine's tongue to give him a loving scratch behind the ears.

In a whisper, she said, "So you give him a high recommendation, do you?"

Bozo grumbled in response. Amanda imagined that the dog said, "He's the best."

On that thought, she plunged into an exhausted sleep.

While drinking his third cup of coffee the next morning, Jeb dialed the numbers of a few friends, in search of help in finding a good attorney. Frank Harrigan, a pal of his brother Ben's in Crystal Falls who raised world-class quarter horses, came through with pay dirt. Frank had hired a divorce attorney years ago to free his daughter, Samantha, from an abusive marriage, and he said Jeb couldn't go wrong with this guy. Jeb promptly called the lawyer to make an appointment. It was only eight o'clock, but a receptionist answered. At first, she insisted that the first opening for a consultation was more than two weeks away, but when Jeb explained the urgency of the situation, the woman said she could juggle the schedule to get Amanda in that afternoon. *Score*.

Seconds later, Jeb was on the phone with his mother. After exchanging greetings, he said, "Mom, I was wondering if you'd mind watching a little girl named Chloe this afternoon."

Silence. Jeb could almost hear the wheels turning in his mother's mind. During the storm, he'd had time for only quick calls to check on his parents, and he hadn't wanted to answer all the questions that would arise if he mentioned his houseguests.

"Chloe? How old is she?"

"Six, and the sweetest child I've ever met."

"And who are her parents?"

Jeb grinned. Though he'd always been discreet, Kate had long since accepted that her sons were sexually active. "She's not mine." He paused. "Not that I don't wish she were. When I say she's sweet, I mean *really* sweet. I met her mom, Amanda, during the ice storm when I was helping people over on Elderberry." Jeb made short work of recounting how dangerous the situation had been. "Anyway, I was afraid to leave them there, especially without a vehicle, so I brought them to my place."

"And they're still there?"

Kate's tone implied that Amanda and Chloe had been in his home for an inordinately long time. "Yes. The next day when I went over to check on her place, half of the roof had collapsed." Jeb explained his near escape.

"Oh, my God!" Kate cried. "You could have been killed, Jeb."

"Yep, but what scares me worse is that the first collapse brought support beams down on the sofa where Amanda and Chloe were huddling for warmth the previous evening."

Kate muttered something Jeb didn't quite catch. "You did the right thing by taking them in. I'm proud of you."

Jeb knew his mom was full of questions, so he decided to head her off with answers. "Amanda works part-time at the elementary school cafeteria, but the hourly wage is low. Even before the storm shut down the schools and got her laid off, she was barely managing to keep the wolves from her door. So I've offered her a job as my housekeeper in exchange for room, board, and a small wage."

"I'll bet she's thanking God for small blessings."

Jeb glanced over his shoulder to make sure Amanda

hadn't slipped downstairs. "She hasn't accepted the job yet. She's—um—wary. But I'm working on her."

"Wary?"

Jeb had already intruded upon Amanda's privacy. It wouldn't be right to reveal every detail of her history to a woman she'd never met. "Bad marriage, a bastard for a husband. Men aren't high on her list of favorite things. I'll leave it at that."

To Kate's credit, she asked for no more details. "Well, in answer to your initial question, I would love to watch Chloe for a few hours. It'll be fun!"

Amanda overslept, and when she got downstairs, Jeb blindsided her with news of an appointment with a Crystal Falls attorney that afternoon.

"Today?" Amanda heard the trill of panic in her voice. "That's awfully fast." She'd been hoping for a couple of days to wrap her mind around the situation and accept that she had no choice but to take Jeb's money. "Are you sure this guy is good?"

"He's been ranked one of the best family law attorneys in the state. He's our man."

Amanda imagined Jeb tucking a thick wad of money in her hand in only a few hours. She wasn't ready for this, but she had no alternatives. "I have no one to watch Chloe, and I do *not* want her to be present in the lawyer's office."

"Got it covered. My mom has agreed to watch Chloe."

Amanda's heart clenched. "I've never left Chloe with anyone, let alone a stranger."

Jeb's hazel gaze held hers. "My mom—her name is Kate—is a grandmother waiting to happen. She raised six kids. I'll bet you ten bucks that Chloe will love her and be calling her Grandma in fifteen minutes or less."

After waking Chloe and getting her dressed, Amanda found her hands trembling as she showered and then fussed over what she should wear. She had nothing appropriate, only worn jeans and tops that had seen better days. A high-end attorney probably considered thousand-dollar suits to be everyday clothes. She decided on her least faded pair of blue denims and a cotton blouse that looked halfway new. Choosing footwear was easy. She pulled on the low-cut boots that Jeb had bought her. *I've never thanked him. Every time I tried, my throat clogged.*

Amanda sank onto the edge of the bed, listening to the musical sound of Chloe's voice and the deeper pitch of Jeb's drift upstairs. *Why is it so difficult for me to accept help?* Amanda had no answers. She knew only that admitting she couldn't make it on her own filled her with trepidation and a horrible sense of inadequacy.

Seconds later, when she entered the kitchen, she saw a beautifully prepared breakfast set out on the table. Jeb broke off a conversation with Chloe to give Amanda a slow appraisal that made her skin tingle. "You look great."

Amanda released a breath she hadn't realized she'd been holding. "From the ankles up, I look like hand-me-down Sue, but the boots are fabulous." She swallowed. "Thank you for buying them for me."

He placed a palm atop Chloe's head, fingering a dark curl as if it were spun silk. "I'm sorry about the white lie. It was the only way I could think of to get you to accept some decent winter outerwear. What you had was completely inadequate."

Amanda shifted her gaze to the platters of food on the table. "Sort of like the white lie you told me about being a lousy cook so I'd accept your offer of a job?" *Shut up, Amanda. He's been nothing but generous. You have no right to be taking shots at him.* "With amazing alacrity, you seem able to switch your culinary skills on or off."

He grinned. "Busted. I'm a great cook. But that doesn't mean all of it was a white lie. When the busy season hits, I have little time for kitchen stuff or for cleaning this huge house. I survive on peanut-butter-and-jelly sand-wiches. During the slower months, I could be making fur-niture if I had help in the house."

"Yum!" Chloe inserted. "I hope I'm here when you're busy, Mr. Jeb. Peanut-butter-and-jelly is my favorite."

"Well, if your mommy accepts the job, she'll do most of the cooking, and I doubt she'll serve that. But maybe we can have them sometimes." Jeb gestured at the table. "Let's eat before our breakfast gets cold."

As Amanda approached the table, she felt like a vic-tim of sudden-onslaught rheumatoid arthritis. Her joints were half-frozen and hurt when she moved. *Pride.* She felt ashamed of herself for speaking harshly to Jeb after he'd been so kind.

She took a bite of the fried potatoes and almost mim-icked Chloe by saying, "Yum." Instead, she rolled the flavors on her tongue and swallowed before saying, "These are better than mine. What's in them?"

"Diced green onions, some flakes of fresh garlic, salt and pepper, and a dash of my secret ingredient, sugar. At the last, I toss in some grated cheddar, but only a little. But I have to correct you. Your fried potatoes and gravy are *spectacular*."

"So are these." Amanda took a bite of bacon. "I think I've gained a pound by merely breathing the air here."

Depending upon road conditions, the drive to Crystal Falls took from thirty minutes to an hour. In Mystic Creek, long icicles still hung from tree limbs, eaves, and power lines, lending the quaint town a fantasy appeal. Everything glistened as if it had been sprayed with liquid silver. Fearful that Highway 97 might be treacherous, Jeb wanted to leave early for Amanda's appointment. And rather than drop Chloe off with his mom and hurry away, he wanted to spend some time there while the two of them got acquainted. For one thing, he didn't want to leave the girl feeling fearful, and second, he knew Amanda would be worried sick all afternoon if she didn't first see Chloe settled in comfortably with his folks.

Jeb hadn't underestimated his mom's ability to win over a child. Kate met them in the entryway. Until that moment, Jeb hadn't realized just how *much* Amanda resembled his mom, both of them petite with dark hair, brown eyes, and delicate features. *Shit, I've got a mother complex.* Jeb quickly shoved the thought aside. The likeness in appearance was purely coincidental. He hadn't latched onto Amanda because she reminded him of his mom.

While Jeb stood there like a stump with deep roots, grasping Amanda's arm, his mom had already sprung into action, shaking Amanda's hand, saying how pleased she was to meet her, and then bending low to greet Chloe, who was leaning against Jeb's leg.

"I figured you'd be here for lunch," Kate said with an

enthusiasm guaranteed to delight six-year-olds. "So hurry and come with me! We're going to make picture pizzas!"

Chloe, who loved to draw, bounced away to enter Kate Sterling's world of childhood delight. She grasped the older woman's hand and, in the process, abandoned her mother.

"What are picture pizzas?" Chloe asked.

"Anything we want to make them into!" Kate replied. "We can try to do a heart pizza, or a dog pizza, or a horse pizza. Plus, I have an idea how we can try to make rooster pizza!"

Amanda looked up at Jeb and offered him a slightly bewildered smile. The question in her eyes said, *Is your mom for* real? Jeb, who'd helped Amanda over the ice outside, released his hold on her arm

He registered Chloe's excited intonations coming from the kitchen without making out all the words. He gleaned only enough to know that his mom had the dough shooter out and her plan was to squirt a thin, gluten-free mixture onto pizza stones.

"Gluten free?" He winked at Amanda. "No one in the family is allergic. I guess my mother is on another dietary kick."

"We can try to make animals, triangles, squares, and people!" Kate exclaimed.

Jeb guessed that Chloe wouldn't care as much about the outcome of her artwork as she would about the fun of trying.

Jeb looked down at Amanda. "I told you. Mom *loves* kids. Chloe will have a great day. She may wish you were here to share the fun, but she won't miss you or feel sad. Are you reading me?"

Amanda's beautiful, soul-deep eyes misted with tears as she nodded. "Your mom is adorable."

He guided her through the house where he'd grown up. "Let's observe the action. Mom can get crazy when it comes to kids. She won't care if she winds up with pizza sauce on the walls. She loves children as much as I love—" Jeb broke off. He'd almost said as much as he loved sex. But it wasn't actually true that he loved sex. Granted, he'd had his share of intimate encounters, but afterward, he'd felt nothing emotional. Besides, the word *sex* wasn't one he should use in the presence of the wary woman beside him.

Amanda noticed his pause and asked, "As much as you love what?"

Thinking quickly, Jeb replied, "As much as I love standing outside at night, staring up at a starry sky and contemplating the magnificence of creation."

Amanda's gaze went blank for a second, as if she were trying to see a starlit sky in her mind's eye. Then she smiled and nodded. "Is there anything more beautiful than a starlit sky to touch our souls?"

Monkey sex with you. All positions, no limits. Hell, if I could swing from a chandelier with you and plunge to my death, I'd die a happy man. Jeb had always spoken his mind and prided himself on the trait. But Amanda didn't need to know what he was thinking at that moment. He suspected that few women wanted to know what a man actually had on his mind. When they asked what you were thinking, maybe they really wanted to hear—well, what they wanted to hear.

He bypassed the formal living room and large dining room on his left and moved into the great room, where, as a boy, he'd kicked holes in the walls during his karate phase and tracked black muck onto the carpet after fixing his motorcycle. The area featured a full-size pool table, a rock fireplace, a comfy sectional in dark brown that created a U shape off to the right, and a spacious adjoining kitchen to the left. It didn't compare to Jeb's kitchen, but his mom and dad had designed the area for large family dinners, with plenty of counter space and an island bar with stools on one side and a work area on the other.

With a kitchen towel already tied around her neck, Chloe stood on the stepstool that Jeb had once used and watched with fascination as Jeb's mom filled a shooter with pizza dough. Today his mom was using what he called the "straight tip," which had always been his favorite.

Jeb motioned for Amanda to take a seat on a barstool beside him, and they watched the pizza-shaping process. With Kate as a guide, Chloe's initial attempt to make a heart resulted in a lopsided one, but her second effort was nearly perfect.

As the child spurted dough onto the stone, Kate said, "We can each choose what kind of pizza we want. I have different cheeses and meat, and plenty of vegetables." Kate hugged Chloe's shoulders and whispered loudly enough for Jeb to hear, "Do you eat meat? If so, you can add some sausage or pepperoni."

"Yes, we eat meat," Chloe replied, "but Mommy and I don't choose to eat animals that are our friends." Already squeezing out another small heart, she added, "That's not okay."

Jeb had another *oh, shit* moment, but he was grateful for the enlightenment. He stiffened on the barstool as Chloe went on, sounding much older than her years.

"For instance, Mr. Jeb raises chickens." The child tipped her head sideways. "But he doesn't *eat* the hens that lay his eggs. So all of them have names, and he goes to the grocery store to buy chicken to eat."

Jeb's mom sent him the piercing look that he remembered from childhood. He gave her an eyebrow twitch in response, praying that she got the message and wouldn't tell Chloe that he'd regularly harvested older hens prior to the child's presence in his home.

Kate visibly collected her composure. "Well, what man with any heart would eat a hen because she stopped laying?" Jeb's mom sent him another straight-into-his-eyes message that said, more clearly than with words, *You'd better live up to the image of yourself that you've planted in this child's mind, or I will make fast work of kicking your fanny.* And Jeb knew he'd let her do it.

If he got lucky and Amanda stayed with him—if he'd finally found the kind of love and commitment that his folks had—he would gladly eat store-bought chicken for the rest of his life.

But—and this was a much larger problem, both literally and figuratively—Jeb also raised at least two steers a year for meat, which he shared with all his family. How would he pull off slaughter day without sending Chloe into hysteria? That was a conundrum of gigantic proportions. The *reason* Jeb raised two steers for himself and his family was because Jeremiah knew that his wife would fall in love with the beeves if he raised them at his place. Kate would name them and give them treats, and then protect the animals with her own body when the slaughter truck arrived.

If Amanda and Chloe stayed with Jeb, he would have

to move his steers to rented pastureland. Then, when it came time for the butcher, he'd tell Chloe that the animals needed more grazing in a distant pasture. *Another white lie.* He was getting much too good at telling them, which made him uncomfortable. But he honestly couldn't think of any other way around the problem. No sane man would feed two steers for their entire lives out of the goodness of his heart. He needed to find a pasture to rent, fast.

Jeb was musing on that, and checking his watch, when his mother announced that lunch was ready. In response to Kate's text message, Jeb's dad came in from the stable to eat. Once Amanda and Chloe were introduced to Jeremiah, the group gathered at the table, said the blessing, and began devouring piping-hot pizza.

"After Chloe and I clean up the kitchen, we're going to make holiday cookies," Kate announced. "Sugar cookies that we can cut into shapes and decorate." Directing a smile at Chloe, she asked, "Won't that be fun?"

"I *love* making cookies!" Chloe crowed.

Amanda, sitting at Kate's left, leaned closer to her hostess to whisper, "She may make a huge mess. She gets a little too enthusiastic with the sprinkles."

Kate laughed. "So do I, and making a mess is half the fun."

Jeremiah dabbed the corners of his mouth with his napkin. "Text me when the first batch comes out of the oven. I want mine warm without frosting."

Chloe flashed Jeb's dad a wondering look. "Don't you like frosting?" The possibility was clearly beyond the child's comprehension. "That's the best part."

Jeremiah chuckled. "I love the frosting. Kate slaps my hands when I get into the cookies because she's afraid

I'll eat them all. It's just that my favorite thing in the whole world is eating cookies still warm from the oven."

"Oh." Chloe shrugged. "We'll make sure to text you then."

Kate gazed at her husband. "You'll eat the whole first batch."

Jeremiah retorted, "Eating the whole first batch is the *fun part* of cookie days."

Chloe chimed in, "Mimi, we can let him eat the first batch if he wants. We'll be making lots and lots!"

Kate nodded. "You're right. He works hard outdoors so he builds up an appetite." She winked at her husband. "Chloe asked if she might call me Grandma. I asked to be called Mimi instead."

Jeb glanced at Amanda. Her shoulders were relaxed. Her eyes shone with warmth. He was glad he'd set aside time for them to linger before leaving for Crystal Falls. Now Amanda wouldn't worry about her daughter while they were gone.

Jeb whispered to Amanda that they had to leave in forty-five minutes. Amanda wasn't about to sit on her bum while Kate cleaned up the kitchen, so she stood to clear the table. Before she could collect a plate, Jeb beat her to the draw. She gave him a quick study, appreciating the fact that he was willing to help. Even more impressive, Jeremiah joined in the effort. Apparently, this was a family that played together, joked, laughed, and pitched in when there was work to be done. As an only child, Amanda had always wished for siblings, the more the better, but her mom had had great difficulty getting pregnant, so Amanda's arrival had been considered a miracle by both her parents. No other kids had come along, and she'd been doted on. Amanda couldn't complain. She'd been a happy kid. But to this day, she still yearned to live in a home that rang with noise and laughter.

She soon found herself working in tandem with Jeb to rinse dishes and put them into the machine. Kate tackled the stovetop. Jeremiah wiped down the island bar. Chloe stood on the stepstool next to Amanda at the sink, *helping* to rinse dishes. She got in the way more than anything, but Amanda wanted her to experience a joint effort and feel part of a family. Someday, when Chloe grew up, Amanda hoped she would jump in to help with meal preparation and cleanup.

Amanda couldn't help but notice how easily she and Jeb established a rhythm. If it hadn't been for the way her heart leaped when they accidentally touched hands or bumped into each other, they might have been doing dishes together for years. It felt strange and yet nice. She got her injured finger wet and was glad that she'd thought to slip some fresh butterfly bandages into her pocket. Before leaving for Crystal Falls, she would re-dress the cut.

All too soon, Jeb signaled that it was time to go. Amanda rinsed her coffee cup and put it in the dishwasher. While Jeb rinsed his, she quickly changed her bandage and went to hug her daughter good-bye. Distracted by a box of clear Christmas tree balls and acrylic paint in an assortment of colors, Chloe returned the quick embrace and resumed her study of the ornaments. Apparently Kate planned to make yet another mess this afternoon, creating tree decorations.

Once outside, Jeb encircled Amanda's shoulders with one arm as they made their way across the ice to his truck. Ever the gentleman, he opened the passenger door and gave her a boost onto the seat.

When he joined her inside the cab and started the engine, he said over the rumble, "On the way, I'm hoping we can have a discussion and make some decisions. We don't get much opportunity to talk about serious matters with Chloe around."

Tension stiffened Amanda's spine and she asked with trepidation, "What are you hoping to discuss?"

She braced herself for his answer.

Chapter Ten

Amanda waited for Jeb's response as he focused on a treacherous curve in the road. When it straightened, he returned his attention to forming a carefully worded reply.

"For starters, I want to readdress the job offer." He turned off Clark Road and headed toward the town center, where he would exit onto North Huckleberry and access Highway 97 at the edge of town. "You haven't accepted it yet, and I personally feel it's the best option you have. For both of you."

Amanda already knew that. She would soon be in debt to Jeb for an incredible amount of money. This employment opportunity gave her the only real chance she had to improve her financial situation and pay him back. She refused to think of his loan as a gift. She'd settle the debt, no matter how long it took.

"I know it's a very good offer," she told him. "It's just—do you want the absolute truth?"

He chuckled. "Hell, no. I want you to lie. Of course I want the truth."

"This whole situation makes me extremely uneasy,"

she confessed. "And I guess my pride is also getting in the way. We barely know each other, and now you're about to give me a huge amount of money. It's insane."

He crossed North Huckleberry Bridge, heading north. "You know what, Amanda? A lot of time isn't always necessary for people to become well acquainted. From the start, we've been in a crazy situation together. Think of it this way. Somewhere on a battlefield right now, men and women are fighting for their country and trying to stay alive. What do you think they do when they've just met and the enemy is coming at them? Do they huddle in a bunker back to back, ready to protect each other with their lives? Or does the woman say, 'You're a total stranger. Why would you want to risk dying for me?'"

Stymied by the question, Amanda studied Jeb's sharply chiseled profile, admiring the straight bridge of his nose, the square strength of his jawline, and the way his toffee-colored hair lay in a wave over his high forehead.

Before she could answer, he continued. "And after the danger has passed, when they have observed each other under fire, do you think they still feel like strangers? Or are the moments they shared engraved forever in their minds, making them feel they know each other better than anyone, ever?"

"We aren't on a battlefield," she pointed out. Saying it gained her a little thinking time.

A muscle ticked in his lean cheek. "The hell we aren't. For us, it's the life of a child that's on the line. I've got her back—or maybe I should say that I *want* to have her back. But you're holding things up, second-guessing my motives, and, well, just generally being a difficult pain in the ass."

A laugh erupted from Amanda. It came so suddenly and with such force that it startled her. "I guess I am," she admitted. "I'm sorry. I'm having a hard time accepting that I need help to protect Chloe. I'm her mother. I should be able to do it on my own, and the fact that I can't frightens me."

"Fair enough. But I do need help with my house, and I think you know it. If you don't take the job, I'll hire someone else. Yet you act as if I'm offering you charity. It's only a job, not a lifelong commitment. As soon as you're financially able, you can quit and move on to bigger and better things, no hard feelings."

"All right!" she cried. "I'll take the damned job. But on my terms. Five hundred a month with room and board."

"Nine hundred," he countered.

"We went over this last night. If I keep my cafeteria job, I can't work for you full-time. That's way too much money to pay me. Six."

"You'll work a lot more than you think," he retorted. "No less than eight."

"Seven," she shot back.

He grinned while keeping his gaze on the road. "Deal. But I have to say, you drive a hard bargain in reverse."

Just then, Amanda recalled that he'd offered her seven hundred last night and realized he'd somehow herded her into accepting that amount. "It's too much, but because *you* are such a difficult pain in the ass, I'll accept it."

It was his turn to laugh. "Call me all the names you like. I'm happy with the bargain. You have no idea just how happy." He glanced over at her. "Now that that's settled, I need to know where I stand for this consultation with the attorney. Would you like me to go in with you, or would you prefer that I butt out?"

Amanda considered the question. She'd be telling the lawyer some of her darkest secrets, which she preferred that Jeb not hear. But this wasn't about her; it was about Chloe. "I need you to go in with me. I might forget to ask a question or, even worse, be so nervous that I'll forget everything he says."

Expression solemn, Jeb stared straight ahead. "He'll probably want to view the photographs. They'll come up on the screen. Unless his monitor faces away from us, I'll see the pictures again. Are you okay with that?"

Amanda swallowed hard. "You've already seen them. I won't like it. I'll feel horribly exposed." She clamped her hands over his knees. "But in the end, all that matters is Chloe. How I feel doesn't count."

"It counts with me," he told her, his voice going husky. "I'm sorry you have to endure this."

"You caused none of it. My mistakes got me and my daughter into this mess. I wore rose-colored glasses when I fell for Mark. I had unprotected sex with him. We were together only once before we got married, but that was all it took. I was pregnant, thought I was in love, and Mark offered to marry me. I was dumb and said yes."

"You were young and innocent, not *dumb*," he corrected. "And it's easy to be fooled by a guy who's all sweetness and charm until he gets a ring on your finger. I've met women who seemed wonderful at first, and then they turned into witches."

"You never married one of them."

"Nope. I wasn't seventeen, and I wasn't pregnant. When you attend university, you grow up and learn a lot.

By the time I graduated and moved back to Mystic, I had a load of experience with women under my belt."

Amanda relaxed against the seat, feeling a vast relief that defied explanation. "You honestly don't think I'm stupid."

"I think you're sharp as a tack. And if you doubt my assessment, take a long gander at Chloe. She's a bright and well-spoken child. *You* raised her. From what I've heard, Mark only showed up to complain, knock you around, and, in the end, abuse your daughter. And, to your immense credit, you managed to get her out of there. And on foot, I might add. When I think of how you waited until the timing was perfect and started getting cash withdrawals off credit cards to collect enough money to run, I'm amazed."

Amanda shot him a startled look. "I never told you about the credit cards. How do you know that? Did Chloe tell you?"

She saw him wince and then witnessed in his expression the battle he waged to tell her the truth. "I read your notes."

"My what?"

"The notes you threw into the wind. About fifty of them landed on my property. I was plenty pissed at first. I thought someone was driving by and tossing trash out the window. Then I noticed there was writing on the strips of paper."

Amanda recalled writing about her credit card scam one night and gleefully wondering how Mark had reacted when he'd started getting all the bills. "I never dreamed I'd meet anyone who'd read those messages."

"Well, you did. I'm sorry I didn't fess up sooner, but I didn't want to embarrass you."

Amanda thought of all the secrets she'd shared on those slips of paper and wished she could melt and be absorbed into the leather of the bucket seat.

"I decided the notes were blowing in from the south, probably from Elderberry Lane. I started to obsess about you, wishing I could find you and at least be your friend. You sounded very lonely. So when the storm hit, and Tony Bradley pounded on my door for help with the neighbors, I chose to cover your road, hoping I'd meet you. Your house was the last one, and it looked vacant. But as I turned around, I noticed disturbed snow in front of the porch. So I pulled over, still not sure that the old house was occupied, and when I knocked, the door cracked open, and there you were."

Amanda remembered how frightened she'd been to let him inside, but in retrospect she now knew it was the best choice she'd ever made. Her voice trembled as she said, "I thank God you knocked. I thank God you refused to let me and Chloe stay there. I thank God for the winter clothes. I just have trouble telling you thank you. I'm sorry for that. I should be thanking you with every breath I take."

"Well, sweetheart, from now on you'll be working and paying your own way." He cast her another quick glance. "And just for the record, I'm thankful, too. Before you came along, I was lonely. Rattling around in that huge house with only a dog for company. My life felt empty and sometimes pointless, though I hated admitting it, even to myself. It wasn't how I imagined it would be when I turned thirty."

"My life isn't what I imagined it would be, either. I planned to become a teacher. English was my favorite subject, and I pictured myself making kids love the language as much as I do. Instead I never even went to college."

"You've done a fine job of teaching Chloe her English, and you're young. You can still become a teacher if that's what you really want."

"My priorities have changed. Raising and protecting Chloe have become my focus. Thank you for helping me do that."

"You're absolutely welcome. This isn't about *charity*, Mandy. I firmly believe it's about fate." He redirected his attention to the icy road. "I'm in love with your daughter. And you may laugh because, according to you, we're barely more than strangers, but I think I'm also falling in love with you."

A long silence followed. She saw Jeb swallow several times as if his airway were restricted by tension. She had a feeling he was thinking, *Open mouth, insert boot.* Warmth pooled in her belly, but along with it came a measure of fear. She had grown fond of Jeb. When he touched her, she felt a strong and undeniable physical attraction. But she wasn't ready to confess her feelings.

Unable to think what to say, she managed, "With all that experience with women under your belt, now you say you're falling in love with someone you barely know."

He flashed her a lingering look that made her skin burn. "Damn straight. I'm not all the way into the hole yet. Let's just say I'm standing over it with one foot inside and the other on a banana peel." He hesitated. "I've never done this before. I'm a virgin. Be gentle with me."

The old phrase, normally said in reference to a woman, made her smile. "I'll try." She joined him in staring straight at the road. Her emotions tumbled within her like marbles being shaken inside a tin can. "I can't say it back, Jeb. Please don't let that hurt you. This whole situation makes me want to run. As far away as possible, in any direction."

From the corner of her eye, she saw him nod. Relief swept through her because he understood.

"Do me a favor?" he asked.

"What's that?" Her voice sounded as choked as if strong fingers had clamped over her larynx.

"When you run, run to me. Or at least give me some notice so I can run with you."

Amanda knew this conversation was crazy, and she stared at the road through a blur of tears. "I'm not going to run. I have nowhere to go and no money to get there."

He sighed, the sound floating toward her like a caress. "You do have somewhere to go. Straight into my arms. I don't want to scare you off, Mandy. But I swear on my grandmother's grave—and I loved her a lot—that I'm not talking about sex. Right now, all I want is to be your friend."

More silence. Choosing her words carefully, she took a stab at changing the subject. "No one except my parents has ever called me Mandy."

"Sorry. If it's special to you, I won't call you that. It's just—well, 'Amanda' seems so formal to me. I've started to call you Mandy a dozen times and bit my tongue. Now that we're talking, *really* talking on a personal level, it's just popping out."

"You have my permission. I like that name. Dad called me that all my life, and I miss it." Amanda considered Jeb's name, which she suspected was a shortened version. "What's your actual first name?"

"Jebediah. I go by Jeb because it's such a mouthful. My middle name is Paul."

"Mine's Marie."

"Mandy Marie. I like that."

"Dad called me that when I was being a difficult pain in the ass."

Jeb chuckled. "I'll remember that. When I tack on Marie, you'll know my patience is wearing thin."

Amanda grinned. "If I call you Jebediah Paul, you'd better duck."

That brought a bark of laughter from him.

Emotions welled within her, all bewildering. "Thank you for being my friend."

"You're very welcome." He executed another sharp curve. "Now, for the appointment with this lawyer. When you're in there, facing him, if you start to lose it, remember I'm there beside you. If you need me to intervene, just reach over and squeeze my hand. I've been told that this guy has a heart of gold, but he also grills prospective clients. He's good, really good. That's why he's such a jerk when you first meet him. He is way beyond accepting cases he can't win merely to pad his pockets. Before he decides to take you on, you'll have to convince him that you have a strong argument and won't fold in court."

Amanda tried to imagine facing a cantankerous lawyer.

"He's older," Jeb went on. "Close to retirement. He's already built his career and reputation. I hope you don't take offense, Mandy, but the truth is, you're a little timid with men. If you start to feel as if you're teetering and about to buckle, grab my hand. Okay? I'll have no problem taking him on."

Amanda appreciated Jeb's offer, because she *was* timid

with men. "I'll squeeze. I promise." Warmth moved through her again. "I appreciate your offer to go in with me."

"No worries. I'll step in if he starts running over you."

Amanda felt the tension drain from her body. She could do this. With Jeb beside her, she almost believed she could take on Mark and win.

The attorney, Clyde Johnson, was a partner in a large firm with offices in an impressive, even glamorous building. Just as Jeb had described him, he was an older man, stocky in build and gruff of voice, with a down-to-business attitude and an abrasive manner. Amanda was instantly terrified of him.

"Right up front, I want you to know that I may not choose to represent you. You'll be charged for this consultation, and I will decide afterward if I want to take your case."

Amanda had no idea what to say. He might not take her case? Panic swamped her. She groped for Jeb's hand, found the warm, thick hardness of it, and squeezed with all her might.

Jeb cleared his throat. "I understand that you don't mess around, Mr. Johnson, and that you aren't willing to waste your time by taking on a loser. But, please, go easy on this lady. She's been severely abused, and she's easily intimidated."

Johnson sank back into his plush leather chair. Amanda looked past him to his monitor and realized with rising panic that the screen faced them. Jeb would see the photos of her nude body again. She had a horrible urge to run, and it was all she could do to remain in her seat. Letting go of Jeb's hand, which seemed to inject strength into her bloodstream, was impossible at the moment. She dug in hard with her fingernails, fearful that he might break her hold on him.

The attorney directed his gaze straight at Amanda. "Okay, so spill it. Why are you here, seeking help? What has your husband done to lose visitation with his daughter? I've gotten only the basic facts from my secretary. She made room for you in my busy schedule today because you claim the matter is urgent."

Without loosening her hold on Jeb, Amanda thrust her right hand into her parka pocket, grasped the SD card, and shoved it across the desk. Anger turned her blood hot, making it move as slowly through her veins as molten lava. "Have a look at these photos and decide if I have a case. Your decision may mean the difference between life and death for my little girl." With a final push, Amanda put the SD card right in front of his bulging upper belly. "If you don't feel I have a good reason to deny my husband visitation with her, I'll be out of here in a nanosecond."

Jeb gave Amanda's shaking hand a two-beat squeeze. She took that to mean that she'd faced the devil and won. She sat hunched forward and stiff as the attorney picked up the SD card and inserted it into his computer. The instant the photographs came up on his screen, he muttered an obscenity.

Jeb bent his head and stared at the carpet, trying, she knew, to spare her some degree of humiliation. Amanda remained on the edge of her chair. When pictures of Chloe came onto the screen, tears filled her eyes. *My fault, all my fault. The child never would have endured such pain if I hadn't married Mark.* Jeb's hand tightened on hers. She held on to him as if her life depended on it.

But in truth it wasn't her life at stake. It was her precious baby's.

As if the attorney sensed Amanda's embarrassment, he hit the "off" button on the monitor, making it go blank. Swiveling in his expensive chair, he folded his hands over his protruding paunch and said, "Those are some very disturbing photos. What prompted you to take them?"

"When Mark—that's my husband—started to speak and act with cruelty toward my daughter, Chloe, I knew it was only a matter of time before he would begin to abuse her physically. I needed to get her out of there, save money for a divorce, and make sure Mark never got unsupervised visitation with our child. I figured the pictures, showing the frequency of and the crazy reasons for his attacks on me, followed by photographic evidence of his attacks on Chloe, would be accepted as evidence in court and help a judge to understand how dangerous Mark is."

"Why didn't you jump in the car and haul ass for help?"

"I had no car."

"No car." He quirked an eyebrow. "So why didn't you call a family member to come get you?"

"I had no phone."

"No phone? In this day and age, even kids have cell phones."

The tremors racking Amanda's body became worse. This attorney would never understand what her situation with Mark had been like, and he clearly felt there were huge holes in her story. She needed a lawyer who believed what she told him, someone who would fight with everything he had to save her daughter.

"I had no phone," Amanda repeated. "If you don't

believe me, perhaps I need to seek other representation."

"I haven't doubted a word you've said," Johnson replied. "But to win this case—and it's going to be one hell of a battle—I need to know everything, and why you allowed it to occur. I also need to see how you hold up under questioning. Believe me, I'm acting like a lamb compared to an opposing litigator. He'll try his damnedest to tear your story apart, and if you lose your cool, the best lawyer in the world won't be able to win this case and keep your daughter safe."

Shaking so violently that she couldn't conceal it, Amanda asked, "Does that mean you'll represent me?"

"I think you need my help—I mean *really* need my help—so, yes, I'll represent you. I require a ten-thousand-dollar retainer fee. A check or credit card is fine. Money matters are handled out front by my staff. As I work and log in hours, your fund may run low. In that event, you'll be notified in time to replenish it."

Not allowing herself to consider her words, she said, "For you to get the full picture, Mr. Johnson, I'll start at the beginning."

He nodded.

Barely pausing to breathe, Amanda started talking. She told him about discovering that she was pregnant after her first intimate encounter with a boy whom she thought was the love of her life. How she'd reeled with morning sickness as she walked across the stage in Olympia, Washington, to receive her high school diploma. How Mark, acting like her savior, insisted on marrying her. How she foolishly believed he was wonderful.

"He hit me on our wedding night," she told the attorney. "He didn't like the lingerie I'd chosen. I was four months along, starting to show, and didn't want to wear anything see-through. So I picked something more concealing. He hit me so hard that he knocked me across the bed and onto the floor. It wasn't until the next morning that I realized all of my upper left molars were loose and that my jaw was fractured. My husband refused to take me to a dentist or a doctor."

The attorney stiffened and shifted his weight on his fancy chair. "But you stayed to let him do it again."

"Not by choice. He hovered over me. If I went near the motel room phone, he dug his fingernails into my arm and said he'd kill me if I called my folks." Amanda swallowed to steady her voice. "It was supposed to be a one-night honeymoon, but my face was such a mess, Mark called his boss and asked for two weeks off for a *real* honeymoon. He lied and said we were going to Tahiti. The boss was a good guy and gave him a leave of absence.

"Mark checked us out of the fancy hotel and walked me through the lobby with the black side of my face pressed against his chest. He told me to make it look romantic or I'd wish I'd never been born." She passed a hand over her eyes, not realizing until then that tears were streaming down her cheeks. "We went house-hunting. He watched me every second. He finally found an old dump clear across town from where my parents lived."

"And it was then that you began living together?"

An overwhelming urge to run washed over Amanda again, but the grip of Jeb's hand on hers gave her the courage to remain seated. "Yes. And during the remainder of our so-called honeymoon, he used me as a punching bag, placing his blows so the bruises wouldn't show.

He used filthy words I'd never heard and didn't understand. He said I ruined his life by getting pregnant. Instead of going to college, he was stuck with a wife he didn't want and a kid on the way. He told me his father had forced him to marry me—to do right by me.

"The house was a long way from my folks. Mark refused to get home phone service. He bought a laptop and paid for Internet, but he took the computer with him to work and kept it locked in the car trunk at night. Sometimes he'd bring it inside to play stupid games, but I was never allowed near it."

Johnson inclined his head, indicating for her to go on.

"One day when I walked across town to see my mother—and that wasn't easy, being so pregnant—he found out and beat me again. After that first night, he was careful not to bruise me where it would show. I'm sorry. I think I told you that." Amanda gulped and forced herself to go back in time. "I think my mom knew something wasn't right, but she wasn't sure what. Dad was getting on in years. I knew he'd kill Mark—or at least try—if he learned what my husband was doing. But I was only eighteen. I didn't want my dad to get hurt. I knew Mark could lay my mother flat with one blow. I was afraid to tell on him."

Johnson shifted again, but now he held his body even more stiffly. "Go on."

Go on? He wanted her to go on? Jeb tightened his fingers over hers. *Do it,* he seemed to be saying. Amanda didn't know if she had the strength.

"If my mother drove over to see me while I was pregnant and Mark found out, he beat me. When I walked to a pay phone and called the cops, he charmed his way out of an arrest by telling them I was emotional and having erratic mood swings because of my advanced pregnancy. After the police left, Mark grew so violent that I feared I might lose the baby.

"Toward the end of my pregnancy, he stopped beating me. I stupidly thought he had turned over a new leaf. In retrospect, I know that he didn't want the doctor or nurses to see bruises all over my body when I went into labor."

"How could they possibly have missed them during your prenatal exams?"

"Mark didn't allow me to have prenatal care. And he started beating me again the day I brought Chloe home from the hospital. He said no one would believe me and if I reported it, he would take Chloe and I'd never see her again."

"Why didn't you seek help while you were at the hospital?"

"I was scared to. When I called the cops on him, he almost killed me. And while I was in the hospital, I had no bruises as proof."

"X-rays would have been evidence enough."

Amanda felt her temper rising again. "I was only eighteen. I'd just delivered a baby. I thought maybe Mark had turned over a new leaf. I was terrified of him! If you don't understand that, you're not the lawyer I need." She looked at Jeb. "I need a woman, not this cranky man who questions me at every turn."

Mr. Johnson leaned forward and curled a heavy hand over Amanda's wrist. "I'm not questioning you to be cruel, Ms. Banning. I need all this information. You've abandoned your husband. You've taken his daughter and not notified him of her whereabouts. You want a judge to deny him any visitation that isn't supervised.

It'll be a tough fight, and I can't go into court without every bit of ammunition you can give me."

"Then you believe me?"

"How could I not after seeing those pictures? But pictures alone, though powerful, aren't enough."

So, dredging deep for strength, Amanda finished her story. The words poured from her like water from a spout. The room around her blurred. When she stopped talking, she couldn't remember if she'd told the attorney everything. She had no recollection of what she'd said.

Johnson sat back in his chair, tapping his chin with a pen. "So he moved you two states away from your folks, rented a house far from town with few neighbors along the rural road. You had no car, no phone, no Internet, and he allowed you to have no money, not even change. The only time you did get your hands on cash was when he took you grocery shopping, and then he demanded the receipt and insisted that you give him back every penny you hadn't spent." His gray eyebrows drew together in a scowl. "Acquiring heaps of credit cards under both your name and his, with pin numbers for each one, and drawing all the cash you could from them by walking into town every day for a month to ATM locations — well, that was nothing short of brilliant." A slow smile curved his lips. "You got out of there before the statements started rolling in." A deep from-the-belly laugh erupted from him. "You had enough money to start over somewhere. But my favorite part is that you screwed him over good by leaving him with all the bills to pay, and, trust me, the interest rate on credit card cash withdrawals is high. My hat is off to you."

Until then, Jeb had remained mostly silent. "Give it to me straight, Johnson. Can you win this case? If you have any doubt, I need to know right now. No matter what it takes, I won't allow that son of a bitch to get his hands on that little girl again."

Johnson shook his head. "Don't even go there. Hiding the child would be a serious criminal offense, and it won't be necessary. I don't know what your relationship with Ms. Banning is, but I get where you're coming from. I won't allow harm to come to this child."

"Do you think Amanda can hold her own under questioning? She got extremely upset while talking with you."

Johnson grinned. "I want her upset. I want the judge to hear her voice quaking. If she breaks down and cries, even better. The *one* thing she *cannot* do is lose her temper." He directed his gaze at Amanda. "Do you understand, Ms. Banning? You can get upset. You can sob. But if you get pissed, the judge may lose sympathy for you."

Amanda nodded.

While hearing Amanda's story, Jeb had grown increasingly horrified. After seeing the photos, he'd known she'd been to hell and back, but he still hadn't understood just how nightmarish it had been for her. That she'd found the courage and the means to rescue her daughter was—well, to Jeb it was incredible. He'd never researched domestic abuse, but over the years he'd read enough here and there to know that most severely abused women became so browbeaten and lacking in self-confidence that they were afraid to leave, convinced they couldn't make it on their own.

Now that he'd heard her story, he better understood her stubbornness about accepting help. To her, needing help proved that Mark had been right. She was too stupid to be independent. It wasn't stubborn pride that drove Amanda; it was terror and an awful sense of inadequacy.

To Johnson, Jeb said, "I've got a few concerns, which I believe are legitimate. Essentially Amanda abandoned her husband and took his child. Isn't it possible that Mark has already filed for divorce, and possibly been granted one, along with full custody of his daughter once he finds her?"

"It's possible," Johnson replied. "I'll check into it." He looked at the wall clock and then at Amanda. "I want you back in my office in one hour—by four fifteen. While you're gone, I'll get the divorce papers drawn up so you can sign them, and I'll file before five. If Mark has already filed, the filing here, with several different charges leveled against him—including spousal abuse, child abuse, child endangerment, mental anguish, to name only a few—will put a hitch in his get-along." He jotted a few notes and passed the paper to Amanda. "Do you have another copy of the SD card?"

"Yes. Jeb made copies."

"Good. You played it very smart by taking those pictures. They're dated. They'll stand good as evidence." He tapped the paper with his finger. "While I'm drawing up the dissolution papers, I want you to go to the state police and file all these charges against your husband. I know several judges in California, including one in Eureka. I'm going to call her and then e-mail her the picture file. She'll also receive a list of the charges you've made, which will be handled in California, the state of jurisdiction. Trust me—when she sees those photos, she'll be so furious that she'll want Mark Banning's head. His only possible defense will be to deny that he committed the abuse."

"And what if he does?" Amanda asked.

Johnson shrugged. "I'll take great pleasure in tearing apart his story when the case goes to trial. I'm licensed to practice in California, which is where he will be tried." Turning to Jeb, he asked, "Do you have a good security system installed in your home?"

"No. I have a mastiff. I always figured he was all the security I needed."

"Not anymore. If you can afford it, get one, ASAP. The instant I file this appeal for divorce, Amanda and Chloe's presence in Mystic Creek will be revealed. It's a small town. I'll use her rental address to throw him off track, but if he's clever, he may discover where they're staying." He turned to Amanda. "The cops will be expecting you at the police station. Once you file those charges, the Eureka authorities will try to arrest your husband."

"Try?" Jeb interjected.

Johnson shrugged again. "They may not be able to find him." To Amanda, he added, "While you're gone, I'll call in a favor from a judge I know to get a restraining order issued against him today."

Jeb saw Amanda's shoulders go limp with relief. Apparently Johnson noticed as well. "The problem with restraining orders is that men like Mark Banning often ignore them. Does he own any weapons?"

"Yes, one rifle and a couple of handguns," she said. "Possibly more by now."

"Until the man is behind bars, you and your child may not be safe." He leveled a look at Jeb. "Are you by any chance a hunter?"

"If you're asking if I have weapons, yes. I keep them locked in a gun safe out in my garage."

"Get them out. Load them to the hilt. Keep a gun within your easy reach in every room of the house, if you have enough weapons to do that."

"I have a six-year-old girl in my house."

"Make sure she can't get to them. Men like Banning can be obsessed and dangerous. I also recommend that you show Amanda how to handle all the weapons and let her do target practice with several of them." He paused. "To be safe, however, you should not leave her and the child alone. It'll also be risky for Chloe to attend public school. The child's father may try to take her. In situations like this, teachers are normally more than happy to allow the child to remain at home and receive assignments online or let someone pick up the lessons."

Jeb leaned slightly forward. "The man would have to be crazy to come after them when he's got criminal charges lodged against him, plus a restraining order."

"You saw the pictures. How sane do you think this guy is?"

"I see your point." Jeb glanced at Amanda. "It's just that this has been really hard for Amanda, and I don't want to make it worse by scaring her half to death."

"Better scared than dead," Johnson retorted.

Chapter Eleven

On the way to the police station, Jeb called his father and cut across the older man's greeting. "Dad, earlier I didn't share a lot of details about Amanda's past, and I don't have time now. I'm calling to give you a heads-up. Chloe may be in serious danger. Knock off work for the day, go inside, lock all the doors, get out your guns, and don't leave Chloe's side."

Not for the first time, Jeb thanked God his dad didn't need his i's dotted and his t's crossed. Jeremiah asked no questions, except, "Who the hell wants to hurt Chloe?"

"Her father. He's a crazy, abusive son of a bitch."

Jeb glanced at Amanda and put his phone on speaker. "Describe Mark to my dad."

Amanda leaned across the console to get closer to the phone. "Dark hair, blue eyes, medium height, slender build. He's smart, so don't let any man who even slightly fits that description near my daughter. *Please.*"

Jeb kept the cell on speaker. "Ask Barney to go by my place to get Bozo and bring him to your place. I put him in the laundry room so he wouldn't devour my house while we were gone."

"I think Barney is doing his deputy thing today," Jeremiah replied.

"Unless he's doing desk duty, he can swing by my house faster than anyone else. If he can't do it, ask Ben. That dog loves Chloe like all get-out, and he'll protect her with his life. He's also got amazing instincts about people. You know that growly thing he does when he tries to talk? Well, his growl when he senses danger is different. You'll know it when you hear it. And if you hear it, trust him and be on guard."

"What the hell suddenly brought this on?" Jeremiah asked. "If the situation is all this critical, why didn't you warn us before you left her here?"

"Sorry, Dad. I didn't think ahead. Amanda is filing for divorce today. I doubt Mark Banning will get served before tomorrow, but right now we're heading over to the state police to file some serious charges against him. The instant he gets cuffed and stuffed, or served with the divorce papers, he may learn that Amanda and Chloe are in Mystic Creek. And if by chance they don't lock him up, he may head straight there. I don't know if he can hop a flight to get here on such short notice, and I don't know how long it takes to drive."

"We'll figure it out," Jeremiah replied. "But, son, he might already know where they are. Nowadays, it's not that hard to find people on the Net. Amanda must have paid for utilities at her rental. That put her on the charts."

From the corner of his eye, Jeb saw Amanda tense. She'd tried so hard to cover her tracks. No wonder she slept with a butcher knife under her mattress.

"I used my mom's maiden name for my utility bills," she said, a hopeful note in her voice.

Jeremiah went on. "If he ran a trace on you and came

up with a blank, he would have done a search on your maiden name and any other family surnames you might have used." Clanking sounds came over the airway as Jeremiah spoke. "Okay, I'm in the house and locking the doors. I'll get my guns out, keeping them well beyond Chloe's reach. Then I'll have one of your brothers bring Bozo over here."

"Thanks, Dad."

"She's one sweet little girl. I won't let anything happen to her."

Without saying good-bye, Jeremiah Sterling ended the call.

Jeb could almost smell Amanda's fear. He needed to say something brilliant to ease her mind. "Listen to me, honey. Will you listen?"

"Yes." She said the word at such a low pitch, Jeb could barely hear her over the truck's engine. "I'm listening."

"We've got the deck stacked in your favor. You're no longer living in the rental. Even if Mark has looked there, he won't know where you've gone. Nobody but Johnson, law enforcement, my folks, and the Bradleys know where you're staying." He pulled into a parking lot in front of the state police station. "While you're filing the charges, I'll call Tony and tell him to keep his lip zipped if anyone knocks on his door asking questions."

Jeb held out his right hand to her, palm up. "Give me your cell."

She hesitated, then handed it over. He pocketed it, saying, "I'm turning this in to the cops."

He exited the truck and circled to help Amanda get out without slipping on the ice.

"Why do that?" she cried. "I need my phone."

"Until this is over, it's safer for you to use mine. If Mark has your number, he may be able to track your phone. I've never actually tried doing that myself, but I'm betting it can be done, and probably very easily if you have the right computer app. Now, if he tracks your phone, he'll wind up at the police station, a place he won't want to be."

This was her nightmare come to life. Amanda had always feared that Mark might find her. He was smart, relentless, and vengeful. She'd tried so hard to put him out of her mind, concentrating on survival and secrecy, and now his malignant presence loomed in front of her like the furies of doom.

She'd cashed her paychecks at the One-Stop Market, a mom-and-pop shop on West Main owned by a widow named Marilyn Fears, who knew the drafts were good because they'd been issued by the school board. Amanda had paid for everything with cash, trying to avoid leaving a paper trail. *Mark's right. I'm dumber than a rope.* She had considered the possibility that he might trace her calls if she dared to contact her mom, but she'd never thought he could pinpoint her location by tracking her cellular device. Jeb's grip on her arm was comforting, but it wasn't enough to ease her mind. As they crossed the parking lot to the entrance, her knees felt as if they'd turned to melted butter.

"How could I be so stupid? I got a cheap phone. It's under my mom's maiden name. I've been paying for electricity with cash. I buy everything with cash. I thought I was being so *smart*, so *careful*. He probably already knows where I am."

"You've done a fabulous job of vanishing," Jeb said. "It's just that modern-day technology makes it difficult, if not impossible, for a person to hide. The only way is to establish a fake identity, and I don't think it's that easy anymore. In fact, with instant information at our fingertips nowadays, it may be next to impossible. At one time, you could take the identity of someone of the same gender who'd recently died and was about your age. Now death records are stored electronically, and it's easier for the authorities to catch when someone starts using a dead person's Social Security number." His expelled breath clouded the air in front of his face. "For now, hold on to the good things. He can't easily find out where you're staying. He'll hit your rental and come up blank. And Bozo is with Chloe, or soon will be."

They quit talking as they entered the police station. Amanda jerked to a stop when she saw the front desk. "I'm scared."

"These are the good guys. I'm sure Johnson prepped them. It'll go just fine." He gave her a slight nudge to get her moving. "Just give them your name, and they'll take it from there. While you're filing the charges, I'm going to turn in your cell, call Tony and Myrna, and check on Chloe."

Jeb proved to be right. The moment Amanda gave her name, an officer emerged and escorted her to a back office. He directed her to take a seat at a gray metal desk, closed the door, and then sat across from her. "Clyde Johnson sent me your information and a list of the charges you'd like to press against your husband. I've got everything ready. He says he wants you back at his office ASAP so he can file your divorce appeal before five. No time to waste."

Amanda's stomach bunched into a painful knot. Had this young officer seen her photos? Surely her attorney wouldn't share them with just anyone, but she wasn't positive of that. *I'm going to be sick all over his desk.*

Amanda had endured plenty of humiliation during her marriage, but never had she been exposed in such a public way.

"You okay?" Without waiting for a reply, he pushed some paperwork toward her along with a pen. "My name's Mike Noir, by the way. Sergeant Noir if we're formal. Given the fact that you look a little pale and shaken, just call me Mike." Inclining his head at the paperwork, he added, "I highlighted everywhere you need to sign and date. It's November thirteenth. Friday the thirteenth, actually, and for me, it's been a doozy. Crunched the fender of my car on the way in this morning. Took out a neighbor's mailbox. I'll pay through the nose to get both fixed."

In a daze, Amanda stared at the papers. Friday the thirteenth. *Oh, God, oh, God.* That had always been Mark's favorite day to make her life hell. *A good day for bad luck*, he'd always said, *and I intend to make sure you get your share.*

Somehow she managed to sign and date the paperwork where indicated. She barely recognized her handwriting. Mike thanked her for coming in, assured her that he would process the charges immediately, and electronically transmit all the paperwork to the Eureka authorities so Mark would be arrested.

Jeb stood in the waiting area. Officer Noir escorted Amanda toward him. "I don't think Ms. Banning is feeling well."

Jeb took her arm. "I'll take it from here. Thank you for your concern."

Moments later as they approached Jeb's truck, Amanda jerked her arm from his grasp to slip and slide over to the bushes growing in the median. Cramps doubled her over. She gagged, and then she vomited, not once but several times, the strain of emptying her stomach leaving her so weak that she dropped to her knees. She felt the heat of Jeb's big body next to her. Normally she would have felt embarrassed, but she no longer had the strength to care.

Murmuring to her, saying words her swirling brain couldn't register, he wiped her mouth with something. She guessed it was his handkerchief. Leaning against him so she wouldn't topple over into the mess she'd just made, she managed to say in a shaky voice, "It's Friday the thirteenth. If Mark is going to come after me, it'll be today."

Jeb wrapped his arms around her. Being enveloped by his strength felt so good that Amanda wished she could melt and be absorbed into him through the pores of his skin. "Let him come. I'm eager to meet the man, and I guarantee that he'll never get past me to harm a single hair on either your or Chloe's head."

He lifted her to a standing position and guided her back to his truck, pushing his key remote before they reached the passenger door. The vehicle's beep made Amanda jump.

Keeping one arm locked around her waist, he opened the door. "Okay, sweetheart, in you go." And before she knew what he meant to do, he swept her up in his arms and deposited her in the bucket seat. Then he drew out the seat belt and shoved the metal tongue into the latch. "All tucked in and ready to roll."

A moment later when he swung up under the steering wheel, Amanda said, "I need to be with Chloe."

"That's where we're headed, honey. But first we have to go back to see Johnson."

Amanda wasn't sure she could handle that. "What if I get sick in his office?"

"You won't," he told her with steady certainty. "You're going to calm down. You're going to stop feeling afraid and have some faith in me and in yourself. You're going to say a prayer or two while we're driving over, thanking God that Chloe is being protected inside a house locked up tight, with Bozo lying beside her. If Mark so much as touches that child, he'll get his gonads ripped off with one bite."

Her mouth still tasted like vomit, but Amanda was able to muster a faint smile. "That dog does love my daughter."

"He's mellow and friendly until some fool pisses him off."

Leaning her head back against the seat, Amanda closed her eyes and followed Jeb's advice, giving thanks that her daughter was safe and that Jeremiah had stepped up to the plate to protect her. When a measure of calm relaxed her body, she asked, "Is one of your brothers really a deputy named Barney?"

"Short for Barnabas."

"Is he allowed to carry only one bullet in his pocket with his gun always empty?"

Jeb laughed. "Trust me, he gets teased about that a lot. He takes it in good humor, but I think he gets tired of hearing the same Mayberry joke repeatedly."

Amanda sighed. "I would, too, I guess. He sounds like a nice guy."

"Yes, he's great." He fell silent as he exited the parking lot into the oncoming lanes of heavy traffic. "You feeling better?"

She had to consider that. "Yes. Still shaky, but much better."

"Good. We'll make fast work of it at Johnson's. Then

we'll head home. I'm as eager as you are to be with Chloe again."

Jeb drove with caution on the icy roads back to Mystic Creek. Mother Nature needed to back off and give central Oregon a short reprieve. Beside him, Amanda slept, her slender body pressed against the door, her head lolling on the window. Jeb was pleased that she'd drifted off. She'd had an exhausting day. At the law firm, she'd ranted at the attorney for sending her picture file to the state police. Johnson had been a gentleman, letting her vent for a minute, and then he'd explained that the pictures were evidence and had been shared with no one else but a female judge he knew in Eureka. He told Amanda that he completely understood how humiliating that was for her, but the pictures couldn't be kept entirely private.

As Jeb navigated the slippery road toward home, images of Amanda's and Chloe's battered bodies flashed through his mind. Without having seen Amanda naked in the flesh, he knew that she had scars. Considering his luck, if he ever made it to third base with her, she'd be inordinately shy about revealing her body, thinking that he'd find the imperfections ugly. He grimaced at the thought. That was a long way down the road, he decided, and not something for him to worry about now.

It was dark when he pulled up in front of his parents' home. The parking area was crowded by all three of his brothers' trucks. Surprised, Jeb grinned. That was real family for you. When a Sterling was in trouble, other family members dropped everything to help. Jeb hadn't asked for reinforcements, but he was glad to have them. Barney had postponed his birthday party this week because he couldn't take time off, Ben had rodeo stock out the yang to tend, and Jonas, going for his bachelor's in psychology, had quarterly finals coming up at the Oregon Institute of Technology in Klamath Falls, a two-hour drive away. None of them could spare the time to be here, but they'd come anyway.

Jeb cut the engine. "Mandy?" He gave her a light shake. "We're back, honey. You need to wake up so we can go in and see Chloe."

She jerked erect as if he'd poked her with a needle. "Chloe?" She struggled with her seat belt. "Oh, God. I'm sorry. I didn't mean to fall asleep."

"You needed the nap. And don't get in a rush. Wait until I come around to help you out. I don't want you falling on the ice."

Jeb swung out of the truck, slammed the door, and walked around to open Amanda's side. Normally, he took her by the arm, ever aware that she didn't care to be touched anywhere personal. But tonight, she extended both arms and fell into his embrace. Grabbing her tightly, Jeb cherished the brief moment of holding her. *Oh, man, I've got it bad. If she can never love me back, I'll have to accept it. But letting her go will half kill me.* He held her for as long as he could, pressing his cheek to the top of her head.

"Don't let my brothers overwhelm you," he told her. "We're a rowdy bunch sometimes. Barney must have called in the troops when he heard Chloe might be in danger."

She glanced up, her beautiful eyes shimmering in the darkness. "If they're like you, they won't overwhelm me."

Jeb shifted his hold on her to grasp her arm. Before they started toward the porch, he slammed her door and used his key remote to lock up. If Mark was out there somewhere watching, Jeb wanted no surprises when he brought Amanda and Chloe back to his vehicle. If the guy was packing, not even Bozo would be any protection.

At the thought, Jeb switched sides without losing his hold on Amanda. Three steps later he shifted sides again. "What are you doing, an ice dance?" she asked.

"Something like that."

She stopped short and shot a frightened glance over her shoulder. "You think he could be out there, don't you? You're shielding me because he may have a gun."

"Something like that," Jeb repeated, and got her moving again. "You told Johnson he has weapons. Is he a good marksman?"

"I don't know," she replied with an edge of fear in her voice. "I never saw him shoot anything. One of his favorite games was to put a gun barrel to my temple and pull the trigger. I never knew if it was loaded or not. One time I got so scared that I wet myself."

Jeb's stomach rolled. Mark Banning was one sick cookie.

Once on the porch, Jeb stood behind Amanda and reached over her shoulder to rap on the door. No point in trying to just walk in as he normally did. He knew the door was locked, with the dead bolt engaged. From inside the house, he heard Bozo give a happy bark. *Good boy.* The dog had caught Jeb's scent, which confirmed his belief that the mastiff could smell danger as well.

The dead bolt inside clicked. The door cracked open, and Barney peered out. He had one shoulder braced against the wood to prevent an unwelcome visitor from shoving his way inside.

"Hey," Jeb said in greeting.

"Hey." Barney pulled the door wide. "Come on in. Supper's almost ready."

Forgoing introductions, Amanda circled Barney and ran to find her daughter. After Jeb entered, his brother closed and relocked the door. "Friendly little thing, isn't she?"

"She's just eager to see her daughter."

Barney grinned. "She's safe as can be. I think Dad is feeling his age. He asked all of us to come, and now he's still paranoid." His smile faded. "It's kind of sad. Growing up, I always thought he could take on anything. Now he's calling on us for backup."

Jeb's throat tightened. Like Barney, he'd had every confidence that his dad could handle protecting Chloe, but apparently Jeremiah wasn't so certain. "That is sad. Especially when I think he can still pin me to the mat."

Barney shrugged. "Same for me. But Dad's self-confidence is apparently in the shitter."

Jeb had long since stopped feeling as if he were looking in a mirror when he was with one of his brothers. But he noted the striking resemblance tonight. All Jeremiah's boys had been poured from his mold. The girls looked more like Kate. Jeb wondered what Amanda would think of the Sterling crew. He made a silent wager with himself that she'd have trouble telling his brothers apart for a while. She would remember Barney because he was in uniform, but the other two would be harder for her. They all had certain dissimilarities, but they were too slight for a stranger to notice right away.

As Jeb crossed the entry hall, he noted that Barney hadn't followed. He stopped, turned, and gave his brother a questioning look. "What's up?"

Barney grinned. "Door duty. Dad has us stationed to

guard every possible entry. We're going to eat dinner in shifts."

Jeb wished he could say that standing guard every second was unnecessary, but then he remembered the prickly sensation on the nape of his neck as he'd helped Amanda over the ice to gain the porch. "Thanks, bro. I can always count on you to have my back."

Chloe sat at Kate's craft table in the great room. It looked to Jeb as if she had gotten more paint on the kitchen towel and herself than she'd gotten into the clear balls. His mom did some kind of swirly thing inside the ornaments with different shades of paint. The spirals of color shone through the glass, looking beautiful, but the outside surfaces were smooth and enduring. She set them in egg cartons, turning them every hour or so to make sure the interior was completely covered. It was a simple process, but apparently a bit more difficult for a six-year-old.

Amanda, crouched next to her daughter, made appreciative noises, saying how beautiful the Christmas decorations were. "I wonder if we might try making some at home. They'd be so pretty on our tree this year."

Chloe gave her mother a disappointed look. "Won't that cost a lot?"

Amanda laughed as if she hadn't a care in the world. "We can afford it, Chloe. I have a surprise for you. Mr. Jeb has hired me to keep his house and cook for him! And even better, we get to live with him!"

Chloe nearly dropped the clear ball she'd been filling with paint. "Really? You mean we can stay there for a long time?"

"As long as he likes my work."

Chloe flashed a grin. "Oh, goody! Then I can stay with Bozo. He's my best friend." In a lower voice, Chloe added, "Be careful with the working bubbles. They make a bad mess."

Jeb saw his mother, frozen in motion, as she took in the conversation. Then she glanced at Jeb and smiled. He walked around the island to give her a hug.

Going up onto her tiptoes, she whispered in his ear, "Score."

Jeb bent to kiss her forehead. "My mother, always the matchmaker."

"It's high time someone wonderful came along," she murmured. "I told you it would happen someday, but you never believed me."

"Put the brakes on, Mom. It isn't like that between us."

"Not yet. But she'll come around." She stepped back and tapped the side of her nose. "I can sense these things."

Jeb could only hope she was right.

Kate yelled, "Dinner! Don't dally. My chili will get cold!"

Amanda asked where the downstairs bathroom was and then guided Chloe along a hallway to the powder room.

"I like it here," Chloe said as Amanda scrubbed off the water-based paint that smeared her daughter's hands and arms. "Mimi is so nice, and so is Pow-Pow." She grinned. "I named him that today because he went outside and made *pow-pow* sounds with a gun."

Amanda assumed Chloe was referring to Jeb's dad. "They both seem like very nice people."

"Oh, they are. They have an old dog. He's black. I can't remember his name." Chloe made a face as Amanda ran a washcloth over her mouth. "He doesn't like to play. He's sleepy all the time. I was glad when Uncle Barney brought Bozo over."

Alarm washed through Amanda. Chloe was claiming all Jeb's family members as her own. "I know you like Mr. Jeb's relatives, sweetie, but don't forget that Kate isn't *really* your grandma, or that—"

"Oh, I know that. Mimi explained. She and Pow-Pow and all of Mr. Jeb's brothers are only my honorary relatives."

Thank you, Kate. Amanda smiled and nodded as she dried her child's hands. "Your *honorary* Mimi is a very smart lady. It's okay to pretend you have a new grandma, grandpa, and uncles, but it's important for you to understand it isn't really so."

"I've got aunts, too! Adriel is the older one. Then there's Aunt Sarah. Mimi says both of them are lots of fun. They'll do my hair and put polish on my fingernails, and if we play dress-up games, they'll let me wear makeup." Chloe threw her mother a questioning look. "Only if you say it's okay, though. Will you say it's okay?"

As Amanda changed the bandage on her finger, her mind spun back through time. At Chloe's age, she'd been fascinated by girly stuff, especially lipstick and nail polish, but the possibility that her daughter might also be curious about those things hadn't entered her mind. Her heart panged. While she'd been with Mark, luxuries like that had been out of the question, and after leaving him, she'd been so focused on survival that she'd never moseyed through a cosmetics aisle to see if there might be a bottle of nail polish she could afford.

"I'll say okay," she assured her daughter, "but only if I get to play dress-up with you!"

Chloe's eyes went wide. "You like to play dress-up?"

"I love it!"

*   *   *

The only male who joined Kate, Amanda, and Chloe at the table was Jeb. Kate had made a huge dish of corn bread to complement the chili, which smelled delicious. Bewildered by the absence of the other men, Amanda bent her head for the blessing and then served Chloe before dishing up food for herself. With one hand on Chloe's knee, she gave the child a squeeze when she reached for her soupspoon.

Bending low, she whispered, "Mimi's our hostess. We must wait to eat until she takes a bite. When the man of the house is present at the table, you must wait for him to take the first bite."

"How come?" Chloe asked.

"Because that is proper etiquette."

"How come Mr. Jeb isn't waiting? Doesn't he know about proper eat it kit?" Chloe whispered back.

"Etiquette," Amanda corrected, glancing across the table at Jeb. She'd heard the expression *wolfing down one's food*, but until now, she'd never seen someone do it. Jeb normally ate slowly to savor a meal, but tonight he ate as if he were in a face-stuffing competition. Kate, who must have overheard the whispered exchange between Amanda and Chloe, tucked into her chili, signaling that it was now okay for her guests to eat.

Jeb muttered, "Please, excuse me."

He went to the sink to rinse his bowl and spoon before putting them in the dishwater, hurried toward the front of the house, and a moment later, one of his brothers took a seat at the table. "I'm Jonas," he said, "the youngest brother." He smiled at Chloe, bent his head to pray, and then filled his bowl, grabbed a piece of corn bread, and began eating with a speed equal to Jeb's.

"I like all my honorary uncles," Chloe said. "I've got

three, Barney, Ben, and Jonas. I wish all of them could have dinner with us."

"They're taking turns," Kate explained. "They're playing a game. They are princes in a castle, and they're guarding all the outside doors to make sure an enemy doesn't cross the drawbridge and get inside the great hall."

Chloe's eyes shimmered with excitement. "When I'm done eating, may I play with them?"

Kate nodded. "I think they plan to continue the game at Mr. Jeb's house, though, after you and your mother finish dinner."

"Maybe I can play the game with them there!"

Until that moment, Amanda hadn't realized just how seriously the Sterling men were treating this situation. They believed that Mark Banning presented extreme danger to her and Chloe. Her appetite for the delicious chili waned. She grew more alarmed with each passing moment. She had lived with her fear of Mark for years. At times during her marriage, she'd grown numb and wondered if she might be the one who was crazy. But now that a crusty old attorney had expressed concern for her and Chloe's safety, all the men in this family took it gravely. Even Jeb, who until now had seemed like a calm, levelheaded man, was acting as if the devil himself lurked outside.

Amanda could only hope that Mark's bid for divorce would look like a Christmas card, filled with pretty lies about how great he was, compared to hers, which would reveal him as a vicious monster. With luck, he was cooling his heels in a jail cell right now.

But what if he wasn't?

Chapter Twelve

Jeb wasn't pleased with the idea that all his brothers were driving over to spend the night at his place and would remain there until he got a security system installed. Jonas needed to attend classes. His education was important, and here he was ditching school. And only yesterday, Barney had refused to take time off for his birthday party at the folks' place, insisting that they celebrate at least two weeks from now because he couldn't be spared at the sheriff's department. Now all of a sudden he had all the shift flexibility in the world. And Ben, who raised rodeo stock for hire, had numerous animals he should be caring for. The last thing Jeb wanted was for any of his brothers to take a hard hit professionally or educationally over family issues. Hell, this wasn't even a *family* issue. Amanda and Chloe weren't related to Jeb, but his brothers and parents acted as if they were.

Well, he couldn't fault his brothers for standing behind him, and they were all big boys who could make decisions for themselves. As he drove, with Amanda in the front passenger seat and Chloe snuggling in back with Bozo, Jeb sensed tension rolling off Amanda. He needed to focus on her concerns and be a good friend to her, since anything more was out of the question right now.

"Hey," he said, reluctant to take his gaze off the icy road. "Don't be worried. Okay? You heard what Johnson said. A certain individual is probably safely tucked away by now. We're just being extra cautious."

"What if he isn't?" she asked in a tight voice.

"Well, if he isn't, and he somehow learns where you're staying, he'll find a house guarded like Fort Knox. I'll call Howdy Gowdy—his first name's actually Burt—this evening to get my place so armed with security that I'll know if an ant gets on my porch."

"It's short notice," she said. "Mr. Gowdy may not be able to get it all done that fast."

"You don't know Gowdy. He's a friend of mine, and his wife, Jerri Lee, who's kept her maiden name, Christi, to avoid being greeted with 'Howdy, Gowdy' like her husband, runs a tight ship for him. When I tell him it's an emergency, he'll put everything else on hold and be all over it. If he doesn't have the right cameras in stock, he'll send someone to Bend or Crystal Falls to pick them up." He shot her a grin through the dash-lighted darkness. "Stop worrying. Is it that you don't want my brothers around?"

"No," she said. "I'm just—" She broke off and glanced over the console at the child and dog behind them. "Well, you know. What if he already split, and the, um, authorities can't find him?"

Jeb considered that possibility and suddenly felt thankful that his brothers were trailing him in their trucks like ducklings in a queue. Nobody in his right mind would mess with all the Sterling boys, especially not when they were armed.

"Or what if he lies so convincingly that he isn't arrested?" she asked. "Or, even worse, what if he gets a judge on his side and wins in court?"

"Didn't you hear what Johnson said? He only takes on cases that he feels are worthwhile and he can win. For tonight, have faith in me, my brothers, and Bozo to keep you safe."

Chloe piped up from the backseat. "Mommy, are you talking about Daddy?"

Long silence. Jeb wasn't sure what to say. Trust Chloe, intelligent as she was, to pick up on unsaid things.

Amanda saved him by replying, "Yes, Chloe, we are talking about your daddy, but you mustn't feel afraid. Mr. Jeb took me to see a lawyer who's really, *really* good at making people safe. And until the lawyer can do his job, Mr. Jeb, Bozo, and his brothers are going to watch over us."

Chloe digested that. "Bozo will sleep with me. He won't let *anybody*, not even my mean daddy, hurt me."

Jeb totally agreed, but not even his faithful mastiff would remain standing with a bullet between his eyes, and Jeb didn't doubt for an instant that Mark Banning would pull the trigger.

Amanda didn't know when Mark would be served with the divorce papers and learn of her whereabouts. Had he already been arrested? And in cases like this, would photographs of the abuse be enough to keep him in jail? She imagined a clever attorney getting Mark out on bail, and her skin crawled. And what if they couldn't find him? He could have moved. Or he could be tracking her down. He could be anywhere.

She cringed when she recalled Jeb seeing all those pictures of Chloe, not only once, but twice. He'd dropped his gaze while Johnson viewed the pictures of Amanda, but he'd looked when Chloe's photos came up. Chloe with bruises all over her body. The horrible wounds on her small hand from when Mark forced her palm onto a red-hot stove burner. Jeb had to be asking himself what kind of woman stayed with a man after he began to hurt her child. In a normal world, things like that didn't happen. How could Jeb, how could anyone, truly comprehend the situation Amanda had been in?

The moment they entered Jeb's home, Amanda hustled Chloe upstairs for a bath before story time and lights-out. Chloe protested. "But I want to play the prince game with them! I'll get to be the princess."

Amanda didn't want her child to see four men guarding the downstairs doors and windows with weapons. It might frighten her.

"Maybe you can play the game with them tomorrow." Amanda hoped she might receive word by then that Mark was behind bars. "But tonight it's late, sweetie, and you've had a long, very fun day. It's time for bed." To lessen the child's disappointment, she added, "As a special treat, I'll read you two stories tonight."

"Can I read one of them? Bozo likes it when I read to him."

Amanda glanced at the dog, who'd followed them upstairs. "Of course. It's good for you to read aloud. You need the practice."

Jeb grew worried when Amanda failed to come back downstairs and went in search of her. He found her sitting on the edge of her and Chloe's bed. A night-light cast a dim glow. Bozo was sprawled beside a sleeping Chloe. The dog's snores reminded him of a chain saw that needed new spark plugs. *Nice background noise for a talk.*

He sat down beside the woman who'd wormed her way deep into his heart. "I know that look," he whispered. "You're ruminating on something unpleasant. Is there anything I can say or do to make you feel better?"

She shrugged and released a drawn-out sigh. "Why do you even care how I feel?"

Oh, boy. "Why wouldn't I? We're friends. Friends care about each other."

"You saw those photographs. You know what a horrible mother I was. If I can't like myself, how can *you* like me?"

Jeb could see the need for Amanda to receive intense and frequent counseling in the near future, but this wasn't the time to bring that up. "You weren't a horrible mother, Mandy. You were a mother trapped in an impossible situation."

"There are safe houses."

"Yes, but you had no phone or Internet to search for one near you. You also had no car. Mark deliberately rented a home in a rural area where you had few neighbors and had to walk a long way to town. He cut you off from all the resources available. How can you blame yourself for that? What were you supposed to do, walk to town and wander around until you found a safe house? Or maybe go to the police station for help, only to have Mark get wind of it and light into you again?"

"I should have called the police anyway."

Jeb tried to think of something more to say. "Fear can be a formidable foe." He went quiet for a moment to gather his thoughts. "I'm no expert on the profiles of abusive men, but I've read a few articles. Abusers are often very charming and quick with believable lies. Cops are in a bad spot. Some women press charges against men who haven't actually harmed them. Mark was careful to leave bruises only where your clothing hid them. He was ready with a story to cover his useless ass. If you'd called the cops again, you would have been taking a huge risk."

Jeb stood and stretched out a hand. "Let's go talk in another bedroom. I don't want Chloe to hear any of this, not even in her sleep."

To his surprise, Amanda put her hand in his and allowed him to help her up. They adjourned to a bedroom down the hall, and Jeb closed the door before taking a seat beside Amanda on the bed.

"I did some reading on the Net," he said. "Most abusers act like princes while they court a potential victim."

"When have you had time to research abusers?"

"It's called lack of sleep. What was more important last night, resting or finding out what that man did to you, not just physically but emotionally?"

Amanda sighed, emitting a sound that epitomized absolute exhaustion.

"Some abusers wait a while before acting out," he told her. "Others turn mean in a blink. Then there are others who pretend at first that the pain inflicted was an accident. Tripping someone so they fall and then apologizing all over themselves. *Accidentally* jamming a woman with an elbow. Swinging around to *accidentally* smack her in the face with an uplifted hand."

"Mark turned mean in a blink," she murmured.

"I'm not surprised, but once they turn the corner, all abusers are dangerous and dream up reasons to justify their actions. They claim the victims *made* them do it. It becomes a horrible mind game for the women involved, and it can take them a long time to regain their confidence and understand exactly what went down."

In this room, no night-light glowed; only a faint hint of moonshine came through the window. But Jeb saw Mandy wipe under her eyes. "Are you saying that I'm that way— that I don't understand what happened to me?"

"In emotional ways, yes. You don't need to work on everything at once, honey. For now, just tackle the feelings that make you blame yourself, and shove them away. Every time you start to think others blame you, shove that away, too. Mark punished you enough. Don't let him continue to hurt you now by believing a single word he ever said."

"But some of it is true."

"No. It's all BS, Mandy. *All* of it."

"Then why do I feel so—" She gulped and gestured with limp hands. "My brain goes in circles. I talk to myself. I pat myself on the back for having found a way to get Chloe out of there. I feel better for a while, but then bad thoughts zoom back in, and I feel so inadequate and guilty. I couldn't stop him from doing horrible things to my little girl. I couldn't get her away from him. Can you understand? It's not that I want to have a self-pity party. I just can't shake the guilt. I was an adult. What Mark did to me, I partly deserved because I married him and didn't find a way to get away. But Chloe? She's never done a wrong thing. It was my job to protect her, and I failed. Instead, Mark beat the hell out of me for trying to interfere, and Chloe ended up being my nurse. Five years old, Jeb, and she had to be the adult because I was curled up on the floor, bleeding and with broken ribs."

Jeb reached up to smooth her hair. "Mandy, sometimes the most difficult part of recovering from horrible things is forgiving ourselves. Why do you think so many soldiers come home from war zones with PTSD? You've got to stop torturing yourself with what-ifs. You did the best you could. And in the end, you did save your daughter. Focus on that."

"Not in time. I didn't save her in time. You've commented on how mature she seems. That's why. The night he burned her hand and turned on me for trying to stop him, he knocked me down and kicked me so many times that I couldn't get up. I bled on the icky old linoleum. I lay there watching my little girl, with a badly injured hand, get on her knees and try to take care of me. Then she tried to clean up the blood because when her father came back, there would be hell to pay if the mess wasn't gone."

Jeb opened his arms and murmured, "Come here." And when she came, he wanted her in a way he'd never wanted another woman. The way she went limp against him was a sign that she no longer abhorred physical contact with him, and, in fact, invited it. It took all his self-control not to take advantage of that. She felt so soft and warm that he wanted to lose himself in her, to taste her skin, to hold her close with both their bodies filmed with sweat, to peak with her into ecstasy. *Bad timing.* She wasn't ready for that, and his gut knotted when he realized she might never be.

She settled against him like a kitten seeking warmth. His eyes burned as he folded his arms around her. He hurt for this woman in ways that he'd never imagined possible. "You hear Mark's voice. Now I want you to shove his away and start hearing mine. Can you try to do that?"

She nodded, dampening his shirt with her tears. "I can try."

"You're beautiful, not ugly. You're smart, not stupid. You never deserved a single thing Mark did to you. You were responsible for nothing he did to Chloe. You plotted and planned and took huge risks to get your daughter away from him. And here you are tonight, safe."

"Only because of you."

"I couldn't have done a damned thing if you hadn't had the guts to come to Mystic Creek. If you hadn't been so ingenious, planning every tiny detail before you ran, you never would have made it this far, and I never would have met you." Jeb pressed a kiss to the crown of her head. "If you think other people blame you, count the heads of the men downstairs. They're here to protect you. They haven't even asked for details. All they know is that you were married to an abusive monster and you managed to get away. They take their hats off to you, and they've got their guns loaded for him. Not one of them blames you. You're a victim. Your daughter is a victim."

"They're your brothers. They're taking your side, not mine."

Jeb felt so frustrated. How could he reprogram her mind? "Your attorney isn't my brother. When we first walked in, he was curt and rude. After he heard your story and saw those pictures, whose side did he take?"

"Mine, but he's being paid a lot of money to—"

"Mandy, the guy is richer than we can imagine. He doesn't need or want your money. Charging you a fee is nothing but professional protocol. He stepped in to be your champion *only* because he sees that you need and deserve his help. He even complimented you on how incredibly smart you were in executing your escape."

She moved away a bit to peer through the gloom at him, her eyes glistening. "I don't remember him saying anything like that."

Jeb tapped her temple. "Mental block. You're hearing Mark's voice and no one else's. He created an off-kilter image of you in your mind. Abusive men often isolate their victims, and then they fill their heads with junk. Making a woman feel stupid, ugly, clumsy, and totally without any marketable talent—well, the list is endless. It helps the abusive man to maintain control. He implants in the woman's mind that if she leaves him, she'll be jumping from the frying pan into the fire."

She nodded. "He did do that. He isolated me from everyone, all my friends, even my parents."

"A classic case."

Jeb knew he was out of his depth. Amanda needed to win a battle against Mark. She needed to walk away knowing that she'd finally smashed him. She also needed professional help to wipe the ugliness from her mind and sow new thoughts. He couldn't help her do that. He wanted to, but he didn't know how.

Releasing her, he pushed himself to his feet. "Mop up that pretty face and come downstairs. I'm going to make something to eat. You barely touched your chili tonight, and one bowl for each of my brothers was barely a drop in their buckets. They'll be taking shifts all night, and they'll need food. My mom swears all of us have holes in the bottoms of our feet because she can never fill us up."

Wiping her cheeks, Amanda stood. "I'll cook. That's my job now. Remember?"

Careful, Jeb. "You're right; it is your job now. But in your job description, I don't recall feeding a bunch of hungry men being part of the bargain. At least let me be the cook's assistant."

She followed him out into the lighted hall. The smile she sent him was faint but warm. Her face was puffy from crying. "What are we fixing?"

"I'm thinking that a gigantic pot of beef stew will keep them happy, and yours is the best I've ever tasted."

Keeping pace with him as he moved toward the stairs, she said, "Along with homemade bread?"

Jeb chuckled. "Damn, Mandy. If you feed them that well, they may move in."

On the surface, Jeb tried to project good cheer, but as he worked beside Amanda in the kitchen, troubling thoughts drifted through his mind. According to the attorney, restraining orders were mostly ignored by abusive men. So, what protection did women truly have? New laws and much stiffer punishments were in order for men who ignored restraining orders.

Now Jeb understood how masterfully Mark had disempowered Amanda. The journey to recovery would be daunting for her. Jeb could only hope that she allowed him to walk beside her over that rocky path.

When Amanda took the bread from the oven, she could have sworn she'd rung a dinner bell. Men converged on the kitchen, grabbed a slice, buttered it at high speed, and then returned to their posts.

"I get first dibs on the stew!" Amanda heard one of them yell from his outlook spot. "I didn't get to eat over at Mom's."

Amanda had seen only Jeb, Jonas, and Barney at Kate's table, so she guessed the voice belonged to Ben. Jeb headed in that direction, and soon a tawny-haired man entered the kitchen. He resembled Jeb, but Amanda could see marked differences.

"I'm Ben. I don't think we were formally introduced." When he thrust out his right arm, Amanda wiped her damp fingers on a towel and turned to shake hands with him. "Amanda. It's good to meet you."

His stomach growled, and he grimaced. "Sorry. I'm running on empty."

Amanda grabbed soup bowls and spoons, and carried them to the kitchen table, where huge mounds of sliced bread filled two platters. While Ben dished up from an oversize silver serving bowl, she tore paper towels from a roll and began folding them.

"Don't bother with that," Ben said, drawing back a chair to sit down. "Our last name may sound fancy, but trust me, we don't claim to be made of silver."

Amanda couldn't help but smile. He reminded her a lot of Jeb. "That's good," she said. "It's plain stew, nothing fancy about it."

He bent his head and silently blessed his meal before taking a bite. "Oh, man, this is so good." His hazel eyes twinkled with humor. "Don't *even* tell me Jeb threw this together. He's a great cook, but his talents don't run to stew."

Taking a seat across from him, Amanda asked, "What things does he like to cook?" She considered this a good opportunity to discover Jeb's preferences. "He just hired me to keep house and cook for him. I could use some tips."

Ben wiped his mouth. "He's off the chart with meats and poultry." His gaze lighted up again. "All store-bought, according to Chloe." He glanced toward the kitchen window and leaned closer to whisper, "All his chickens will now have to croak from old age with that little girl in the house. And he asked me if I knew of any pasture for rent where he can put his steers until they're ready for the freezer."

Amanda rested her elbows on the table and propped

her chin on her folded hands. "It's very sweet of him to protect Chloe's innocent view of where her food comes from. But she won't be here forever. When I get on my feet, we'll find our own place, and Jeb's life can return to normal."

Ben chuckled. "'Normal,' meaning 'lonely'? That's what my brother was before you came along. He'd rather eat store-bought chicken for the rest of his life than lose you."

Amanda's heart jerked. "He can't possibly have told you that. We barely know each other."

Ben refilled his bowl, grabbed another piece of bread, and launched into the story of his parents' courtship. They'd met on the shore of Mystic Creek, it had been love at first sight, and they'd married less than a month later. "They've been together—well, I can't remember how long, but they're as in love today as they were in the beginning. It's not always about how long people know each other. Sometimes they just instantly click. You know?"

Amanda wasn't certain what to say. "What do you do for a living, Ben?"

"I raise rodeo stock. Have you ever been to a rodeo?"

"Years ago."

"Well, all those bulls, calves, and horses are often rented from guys like me who raise rodeo stock. It puts me on the road a lot during the season. The rest of the time, I care for the animals, train them, and do my best to keep them in shape for competition." He shrugged. "Out on the road, it's my job to make sure my animals aren't mistreated. There are laws to protect them, but some people ignore them if they can."

After Ben rinsed out his dishes and stowed them in the dishwasher, Jonas came to the table. "I'm studying for a bachelor's degree. I really don't want to talk about that because I'm facing finals at the beginning of December." He flashed a grin. "Yes, I overheard your conversation with Ben and heard you change the subject on him. I'm sorry Jeb is relieving us of duty so we can eat. Otherwise he'd play referee."

"Um, so far I haven't felt I needed one."

"You will," he replied. "All of us hope you'll hook up with Jeb. He's our big brother, you're perfect for him, and it's hard for us to keep our noses out of it."

After blessing his food, he took a bite of stew and made appreciative noises. He winked at her. "For me, talking about my major is the equivalent of shop talk. I've been studying to the point of near blindness, and when I get a break, it's the last thing I want to think about."

The gleam of intelligence in his hazel eyes told Amanda that he'd probably ace his tests without half trying. "Okay. No questions about your major. How about your social life?"

He shook his head as he swallowed again. "No time for one."

"Not even dating occasionally?"

"Nope. My first year of college, I messed around. Partied. Went out with girls. Cut classes. And before a test, I crammed. My dad let me screw around and didn't complain about my grades. The following summer, he waited until it was almost time for me to go back before he brought down the hammer. He'd given me time to sow my wild oats. From that point forward, if I messed around, I'd do it on my own dime. I knuckled down, kept my nose in the books, missed few lectures, and my grades shot up so high it surprised even me."

Amanda smiled. "So now you're all business."

"Mostly. Dad's paying for my education. I work for

him all summer, he pays me a decent wage, but that's barely enough to take care of my truck and pay for insurance. If he's paying the tab, I don't goof off anymore."

"That's admirable."

He spread butter on some bread. "No, that's smart. Otherwise I'd be going to school on loans."

Drawn by the smell of food, Bozo appeared at Amanda's elbow. She rose to pick out edibles from the stew for him and set the bowl on the floor. After a quick gobble and a hunk of bread for dessert, the dog lumbered back upstairs. Amanda was relieved. Even with men watching the property, Chloe would be safer with Bozo beside her.

As she resumed her seat, Jonas was refilling his bowl. "So, what's the deal between you and Jeb? Please tell me you've got feelings for him. If you don't, he's going to get his heart broken."

Amanda propped her chin on her hands again. "So what did you say your major in college is?"

He narrowed an eye at her, and then they both laughed. "Okay, I'll back off," he conceded. "You can't blame a guy for putting in a good word for his brother, though. I love him."

"I didn't hear a good word," she countered.

Jonas frowned. "You're right. I went straight past those and got to the point." He took a bite of stew and swallowed. "Jeb has a good heart. His character is as sterling as his last name. He'll never lift a violent hand to you or your daughter. I guarantee you that."

By the time Barney came to the table, Amanda had decided she'd be better off doing dishes rather than visiting. She was beginning to trust Jeb. It was nearly impossible not to grow fond of him. But she wasn't ready for any kind of commitment, short term or otherwise.

When Barney came into the work area with his dishes, she took them from him. "I'll take care of the cleanup," she told him. "I hope you enjoyed the meal. Jeb plans to put the stew in the warmer, so it'll be available all night. You probably know better than I do where all the snacks are, but I'm sure Jeb will want all of you to help yourselves."

Moments later, Jeb reentered the kitchen, rolled up his sleeves, and began helping her clean up. Giving her a sidelong glance, he said, "What?"

Amanda guessed he'd read something in her expression that concerned him. "It's nothing."

Jeb turned on a faucet. "Uh-oh. Have my brothers been singing my praises?"

Amanda relaxed slightly. "Actually, I think they'd plan the wedding if I gave them the go-ahead."

He chuckled and shook his head. "Don't take them seriously. It's just that I always strike out with women." He leaned sideways to drop a table knife into the flatware basket. "Well, actually, that's not true. Women normally strike out with me. I guess I'm too particular." He grabbed a damp cloth to start cleaning the stove. "All of my bros think you're special. They know I'm falling for you. They're just trying to hit a few homers for me."

Amanda took her time before replying. "I'm still a married woman. I've been away from Mark for only three, almost four, months. I've got a lot of baggage. Don't fall for me, Jeb. I'm a really bad bet."

He turned to study her. "I'll decide if you're a bad bet. I'm a big boy. The last thing you need right now is to worry about hurting me. No strings, no expectations. Ignore my brothers. Let's take it step by step and see where time leads us. Deal?"

I'm falling for you. Those were the words that rang loudest in Amanda's mind. She didn't want to wound this man with his gentle hands and generous heart. She wasn't the special one; *he* was. "Deal," she agreed.

He resumed scrubbing the Viking stovetop. "Gowdy will be here first thing in the morning. I called him while I was standing guard to let my brothers eat. He's got some high-quality cameras and monitors on hand. He'll bring in a crew and have a top-notch security system installed by tomorrow night. My brothers will be able to leave as soon as it's in."

"It's not that I dislike your brothers. I just—"

"I understand. They're nice guys, but they're trying to push you in a direction you're not quite ready to go."

"It's a direction I may never feel ready to go," Amanda clarified.

Jeb nodded. In the golden wash of overhead light, he looked so handsome in profile that Amanda wondered if she was out of her mind to discourage him. He'd be such a good father to Chloe, and any woman who snared him as a husband would be lucky. "I understand that, too," he assured her.

Amanda wasn't certain he did. Stepping close to him, she forced herself to utter words she'd never dreamed she might. She whispered, "I hate sex."

He stiffened and shot her a startled look. "You what?"

"I *detest* sex," she reiterated. "I will *never* allow another man to so much as *touch* me that way. Before we got married, it happened in the backseat of Mark's car, and it was *horrible*. I vowed then that I'd never do it again, but then I realized I was pregnant, Mark offered to marry me, and my folks, believing he was a nice boy, encouraged me to accept. I did, and my second time with him was a *nightmare*. I will never go there again."

Jeb glanced over her shoulder to make sure none of his brothers was eavesdropping. "I totally understand why."

Relief washed through Amanda. "You do?" That was good, she thought. In fact it was excellent. No man in his right mind wanted a frigid wife. "I'm so glad. You can push aside any romantic notions you may have and know that we can never be more than friends."

His lips twitched as if he were suppressing a grin. "Don't put words in my mouth. I said I understand why you never want to go there again—being hurt, humiliated, and beaten to within an inch of your life by a man who should have loved and protected you. But I'm not Mark. You'll never walk that road with me." He bent to plant a quick kiss on the end of her nose. "Stop worrying, Mandy. We aren't racing toward a finish line. We've agreed to take one step at a time and see where we end up. What's wrong with that?"

"I'm just afraid your goal and mine may not be the same."

"You're right," he told her. "I'm fine with being only friends for right now, and if you still feel that way later, I'll accept it. Just don't throw up any barricades before you reach that stretch of road. There's a country song I love about life being a dance that we learn as we go. You ever try to learn how to dance?"

Amanda didn't like the direction this conversation had taken. "Yes, back in high school. I was lousy at it. I tripped over my own feet."

"No worries. I'll let you stand on my toes until you get the moves down pat."

Chapter Thirteen

The following morning, Amanda was relieved to see no weapons in sight, except for the one Barney wore holstered on his hip as part of his deputy uniform. The other men had hidden their guns somewhere. With daylight came a more relaxed vigilance. The men strolled casually from window to window, surveying the grounds around the house, but they weren't obvious about it. As a result, Chloe forgot about playing prince and princess with them and began stowing the Thanksgiving cookies she'd made with Kate into freezer bags while Amanda started breakfast for a large crew.

At one point, she heard the unmistakable sound of a shotgun being opened and jacked closed, something Chloe didn't recognize. Raised around guns, Amanda felt no alarm. She knew Jeb would make sure that Chloe had no access to a loaded weapon.

Trust. She wasn't sure when she'd come to trust Jeb, and intellectually she knew it was too soon, but her heart wouldn't heed the warning. Recalling his analogy from yesterday, she decided the two of them were, in some ways, like soldiers in a war zone. The usual time required to grow well acquainted had been nixed by their circumstances. She'd seen how Jeb stood his ground when danger threatened. As a kid, she'd taken for granted the feeling of safety her parents had provided, but until coming to this house, she hadn't felt secure since marrying Mark. It felt incredible to be relaxed and have no urge to look over her shoulder.

Jeb. He came in to assist Chloe with her cookies, admiring the lopsided turkeys and appearing to be in no hurry, but Amanda knew his true goal was to get the kitchen table cleared for breakfast. When the holiday treats were safe in the freezer, he moved in on Amanda, took stock of the works in progress, and then jumped in to help her by peeling potatoes. Even in so large an area, Amanda found herself brushing against him as she used the side-by-side sinks. The accidental touches unsettled her, and she experienced that butterfly-wing sensation in her stomach again. *Physical attraction.* She could lie to herself and pretend she felt nothing—and that he didn't—but the electricity that snapped in the air between them was undeniable. She wondered how it might feel to surrender, to have his hands moving over her skin, to let him kiss her. The images that flashed through her mind made her knees weak.

"I thought I'd make your kind of fried spuds," she told him, determined to stay focused on cooking.

"No way." He flashed her a grin. "My brothers have tasted mine lots of times. Yours with gravy will be a real treat for them."

Warmth pooled low in Amanda's middle. He wasn't pretending to enjoy her cooking. He truly liked it. She began frying a pound of bacon.

"Two," Jeb told her. "A pound will be only an appetizer for this crew."

Amanda grabbed another package from the meat drawer, noting that it was wrapped in butcher paper and marked as bacon with red ink. *Homegrown pork*. She glanced over her shoulder to make sure Chloe had left and then heard the child's voice coming from a distant part of the house.

"You know, Jeb, as much as I appreciate your guarding Chloe's innocence about the fate of your livestock, perhaps she'd be better off learning the truth. It isn't realistic for her to grow up believing that meat, poultry, and eggs magically appear in Styrofoam trays or cartons."

Jeb paused in his task. "I'll tell her someday. All of us need to know where our food comes from."

"When?" Amanda asked.

"Oh, I don't know. I'm thinking maybe when she's sixteen. Better yet, twenty-one."

She laughed. "You may not even know her when she's twenty-one."

He grinned. "If I don't, then I'll happily leave the job of educating her to you." He resumed peeling. "Johnson called this morning. He tried your cell first and got no answer. So then he dialed mine. The short version is, Mark couldn't be found."

A dreadful cold trickled into Amanda's middle. "Oh, dear God."

"He's quit his job. Apparently he's still renting the house. The cops got in and found some of his things still there."

"Do you think he's tracked me down?" Her voice quavered.

"Impossible to say." The paring knife went still again. "But Johnson filed for the dissolution using your rental address. All Mark will find is a caved-in house. And Gowdy will arrive soon. We'll have state-of-the-art security before the day ends." He held Amanda's gaze. "Mark may know where you work and where Chloe attends school. As soon as classes resume, you need to call your boss and ask for a leave of absence. Just explain what's going on. And then you need to contact Chloe's teachers to get her assignments ready for pickup. We'll work with her here until the danger is past."

Amanda agreed that going to the school would be dangerous for both her and Chloe. "What if he finds us?"

Jeb narrowed an eye at her. "As long as he minds his manners, he'll be fine. But if he makes one move to harm either of you, I'll make him wish he'd never been born." He relaxed his shoulders. "On a bright note, Johnson created a flyer and sent it electronically to our county sheriff here in Mystic, so a picture of Mark will soon be posted all over town. The image will be underscored with WANTED AND DANGEROUS. People will be warned not to let on if they recognize him. They're to do nothing until he's gone, and then they should call the police."

"How did Johnson get a picture of him?"

"You've been out of the Internet loop for too many years. It's easy to find information on individuals now, especially if you have the resources that Johnson has." A grin teased the corners of his mouth. "In truth, Johnson got a picture off his Facebook page, which I could do. Better than a mug shot. It shows his face and body build."

Amanda struggled against the tremors that tried to overtake her body. "He's after me. I'll bet you anything he went to my house yesterday."

"Because it was Friday the thirteenth, and that was

his favorite day to make you miserable. I remember you telling me that. But his days of making you miserable are over. I know it'll be no picnic for you to see him in a courtroom, but with Johnson at the helm, I don't think Mark has a chance of winning. He'll be lucky to get supervised visitations with his daughter instead of doing hard time."

Amanda turned the strips of bacon in the extra-large skillet. "I wish Chloe never had to see him again."

"There's every likelihood she won't. He'll be unable to do anything out of line in front of a caseworker, so the visitations won't fulfill his needs. I'm guessing he won't show up. He'll move on and find another woman to victimize."

Amanda couldn't bear to meet Jeb's gaze. "If Mark isn't locked up, he'll never stop trying to make me pay. Chloe, too. He won't rest until I'm dead."

Shortly after breakfast, Gowdy arrived at Jeb's with six helpers. Blond with friendly blue eyes, he was a stocky young man with a winning grin. In short order, he informed Jeb that keeping the doors and windows locked while they installed a security system would be impossible.

With a nod of greeting to Amanda, he told Jeb, "We'll do a little hardwiring, but we'll also be going wireless wherever we can. That requires opening windows and doors repeatedly to make sure the magnetic devices are making good contact, testing the alarm, and all kinds of stuff. Some ditchdigging, which is noisy, will be necessary to install cable to the outside cameras. I brought a trencher, but it'll take time to penetrate the ice and the frozen ground. Once you and I decide where you need visual coverage, I think all of you should leave and go someplace more secure."

Jeb agreed. "You still think you can get everything done today?"

"I've got three more guys coming in from Crystal Falls. I think ten of us can knock it out and be finished by five or six."

Ben spoke up to say, "I'll call Mom. She'll be happy to have us at their house."

As he turned away, lifting his cell phone to his ear as he walked, Chloe chimed in with, "Yay! We'll be with Mimi all day long!"

The day at the Sterling home passed with amazing speed for Amanda. Kate was energetic beyond belief. While the men visited, ate snacks, and watched the property perimeters, Kate came up with one project after another to entertain Chloe. First, they made more cookies, decorated for Christmas this time, and then they adjourned to the craft table to create another dozen beautiful tree balls. At first Amanda worried that her daughter would pick such awful color combinations that her attempts would look like goulash, but instead, the six-year-old girl went for bling, choosing metallic gold and shimmery burgundy. The result was outstanding.

"Oh, Chloe, that's my favorite one yet!" Amanda said.

Chloe beamed. "Mimi said yesterday that it's better to use only two colors. Sometimes I can use three. But if you use too many, the paint runs together and makes one icky color inside the ball."

Hats off to Mimi. Amanda relaxed to focus on her own efforts.

"You can keep the ones you make," Kate said. "I already have so many that my tree looks as crowded as Times Square on New Year's Eve."

"Oh, we can't just take them!" Amanda cried. "The materials cost money."

"At most, only two bucks apiece. I got the clear balls on sale. The paint isn't that costly per bottle, and you're only using a little." She leaned across the table to turn a few in the egg carton. To Chloe, she said, "That's the most important part. By turning them, we can make sure the colors spiral to make a lovely design inside each ball that shows through the glass." To Amanda, she added, "I sell these for a nice profit at the Christmas bazaar, twenty bucks a whack. The bazaar is held each year at the Mystic Creek Menagerie. That's where Dizzy's Roundtable Restaurant is. The building is gigantic, and all our churches put up tables there for a small fee. It's fabulous. The eateries remain open. People can shop, eat, and shop some more."

Amanda had grown excited for a moment because these gorgeous balls were very easy to make, and eighteen dollars of profit per sale sounded like a grand way to make money fast. *Dreaming*. With Mark at large, she couldn't have a table at the bazaar.

Amanda watched the paint swirl inside her ball to create a magical blend of black and gold. As if sensing Amanda's turn of thought, Kate said, "I know this is a trying time for you. But you can rest assured that everyone in town will be watching out for you, however long it takes. Barney says posters are up everywhere, and a few of my friends have even called to tell me about them. I pretend to know nothing."

"What kind of posters?" Chloe asked, turning the ball she held to cover the inside with paint.

Amanda could only think to answer truthfully. "The posters show a picture of your daddy. If anyone sees him in Mystic Creek, they'll call the sheriff's office."

Chloe set her ball in the egg carton. "Good. My daddy is mean, and if he finds us, he'll try to do bad things."

Glancing at her watch, Kate changed the subject, saying, "I think it's time to make afternoon snack trays."

As promised, Gowdy called Jeb at five to tell him the security system had been installed and gave him the temporary passcode to disarm and reset the panels. By then it was dark, so all of Jeb's brothers followed them back to the newly armed house. It didn't escape Amanda's notice that she and her daughter were surrounded by a gaggle of large men as they walked from the truck to the front door. It unnerved her to realize their aim was to protect her and Chloe from a bullet. With their own bodies.

Once inside, Jeb stepped over to a beeping security panel to punch in the passcode. Jonas, the last person to enter, turned to bolt the door. As Amanda helped Chloe take off her jacket, Barney said, "Well, bro, now that our services are no longer needed, I'd better head back to work."

Nodding, Jeb said, "I really appreciate this, guys. It's a big house, and I couldn't have covered all the entrances by myself."

"No big deal," Ben replied. "We were happy to stay over. But now that we're past the hump, I need to boogie, too. A neighbor kid is taking care of my livestock, but with these low temperatures, I worry anyway."

Before Amanda saw it coming, she and Chloe received hugs from men who had been strangers to them yesterday. Jonas's farewell made Amanda smile. Arms locked around her, he bent low to whisper, "I'm going for my bachelor's in psychology, focusing on human services. Later, I hope to get my master's."

She leaned back to search his gaze. "Wow. When can you set up shop? I think I'm going to need some counseling."

He grinned and kissed her forehead. "Soon. But if you stick with my brother, I'll refer you to someone else. Conflict of interest." He winked.

Once the men left, Jeb relocked the front door and then, after fetching a stool for Chloe, gave her and Amanda lessons on how to operate the system. Together they came up with a permanent numerical passcode that all of them could remember: Bozo's birth date. Chloe loved that idea.

When Jeb went outside moments later to care for his animals, Chloe stood on the stool under the kitchen security panel to turn off the system. Jeb paused at the back door and met Amanda's gaze. "If I'm not back in an hour, hit the panic button. Same goes if anyone tries to get inside."

Amanda nodded, locked the door behind Jeb, then supervised Chloe as she reset the alarm to Stay.

"Now we're safe as can be," she told the child. "And I need to get started on dinner!" In the kitchen, she set an oven timer for fifty-nine minutes. If Jeb didn't return before it went off, she would do as she'd promised and alert the authorities. "Do you want to help me cook?" she asked Chloe.

"Yes, please."

Amanda reached up to turn on the kitchen TV and froze in midmotion. A larger monitor had been installed next to it. Divided into squares, pictures of the house, both inside and out, graced the screen. She could see Jeb walking toward the sheep enclosure, clear as day, even though it was dark. There were views of the front yard and porch, the upstairs hall. No area where an intruder could approach the house or be seen inside had been missed.

"Oh, my, infrared cameras," she said in a low voice.

Chloe turned from positioning her stool near the sink to stare with wide eyes at the pictures. "Wow, Mommy, we're on TV! Does that mean we're movie stars?"

With a start, Amanda located the kitchen view and laughed. "No, sweetie. It only means that Mr. Jeb spent a passel of money to make this house secure." She pointed. "See? That's the upstairs hallway. Right now, it's empty, as it should be. If we saw someone in the hall when all of us are accounted for, we'd know we had an intruder."

Chloe's face went pale. "Then what would we do?"

Amanda gave the child a quick hug. "We'd press the panic button and lock ourselves in the downstairs bathroom until the police arrived."

"We can't forget to take Bozo in with us."

Amanda decided to quick-thaw hamburger and make an oven casserole with noodles and cream of mushroom soup with a little cheddar cheese tossed in for yum effect. It wouldn't be haute cuisine, but it would fill their empty stomachs and be ready to eat quickly. As she worked, giving Chloe small chores and circling Bozo, who lay on the slate near the child, Amanda glanced often at the monitor to check on Jeb's whereabouts. If Mark lurked in the dark, ready to pounce— Well, Amanda couldn't even finish the thought. If something happened to Jeb, she wouldn't know what to do.

A sudden ache filled her chest. *What's happening to*

me? As she put the baking dish into the oven and set a second timer for thirty minutes, she saw that her hands were trembling. She'd never dealt with emotions that ran this deep for a man. She'd adored her father, but that had been different, a bond formed by flesh and blood.

When Jeb knocked a moment later, Amanda could see him on the monitor. She hurried to the security panel to disarm the system and then moved to open the door. Jeb shouldered his way past her, closed and locked the door, and said, "You didn't ask me to identify myself. Never open the door unless you know for sure who's there."

Amanda gestured toward the monitor in the kitchen. "I knew for certain. The picture wasn't clear enough to count your chin whiskers, but I could identify you."

Shedding his heavy jacket, Jeb regarded the screen. "It's awesome, isn't it?" He went to hang his coat on the tree, then returned to give the monitor a closer study. "Gowdy told me he installed high-end cameras, but I never expected the infrared views to be this clear." Grinning, he added, "We've got four monitors like this in the house, one here, and one in my office, the living room, and the master suite. Each screen shows all the same pictures, so as we walk through the downstairs, we can keep an eye out for trouble no matter where we are."

Chloe turned slightly on her stool. "Mommy, you and Mr. Jeb forgot to reset the alarm."

Both adults moved toward the panel at once, collided, and Amanda would have been knocked off her feet if Jeb hadn't caught her. "Are you okay?" he asked.

"I'm fine." Amanda rubbed her shoulder. Giving him a measuring glance, she added, "I think the security system is overkill. You're as hard as a brick. Mark wouldn't stand a chance."

Jeb put a hand on the shoulder she'd just massaged. His touch made her skin burn, yet she shivered, only not from a chill. His voice pitched low for her ears only, he said, "The security system is just another layer of protection. If anything happens, lock yourself in a room and barricade the door. Downstairs, my bedroom is your best bet for moving furniture to help keep him out."

Amanda followed him to the panel. "I was thinking the bathroom."

"No. If you get caught in that side of the house, run for my office. I have some furniture in there that can be moved. Let me show you."

Amanda trailed behind him to the office, where he pointed out pieces of movable furniture. "Hide Chloe in here." He reached up to grab the handle of a large cabinet Amanda had thought held office supplies. He pulled it down to reveal a Murphy bed. "I designed this for extra sleeping and never bought a mattress. Chloe's tiny enough to fit inside, and once it's closed, Mark will never know she's there."

"Chloe comes first," she said.

"Damn straight." He chucked her under the chin. "That isn't to say I don't count your safety as important. But in the end, we're the adults and she's the child. It's our job to make sure she's safe, and to hell with ourselves. Right?"

This time, Amanda couldn't blink away the tears that filled her eyes. He rubbed the spillover on her cheeks with work-roughened fingertips. "Shit. I didn't mean to make you cry. I'll build a hiding place in all three rooms for you, too. It's not that I don't care about you."

Amanda couldn't help herself; she started to giggle through the tears. "No, no, you don't understand. This is the first time, *ever*, that anyone has cared as much about my daughter's safety as I do. Until now, I had to worry alone. You are the most incredible man, Jeb Sterling. Hands down, no competitors. You're wonderful."

He bent to kiss her forehead. Amanda couldn't move or even think clearly. There it was again, the fluttering in her stomach—only this time, molten heat pooled in her pelvic area. She took in his strong shoulders, the breadth of his chest, and the powerful contours of his arms. Oh, how she wanted to sink against him and run her hands over his body. Her feminine parts were wet, and deep inside, her flesh throbbed with yearning.

A glint crept into his eyes. He lifted a hand to smooth a tendril of hair from her cheek. "Don't be afraid. Nothing's going to happen between us that you don't invite."

Her cheeks went hot. He *knew*. Was she sending out signals? *That* was humiliating. And even worse, he might interpret them as an unspoken invitation.

"I'm not ready," she blurted.

"I know." He ruffled her hair. "Don't get panicky."

He motioned for her to follow him out of the room. Amanda had never entered the downstairs master suite. The instant she did, she couldn't stop staring at the king-size bed. Giving herself a hard mental shake, she compared this space to the gigantic kitchen. All told, the square footage of the bedroom, his-and-her walk-in closets, and the bathroom had to be larger than the rental she and Chloe had lived in.

"This is amazing."

Jeb led the way into his closet. At the back, where clothing hung from a rod, he showed her a hidden compartment, presently empty. "I meant to put in a covered safe and never got around to it. Show Chloe how to hide in here. From inside, she can get the cover back up. Mark will never think to look for her here."

Amanda bent to peer inside. "In a pinch, I think it's big enough to hide *me*."

"But not big enough for both of you." He sighed. "If I had time, I'd build a safe room and install a second phone line, buried underground." He sent her a dark look. "That's the first thing the bastard will try to do, cut the phone lines. I tried to hide mine, but if Mark is clever, he could find them. On Monday, we've got to get you a new cell phone under my account."

Amanda trailed behind him from the closet. "I'll be mostly staying inside, and you have landline phones all over the house."

"Which won't work if he figures out where the junction is and cuts the cable."

"Then how will the security system work?" she asked.

"It has cellular backup." He drew his iPhone from his pocket. "Give me a minute. Gowdy loaded OpenEye on this today, but I haven't tried to use it yet."

He tapped an icon, filled in some computer-type addresses, pressed "Local Connect," and suddenly all the same pictures from the kitchen monitor popped up on the screen. Amanda gasped in amazement.

"Inside the house, you connect locally. If you're downtown, you connect by remote. That way, you can see what's going on at your house, inside and out, no matter where you are. If this mess with Mark drags out in court and I have to work in the field, I can check on you here through my cell." He glanced up. "This'll come in handy if we're gone shopping. From the driveway, we can check all around the property and inside the house. If we see Mark, we'll call the cops."

Amanda's throat went tight. "So you believe he's going to come after us?"

"After hearing your story, yes. He's beyond dangerous. I think he's a psychopath."

Amanda set the table, drew a freshly made salad from the fridge, and filled a pitcher with ice water after pouring a glass of milk for Chloe. *No Jeb.* She assigned her daughter the job of filling the adults' tumblers, then went to find her missing diner. He was in the living room, laying a shotgun atop the built-in entertainment center.

"I'm glad you saw where I'm putting it," he said. "Too high for Chloe to reach, but an easy grab for me and accessible to you." After the weapon was out of sight, he turned toward her, his gaze moving slowly over her face. "You look like you've been dragged through a knothole backward."

"It's been an interesting couple of days."

He opened his arms, inviting her to step close for a hug. Amanda hesitated, but then he smiled, and the next thing she knew, she was enfolded in his strong embrace. Breathing in the scent of him, an intoxicating blend of fresh air, hay, grain, and piney cologne, she wondered if she'd completely lost her mind. But being held close to him felt so wonderful. *Safe.* That was how Jeb made her feel. But he also ignited sensations within her that were dangerous. He lightly touched her spine, every drift of his fingertips sending zings of need through her.

"What's happening between us?" she whispered.

A low laugh rumbled through his broad chest. "I've been asking myself the same question," he whispered. "Sometimes I think we need to stop doubting and just go with it."

"Is that how you handle things like this with women, by just going with it?"

"Nope. Never, which is why I'm still single. I've never met someone who gave me the urge to throw caution to the wind." He paused. "Until now."

Amanda closed her eyes, holding those words fast in her heart. *Until now.* This man was totally obliterating the walls she had erected over the years. Mark, who had loomed in her mind like a monstrous specter, had been reduced to a faint shadow.

While they ate dinner, Amanda heard a faint meowing sound coming from outside. Bozo, lying next to Chloe's chair, snapped erect and tried to cock his floppy ears. Jeb stepped over to the hall leading to the front door, listened for a moment, and then fetched a .357 Magnum revolver from atop the kitchen cupboard.

"Don't shoot it, Mr. Jeb! It's a tiny baby kitten!"

Following her daughter's gaze, Amanda realized the child was staring at the kitchen monitor. "She's right, Jeb. It's only a kitten."

Jeb joined them in studying the screen image of the tiny creature on his front porch. "It could have been planted out there," he mused aloud. "Bozo and I will rescue the kitten, but until I call out that it's safe, I'd appreciate it if you two would go into my bedroom and lock the door."

Amanda almost protested. It was only a tiny baby and posed no threat. But then she remembered hearing tales of burglars and rapists tricking women into opening their doors by producing the sound of a baby crying on their porches. Jeb was right. Mark could have found the kitten and deposited it on the stoop.

"Come along, Chloe." Amanda lifted her daughter into her arms and hurried toward the bedroom.

"But a kitten won't hurt us!" the child cried.

Amanda ignored the protest, entered the master suite, and locked the door. "See!" she exclaimed to Chloe, pointing at the other monitor. "Mr. Jeb has turned off the alarm and is opening the door. We can watch the rescue from here."

"Oh, Mommy," Chloe said as Jeb picked up the bedraggled feline. "Look how little!"

Keeping the kitten cupped against his chest, Jeb relocked the front door and reset the entry hall alarm panel. They had an inside view of the entire entry hall. "Okay," he yelled. "It's safe. Come on out."

The .357 had vanished by the time Amanda and Chloe returned to the kitchen. Jeb bent to carefully deposit the tiny, wet kitten on the floor. It had gray and white markings and an adorably round face, showing Persian heritage.

"Her fur is frozen," Jeb said. "We need to get her thawed and warm, ASAP."

Amanda raced for the bathroom to grab two towels. Dinner sat forgotten as they tended to the bedraggled baby, drying her frost-encrusted fur into fluffy spikes. Jeb went into the kitchen to put together a mushy meal of powdered milk, rice pabulum, and jarred baby meat.

As he returned with the offering, Amanda asked, "Why do you keep stuff like that on hand?"

"I get an occasional barn kitten that wanders in. I think they venture too far from shelter and their mothers, get turned around, and don't know the way home. This mixture always seems to agree with them."

Studying Chloe, who sat cross-legged on the floor,

holding the kitten while it lapped up the food, he mused aloud, "Normally I find homes for them. I have a feeling that may not be an option this time."

Warmth radiated through Amanda's chest. Mouthing the words, she asked, "You'll let her keep it?"

He lifted his big hands in a gesture of helpless surrender, which caught Amanda by surprise and made her choke back a laugh. He outweighed the child by heaven-only-knew how many pounds.

Jeb stepped out into the adjoining garage, which Amanda had noted previously was crowded wall to wall with woodworking equipment, and returned a moment later with a shallow plastic tub filled with gray and bright blue granules.

"Do you want the kitten to sleep with you tonight?" he asked Chloe.

The child's eyes went round with wonder. "Yes, my kitten should sleep with me. That way, he'll stay warm."

Jeb carried the potty box upstairs to Amanda and Chloe's room. Once back downstairs, he found another durable plastic tub, approximately the shape of a litter box, and, after filling it with kitty gravel, placed it in the laundry room.

Hunkering down by Chloe, he said, "In order to box train your kitten, you must show her where she is supposed to go potty. Can I count on you to do that?"

Chloe gave him a questioning look. "How do you know it's a she and not a he?"

Jeb chuckled. "Trust me, it's a girl, and she must be trained so she doesn't go potty on the floor. Girl kitties are very smart and remember where their boxes are. All you need to do is show her once. Just set her on the litter. She'll know what it's for."

"All girls are smart," Chloe replied, giving Jeb a defiant look.

Amanda nearly intervened; Jeb wasn't aware that Mark had frequently told Chloe that all females were born with half a brain.

Jeb nodded. "You're absolutely right, Chloe. Most girls are very smart."

"Frosty is *extremely* smart," the child insisted. "She knew right where to go when she got lost in the dark." She lifted an adoring gaze to Jeb's sharply carved face. "She knew Mr. Jeb would give her food and be kind to her."

Bozo moaned, his mournful gaze fixed on Chloe.

"Uh-oh," Amanda said. "I think you have a gigantic furry friend who's feeling a little jealous, Chloe."

Chloe lifted an arm to invite Bozo closer. "Don't be jealous. Just because I like Frosty doesn't mean I don't still love you!" Bozo plopped down beside the child, eyed the kitten for a moment, and then began licking her still-wet fur. "Be gentle," Chloe warned. "She's way littler than you."

"That's what she needs," Jeb said. "The licking will stimulate her system and bring her body temp back up." He pushed himself to his feet and regarded their now-cold meal. "Thank God for microwaves."

After scooping their salads onto dessert plates, Amanda reheated the portions of casserole and returned them to the table. Chloe reluctantly left Frosty in Bozo's care while she resumed her meal. The conversation revolved around the kitten, Bozo's gentleness with her, and things the small creature might need during the night.

"Food, for sure," Jeb said between bites. "The pabulum mixture should do the trick. She looks pretty young and may not be completely weaned yet. It'll settle well on her tummy. At least I've never had a kitten get sick from it yet." To Chloe he said, "If she isn't weaned, she'll need to eat every couple of hours." He directed a twinkling look at Amanda, his message clear. Night feedings would probably fall to her.

"What does 'wean' mean?" Chloe asked.

Amanda fielded that question. "Most baby mammals need milk from their mothers, who have teats on their tummies where the little ones can suckle. Over time, the mommy encourages her babies to eat more grown-up food and drink less milk until the babies are finally weaned."

"Did I need milk when I was a baby?" Chloe asked.

Amanda felt her cheeks flush. "Yes, you did."

Chloe frowned. "Mommy, all you've got on your tummy is a belly button."

The heat in Amanda's cheeks radiated down her neck. She felt sure she'd gone as red as a candied apple. Jeb cleared his throat, excused himself, and went to scrape his plate while the mother-daughter conversation continued.

Lowering her voice and leaning close to her daughter, Amanda explained that human mommies had breasts just above their tummies.

Chloe asked several more questions and Amanda did her best to give straightforward answers. Soon after, Chloe resumed her position on the floor with Bozo and Frosty, leaving Amanda free to gulp down the rest of her meal and hurry into the kitchen.

"It's not your job to be cleaning up," she told Jeb as she nudged him aside to scrape what remained on her plate into the slop bucket Jeb had brought in from the laundry room. "If this continues, I'll renegotiate my wages down to five hundred a month."

Jeb grinned. "Like hell. We made a deal. No reneging now!"

Amanda settled in beside him to take the dishes he rinsed and put them in the dishwasher. Battling a smile, she said, "Thank you for doing the disappearing act. Her questions came at me from left field."

With a chuckle, he said, "Around here, with farm critters giving birth left and right every spring—well, Chloe will be catching both of us off guard with questions we don't expect." At Amanda's alarmed look, he laughed again. "I'll send her to you for answers if you like. But I'm pretty sure I can handle them on my own. I was trained by one of the best—my mother."

Amanda was coming to love Kate Sterling. "So what did she say when critters were born on your farm?"

Jeb's teeth flashed in a broad smile. "She told us that Dad found all the newborns under a cabbage leaf in the garden. I actually believed it until I was about eight and one of Dad's expensive brood mares dropped a foal when I was alone in the stable. It scared the bejesus out of me."

Amanda sniggered. "Your poor mother. How did she explain that one?"

Jeb leaned around her to stick a plate in the rack. His chest grazed her back, making her acutely aware of his nearness. "All she did was threaten me with death if I blabbed to my younger brothers and sisters. According to her, kids should remain innocent for as long as possible. Reality comes calling soon enough."

Amanda took Jeb's place at the right-hand sink to

scrub the casserole dish. "In a way, I see her point. On the other hand, I'm not so sure I want Chloe to miss out on the beauty of nature. Seeing a lamb born—well, *that* has to be something."

"I'm glad you feel that way because I'll have babies popping out all over the place in a few months, and my vegetable garden won't be planted yet. I keep my starts in the greenhouse until well beyond the last frost." He gave her a sidelong glance. "Even worse, I don't plant cabbage."

"Why not?"

"I detest the stuff. Who wants to eat something that once had a gooey, bloody baby under it?"

Amanda laughed until her sides ached.

School resumed on Monday, but the decision had already been made that Amanda and Chloe should remain at home. Amanda hated missing work, but the small amount she made in wages wasn't worth taking any unnecessary chances. She called Mystic Creek Elementary, asked to be put through to the cafeteria, and, after Delores answered, requested a leave of absence.

"Not having you here will put me in a pinch," the head cook said, "but take all the time you need, Amanda. Nobody in town is sure what that monster did to you, but you and that child need to stay away from here until he's caught. I'll get a temp in to cover for you until this is over."

Amanda paced inside Jeb's office, squeezing the portable phone so hard that her knuckles ached. "I really appreciate this, Delores. I'll keep in touch. If you get in a bind, I'll show up no matter what. I promise."

"No, don't call here again. There's caller ID on the phone lines. I don't want every staff member in this building to know where you're hiding out."

It hadn't occurred to Amanda that her call to the school would show under Jeb's name. Whoever had answered the phone and spoken to Amanda now knew where she and Chloe were. She'd just compromised their safety.

Chapter Fourteen

Jeb sat at the kitchen table drawing pictures with Chloe. The little girl's cheek was close to his, and her breath came between slightly parted, upturned lips. She was enraptured with his efforts, even though Jeb thought his drawing of a horse looked more like a dinosaur. It was humbling when a six-year-old totally eclipsed his artistic endeavors. There was no mistaking what she was drawing. He could almost hear Bozo bark.

"Yours is really good," he said, and was rewarded by a smile from beneath Chloe's glowing eyes. The child had evidently had little praise from men, and she reacted like a flower bud accustoming itself to the warmth of the sun.

"So is yours," she said loyally. "But its nose is kind of funny-looking."

The nose wasn't the only funny-looking part. Jeb was frowning in feigned disapproval of his drawing when he heard Amanda's light step on the slate floor. Glancing up, he took one look at her face and immediately set down his pencil.

"Excuse me for a minute, princess," he said to the child. "I need to talk to your mommy in private."

Chloe barely glanced up from her drawing, which depicted Bozo and Frosty snuggling together on the floor beside her chair.

Jeb grasped Amanda's elbow and led her to the living room. Her arm was rigid and her face was blanched. Once they were safely beyond Chloe's earshot, he said, "What's wrong?"

"I gave away where we're staying. I didn't mean to! I'm just not used to all the phones having caller ID."

Jeb winced. He wanted to say, "Oh, *shit*." Instead he looped an arm around her taut shoulders. "You called the school on my landline," he guessed aloud.

"I didn't *think*. I should have been smart enough to use your cell."

Bending low, Jeb pressed his forehead against hers. Her scent surrounded him, a heady combination of shampoo and woman. He wished he might hold her for hours. "It has nothing to do with how smart you are, Mandy. I knew you meant to call in and ask for a leave of absence, but I never considered the damned caller ID thing, either. As for using my cell phone, same thing. My number and possibly my name would have shown up on the school's line."

She went limp against him. "Delores said not to call there again until I'm sure it's safe. Someone else had to put me through to her, and whoever it was might blab."

"Did you give your name to the other person?"

"I think I just asked to be put through to the cafeteria."

Jeb tightened his arms around her. "There's no reason to panic, then. To whoever first answered the call, you were just a female voice on the line, and I know Delores will keep your whereabouts secret."

"How will we get Chloe's homework?" she asked. "If you go in to get it, everyone will know where she's staying."

Thinking fast, Jeb said, "First off, I'm calling Ben to come over and stay with you. Then I'm going into town to get you a cell phone, which I *won't* put under your name or mine. Second, I'm stopping by the sheriff's department. Barney can have another deputy pick up Chloe's work from the school. Then Barney can get it from him and drop it off here."

"But then the other deputy will make the connection and guess where we are!"

"The deputies already know where you are," Jeb replied. "And trust me, they'll tell no one. They're used to dealing with creeps, and they know about the charges you filed against Mark."

No sooner had he spoken than Jeb wished he could call back his last words. Having all her dirty laundry aired in public had to be humiliating for Amanda. She probably wondered how she would ever be able to hold her head high in this town again.

She withdrew from his embrace and straightened her spine. "That's good. After seeing those charges, they'll do everything within their power to protect my daughter."

There it was again, her tendency to put Chloe first. To hell with her own feelings. "You're really something— you know that? Chloe is lucky to have you as her mother."

"She wasn't always lucky, but now, yes, she's finally gotten halfway lucky."

As Jeb watched her walk back toward the kitchen, he wondered how long it would take before she stopped blaming herself for things that had been beyond her control. He wished he knew how to wash away her bad memories. But that wasn't possible and never would be.

*   *   *

"This phone is a nightmare," Amanda complained after getting Chloe into bed that night. She touched the screen and rolled her eyes. "Where on earth did you come up with the name Onrietta Parker? Is Onrietta even a name?"

Jeb, sitting beside her at the table to show her how to operate the Apple device, felt unsettled by the question. Though Ben had come to stay with Amanda and Chloe while he was in town, Jeb had still been worried and distracted when he reached the Verizon store. "I pulled the name out of my hat as they set up the phone. I, um . . ." He tugged on his ear. "Don't get mad. Okay? I had to come up with something fast, so I named you after a chicken."

"A *what*?" She gave him a startled look.

"A chicken," he repeated. "I've been naming my hens for Chloe, and that one stuck in my brain. Actually, the chicken is named Ornrietta because she pecks the other hens, but I left out the ornery part."

Jeb saw her lips twitch. "Well, I guess I can be thankful you left that bit out." She gave him a quizzical look. "A chicken? It suits me, I guess. I'm the biggest chicken you'll ever meet."

"I never meant—"

"I know you didn't. I'm joking. Want to hear me cluck?"

He grinned. He enjoyed seeing her spunky side. "I think you're one of the bravest people I've ever known," he told her, "and I'm *not* joking."

As if he hadn't spoken, she resumed her study of the device. Jeb guessed she disliked receiving compliments almost as much as she did accepting help.

"And Parker? What hat did you pull that from?"

"It's my mother's maiden name."

Amanda nodded. Then she gave Jeb a sideways look, the twinkle in her eyes telling him he was off the hook. "I don't suppose the name matters. The important thing is that the phone can't be traced back to me."

"If the name bothers you, I can go online and change it."

She shook her head. "No. In retrospect I just wish you'd left the *ornery* part in. I could use a good dose of it, I think."

Jeb agreed. He'd often wished that she'd had a baseball bat handy when Mark Banning came after her with his fists and boots.

"Does it cost a lot to make phone calls under your plan?"

He detected a hopeful note in her voice and suspected that she wanted to call her mother. "I pay a monthly fee for unlimited calling and texting. You can use your new phone as often and for as long as you like. It won't add to my bill."

That was the truth. Jeb had signed up for a family plan that morning, purchased the device for a hefty chunk of change, and from now on, the additional phone service would cost him more money each month. But her usage wouldn't add to the tab. *Now I'm lying by omission.* He wouldn't allow himself to feel bad about that. She'd needed a cell under a different identity, and he'd gotten her one.

"How much do these things cost?" she asked. "I need to pay you back."

"I was due for an upgrade." *Another lie of omission.* He *had* been due for an upgrade, but he hadn't used it to get the phone.

She searched his gaze. "Even so, I need to offset the cost."

"Are you going to be impossibly stubborn about this?" he asked.

"Yes."

Jeb burst out laughing. "Am I supposed to act surprised?"

After the iPhone lesson, Jeb handed Amanda the revolver that he'd recently started hiding atop the kitchen cabinet. The piece looked gigantic in her slender hands. He expected her to act as if it were a bomb about to detonate, but instead she grasped the handle with a firm grip. Keeping the barrel directed downward at the outside wall, she sighted in on an imaginary target. Jeb noted her stance and how she held the butt.

"You've been around weapons?" he asked

"All kinds." She disengaged the cylinder and twirled it with a fingertip to make certain it was fully loaded. "My dad was a hunter and had a huge collection of guns. When I was in my teens, we had gun-cleaning night once a week. We took a weapon apart, cleaned it, and reassembled it, timing each other. I could do this one in five minutes flat. Well, it might take me a bit longer now. It's been a while since I practiced."

"Are you a decent shot?"

Jeb saw the proud lift of her chin and guessed her answer. "Way better than decent."

Now that Jeb had learned Amanda knew how to handle firearms, he apparently felt better about leaving her and Chloe alone in the house for a few minutes, because he began measuring the downstairs windows. He explained as he took notes on his phone that he intended to go out to his shop to cut some lengths of square trim.

"Call me paranoid," he said over his shoulder, "but as safe as I believe we are with this high-tech security system, I see no harm in taking some old-fashioned precautions. Wood in the window slides stops the panes from opening. In order to get in, you'd have to shatter the glass, and the sound would set off the glass-breakage detectors."

Amanda couldn't help but admire his physique as he bent and shifted to study the measuring tape time and again. He worked with a fluid economy of movement for so large a man. His wash-worn flannel work shirt clung to his skin, revealing a play of muscle in his back, shoulders, and arms every time he changed position. Watching him gave her a strange, tingling sensation low in her stomach. She'd once been attracted to Mark, but never with the intensity that she now felt toward Jeb. Even his scent, distinctly masculine, filled her with yearning.

"I appreciate your taking such good care of us."

He flashed the dazzling grin that always warmed her. "For my ladies, I cover all the bases."

His ladies? Amanda felt as if she were standing on a rickety raft in the middle of a lake with boards breaking away beneath her feet. She remembered Jeb saying that life was a dance. But for her, moving with the rhythm presented a challenge that she wasn't certain she could take on. She'd fallen into the metaphorical lake all too often.

He donned his jacket and then stepped over to the kitchen security panel near the back door. "I'll be gone only a few minutes, but just to be safe, reset the alarm after I go out. Okay?"

Keeping the system on all the time had already become a habit. "No worries. I'll watch the monitor. When you get back, I'll let you in."

He bent to kiss her just below her ear. Until now, Amanda hadn't realized how sensitive that spot was, or how the tickle of his breath against the side of her neck would tantalize her. "When I get back, will you help me dream up some passcodes for my computer and network? I put in some temporary ones, but they aren't as strong as Gowdy thinks we need. He wants letters, numbers, and symbols. I haven't had time to sit down and do it."

Trying to collect her composure, she said, "Sure. We'll think of some humdingers."

Amanda locked the door after he exited onto the back porch. Then she returned to the panel to reset the system. But when she selected Stay, the screen flashed Fault!

She frowned, wondering what that meant. Toward the bottom of the menu, she saw a choice that read, View Faults. When she pressed the button, an alert popped up, saying that the front door was open. *What the heck?* She knew good and well that it was closed and locked. She turned to check that zone on the monitor, only to see that the kitchen screen had gone blank.

A jolt of fear shot up her spine. For an instant, she stood frozen in place. Then she ran toward the door to call Jeb back. *No, no, no.* The gun. She needed to get the gun! She changed directions so fast that she nearly tripped over her own feet. Once at the cabinet, she went up onto her tiptoes to grab the Magnum.

"Well, well, well," a familiar male voice said from behind her. "Nice digs, sweetheart."

Amanda whirled, gripping the butt of the .357 with both hands. Mark stood at the opposite side of the kitchen table. He wore faded jeans and a red T-shirt topped by a black jacket. His stance was relaxed, his expression smug, and his lips were curved into the smile she'd learned to dread. It made him look almost angelic, and he always sported it right before he did something evil. How many times had she seen him flash it at Chloe right before he slugged or kicked her?

Compared to Jeb, Mark looked insubstantial, but Amanda had felt the strength behind his fists too many times to be fooled. His cheeks were flushed as if he'd been running, and his dark hair was a tousled mess. It was his eyes that made her blood run cold. The blue irises glinted like glass in harsh sunlight, but you saw no emotion when you delved deep. It was like locking gazes with a lizard.

"Your cowboy finally dropped his guard. I knew he would sooner or later. And I've been waiting. I'm a very patient man."

His smile deepened. This was Mark at his most treacherous—clever, self-assured, and certain he was invincible. The air between them felt oily, filming her nostrils each time she breathed. If malignance had a smell, this man exuded it from every pore. She could almost feel his brutal fingers closing over her throat, squeezing until her lungs burned for oxygen and her vision went black.

Shoving away the images and gathering her courage, she cocked the weapon and sighted in on his forehead. "Get out of this house, Mark, or I'll bury a bullet right between your eyes." The calm resolve in her voice surprised even her. "Now. If you think I don't have the guts, you're dead wrong. Your reign of terror is over."

Still smiling, Mark brought up his right hand. In it, he

held the revolver that he'd often pressed to her temple for nasty games of Russian roulette. "It appears we have a standoff. Play it smart, Amanda. Come with me without a fight, and I'll leave Chloe alone. It'll be just you and me, and we'll settle this."

Amanda knew better than to fall for that. Mark would kill her, making it look like an accident, and then he'd get sole custody of their daughter. "Not on your life."

"Don't be stupid. Your only hope is to shoot firs—"

From out of nowhere, Bozo appeared, his massive, mottled brown body going airborne. Mark had no time to react. In a fraction of a second, the dog collided so hard with the man that he went flying. Amanda lurched forward, terrified that Mark might shoot the mastiff, and true to form, he tried, even sprawled on his back and anchored by the animal's weight. He swung the gun up, trying to level it at Bozo's head.

"No!" Amanda screamed. She aimed the .357, but she couldn't get a clear shot. Bozo was in the way. *"No!"* she cried again.

The mastiff lunged and sank his fangs into Mark's wrist. Knocked off target, the gun barrel was now pointed at a wall, then at the ceiling. Mark emitted a ragged scream. The weapon went off, the report so loud that the repercussion pounded against Amanda's eardrums. At the sound, Bozo's fury increased, visibly vibrating through his huge body. He shook Mark's arm. The pistol flew from his grasp and landed about three feet away.

Bozo released Mark's wrist and clamped his jaws over his throat. The snarls that rumbled from the animal's massive chest bore no resemblance to his conversational growls, but they conveyed his meaning with absolute clarity. If Mark tried to move, Bozo would kill him.

"Lie still!" Amanda cried as she ran toward the security panel. "If you even twitch, he'll rip your throat out."

The instant Amanda pressed the panic button, the siren went off, the shrill sound bouncing off the walls. To her horror, she saw Chloe hurtling down the staircase. Before the child reached the kitchen, Amanda yelled, "Go to Mr. Jeb's bedroom, Chloe. Remember the hiding place I showed you? *Go!*"

Chloe wheeled, tripped, and sprawled on the floor. But she scrambled back to her feet in short order and bolted for the bedroom. Amanda stepped around the table to keep her weapon trained on her husband.

Mark moaned. The sound incited the dog to bite down harder.

"Hold him," she shouted to Bozo. "Don't kill him. Just hold him."

Bozo didn't need direction. Every time Mark wiggled or tried to speak, the mastiff increased the pressure on his throat. Amanda heard a thud at the back door. *Jeb*. He must have heard the gunshot or the siren. She ran to let him in. The instant she disengaged the lock, he burst into the room.

"It's Mark," Amanda cried, hoping Jeb could hear her over the wailing horn. "I don't know how he did it, but he got the front door open, and I couldn't reset the system!"

Jeb gave Amanda a quick once-over to check for injuries. Then he strode around the table, retrieved Mark's weapon from the floor, and took stock of the situation.

Amanda wasn't sure what she expected Jeb to do, but laughing wasn't on her list. His hair gleaming like molten gold in the overhead lights, he gave his dog a thumbs-up. "Good job, Bozo! I always knew I could count on you."

Jeb circled the snarling mastiff and the visibly terrified Mark. "Wow, I don't envy you! One wrong move, and he'll rip out your jugular." Jeb pocketed the gun and planted his hands on his hips. More clearly than words, his stance conveyed that the mastiff needed no backup.

Just then, the house phone rang. Jeb signaled Amanda to answer it. She hurried over to the base unit, put the Magnum on the counter, and grabbed the receiver. A woman said, "This is Deb at central station. Is everyone okay there?"

Amanda blinked. "A man broke into the house and threatened us with a gun, but he's been subdued and we have the situation under control now."

The woman asked for the password, and Amanda gave it to her.

"The police are on their way," she said. The siren suddenly stopped shrieking. "There, that's better on your ears. Would you like me to stay on the phone with you until help arrives?"

Amanda couldn't see any point. "No, I don't think that's necessary. The intruder is on the floor and being held—at gunpoint." She preferred not to paint Bozo as being vicious. "The authorities should be here soon."

"Do I hear a dog growling?"

"Yes. He's very protective, and right now he's upset."

When Amanda ended the call, Jeb still stood over Mark but was no longer laughing. "I'd call him off, but then I'd have to take over. Given that I'd rather kill you than look at you, I think you're safer with the dog. Besides, it's never too late to learn a hard lesson. Now you know firsthand how it feels to be bullied by somebody bigger than you."

The glare Mark gave Amanda terrified her. She knew she was safe now, but no amount of logic could erase from her mind all the memories she had of this man. He was afraid of the dog and too scared to move, but his rage and hatred were almost palpable. Amanda hoped the police hurried. You could never underestimate Mark. He'd just proved that again.

She felt as if her legs had turned into limp noodles. Unable to remain standing, she plopped onto a chair. To her, every second seemed to last a small eternity. *Mark*. He lay only a few feet away. As the realization sank in, she started to shake. *Delayed reaction*. She thanked God for keeping her hands steady to hold the gun.

Just as she heard the distant wail of police sirens, a short, stocky man holding a shotgun burst into the kitchen.

"Is everybody all right in here?"

At a distance, Amanda had seen the farmer across the road. *Tony Bradley*. And he had come loaded for bear.

Jeb arched an eyebrow at Amanda. "Where's Chloe?"

"Hiding," she replied with a wobble in her voice. "In your bedroom."

Jeb turned back to his friend. "Thanks to Bozo we're all fine, Tony, but I appreciate your coming over. You're the best."

Tony lowered the shotgun barrel, studied the prostrate Mark, and scowled. "If ever a throat needed rippin' out, it's his. You oughta tell that dog to go for it. All the lady's troubles would be over."

"It's tempting, but unlawful. Barney would probably throw me in the hoosegow." Jeb motioned at Tony's shotgun. "Can you stand guard over him? I've got a little girl I need to check on."

Tony brought the gun barrel back up. "It'll be my pleasure. Long as he doesn't move so much as a whisker, him and me will get along fine."

"Just don't shoot my dog." Jeb laid Mark's weapon on the table in front of Amanda. "Make sure you hand that over to the sheriff. It'll stand as evidence that Mark entered this house with deadly intent."

At the words, Amanda shuddered. *Deadly intent.* She'd come so close to dying tonight. So *very* close. If it hadn't been for Bozo's surprise attack, Mark would have shot her. Even worse, she knew this wasn't over. Mark was subdued right now and he'd surely go to jail, but the authorities couldn't keep him behind bars forever.

Jeb found Chloe in the closet hidey-hole. When he opened the cover, she bleeped in terror, which made him want to kick himself. *I should've told her it was me.* "Hey, hey, hey," he said when she ducked into the corner. "It's Mr. Jeb, princess. I just came to make sure you're all right."

Chloe launched herself into his arms. "My daddy—my mean daddy—he's—in—the house!"

An ache spread through Jeb's chest as he gathered the trembling child close. "I know, but Bozo is making sure he can't harm anyone, and your mommy pressed the panic button to call the police." He tightened his embrace. "You're safe. Your mommy is safe. There's no reason to be afraid."

She shrank against his thick jacket. "You don't know. He does awful, horrible things."

"Not anymore, he won't. Your uncle Barney will lock him up in jail and throw away the key." Jeb heard heavy footsteps rushing into his kitchen and guessed that the deputies had arrived. He needed to get back out there, but he couldn't bring himself to abandon Chloe. So instead he sat on the floor, braced his back against the cedar wall, and cradled the child across his chest. Sometimes a guy had to set priorities, and the importance of holding Chloe right now outweighed everything else. "I sure am proud of you, princess."

"How come?"

"Because you came in here to hide. You minded your mommy and didn't panic. You're a very smart girl."

She sniffed and nodded, which made Jeb smile. This little gal wouldn't grow up to be a woman with no self-confidence, not if he had anything to say about it.

"I think Uncle Barney is here," she whispered. "His voice sounds almost like yours."

Jeb cocked an ear and heard his brother speaking. The tension eased from his body. With Barney here, Mark Banning would be cuffed and stuffed before he could blink. Jeb's thoughts turned to Amanda. She undoubtedly needed some comfort, too, but there was only one of him to go around.

Amanda felt as if her posterior had been glued to the chair. Cops swarmed through the house, their voices droning in her ears like the buzz of hornets. She forced herself to reconnect with reality. *Shock*. She'd felt this way before—numb, separated from everything by a fog. But now wasn't the time to succumb to it.

Barney dragged Bozo off Mark, and two deputies dived in to take the dog's place. Mark was rolled onto his stomach. A knee, backed by a man's weight, dug into his spine.

"Hey!" Mark yelled. "Easy on my arms!"

The officers ignored him and shoved both his wrists up his back to rest just under his shoulder blades as they handcuffed him.

"That *bitch* invited me here for visitation with my

child!" Mark cried. "I have a letter to prove it! She set me up! I'll have your jobs for treating me like this!"

Barney stood near Amanda, bagging Mark's weapon as evidence. "Do you always come for visitation armed with a deadly weapon?" he asked Mark.

"I have permits to carry concealed!" Mark shouted. "A man has a right to defend himself in this country. Check my wallet, asshole! I'm legal in both Oregon and California!" He cried out in pain when the two deputies grabbed him by the elbows and dragged him to his feet. "Jesus Freaking Christ! You dislocated my shoulders!"

A husky older man entered the kitchen. He carried himself with an air of authority. Amanda decided he must be the sheriff. "If they'd dislocated your shoulders, you'd be in so much pain, you wouldn't be able to talk, let alone yell."

Mark sent Amanda a glare that cut through her like a razor. "You'll pay for this. In your letter, you asked me to come! You'll pay! I won't rest until you do!"

Amanda had written no letter. The very idea that she might have was ludicrous. But she couldn't form the words to contest the accusation.

As the deputies shoved Mark into a walk, he shouted, "I didn't pull the gun until the damned dog jumped me! I was invited here, I'm telling you! I was only trying to protect myself!"

"Put him in a car," the sheriff ordered the two deputies. "And don't take your eyes off him."

Jeb didn't know how much time passed. He only knew that Barney finally entered the closet and crouched in front of him. "You need better locks, bro. Yours are sturdy, but the mechanisms can be picked. You also need to watch those monitors you had installed. If you had been paying attention, you'd have noticed when the screen went blank."

Jeb narrowed his gaze on his brother's burnished face. "You mean he picked the front door lock? Why didn't that set off the alarm?"

"What triggers the alarm is the magnetic connections being broken. When the doors or windows are closed, the connection is intact. You can pick the lock or disengage it with a key. The system senses nothing until a perimeter is actually breached. Then the little magnets aren't touching anymore."

Jeb's brain felt as if it had been put through a blender.

"Banning's lying through his teeth right now, saying that Amanda let him in," Barney continued. "But my take is, he picked the lock after he hacked into your system, probably sometime after dark, and then he watched through the windows, hoping for an opportunity to open the door without setting off the alarm."

Jeb recollected the string of events that had transpired before and after he had left the house through the back door. He'd turned off the alarm and reminded Amanda to reset it. Then he'd kissed her under the ear, asked her to help him dream up better passcodes, and stepped outside. Before setting the alarm, Amanda had locked the door behind him. If Banning had been watching through a window, he would have known the security system was momentarily off. If he'd already picked the front door lock, those seconds had given him time to race back to the porch and open the door before Amanda tried to reset the alarm. She must have been terrified when the panel screen told her there was a fault.

"Man, he's a sneaky piece of work," Jeb said. "He must have plotted and planned this for hours."

"And he had to have been watching the house, possibly for a day or more." Barney rubbed beside his nose, a nervous habit when he was about to say something that made him uncomfortable. "Jeb, you gotta remember that those monitors are useless unless you keep an eye on them. When the screens go blank, something's up."

Jeb couldn't argue the point. Sometime tonight he'd dropped the ball and allowed Banning an opportunity to get in. "I can't believe this happened."

Barney sighed and reached out to pat Chloe's head. "All's well that ends well. I'll do my best to keep him behind bars."

Jeb's skin tingled. "What do you mean, your best? He broke into my house while armed with a deadly weapon. And what about the restraining order?"

He rubbed his nose again. "It's complicated. He's got a permit to carry concealed in two states. He's Amanda's husband. He claims she sent him a letter, inviting him to come for visitation, and that she let him inside. He also claims he didn't pull the weapon from his pocket until the dog attacked him. We've got no physical proof that he broke in or threatened Amanda with a gun. There's no damage to the door. It could come down to Amanda's word against his."

"Are you telling me you don't believe her?" Jeb's voice rose dangerously.

Barney shook his head. "It's not about who I believe, Jeb. It's about the law, and in order to press charges against this dude for breaking and entering with malicious intent, the burden of proof is on us."

Jeb tensed. "The cameras. The playback will show that he broke in."

"Didn't you hear me? He hacked your network and

turned off the cameras. At least that's my best guess. The guy's smart."

"How in the hell did he hack into my network?"

Barney swept off his hat to scratch his head. "Have you ever called a computer company to ask for help with your system and authorized a technician, using Go to Assist or some other remote access application, to get on your computer?"

"Yes, a couple of times. You see their cursor going everywhere, looking at files as they fix problems."

"Well, it's possible for someone to get on your computer using remote access *without* your permission. I don't know *how* they do it. I only know it can be done, and once they gain access, they can do almost anything, even disconnect your security cameras from your DVR. It's the only explanation, unless you disconnected the cameras yourself." He settled the dark brown Stetson back into place. "You've got access to the Internet from a tower, not through an underground cable. If someone gets within a certain range of your receiver dish with a wireless device, they can pick up the signal. I think Banning did exactly that, somehow logged on to your network, and disconnected the cameras before he picked the lock. The minute he started saying that Amanda invited him in, I went into your office and tried to do a reverse search of the recordings. Nothing, nada. When he entered the house, your DVR was getting no signals from your cameras. They stopped working at a little after eight."

A bitch of a headache took up residence in Jeb's temples. "Where's his laptop? Surely there's evidence on there that he hacked in."

"It was in his car, which is parked out on the road next to your driveway. Like I said, I'm no expert with computers, but when I turned it on, I saw no evidence that he'd hacked in. I checked the history. He apparently erased all of it. I'm impounding the vehicle, and I'll take the computer back to the department so our tech guys can have a look at it."

"He parked right next to my driveway to watch the house? Why didn't I notice it on the monitor?"

"It's barely visible. I got the cameras turned back on, and even with the infrared lens that covers your driveway, the vehicle is far enough away that it's difficult to spot. It's a gray sedan and blends in with the road. Mostly all you can see are bits of chrome glinting. If I hadn't known I was looking at a car, I wouldn't have guessed that was what it was."

Jeb forgot he was holding Chloe and said, "Son of a bitch."

Barney inclined his head at the child. Jeb clamped his lips tight.

"You need to get Gowdy back out here to put up some stronger firewalls, and once he does, you need to dream up a lot better network password than the one you have right now."

Jeb closed his eyes. "I have temporary password protection on my computer and the network, and I intended to create stronger codes later tonight."

"What are your temporary codes?"

"For the computer, I changed it to my house number tacked onto the end of my first name. For the network, I used my middle name, Paul, followed by the same numbers."

Barney gaped at him as if he'd grown a third ear in the middle of his forehead. "Why would you choose such easy-to-guess passcodes?"

Jeb shrugged. "They didn't seem that easy to me, and I had to come up with them off the top of my head. Gowdy said I needed stronger ones, and, like I said, I meant to create them later tonight. Amanda was going to help me."

"Jeb, you have a radiant signal, and you left yourself wide open to a breach? As a temporary code, you would have been better off using your Social Security number. At least that's harder to find online. Not impossible, but harder. Lots of people use their names followed by numbers, and your street address is way too obvious."

Jeb's headache went from bad to worse. "Hello, Barney, we live in Mystic Creek. I know and trust my neighbors. Who in this town would park outside my house and try to hack into my network?"

"A stranger named Mark Banning," Barney retorted.

Chloe looked up. "Does that mean you didn't lock your computer door, Mr. Jeb?"

Jeb thumped the back of his head against the wall. "Yes, princess, that's pretty much what it means."

"Oopsy-daisy."

"Yeah, a big oops."

Barney interjected, "How can someone as brilliant as you are professionally be such an idiot?"

"No name-calling," Jeb warned. "I already feel bad enough." Jeb met and held his brother's gaze. "Don't let him walk. We've got the photographic evidence that Amanda collected, and she's pressed charges. Her file was sent to a Eureka judge. The police, both here and there, have been looking for him. If we can't get him one way, we can get him another."

Barney huffed and stood up. "You're right, Jeb, but that doesn't mean I can keep Banning in our jail."

"Why the h—" Jeb remembered Chloe. "Uh, why not?"

"Amanda filed charges against Banning here, but the crimes she documented occurred in California. Read the Sixth Amendment. Put simply, it says that a person must be tried in the state and district where the alleged crime was committed."

"So you can arrest Banning in Oregon, but he'll be prosecuted in California?"

"Yes. Oregon will extradite him to California to face the charges there. At that point it's out of our hands. The only way we can keep him here is if we can prove that he committed more crimes in Oregon."

"The law sucks."

"The law is complicated," Barney revised.

"I get what you're saying," Jeb inserted. "But right now, all I feel is frustrated. The jerk could make bail and head straight back here."

Barney nodded, his expression weary. "I wish I could stop it from happening, but California has jurisdiction."

"There's still the restraining order that Amanda filed. He totally disregarded it. Why can't we get him for that?"

Shifting his stance, Barney replied, "He's got a letter, supposedly written by Amanda and postmarked in Mystic Creek, that invites him to come here. Amanda denies writing the letter, but even she admits that the cursive resembles hers. I can't prove she didn't send Mark the invitation until I get a handwriting expert on board. That could take some time."

"Even if Amanda *did* invite Banning here, the restraining order is still valid. I've heard of women inviting an ex to come see them and then pressing charges because restraining orders were violated."

"True, but in this instance, Banning has an actual written letter as evidence. That complicates things. Unless we can prove he forged the handwriting, a judge may read it and think Mark was tricked into coming here. Women do that kind of thing all the time to get revenge."

As Barney walked away, Chloe stirred on Jeb's lap and asked, "Does that mean Uncle Barney can't throw away the key?"

Jeb looked into her trusting brown eyes and swallowed hard. "Yes, honey, that may be what it means."

Chloe mulled that over. "It's okay, Mr. Jeb. Even if they turn my mean daddy loose, I won't be afraid. I've got Bozo to protect me and Mommy."

Definitely a smart girl. She knew who she could count on, and it wasn't Jeb.

After the deputies took Mark away, Jeb was left to ponder what he'd done and what he'd failed to do. Barney was right; he was an idiot. He'd spent thousands of dollars on a security system, and then failed to protect the network from a hacker.

Amanda remained shaky long after Barney took off. Jeb wished he could reassure her, but right then, he felt like such an abysmal failure that he needed to lick his own wounds. While she was upstairs trying to get Chloe settled again for the night, he slumped on the family room sofa and stared at the ceiling. He'd tried so hard to keep them safe, and he'd screwed it up so badly that he wondered if he'd ever get over it.

Amanda came back downstairs and sat on the ottoman in front of him. She braced her elbows on her knees and clasped her hands, studying him in a way that made him feel naked to the bone.

"What's wrong?" she asked, her voice pitched low.

Jeb hated to tell her that he'd left his network wide open to Mark's attack, but when it came to something this awful, trying to dodge the bullet didn't seem right. So he told her the truth, leaving out nothing.

"You intended to create stronger passwords this evening," she reminded him. "And I don't think your temporary ones are really that weak."

"Barney says they are. He's the criminal investigator, not me. I should have come up with some stronger ones right away."

"It's been a little crazy around here."

Jeb appreciated her effort to make him feel better, but he couldn't let himself off the hook.

Amanda sighed. "You're not going to turn loose of this, are you?"

Jeb released a long breath, too. "I let you down. I tried to keep you safe, and I let you down."

She sat erect. "Now maybe you can understand how I feel. I let Chloe down, not just once but many times."

He hadn't thought of that. *Whammo*, right in the solar plexus. How many times had he told Amanda to turn loose of her guilt? It would be a cold day in hell before he let go of *his*. He felt like a fool. He suddenly understood her in a way he hadn't before.

"I'm sorry," he said, knowing that was inadequate. "I totally screwed up."

"If it will make you feel better, during our marriage Mark took night classes in computer programming. He also hung around with some guys who called themselves crackers and infiltrated people's networks just for fun. In his own way, Mark's also smart." She lifted her shoulders. "I don't think he's a genius or anything close, but he is obsessive and capable of hyperfocusing when he wants to inflict harm. I got away from him, and now he will go to any lengths to get his revenge."

"In short, he's an asshole," Jeb observed. "I can't believe he figured out how to invade my network and gain control of my DVR. Sometimes my phone will pick up signals from an unprotected network, but I'd never for a moment think about hacking in."

"You have scruples. Mark doesn't."

Jeb guessed he should be happy that Amanda believed he had scruples, but right then, he ached with regret, and he couldn't rejoice about much of anything. "I'm sorry I didn't get better passwords up sooner."

"You've done your best. Now you have to move on."

Jeb shifted on the cushioned seat. "You mean I have to follow different rules than you do?"

"I don't understand."

"You did everything you could to protect Chloe, and you can't forgive yourself for failing. Now I've stumbled into Mark's twisted world, and I've failed to protect both of you. Why are you allowed to hold on to your guilt, but I'm not?"

She stood and gazed down at him for a long moment. "You just answered your own question. You stumbled into Mark's twisted world. I walked in with my eyes wide open."

Jeb watched her step into the adjoining kitchen, where she collected the Magnum .357. "If you don't mind, I'd like to borrow this. You can use the shotgun, right?"

"Right." He glanced at the revolver. "If you're taking that to bed with you, put it where Chloe won't find it."

She circled the counter and paused to search his expression. "You think he may get out on bail, don't you?"

Jeb hated having to admit that. "My brother isn't sure

he can keep him behind bars here. Mark thought of nearly everything—a forged letter from you that invited him here; a permit to carry concealed; hacking into my network to turn off the cameras. We've got no real evidence against him."

"But he'll be extradited to California to be prosecuted for the charges I filed against him. And he might be allowed to post bond there."

"Pretty much, unless Barney can make something that he did tonight stick. He'll try to nail him on disregarding the restraining order, but your letter makes that iffy."

"It's not *my* letter." She headed toward the stairs. "I'm sorry to leave you alone when you're feeling down, but I need to be close to my daughter right now."

"He won't be released tonight, Mandy."

She paused with her hand on the baluster. "I know you're only trying to reassure me. You might even believe it, Jeb. But you don't know Mark."

Chapter Fifteen

With one eye open, Jeb slept on the sofa that night. Earlier he'd set up better password protection on his computer, using random numbers, symbols, and letters, and taking diligent notes. Surely that was now impenetrable, but he didn't know how strong his firewall was.

Jeb rolled onto his back and then onto his side again. *I hate sleeping on this sofa. It's too damned short.* He thanked God that Bozo was upstairs in Amanda's bed. If Banning somehow escaped custody and slipped inside again, the huge dog would at least slow the bastard down, giving Jeb enough time to race upstairs. Letting his arm drop over the edge of the cushion, he curled his fingers over the shotgun lying on the floor. He wouldn't get caught off guard again.

The next morning, the bedding on the couch didn't escape Amanda's notice. While working in the kitchen to help fix breakfast, Jeb endured questioning looks from her. When Chloe ran to the bathroom, she whispered, "Is he out on bail?"

"Not that I've heard. I'm just being cautious."

Amanda tipped her head to study his face. "You look exhausted."

"I had trouble drifting off." In truth, Jeb hadn't slept much. He'd been too wound up. "I'll grab a nap later."

That plan went south. Gowdy showed up to work on Jeb's network security. He installed a router guaranteed to block all invasions, and then for good measure, he loaded two different firewalls. In addition to that, he checked Jeb's passwords and gave them high marks. Shortly after Gowdy left, Barney showed up.

"I bring new locks," he said with a smile. "These can't be picked, not easily anyway. I got off early to help you install them." He glanced past Jeb toward the kitchen. "I also brought Chloe's homework, and before you ask, no, I didn't pick it up. I sent a fellow deputy. If you're still speaking to me when we're done, maybe I can bum a beer and dinner off you tonight."

Jeb's stomach knotted. "He made bail," he guessed.

Barney shook his head. "Not yet. The California boys came this afternoon to haul him back to Eureka. He's still in custody, but I don't know for how long. He's got a barracuda attorney and used his one phone call last night to contact him. Around noon, the lawyer showed up. He argued that we have no proof Banning did anything wrong, and he told Sheriff Adams that he'd have his badge if he tried holding the creep until we find a forensic handwriting expert." With a shrug, Barney added, "I did my best to keep him, Jeb, but now it's out of our hands."

"It's not your fault."

"I paid him a visit in his cell before the California officers took him into custody. I told him if I see him in Mystic Creek again, I'll kill him and make it look like he fired a shot at me first. I'm pretty sure he believed me, because he turned as white as snow."

Jeb rested a hand on his brother's shoulder. "Thanks for that."

Barney nodded. "Come to find out, I wasn't the only one who went back to threaten him. Even the sheriff did. If Banning comes back here, he's crazy."

"That's the problem. He's nuts." Jeb took the sack and homework from his brother. "How much do I owe you for the locks?"

"I'll take it out in dinners. I enjoy that little girl. She's cute as a button. I like how she turns you into melted butter. I always thought you were a tough guy, and then, bang, you went soft."

Jeb dredged up a smile. "Gird your loins, bro, or she'll have you melting like butter, too."

Jeb took the homework into the kitchen. Then he decided he and Barney should change the locks on only one door at a time, one man working while the other stood guard. Mark Banning had gotten the better of Jeb once; he never would again.

Barney said several times, "Even if he's back in Eureka, it'll take a while for his attorney to get him out on bail."

"I'm not taking any chances. He's as slippery as an eel." Jeb glanced up at his younger sibling. "What's the matter with people, believing a slimeball like him?"

"From a cop's perspective? Here in Mystic, things are boring, but while working for the state, I saw things you wouldn't believe." Barney warmed to the subject. "After being jilted, some women hate their ex-lovers so much, they'll bang themselves up to get the men arrested. Bust their own noses, blacken their own eyes. And they're pretty convincing, crying and shaking. Cops have to look beneath the surface and question a story." He relaxed his shoulders and leaned back against the doorframe. "Don't get me wrong. I know Amanda. But when it's a stranger, how can a cop know if a woman is telling the truth or trying to get even?"

"What is it with this getting-even bullshit? Why can't people just call it curtains?"

Barney shifted his weight onto one foot and crossed his ankles. His brown boots shone like buffed wax. "The world is filled with all kinds of people. Some are crazy, or just self-absorbed and can't handle rejection. They have to strike back. Right here in Mystic, I've seen people slander each other publicly. About six months ago, we had a dude who got dumped by a gal, and in retaliation, he posted on Craigslist under her account, uploading risqué pictures of her and inviting all comers for a one-night rodeo. She got calls from men all over the country. Jilted lovers often have no stops."

They switched the locks out in an hour, and by then the delicious smell of baking bread filled the house. Adjourning to the kitchen, Barney sat with Chloe to help with her lessons while Jeb gave Amanda a hand in the kitchen.

Jeb felt better with Barney there to provide backup, but all too soon dinner was over and his brother left for home. Jeb made sure to lock up and reset the security system, but after last night, he didn't trust the electronics much.

Once Chloe was settled in for the night, Amanda came downstairs to get the skinny. Jeb knew by the haunted expression in her eyes that she suspected Mark was no longer in the local jail, but that didn't save him from having to say the words. Shortly after he told her, she rushed past him to the bathroom. He heard her gagging and wished he could do something. Problem was, he didn't know what.

When Amanda returned, she had a little color back in her cheeks.

"What are we going to do now?" she asked.

Seated at the table, Jeb felt helpless. "We have to wait it out. Right now, he's still in custody." He wanted to assure her that Mark would stay behind bars, but in reality, it was a crapshoot. "Johnson is trying to get an early date for the divorce-and-custody hearing in Crystal Falls. I can't imagine a judge ruling in Mark's favor."

"It may be a long wait, Jeb. And even if a judge denies Mark unsupervised visitation, what good will it do? He has no stops." She folded her arms, her stance rigid. "You can't spend the rest of your life standing guard over us. What about your business? At some point, you'll have to work."

Jeb was glad to know she'd started thinking long-term in regard to their relationship. If he had the honor of protecting her and Chloe for years, he'd count himself one lucky man. "Gowdy wired the shop and put in a security panel. If an important job comes in, I'll take you and Chloe out there with me while I work."

"Which will mean I can't do the job you've hired me to do inside the house."

"For now, can we forget about that?"

"No. This is a mess with no light at the end of the tunnel."

"We'll work it out," Jeb insisted. "If nothing else, you

can help me in the shop, and when we come back in, I'll help you with the house."

He anticipated an argument, and the thought made him feel like a dog chasing its tail. He wasn't sure he had it in him to go over the same old points again.

Instead, she surprised him with, "You're a difficult man not to love, Jeb Sterling."

"Then stop fighting it."

She bent her head. When she looked back up at him, her eyes had gone warm and shiny. "I think I already have." She held up a staying hand. "Don't take that to mean I'm ready for anything physical."

"You're attracted to me." Jeb knew he was pushing her, but his male radar told him it was time to give her a nudge. "I feel the electricity snap between us, and I'm no kid still wet behind the ears. I know you feel it, too."

The faint color in her cheeks deepened to rose. "Yes, I do." She glanced away, then back at him. He saw her struggle and wondered if she could muster the courage to go on. "I wonder how it might be if you kissed me. Sometimes I want to touch you in ways I shouldn't. I used to have nightmares about things Mark did to me, but they stopped when I came here. Now I have only lovely dreams about you. And other times, being near you makes me feel as if I just swallowed a cup of live minnows."

Jeb had been thinking, *Oh, yeah*. But that last bit shocked him out of his hormonal reverie. "Sweet Lord." He gulped, telling that part of his body with no connection to his brain to stop pushing against the fly of his jeans. Since adolescence he'd privately called that unruly body part George, and George was certainly active now. "That must feel awful."

She shook her head. "It's actually not awful. Bad wording. It's how I feel when I—um—yearn to find out how it might be between us."

"Just say when, and we'll find out," he said.

"I can't. For me, it's like standing on a cliff, looking at jagged rocks far below and thinking about jumping."

Though Jeb felt proud of her for having the guts to be truthful, now it was his turn to struggle, to try to wrap his mind around this sweet but complicated lady's emotional processes. *Jumping off a cliff?* He'd always found sex pleasurable, and his partners had never complained. Hello, it felt *good*. But his Mandy had never experienced sex as good or even okay.

He searched her lovely eyes and saw that the thought of having sex frightened her. He suspected Mark had used physical intimacy as another way to make her pay for screwing up his life. "Don't jump off the cliff," he told her, his voice so gravelly he barely recognized it. It wasn't what he wanted to say, but, damn it, it was what she needed to hear. Borrowing her analogy and changing the picture, he added, "When you feel as if you're standing on a boulder, and all you see is me there to catch you, then go ahead and leap."

Her eyes filled with tears. "When will I feel that way? You're everything I ever dreamed of, and—" She wiped her cheeks, looking miserably unhappy, not with him but with herself. "I'm such a coward. I know you won't hurt me. I tell myself it'll be nice, but just as I think I'm ready, I want to run. And what if you get fed up with me and run before I do?"

Jeb had a hard-on now that throbbed. He'd known she wanted him, but hearing her admit it—well, George never had listened to a thing Jeb told him. "Mandy, I'm not going to run. The first time I met you, I felt drawn to you, and that hasn't changed."

Her swimming gaze clung to his. "Really? You're not impatient with me? I know I've sent you signals, and then I've backed away. Men don't like a tease."

Jeb didn't know how to deal with her fears. She wasn't just carrying baggage; she was towing heavy freight. Right now, she felt threatened by Mark, and the last thing she needed was to be pressured by Jeb for sex. How in the hell had the subject even come up? He'd started it. *Damn it*. He was *such* an ass, nothing like the prince she'd wished for in her messages.

Okay, so I want her. What would it take to make him understand she wasn't ready, a blow on the head? She needed no more stress. Mark Banning was enough to push almost any woman over the edge into a nervous breakdown.

But somehow Amanda had stood strong. Looking at her, Jeb felt ashamed for adding to her worries. "I told you I'll wait, and I meant it. No pressure, no expectations, *nothing*." Jeb wanted to whack George and could only pray she didn't glance down. "I'm in no hurry. Let's just go with the flow and see where it takes us."

She gave him a pleading look. "I don't know right now if I'll ever be ready. But I do care for you in a way I never would have thought possible. You're everything that Mark isn't. I don't know how any woman could spend time with you and not fall in love. I'm sorry I can't give you more, but I've dipped my well dry."

"I'll take whatever you can give and be glad of it." Jeb cleared his throat. "As for Mark, I'll do whatever it takes to keep you and Chloe safe. Gowdy says my passwords are now such strings of gibberish that only someone with a special application could hack them. If you end up helping me in the shop, you'll get a few calluses, and I'll have a great helper." He stood and cupped her chin. "We're going to get through this, Mandy. It may seem to you right now that there's no end in sight, but I believe God is up there orchestrating events. I think He led you to Mystic Creek so I could find you. We need to trust that everything else will work itself out."

Over the next couple of days, Amanda held Jeb's words close in her heart. He'd done so much for her and Chloe, yet he expected no paybacks. She wasn't sure when, but she'd come to believe that. Jeb wasn't a taker or a controller. He knew how to love with no strings attached. She suspected he'd learned that from his wonderful parents.

Amanda had once been able to love without condition. Her mom and dad had taught her how. But that period of her life seemed so distant now, almost beyond her reach. Now that Mark knew where Amanda was, she yearned to call her mom. He'd no longer be watching to pounce on Emma Lang for information. But every time Amanda started to dial her mother, she lost her nerve. During her marriage, it had seemed safer to keep her mom in the dark.

Now the situation had changed, and Amanda would have to find the words to explain all the deceptions. It would be a difficult conversation.

Trying to chase the worries away, Amanda focused on Jeb's house. A typical guy, he hadn't washed the baseboards in God knew how long, and his doorframes had dust on top that had gone gooey. His cupboards and kitchen drawers also needed attention.

As she cleaned and found built-up dirt in hidden

places, she accepted the fact that Jeb did need her help. The stairway banister hadn't been nourished with beeswax for a long while. The beautiful wood had grown dry and would soon start to crack if she didn't take care of it. She had no idea who'd last worked for him, but the person had done a crappy job.

As Amanda treated the wooden trim, she thought of Jeb creating all these surfaces. The finishes had been applied by his big hands. He'd known to add a layer of wax over the stain, but somehow he was clueless about how to care for a masterpiece after he created it. His house needed a woman who would love every nook and cranny. Amanda couldn't help but wonder if that woman might be her. With each passing day, she felt more drawn to him. She trusted him and enjoyed his company, and her little girl adored him. And most important, he didn't press her. Why couldn't she forget Mark and embrace this opportunity with Jeb?

Jeb noticed her housekeeping efforts and thanked her. "I just never seem to find time. I know I'm neglecting stuff."

Amanda replied, "Your work is beautiful."

"Thanks," he said. "I enjoy the artistic aspects of it, which is why I don't hire out anymore to a home builder as a cabinet-and-trim man. I learned the hard way that most contractors have two or three house plans, and making cookie-cutter cabinets, with slight variations, bored me to death. Now I accept only custom jobs, which allows me to use my imagination. People who pay me to make cabinets deserve a bang for their buck, and I try to give them that."

"I've found some pieces of furniture in this house that scream 'Jeb Sterling.' Am I wrong about that?"

He laughed. "My sofas and easy chairs are run-of-the-mill furnishings, but all the wooden pieces in this joint are handcrafted."

They joined Chloe at the kitchen table, helping with her lessons when needed and chatting in between. Jeb had worked indoors for the last couple of days on his computer, creating new furniture designs and never leaving Amanda and Chloe alone in the house. As they talked about his business, and he spoke about this project or that one, Amanda enjoyed the expressions on his face. He truly loved what he did for a living.

"Not many people can say that," he told her. "Well, maybe Tony across the road. He loves farming. I swear, that man's having an affair with his tractor. He's even named her Betsy."

Amanda had never met Myrna Bradley, but she knew that the older woman had a heart of gold. "Is he so obsessed with his tractor and farming that he neglects his wife?"

"No. Myrna is passionate about her little house and yard, so she stays as busy as Tony does. She keeps telling him to replace Betsy, but he just keeps fixing her."

"Why do men refer to vehicles and equipment as females?"

Jeb chuckled. "Good question. I can only say it didn't start with me."

"Well, I'm glad to know Tony and Myrna are happy."

Amanda envied Myrna. As that thought settled into her brain, she realized she was developing a passion for Jeb's home and felt excited about other things as well. "I want to make Christmas balls and sell them," she suddenly said.

Chloe's head jerked up. Jeb arched an eyebrow and said, "Uh-oh, my mom is a contagious disease."

Amanda smiled. Kate's enthusiasm *was* contagious. "Can I have a small corner of your house to set up a worktable where there will always be a mess? I'd like to create things, just like you do, but I'll understand if you say no."

He leaned back on his chair. "Mandy, I've got a separate room in my shop, and the place is wired for security. If you want to do arts and crafts, and you can keep Chloe interested, that's a perfect solution. While I work, you can work. I think it'd be good for you, and with the alarm set, I can focus on my projects without constantly watching the doors."

Melting warmth moved through Amanda. He truly didn't care if her focus wasn't on only him. For her, that was such a marvel. "I think I can make some money. Your mom says she sells the balls for a huge profit at the Christmas bazaars, but if I knew how to set up a Web site, I could sell them all year long."

He searched her gaze. "Sounds like a plan to me. I have a Web site development app. I created a page for my business, and I get many orders. I don't see why I can't do the same for you. I'll need pictures of your merchandise, though, so you need to get to work."

Amanda lurched to a stop in her dreaming. "I can't spend too much time on crafts. I'll have the house to take care of, plus meals and cleanup." She shrugged. "If I keep my cafeteria job, my schedule will be packed."

He leaned forward. "Earth calling Mandy. Where have you been in this relationship? I've moved way past thinking of you as my employee."

"We don't have a relationship yet."

Jeb shook his head. "We *do* have a relationship. You just don't want to face it. I'm good with that, but the bonds forging between us are no less real. As for your cafeteria job, just quit. There's no telling how long it'll be before it's safe for you and Chloe to be at the school. It isn't fair to make Delores work shorthanded for too long."

"I think you can make more money selling Christmas tree balls, Mommy." Chloe grinned. "I can help. I'm really good at it."

"Chloe has to go back to school eventually," Amanda insisted. "She'll fall behind."

"Until we're sure it's safe, we'll homeschool her. Oregon has fabulous online education."

"Yay! I'd like to do homeschool and make Christmas balls with Mommy."

Jeb tousled the child's hair.

"What about your friends, Chloe?" Amanda asked.

"We'll have playdates! I'll see my friends a lot!"

Jeb held out his hand and asked for Amanda's cell phone. When she handed it over, he loaded an app called OpenEye. To Amanda's amazement, she suddenly had a duplicate of the house monitors, which all showed the same camera views, on her iPhone. Because the screen was small, she had to scroll through the panes to see everything, but it was there, and it was live. On her cell, she saw Bozo lift a hind leg to scratch, and when she glanced down, he was flapping one ear with a back paw.

"Gowdy showed me how to load that the other day," Jeb said.

"This is awesome. I'll be able to see the whole house, inside and out, even while I'm cleaning a bathroom. It'll be like having a big monitor in my pocket."

As Amanda moved from the table into the kitchen to start dinner, she thought about how quickly the three of them had started to act as if they were a real family. It felt good. Even better, it felt *right*.

On Monday before Thanksgiving, Amanda's attorney called. Jeb drew her into the living room and put the lawyer on speakerphone. Judging by what Clyde Johnson said, Amanda determined that Jeb had notified him of Mark's break-in. Why *she* hadn't thought to do that, she didn't know. He was her attorney and Chloe's only hope, but he wasn't her friend. When bad things happened, she didn't think of him as someone she should call. She needed to get over that, accept him for who he was, brusqueness and all, and depend on him. Jeb was certainly paying him enough to be attentive and available.

"The good news is that Mark hasn't filed for divorce," Johnson told them. "The bad news is that after he was held for a few days in Eureka on the charges filed against him, his lawyer got him out on bail today. The photographic evidence is strong, but none of the pictures shows Mark inflicting the injuries. Until the judge hears Amanda's testimony, she's reluctant to make a decision. I'm still pushing for an early date for the divorce hearing. Because Amanda filed in this county, that hearing will take place here. Mark's attorney argues that the couple lived in California, and he's screaming for a change of venue, but he isn't likely to get it."

"How does it benefit him to have the hearing in Eureka?" Jeb asked. "I don't get why his lawyer is fighting for that."

"Some attorneys believe venue is important—that a local judge may lend Amanda a more sympathetic ear. In small towns, it's assumed everybody knows everybody, although that's seldom true. Most judges strive to be unbiased, but many attorneys still prefer a *home* hearing because the presiding judge knows them. They feel it gives them an edge."

Amanda wasn't surprised that Mark hadn't remained in jail, but she could tell that Jeb was worried. The stark reality suddenly hit her. *Mark is loose again, and he knows where I am.* Nausea washed over her. She ran to the bathroom and vomited to a dry heave, leaving her face flushed and clammy.

Jeb tapped on the door. Amanda grabbed a washcloth to wipe her mouth. "I'm fine. Sorry. I must have eaten something tainted."

Eaten something tainted? She'd *married* something tainted.

Feeling weak, Amanda stared at her reflection in the mirror and saw a trembling, inadequate, miserable woman who should have some backbone. She needed to pull herself together, get some steel in her spine, and forget the images of herself that Mark had drawn for her.

When she left the bathroom, she found Jeb standing just outside. "Are you okay?"

"Yes," she replied, feeling stronger and braver without knowing exactly why. "What else did Johnson have to say?"

"He spoke with the judge who let Mark out on bail." A faint smile touched his mouth. "It's probably more accurate to say that he gave her hell. She told him she'd had to consider the distance Mark must travel to get here. The letter, supposedly from you, indicates that you invited him here the night he broke in and clouds the issue of the restraining order. She also said that as strong as the photographic evidence is, no picture shows Mark actually committing the violence. In short, she needs to hear your testimony before she makes a judgment, and she didn't feel it was fair to keep a possibly innocent man behind bars until the trial, which could be months from now. She warned Mark that the consequences will be severe if he returns to Mystic Creek, but that was all she could really do."

"So we're screwed."

"If he comes back here, he'll be the one who's screwed."

Amanda reached deep for strength. "You're right. I should flip things around and think optimistically."

"We need to keep an eye out and never let our guard down, though. Johnson has dealt with a lot of Marks. He says they rarely turn over a new leaf, and they become addicted to violence. Mark sees himself as invincible, and he has no internal brakes. He doesn't consider the risk of going to prison. In his mind, he's right, and the whole world will see that in the end."

"That sounds like Mark. Johnson has him pegged."

Jeb's phone chirped. He drew it from his pocket and smiled as he read a text message. "My dad," he told her. "He's got Gowdy over at his place installing security so you and Chloe will be safe there on Thanksgiving."

"We're invited?"

"Of course you're invited. And it'll be fun. With all the Sterlings under one roof, it's a madhouse."

"Jeb, I've been thinking—I need a holster for the Magnum. I'd like to start wearing it most of the time so I don't get caught off guard."

His gaze bored into hers, but he asked no questions. "Okay. I'll get you one."

"You don't think I'm nuts?"

"No, I think you're finally ready to fight back, and that's a good thing."

"No matter where I am in the house, I need to be armed. I don't know when, and I don't know how, but Mark *will* try again."

"I know, and being prepared is the smart thing to do."

"I need you to promise me something."

"What's that?"

"If anything happens to me, will you raise Chloe? I've got my mom, but she's a bit old to take on a six-year-old."

His jaw muscle started to tic, and for an awful moment, Amanda thought he might say no. "I'm honored that you trust me enough to ask, and my answer is yes. But just for the record, I won't let anything happen to you."

Amanda realized that Jeb still felt guilty about his one failure to protect them, and she regretted making him remember. But facts were facts. Mark mainly wanted to make her pay. Chloe had only ever been a weapon he used against her. Amanda knew that in the end, she might wind up dead. She needed to know that if that happened, Chloe would have a wonderful life.

And Jeb was her only hope.

Kate Sterling called the next morning to officially invite Amanda and Chloe to Thanksgiving dinner.

"I'm sure Chloe would love it," Amanda said. "But traditionally, it's a time for family."

"Nonsense," Kate replied. "For us, the more, the merrier."

"Then I accept," Amanda conceded. "But please let me bring something for dinner."

Kate laughed. "My boys say your homemade bread is

fabulous. My oven will be otherwise occupied. I'm baking pies today, and tomorrow, heaven knows."

Amanda agreed to bring bread and then had misgivings the moment she hung up. What if her loaves fell? The rising stage could be tricky. Jeb chuckled when she told him how nervous she felt.

"There'll be so much food, they'll never miss the bread if something goes wrong. Don't worry about it. It's supposed to be a happy time."

And it *was* a happy time. Amanda's bread turned out perfect, and she enjoyed the gathering. Jeb's sisters, Adriel and Sarah, whom Amanda was meeting for the first time, were delightful and instantly took Chloe under their wings. Both girls had Kate's delicate features and build, along with her energy, but they had inherited their father's tawny hair. Amanda admired how the entire family pitched in to cook. Even the men got involved. Kate had a no-television rule on holidays. Sporting events, she maintained, could be recorded. Ten people sat down for dinner.

The only sadness for Amanda that day came from knowing her mom was probably celebrating alone. She sneaked off to a bedroom, collected her courage, and dialed the number to her childhood home. No answer. Was her mom working or possibly at a friend's house? She hoped for the latter.

On the Friday after Thanksgiving, Jeb took Amanda, Chloe, and Bozo out to find a Christmas tree. Jeb wore a holstered Glock on his hip, and Amanda carried the Magnum on hers. She'd never gone into the forest for a tree, but with their warm winter outerwear, both she and Chloe enjoyed the activity, trudging through deep, crusty snow to find a blue spruce they all deemed perfect. When that mission was accomplished, they searched for a second gorgeous tree that Jeb would drop off at his parents' place on the way home.

Chloe kept clapping her hands and saying, "Yay! That's the prettiest tree *ever*, Mr. Jeb!" When Jeb began putting tags on the evergreens, Chloe asked, "What do the tickets mean?"

"They're cutting permits. People must have them to take trees from a forest. If Uncle Barney stops me on the way home, he'll check to make sure our trees are tagged."

"Would he put you in jail if they weren't?"

Jeb chuckled. "No, but he wouldn't hesitate to make me pay some money." He winked at Amanda. "He's a stickler on the law."

That night after dinner, Jeb insisted on a tree-trimming party. He turned on Sonos, a piped-in stereo system that offered different kinds of Christmas carols. They settled on Classic Holiday from SiriusXM, and music rang merrily through the house. While Jeb unearthed boxes of decorations, Amanda and Chloe made cookies.

Amanda hadn't enjoyed trimming a tree for years, and Chloe never had. The child's joy shimmered in her big eyes and lent a flush to her cheeks. Before stringing the lights, Jeb lifted Chloe in his arms so she could put the angel atop the tree, and everyone burst out laughing when an ancient song came on about Sweet Angie, the Christmas tree angel on the tippy-tippy-top of the tree.

More than once, Amanda blinked away tears while watching her daughter. To Chloe, who'd never had a happy Christmas, hanging ornaments on evergreen branches while laughter mingled with the Santa songs was magical. Every time Amanda looked at Jeb, her throat went tight, because if not for him, there would have been nothing magical for them this month. At best, she would have purchased a tiny tree and one pathetic string of lights, and all their decorations would have been home-made.

When the spruce boughs drooped under the weight of too many decorations, Jeb insisted that they make heaps of popcorn, and they sat before the fire to string it. Chloe ate more popcorn than she got strung, and Bozo ate his share, too.

"Uh-oh!" Jeb said.

Amanda followed his gaze to see that Frosty had climbed to the top of the tree. The spruce leaned one way and then jerked another, sending a few ornaments crashing to the carpet. Upon impact, they shattered. Amanda feared Jeb might get angry.

"It's fine," he said. "I have too many decorations any-way."

He took a darling picture of the kitten peering out at them through the branches. Then he gently collected Frosty and deposited her in Chloe's waiting arms.

"How will we keep her from climbing up again?" Amanda asked him in a whisper.

"We can't," he replied, "but I know how to keep her from making the tree fall over."

His solution was fishing line, which he wound around the top of the trunk and tacked to the wall. It was nearly invisible, and the next time Frosty went for a climb, the spruce remained stable.

"A trick of my dad's," Jeb explained as they laughed at Frosty's antics. "Mom always had cats, and they all had high aspirations."

Amanda sighed and smiled. This was one of the most wonderful nights of her life.

"Thank you, Mr. Jeb," said Chloe. "Now my kitty won't get into trouble."

Jeb handed the child his cell phone and showed her how to take a picture of Frosty. It turned out so cute that he grinned. "You know what I think?"

"What?" Chloe asked.

"I think we should print that picture and hang it on your bedroom wall. Frosty's your first kitten, isn't she?"

"Yes!" Chloe clapped her hands. "And Bozo is my very first dog. I had a tiny puppy once, but not for very long. Can I have Bozo's Christmas tree picture on my wall, too?"

Jeb managed a half-convincing scowl. "Whoa. I thought Bozo was *my* dog."

"He is your dog," Chloe conceded, "but he likes me lots, too. I hoped maybe you might share him with me."

With a grin, Jeb tousled her dark hair. "Now there's a plan. We'll split him, fifty-fifty."

After they hung the popcorn garland on the spruce tree, Bozo grabbed an end and started to eat it. Amanda laughed until she almost cried. The expression on Jeb's face was priceless.

After getting Chloe into bed, with Bozo stretched out beside her and Frosty cuddled in her arms, Amanda went back downstairs. She found Jeb sitting on the sofa gazing into the fire. He had poured them each a snifter of brandy. As he handed her a glass, he said, "Now it's time for the adult version of the party."

Gazing down at his burnished face and twinkling hazel eyes, Amanda realized that she could easily fall in love with this gentle giant of a man. Strike that. She was already in love with him. Maybe it was true that the way to a woman's heart was through her child. He was so wonderful with Chloe, a natural-born father, the kind of dad Amanda wished her daughter had had since birth. Madness. She was in love with Jeb.

Keeping distance between them, Amanda joined him on the sofa and warmed the glass between her palms. "I can't think how to thank you for making this day so special for me and Chloe. My daughter's previous Christmases have been grim affairs."

Jeb swirled his glass. "Christmas has always been a special time in my family. Even as a bachelor, I've decorated and put up a tree. Some years, I haven't bothered with outside lights or putting the Nativity scene on the lawn. Mostly there's no one here but me to enjoy the extras."

"That won't be the case this year. All of this is pure magic to Chloe."

"Are you going to go all stubborn on me if I buy gifts?" He shifted closer and looped an arm over the sofa behind her, the tips of his fingers brushing her shoulder. "I've never had a little girl to buy for, so you'll have to bear with me because I'm really looking forward to it."

Amanda felt his forefinger circle over her blouse, a light, tantalizing caress. How could he set her skin afire with so innocent a touch? She tried to focus on the conversation. "You've already done too much. I owe you for the ten-thousand-dollar retainer fee, the phone, and so many other things I've lost track."

He took a sip of brandy, continuing the almost imperceptible motion on her shoulder with his free hand. "I love that kid. Let me enjoy spoiling her a little bit." He gave Amanda his best stab at a fierce scowl. "Quit being such a scrooge, Mandy Marie."

She laughed and took a taste of her drink.

Jeb wiped her brain clean by saying, "I'm also in love with Chloe's mommy. I finally slipped on the banana peel. Head over boot heels, totally in love. I hope you aren't going to feel uncomfortable now that I've admitted it."

He took her snifter and set it with his on the gorgeous coffee table. With a jerk of her stomach, Amanda realized that he intended to kiss her.

Chapter Sixteen

Sex with her husband had been such a nightmare that even though Amanda had deep feelings for Jeb, she felt a stab of panic. Her misgivings must have shown in her expression, because he framed her face with his hands and whispered, "I'm not Mark."

He bent his head and feathered his lips over hers, initiating a kiss that was sweet, lingering, and arousing. Amanda had experienced desire once, but it had happened so long ago that feeling it again, this *strong*, was unsettling.

When Jeb drew away, he smiled and said, "Wow. No, let me restate that. *Big* wow. I've kissed a lot of women, but I never felt this way with any of them." He toyed with a tendril of hair at her temple, which she recognized as an attempt to soothe her, but instead it only gave her that fluttery, hot feeling low in her belly again. "Now when you wonder how it might feel if I kissed you, you'll have a sample to remember."

"Don't forget I'm still married." *That was a stupid thing to say,* she thought. He was financing her divorce.

His grin broadened. "Married, but soon to be free.

And as far as I'm concerned, your union with Mark was never a marriage. Instead, you spent nearly seven years in a concentration camp."

Amanda couldn't think how to reply, and Jeb saved her the necessity by reclaiming their snifters and proposing a toast. "Merry Christmas, Mandy. May this be the first of many we enjoy together."

She couldn't refuse to take a sip of the brandy, so she toasted to their future.

The next morning, Amanda awakened with a new resolve. From this moment forward, she refused to worry about Mark or allow him to ruin this Christmas, too. After making breakfast and cleaning up, she and Chloe helped Jeb hang outside lights.

Bozo gave no indication that Mark was anywhere around, and Amanda drew comfort from that. The dog had proven that he sensed danger. Mark hadn't made any unusual noises when he'd gained entry to Jeb's home, yet Bozo had known someone evil was present in the house.

Jeb's eaves were two stories off the ground and slick from the silver thaw. Amanda's job was to steady the ladder while he strung lights over hooks he left screwed into the overhang from year to year. He didn't seem frightened when the ladder wobbled, but Amanda was terrified for his safety.

"Don't worry, honey. If it goes sideways, I'll grab the roof and wait for you to get it back under me." He began to sing, "'You'd better watch out! You'd better not shout! Santa Claus is coming to town!'"

Chloe frowned up at him. "My daddy doesn't believe in Santa."

Jeb cast the child a warm look. "I'm not your daddy,

princess. And I *do* believe in Santa. Heck, I've even met him!"

Chloe's eyes went round. "You have?"

"Of course I have."

"Where?"

"He comes here every December and sits in the Mystic Menagerie to let children tell him what they want for Christmas."

Chloe's eyes went even rounder. "Is that where the merry-go-round is?"

Jeb laughed. "You nailed that one, only I never thought of it as a merry-go-round."

"Mommy says someday when she's rich, she'll take me there to eat! Do you think, maybe, if we didn't spend any money on food, I could go there to meet Santa?"

Jeb strung another section of lights and started to descend the ladder. "Absolutely not."

Chloe's face fell.

Jeb reached the ground and swept the little girl into his arms. "We can't go to the merry-go-round place without eating food! What fun would that be?"

Chloe gazed up at him with incredulity stamped all over her face. "Are you rich enough for us to eat there? We only go to Taco Joe's."

Jeb planted a kiss on her cheek and swung her back to the ground. Looking on, Amanda had to admit her daughter was beyond adorable in her pink snow outfit. Little wonder Jeb had lost his heart to her.

"I can afford to take you there for lunch every day of the week," Jeb said. "That doesn't mean I'm rich, though, only well-fixed."

"What does well-fixed mean?"

He bent over to get eye-to-eye with her. "It means

that, within reason, I can afford to do fun stuff. I know you haven't seen me do much work, because I already finished all the Christmas orders and this is my off season unless a late request comes in. But in February or March, I'll get heaps of orders, and people pay me lots of money for the stuff I make."

Chloe shot Amanda a sideways glance, as if asking for permission to push for a merry-go-round meal, plus meeting Santa. Amanda didn't have it in her to wag her head no. All she could do was smile. Around Jeb, she found herself doing that often.

Chloe loved setting up the life-size Nativity scene in Jeb's front yard. She wanted to put Baby Jesus in the manger, but Jeb explained that they needed to wait until Christmas morning, when it was officially Jesus's birthday. Chloe was disappointed, but Jeb distracted her by powering up the icicle lights strung along the eaves. It was nearly dusk, and with snow on the roof, the house looked like a winter wonderland postcard. Holding hands, the three of them stood at the edge of the road, Chloe hugging Jeb's leg with her free arm. Taking the child's cue, Jeb wiggled his fingers free of Amanda's and curled a hard arm around her waist.

Locked together, they gazed at the house like first-time visitors to the Grand Canyon.

Moments later, as Jeb guided his ladies onto the front porch, he saw a pink slip of paper caught in a bush at the corner of his house. It was the first message he'd seen on his land since Amanda had come to stay.

"I just thought of something I didn't put away," he told them. "Set the system, and I'll be with you in a minute."

When the door closed behind them, Jeb went to collect the message. *He kissed me last night, and it was so wonderful it terrified me.* Jeb crumpled the note, pleased that she'd enjoyed the kiss but disappointed that she'd found it frightening.

Chloe's birthday fell on December 22, and Amanda, accustomed to being flat broke all the time and unable to buy the child very much, hadn't spared a thought for what gifts to get her. She wasn't used to having extra money to spend on frivolities. After the child was in bed one evening, she joined Jeb at the kitchen table for their nightly libation.

"Chloe's birthday is right around the corner," she announced with a trill of panic in her voice. After mentioning the date, Amanda added, "I'm not used to having money to buy her gifts, and it just hit me like a ton of bricks that this year can be totally different. She'll be seven, and I'd like to throw her a real party. This'll be her very first one."

His brows drew together in a frown. In the golden glow of the overhead lights, his hair looked nearly the same color as the liquor in his snifter. "You still have plenty of time to buy her heaps of presents, Mandy, but this is no time to invite kids over for a party. With Mark on the loose, we'd be endangering any child who came to the house."

The moment he spoke, Amanda knew he was right. Her stomach felt as if it dropped to somewhere around her ankles. *No party? Poor Chloe.* She seemed destined never to have a proper birthday celebration.

"It's a really bad time of year for a party, anyway," Jeb went on. "Adriel was born on the twenty-first, and her birthday always got lost in the shuffle. Few parents can work a party into their schedules right before Christmas. My mother finally started celebrating Adriel's birthday on May seventh. My maternal grandmother was born on that day."

"Chloe already knows her birth date. I can't change it on her now."

"We can still celebrate on the actual day. We'll just postpone the party until later."

Amanda bent her head to study the amber depths of her drink. Even from a distance, Mark was once again ruining Chloe's special day.

"Hey," Jeb murmured. "Look at me."

Amanda locked gazes with him.

"This is really important to you, isn't it?"

Voice taut, she said, "I know it's risky to throw a birthday party now, but it still hurts my heart. Now that I have a little money to spend, I'd like to do it up right for her this year." She shrugged and gazed beyond him at nothing. "When will my daughter ever have a normal life?"

He sighed and swirled his brandy. "Okay. We'll make it happen." He looked up at her. "I'll call Barney and arrange for a gaggle of deputies to guard the house during the party so Mark can't breach our perimeters. But we have to keep it small, Mandy. Please invite only her best friend. What's her name? I forget."

"Molly." Amanda took a sip of her brandy, too upset to enjoy the taste. "Only one child can come? It won't be much of a party."

"We'll make the most of it. I'll even hire a clown. I can't have a bunch of kids here. They'd be running in all directions. One or two might even slip outside. We can't put innocent children at risk."

Mark couldn't get to Amanda or Chloe right now, but he wouldn't hesitate to do collateral damage if he saw an opportunity. Amanda knew that he'd stop at nothing to get even with her. Her skin crawled at the thought of him hiding on the property and nabbing a child who happened to pass him.

Amanda glanced over her shoulder at the kitchen monitor.

"He's not out there," Jeb assured her. "That's why I always sit at this side of the table. I can see the monitor as we talk."

If any motion was detected, a red frame popped up around that zone. They often got false alerts due to their own movements inside the house or because of Jeb's livestock wandering around their pens. With a quick study of the highlighted picture, they could make sure no danger was afoot. One evening while they ate supper, a bull elk had been the culprit, and Chloe, never having seen an elk, had been captivated.

"It's like living under house arrest. Will we ever get past this?" Amanda asked.

A smile tugged at the corners of Jeb's mouth. "Sure. I know you think Mark will never turn loose of it, but I believe he will eventually. We've crippled him. He can't get a high by hurting one of you. And he *craves* that, *needs* it. Over time, he'll find another victim to feed his addiction."

"I hope you're right." Realizing what she'd just said, she added, "How horrible. I wouldn't wish Mark on anyone."

"Whatever he does in the future isn't your fault, Mandy. If he finds himself another woman to beat on, that'll be his sin, not yours."

"I know. I just hate to think that we'll be safe only at the expense of someone else."

Jeb reached across the table to trail a fingertip over her wrist. As always, his touch electrified her skin, only now she was starting to yearn for more. "Then don't think about it," he said. "Focus on Chloe's party instead. My family will show. We'll have a clown, a cake, gifts, and all the trimmings. To you, it may seem small, but to Chloe, who's never had a party, it'll be a big deal." He lifted his glass to her. "If this is all over in May, we'll have a huge bash. I'll hire a clown *and* rent ponies. Kids her age love pony rides."

Amanda couldn't help but smile. "How do you know what kids her age love?"

He chuckled, the rich, deep sound curling around her like a warm blanket. "I've seen kids going nuts over pony rides at our summer fairs. I was also a seven-year-old once and I loved my pony."

He took a sip of brandy. "If you're hoping Molly will attend the party, you should call her mom in the morning so she can put the date on her calendar."

Amanda nodded. "What if there's a glitch in getting some deputies to stand guard?"

He grinned and rubbed his fingertips together. "No glitch. I'll make it worth their while. It won't cost much, and after Molly leaves, we can tip them with dinner. I reserve the right to remove my party hat before I invite them in, however. I'll act like a goof for the kids, but when men outside my family enter the house, all bets are off."

"*You* plan to wear a cone hat with squiggly bits on top?"

He laughed. "Of course. For Chloe, I'm up for anything."

Amanda believed he truly was.

"In future, though, let's do a bigger party in May. Is that a deal? She'll be happy, and so will I until she turns sixteen. Then I may have a coronary, worrying about boys."

She cast him a curious look. "You talk as if we'll all be together far into the future."

He caught her hand and pressed a quick kiss to her knuckles. The silken brush of his lips over her skin made her heart skip a beat. "That's my plan."

The following evening, Jeb announced that tomorrow they'd go for a merry-go-round lunch and a visit with Santa. Chloe got so excited that Amanda had to read her four stories before getting her to sleep. The next morning, Chloe hit the floor and bounced around like a yo-yo. Amanda could barely manage to get her dressed.

"You need to calm down, sweetness."

Her eyes as round as dimes, Chloe cried, "But, Mommy, today I get to meet Santa! And Mr. Jeb is buying us lunch on the merry-go-round!"

Amanda knew how thrilling that was for Chloe. She'd never gotten to sit on Santa's knee, and she'd long wished to eat at Dizzy's Roundtable Restaurant. Crouching to fuss with her daughter's hair, Amanda said, "I know it's *very* exciting, but if you don't calm down, you'll forget to tell Santa what you want for Christmas!"

Chloe shook her head. "Nope! I know exactly what I want most, and I won't forget."

"And what is that?"

Chloe made a face. "I can't tell *you*, Mommy. I can only tell Santa."

Amanda's heart squeezed. If Chloe didn't reveal her

Christmas wish, she might not get what she wanted. "Sometimes," she tried, "Santa needs a little help from mommies."

She shook her head. "Mr. Jeb says Santa has heaps of helpers, elves making toys and Mrs. Claus keeping track of children's wish lists so he doesn't forget anybody."

Amanda needed to have a talk with Mr. Jeb.

He had already started breakfast when they got downstairs. He prepared Amanda a coffee with cream and sugar, just the way she'd come to like it, and then he made Chloe hot chocolate with miniature marshmallows. Amanda sipped her java while she helped finish the meal. Chloe sat at the table, writing down her Christmas wishes. When Amanda sidled close, the child covered the list.

Under her breath, Amanda informed Jeb of her dilemma. He grinned and bent low to whisper, "You worry too much. I'll take care of it. The secret is a tip."

"A what?"

He grinned. "A tip, as in a gratuity. If I slip Santa a twenty, he'll spill his guts."

Amanda almost choked on an unexpected giggle.

It was gratifying for Amanda hours later when Jeb was the one in a panic. After tipping Santa to share Chloe's Christmas wishes, Jeb gave Amanda and Chloe a tour of the menagerie, briefly visiting Treasure Adventure Antiques, Mystical Confections, a couple of travel agencies, Betty's Hair Affair, and the Morning Grind, a coffee and pastry shop. Except for the hair salon and bookstore, the places of business were operated by enterprising young people ranging in ages from mid-twenties to early thirties.

The last stop before having lunch at the revolving round table was Old and Antiquarian Books, a cavernous place rumored to be haunted by the ghost of a man who'd been killed on that spot years ago when the sawmill was still running. As Chloe scampered ahead of them to see Pop, real name Paul Kutz, an old man who seemed to live his life between the pages of musty books, Jeb drew Amanda to a stop.

"We've got trouble. She wants a dollhouse, complete with furniture and residents."

Amanda smiled. "That's doable. We can order everything online." Now that she'd received her first bimonthly payment from Jeb, she felt borderline rich. No outlays for rent, utilities, or groceries! Amanda couldn't say the sky was the limit for Chloe this Christmas, but she had enough money to make sure the child had lots of birthday presents and Santa gifts under the tree. "I'm sure you can get furniture and dolls online as well."

He looked appalled. "My father built my sisters' dollhouses and made all the furniture. My mom helped him decorate and got the dolls, complete with outfits." He studied her face. "Don't you get it? It needs a yard. It needs stuff on the porch. It needs landscaping. Hello, it has to look *real*, only in miniature."

At that moment, Amanda completely lost her heart to this tall, wonderful man. "All right. We can make that happen."

Jeb arched an eyebrow. "We don't have much time, Mandy. It'll be a lot of work."

"I'll help."

"Deal." Jeb's brows drew together. "For Sarah, Dad got a dollhouse kit, but it took hours to assemble, and then he had to glue the precut furniture pieces together."

Amanda glanced after Chloe, feeling uneasy. With all

the precautions Jeb had taken, she had been able to forget Mark for large blocks of time, but being careless was foolish. "We're letting our guard down," she told Jeb.

"My guard isn't down, Mandy. Three deputies in plain clothes are tailing us. They have Mark's face memorized, and they're watching for him." He sprang into a long-legged trot and headed in Chloe's direction. "I'll go get her, though."

Amanda looked around the cavernous building and immediately spotted Barney. He wore jeans, a ball cap, and a green parka, under which, she felt sure, was a police-issue gun. When he caught her studying him, he winked at her.

Amanda was about to race after Jeb when her cell phone rang. She drew the device from her pocket to see that it was Clyde Johnson calling. The conversation was short and to the point. The divorce hearing would take place on January 11. He had no doubt that Amanda would succeed in denying Mark unsupervised visitation, but this wouldn't be a trial for his criminal offenses, only a dissolution of the marriage.

"What does that mean, exactly?" she asked.

Johnson answered, "It means that even if he loses, he'll still be at large and royally pissed."

Amanda's shoulders slumped under a crushing dread.

"I got this on the court dockets three months early by calling in a favor from the judge," Johnson continued. "If she rules that Mark isn't allowed unsupervised visitations, he won't be able to file for temporary visitation privileges with Chloe before the divorce is final."

Amanda clung to those words. "Thank you, Mr. Johnson. Protecting Chloe is the most important thing."

"You sound as if you're pretty shaken up. Don't get

nervy. By the time you take the stand, you'll be so well briefed you'll slam-dunk your testimony."

Amanda expressed her gratitude, but the moment they hung up, she went into a panic. The hearing date wasn't that far away. Despite the restraining order, Mark could legally show up in court to argue his case, and she knew he wouldn't miss a chance to torment her. That meant she'd have to testify with him in the room. He'd smirk when she told the truth. Then he'd lie through his teeth and put her through sheer hell.

The wonder of Christmas seemed to have slipped through her fingers and been lost to her. *No.* She wouldn't let Mark ruin this holiday. She *wouldn't*.

After bringing his ladies back from the Mystic Menagerie, Jeb took Bozo out for a quick potty run. He circled the house, looking for pink slips of paper. His search didn't go unrewarded. Pressed against the south end of the concrete foundation, he found a message. *Every day, I grow more attracted to him. At night while we talk, I almost tell him, and then I chicken out. I'm afraid he'll interpret it as an invitation to make love to me, and as much as I want that, the thought still makes my insides go cold.*

Jeb smiled, sad and happy at once. It was good that she felt attracted to him, but it was a shame she was afraid to share her feelings. *Two can play this game.* Jeb folded her message and tucked it in his pocket. Later, when he found a moment alone in his office, he wrote on the back of her note. *Be careful when you toss messages into the wind. Do it fast, get back in the house, and reset the alarm.* He considered what to say next. *Don't stop writing the notes. I like finding them again. You can tell me things on paper that you aren't yet ready to say to me in person. You're beautiful. You're special. I want you. But anything worth having is worth waiting for, and you are definitely worth waiting for.*

Jeb sneaked upstairs to the bedroom Amanda shared with Chloe. He tucked his reply to her message under her pillow, where she'd find it that night when she turned in.

That evening after Chloe was asleep, Amanda found Jeb waiting for her at the table with their customary snifters of brandy. Instead of sitting across from him, she drew a chair around to sit beside him. Feeling the warmth of his body and smelling his cologne helped ease her anxiety as she told him about Johnson's call and the hearing date.

"I'm going to have to face him in the courtroom." Anger laced her mounting hysteria. "Even though he broke in here and meant to kill me, he's still free as a bird! And in January, not even the restraining order will be able to keep him away. He has a legal right to present his side before a judge."

"Hey, hey, hey," Jeb said, his voice husky and warm. "Come here."

Amanda felt his hard arm slip around her, and she moved toward him without hesitation, needing to feel his strength. She'd struggled to hold her feelings for him in check, but as she moved onto his lap and clung to him, she knew that not only had she lost the battle, but she didn't care. She'd fallen in love with this man, and she trusted him as she'd never trusted anyone. *Jeb.* He was everything she'd ever dreamed of, and more.

"It's going to be okay," he murmured against her hair.

"How? When he goes to trial in California, the judge may only slap his hand!" Amanda tried to control the shrill edge in her voice. "Chloe and I will never be safe."

"Here, with me, in Mystic Creek, you'll be safe." He shifted her weight so he cradled her more comfortably against him, and then lifting her altogether, he carried her to the living room. After settling on the sofa, he continued. "Remember how, when we first met, you couldn't understand our neighbor-helping-neighbor motto? Well, there's another underlying creed. Here in Mystic, we protect each other."

Amanda pressed her face against his neck, loving how the vibration of his voice thrummed through her as he informed her that the sheriff and all his deputies had spoken privately with Mark before he was released.

"I don't know precisely what each man said," he confessed, "but I do know Sheriff Adams told him never to enter the Mystic Creek city limits again. They'll give him a pass for the hearing in Crystal Falls, but if he comes to our town, he'll regret it."

"Can someone be forbidden from entering a town?"

Jeb chuckled. "By the letter of the law, I doubt it, but Sheriff Adams considers Mark a threat to your safety, and he'll fall back on the good-old-boy system. He'll tell his deputies to arrest Mark, even if they have to fabricate a reason."

"Fabricate?"

"I know it sounds bad, but if Mark comes here, he'll have malicious intent. A deputy may arrest him for breaking the restraining order and swear he caught Mark near this house even if he was two miles away. Mark will have a hard time proving that an officer is lying."

Amanda shuddered. "Mark will just have another forged letter from me, inviting him to come for visitation, and he'll be free in a blink."

"Nope. Adams submitted the original letter to a handwriting expert, and the guy sent back a document this morning declaring it a forgery. He says it was definitely not your writing."

Amanda frowned against his shirt. "But I never submitted any of my own writing so he could compare the faked against the real."

"I submitted a sample of your writing. It's amazing how useful a grocery list can be sometimes."

Amanda released a startled giggle. "You *stole* that grocery list? I looked for it all over."

"Sorry, but it was a perfect sample, showing how you form all your lowercase letters and a lot of uppercase. Why you capitalize the first letter of every item is a mystery, but I was glad of it. I slipped it to Barney the night he helped change the locks. He took it to the sheriff. We now have documented proof that Mark forged the first letter, and he'll never get away with that trick again. If he breaks the restraining order, Adams will be able to keep him in jail."

"For how long?"

"Up to six months, I think," Jeb replied. "Until the abuse trial, if we're lucky, and if he's found guilty then, he should do prison time."

Amanda sighed, amazed that he'd somehow managed to wipe away her mounting anxiety.

"What if he slips past our guard again without anyone in the sheriff's department realizing he's in town?"

Jeb pressed a kiss to the top of her head. Amanda realized that she wished those lips weren't being wasted on her hair. "I won't be unprepared for him again. Next time, Bozo will kill him if I don't get to him first."

"I hope Bozo isn't first. They might euthanize him."

Jeb chuckled. "Over my dead body. If a dog bites the

mailman, that's one thing. But if he goes after a killer, that's different. Sheriff Adams would probably award Bozo a medal and make him an honorary canine cop."

Amanda felt as if her bones had melted. "Have I told you that I love you?"

A brief silence followed. "Not in so many words."

"Well, I do, Jeb. I used to write my dreams on slips of paper and send them flying away on the wind. Now I have you, and all my dreams have come true."

His mouth curved in a smile. "I never sent my wishes flying away on the wind, but I did cling to what my mom always told me, that I'd find the woman of my dreams when I least expected it. And in a tumbledown house, I finally stumbled across her."

Amanda made fists on his flannel shirt, thinking that the cloth, sturdy and durable, was also soft and soothing against her skin, just like its owner. Now that declarations had been made, she expected and accepted that Jeb might want to seal the bargain with sex. But, no. He'd surprised her at every turn since she'd met him, and he didn't change tactics on her now.

"Have you called your mom yet?"

She squeezed her eyes closed. "I've tried, but I can't do it. It will be so hard to tell her everything over the phone. I won't see her face. She won't see mine. I lied to her, you know. Repeatedly. I wanted to keep her safely out of Mark's world. Before Dad died, I lied to him, too. My parents loved me. They adored Chloe. Daddy would have tried to take Mark on, and after he was gone, my mom would have done the same."

Jeb ran a big hand along her side, carefully avoiding her breast. That didn't lessen the fiery sensation that raced over her skin or prevent her nipples from pebbling. "You shouldn't blame yourself for protecting your parents. It was the right thing to do."

The guilt of having lied and covered for Mark had long eaten at her. "Do you really think so?"

"I know so." She hung there, waiting to hear the rest. "You tried the cops. That backfired. Way I see it, you got shanghaied. All you could do was wait for a port of call to jump ship. When you saw your chance, you got away."

Amanda needed to hear him say the words that she'd recently said to him. "I told you I love you, but you didn't say it back."

This time his chuckle was a deeper rumble. "I love you, Mandy, with my whole heart. And for me, your daughter is a part of the package."

"Chloe will be *so* upset."

She felt him go tense. "She will?"

"Oh, yes. Since moving to Mystic Creek, she firmly believes that true love can occur only when two people meet on the natural bridge."

His lips grazed her temple. "That's a twist on the actual legend. In truth, the story goes that any lonely stranger who stands along the stream or on the bridge will find true love. I'll be sure to set her straight. Or, once Mark is neutralized, we can meet on the bridge so she's convinced we've got the real deal."

Amanda absorbed those words. "Do you think we've found the real deal?"

She felt his muscles tighten around her. "Sweetheart, I'm willing to bet the rest of my life on it."

In Amanda's mind, this was when a man lifted a woman into his arms and carried her to bed. She felt nervous to the point of nausea, and yet another part of her was crestfallen when he only held her. In romances, this wasn't how it went.

Almost as if Jeb sensed her thoughts, he murmured, "You're not quite ready yet, Mandy. For now, let's get back to your mom. You need to call her."

"I dread it."

"I doubt you'll tell her anything she hasn't already suspected. Was she a loving mom?"

"The very best."

"Do you have her number on your phone?"

"Yes."

"Then why don't you bite the bullet and call her?"

Amanda knew he was right; it was time. She drew away from his embrace and stood. "Do you mind if I use your office? For this conversation, I'll need some privacy."

Jeb nodded, and Amanda adjourned to the other room. After closing the door, she took a deep breath and dialed her mother. Would she answer this time?

"Hello, Lang residence."

"Mom, it's me."

Emma gasped. "Oh, thank God. *Finally*. Are you all right? Is Chloe okay? My caller ID says Onrietta Parker. Talk to me, Mandy. Where has Mark taken you? Tell me all is well."

"I left him, Mom. We're finally safe."

The rest of the story poured from Amanda, not necessarily in chronological order. Emma didn't ask questions. She only listened, interjecting here or there.

When Amanda ran out of words, she realized her face was swollen and wet from crying. "I'm so sorry for all the times I lied and said things were fine."

"Don't worry about it. Dad and I knew something

wasn't right. All that matters now, sweetness, is that you're safe." She sighed. "So tell me about this Jeb fellow."

Amanda smiled through her tears. "He's wonderful." She told Emma how Jeb had stepped forward with the money to hire a great divorce attorney. "The best thing about him is that he expects nothing in return. I'd like to pay him back someday, but he doesn't want me to worry if I'm unable to."

"I can't wait to meet him. But I'm especially eager to see you and my granddaughter again. Chloe won't remember me." Emma's voice rang with sadness. "That'll break my heart."

"I can't travel to see you until Mark is behind bars. It isn't safe."

Emma agreed. "And with this bad hip, I don't think I can make the drive from Olympia down to see you. If I could afford it, I'd fly, but I'm stretched just to make it from payday to payday with a little extra. Your father left me some money for a rainy day, but toward the end, his illness ate most of it."

"I'm so sorry I couldn't be there. I didn't get your letter saying that he'd passed on until New Year's Eve, not that Mark would have let me attend the funeral, anyway."

"No more regrets," Emma said. "The past is behind us. Let's move forward."

After the call ended, Amanda sat in the office until she collected her composure. She found Jeb in the kitchen and gave him a recap of the conversation. He listened, nodding occasionally.

"I wish I could see her," Amanda told him. "Her hip is really hurting her now, though. She can't make the drive. We both agree that a visit will have to wait." She felt drained from the long talk with her mother. "Would you mind terribly if I don't finish my brandy and just go to bed?"

"Not at all," he said. "I hope you have sweet dreams."

Minutes later, Amanda slipped into bed beside her daughter and felt something crinkly under her pillow. She curled her fingers over the paper, recognizing the shape even in the darkness. *One of my notes. What's it doing under my pillow?*

Easing from under the covers, she crossed the room and crouched by the night-light to read the message. On one side, she saw her own writing. On the back was Jeb's masculine print. As she took in what he'd written, she smiled. "You're not quite ready yet," he'd told her downstairs, and now she understood how he'd known that.

She experienced a brief stab of embarrassment because he'd clearly been finding some of her recent messages wherever they'd landed outside. She'd poured her heart out in those missives, expressing her most secret thoughts and feelings. *Don't stop writing the notes. I like finding them again.* She smiled, appreciating that he'd left his reply under her pillow where she wouldn't miss it. Maybe she should follow his example. That way, only Jeb would read what she wrote.

She reached into the top dresser drawer for a pen and slip of paper, went to another bedroom for light, and wrote, *Thank you for being so patient and understanding. I want to feel ready. I* really *do. But something keeps holding me back.*

She crept downstairs and left the note in front of the coffee machine, the first place Jeb went when he woke up.

*   *   *

In the morning, Amanda grabbed her cell phone, which she'd charged on the nightstand, and hurried downstairs. Sitting at the kitchen table, Jeb saluted her with a mug and greeted her. Murmuring a reply, she placed her phone on the peninsula bar and moved to the coffee machine. Her note had been turned over, and Jeb had written on the back of it.

We aren't on a time schedule, Mandy. When we make love, I want you to have no reservations. Only then will it be perfect between us. I'm willing—no, determined—to wait for perfect.

Taking advantage of Amanda's distraction as she read his message, Jeb rose from the chair, grabbed her cell, and sent her mother's contact information to his iPhone.

She turned from the coffee center to beam a smile at him. "Maybe we should start saving these," she said, clutching the pink paper over her heart. "We're probably the first couple ever to fall in love by writing notes. Years from now, we can read them and remember every twist and turn of our relationship."

Jeb was glad to hear her say they had a relationship. "That's a great idea. For now, let's put them in the cookie jar. Around here, no cookie has a long enough life span to sit in a container anyway."

She laughed and did as he suggested.

That evening while Amanda was upstairs bathing Chloe and coaxing her to bed, Jeb slipped into his office, closed the door, and called Emma Lang.

"Hello." Uncertainty laced her voice. "Mandy?"

Jeb liked hearing someone else use Amanda's nickname. "No, this is Jeb Sterling, the man Mandy and Chloe are staying with. This may sound odd, but your daughter has no idea I'm calling you."

After a short get-acquainted session, Jeb got to the point. "I think you should fly down to spend Christmas with us here at my place, Emma."

"Oh, I can't afford—"

Jeb cut her off. "It'll be my Christmas present to Mandy. She really needs to see you. Of all the things I might get for her, I think she'll enjoy a visit with you the most."

"That's very kind of you."

"Not a bit. I'm in love with your daughter. Making her happy makes me happy."

Emma finally agreed to let Jeb purchase plane tickets to Redmond, just north of Bend. "I want it to be a surprise," Jeb stressed, "so Mandy won't know who we're picking up at the airport on Christmas Eve day. I'll say a friend is flying in."

Emma chuckled. "If she calls again, I won't tell her I'm coming. I love surprises, especially for someone I love."

Jeb was glad to have leaped that hurdle. "Mandy doubts that Chloe has any memory of you," he said. "I think Christmas will be much more enjoyable if your granddaughter can see you and talk with you several times before the holiday. So she'll know you by the twenty-fifth."

A long silence followed. Finally Emma said, "How on earth can we manage that?"

Jeb told her about placing video calls on a computer using Skype. Emma retorted that she had no computer and wouldn't know how to operate one if she did.

"I can have an inexpensive laptop sent to you by two-day mail, and when you get it, I can walk you through setting up Skype over the phone. Video calls are fabulous, Emma. Chloe will be able to see and hear you, and the same in reverse, almost as good as being in the same room together."

"Oh." There was a world of yearning in that word. "But I can't allow you to pay for my flight and buy me a laptop! I can afford to get Internet, but not a computer."

He grinned. Now he knew where Amanda got her stubborn pride. Luckily he'd become an expert at waltzing around it. By the time he ended the call, Emma had agreed to get Internet service and would eagerly await the arrival of the laptop.

Chapter Seventeen

Over the next two days, Chloe's Christmas wish list grew. Jeb figured that Amanda now had the money to handle those expenditures, and he helped her navigate the Net to order most of the gifts online, using his credit card and reimbursing him for the charges. They also went shopping in Mystic Creek. In addition to hiring three deputies to guard them, Jeb took Bozo along. Because of Bozo's overproduction of drool, Jeb left the dog just inside the doors and commanded him to stay. That way no merchandise would be inadvertently damaged, but the mastiff would still be right there if Mark showed up. None of the shop owners complained about the huge animal's presence. They'd all heard one version or another of Amanda's marriage, and knew that both woman and child were in possible danger.

The dollhouse kit Jeb had ordered arrived by express delivery. He chose one of the unused upstairs bedrooms as his work area, which allowed him to lock the door but still be within earshot if Amanda or Chloe needed him. When Chloe was awake, she couldn't burst in and see her surprise in various stages of construction. After the child went to bed, Amanda came in to help, but her time was limited.

"Oh, Jeb, I've never seen anything so adorable."

Jeb enjoyed every second of the imaginary reality he was creating for the girl. His mind swam with ideas as he glued shingles to the roof. "It's going to be awesome!"

On the third day after talking with Emma, Jeb called the woman again from the privacy of his office. The laptop had arrived, and Emma sounded panicky. Apparently she thought the computer might go haywire when she touched it. He calmed her down and guided her step by step to set up her wireless connection and then load Skype onto the machine. When they finally made screen-to-screen contact, Emma squealed in amazement.

"Omigosh, I can see you!" she cried.

Jeb chuckled. "Isn't it great?" He held up a staying hand. "Sit tight. Okay? Don't touch any buttons. I'm going to fetch your daughter and granddaughter."

Amanda had no idea why Jeb wanted her and Chloe in his office. When he pressed her into his castor chair and she saw her mother on the monitor, she started to cry. Then Emma sobbed. Jeb picked up Chloe.

"It's okay, honcy. That lady is your grandmother, and it has been a long time since your mommy has seen her. So they're crying happy tears."

Chloe studied her mother and the face on the screen. "They don't look happy," she pronounced, but even as she spoke, she squirmed to get down. Approaching shyly, she gave a start when she saw herself in a square at the bottom corner of the screen. "Hi," she said. "My name's Chloe."

Emma burst into tears all over again. "Oh, Mandy, she's so *beautiful*, the very picture of you at that age!"

Jeb rested his hip against an office counter, folded his arms, and enjoyed watching the conversation. Chloe overcame her shyness, and the next thing he knew, she was showing off her fluffy kitten, Frosty.

"Mr. Jeb, can you help me show Bozo to Grammy?"

Jeb turned the camera atop his monitor toward the dog, who was already snoozing on the office floor, his jowls splayed, gleaming wetness around his nose.

Chloe did the honors. "Grammy, this is my best friend, Bozo. He is my protector."

"My goodness, he's very big," Emma observed.

"Yes. He's a mastiff. Mr. Jeb says he weighs two hundred and thirty pounds! When my mean daddy broke into Mr. Jeb's house, Bozo was our SWAT team."

Emma laughed. Jeb, who hadn't heard that version of the story, grinned. He suspected that Chloe had seen a SWAT team on television or her mother had used the expression. When the camera was refocused on Amanda, Jeb caught Chloe's hand and slipped out of the room with her, saying, "Let's give your mommy some alone time with Grammy. Then you can come back to talk."

Chloe nodded. "May I have hot chocolate with mini marshmallows while I wait?"

That was a request Jeb could deliver on.

For Amanda, it was a fabulous conversation. She'd never felt free to talk honestly with her parents about Mark, but now that her dad was gone, she no longer feared a confrontation between them. She could at last look into her mom's eyes and tell her everything.

"I once saw bruises on your arm and suspected that

Mark had put them there," Emma confessed. "I wanted so badly to tell Dad, but like you, I feared he would fly into a rage, go after Mark, and get either seriously hurt or arrested. So I kept it to myself, a decision I've regretted ever since. Shortly thereafter, Mark spirited you two away to California. I had many sleepless nights, worrying about where you were and what he might be doing to you. I received only one letter from you in Eureka, and you made it sound as if everything was fine, but I knew it wasn't. You gave me no phone number, only your address. I tried to find Mark's number through information, but I couldn't."

"Mark allowed me no access to a phone. He had a cell, but he always carried it on him. I tried to sneak enough quarters from his pocket to call you collect from a pay phone, but he caught me. I did manage to steal enough to buy a stamp and write you that one letter."

"Oh, sweetness, I'm so sorry I wasn't there for you."

Amanda felt they'd both endured too much sorrow because of Mark. "The good news is, Mark will never hurt me or Chloe again. Jeb is a big man. His dog is a huge old love—unless someone threatens a member of his family. He's very like Jeb in that way." Amanda chose not to tell her mom that Mark had been carrying a gun when he broke into the house. "Now Jeb has installed a security system with camera surveillance. His network is protected with firewalls and strong passwords. Chloe and I are safe."

Emma sighed and briefly closed her eyes. Then she grinned. "You forgot to tell me how handsome Jeb is! If I were thirty years younger, he'd give me heart palpitations."

Amanda's throat went tight. "I'm in love with him.

And he says he loves me. But it seems so fast. Do you think I'm nuts for thinking about going to bed with him?"

Emma laughed, a long, from-the-gut peal of mirth. When she quieted, she said, "I gave you bad advice when you got pregnant by Mark. I don't want to make the same mistake again. But I have gotten to know Jeb. I think he's a wonderful guy."

"How have you gotten to know him?"

Emma confessed, "We've been chatting on the phone. He loves you, sweetie. I hear it in his voice."

Amanda had heard it in Jeb's voice as well—and seen it in his eyes.

With Christmas fast approaching, Jeb spent more and more time upstairs to finish Chloe's dollhouse. The little girl was accustomed to him working in his office, so she didn't seem suspicious when he vanished into another room. He'd found a miniature wiring kit and light fixtures online, along with other accessories. He used safe acrylic paints inside and out. Victorian in style with intricate trim, the house was mounted on a square of plywood and begged for a gingerbread-brown exterior with pink accents.

One afternoon, Kate and Jeremiah came to visit. As Jeb disarmed the security system, Chloe raced into the entry hall to greet them. Trailing after the child, Jeb unsnapped the holster strap of his Glock. Though he doubted Mark was anywhere near his property, he'd never be caught off guard again. "You can let them in now, sweetheart."

Excited, Chloe drew open the door. "Hi, Mimi and Pow-Pow!"

While Jeb's parents hugged the little girl, he reset the system on the entryway panel before accepting embraces himself.

Thrusting a paper sack into her son's hands, Kate whispered, "Yardage remnants for the you-know-what. Don't let Chloe see them."

Jeb took his mother's coat, and as he hung it in the guest closet, he tucked the bag behind his extra boots. Kate had already gone to the kitchen with Chloe when Jeb turned to take his father's jacket. "Pow-Pow? Where the heck did that come from?"

Jeremiah pulled off his stocking cap and smoothed his hair. "I think it started that first day when you called and told me to get out my guns. I hadn't fired any of them in a long while, so I needed to make sure the sights were still aligned. After your brothers got there, I went out behind the barn to shoot a few targets." He shrugged. "The sound of my rifle must have reached the house."

"Ah." Jeb chuckled. "So now you're Pow-Pow. It beats being called Bang-Bang."

"True."

That night, after Chloe fell asleep, Jeb and Amanda took the sack upstairs to look at the scraps of cloth Kate had brought.

"Oh, Jeb!" Amanda cried, keeping her voice low so as not to awaken Chloe. "This tiny rose pattern will make perfect wallpaper in a bedroom!"

From that point forward, Jeb had a partner with an eye for decorating who couldn't wait to get Chloe off to bed so she could help with the dollhouse. While Jeb added finishing touches to the interior, Amanda wielded needle and thread to make tiny bed linens, coverlets, bath towels, tablecloths, and throw pillows. Whispering and giggling like kids, they let their imaginations run wild.

One evening, Amanda circled the miniature house, studying it from every angle. "It's absolutely beautiful." She trailed her fingertips over the faux grass in the front yard and then leaned closer to examine the stepping-stones that led to the veranda, which sported a swing and two tiny rocking chairs. "How on earth did you make stepping-stones?"

"I used plaster of Paris and bottle caps as molds. Once the rounds were set, I popped them out of the caps, sponged on mottled gray paint, and glued them down."

"Very clever!"

She came to stand beside him and peered into the rooms. Her soft breast grazed his shoulder. It took all Jeb's control not to carry her to the bed and make love to her. All that held him back was his promise to wait. Amanda had lived through a nightmare most women couldn't begin to imagine, and Jeb didn't want to push her. When she was ready, she would give him the signal or tell him in a message. Until then, he'd keep his word—even if it killed him.

"Is that how you made the fireplace, with plaster?"

"Yes. All it takes is imagination to create a mold." He thumbed his iPhone to check the security cameras, a habit he'd cultivated because there was no monitor in the bedroom where he now worked. Because of the small screen, he had to scroll sideways to see all the camera shots displayed on the large monitors, but in seconds, he'd checked every view of the house, inside and out. "Next I need to focus on the backyard landscaping. What do you think about a fishpond? It'd be easy to make a mold, and I can fill it with clear resin, tinted blue, to make it look like water."

She laughed, the sound soft and musical. "I think Chloe is the luckiest girl in the world."

As the days swept by, Jeb's home became aromatic with the scents of Christmas baking. He often found money on his bedside table to pay him back for Amanda's credit card purchases. Nearly every afternoon, a UPS driver delivered packages. Jeb took them upstairs and stashed them in the closet. He had no idea where Amanda hid hers.

As a bachelor, Jeb had enjoyed the holidays, but never so much as this year. In nearly every room, Amanda had added decorative touches and scented candles. His office became the gift-wrapping station, with paper and bows scattered everywhere. Beribboned presents were stacked beneath the tree in the living room, and he often found Chloe crouched near the spruce, shaking or feeling packages that had her name on them. Stockings were hung from the juniper mantel, and one of them bore Jeb's name. *Oops*. He'd forgotten to order stocking stuffers.

Jeb helped Chloe go online to buy Mommy a present. It wasn't quite as enjoyable as taking the child shopping in town, but he was reluctant to push his luck on that front.

"This is so fun!" Chloe exclaimed. "Mommy will love having new jammies."

Jeb would have preferred sexy lingerie over flannel, but if and when Amanda slipped into his bed, he wouldn't complain if she wore burlap.

*   *   *

That night when Amanda joined Jeb upstairs, she noticed that new dollhouse accessories had appeared. A tiny skillet sat on a stove burner. Miniature dishes filled the cupboard shelves. A rolling pin and a cookbook lay on the counter. Even a mailbox, mounted on a post, stood at the edge of the front lawn, and when Amanda lowered the flap, she found miniature envelopes inside.

"Oh, Jeb. How much have you spent on all this stuff? It must have cost a fortune."

"I haven't kept track, and I don't plan to worry about it. This is Chloe's Santa gift, and it's her first Christmas without Mark the Scrooge spoiling it for her. If you want to help, you can make curtains." He inclined his head at the interior of the dollhouse. "I installed the rods this afternoon."

Amanda bent low to see. "Oh, how darling! Where did you find brass ones?"

He grinned. "Online, you can find just about anything." His smile faded. "Have you ordered any Christmas gifts for your mom yet?"

"No." Amanda's stomach clenched. "Oh, Jeb, I never even thought of that. It's been so many years since — "

"It's not too late. Order her something, and after you get it wrapped, I'll ask Barney to take it to Pack and Mail in the town center. They'll overnight it to her."

Amanda hurried downstairs to Jeb's office. A gift for her mom. She wasn't sure what size Emma wore now, so clothing was out. She remembered that her mom loved to drink her coffee from dainty teacups with matching saucers, so she searched for china. The pattern she loved was embellished with mauve roses and real gold trim. The cup and saucer cost nearly seventy dollars.

She jumped with a start when Jeb spoke from behind her. "That's gorgeous."

"I think she'd love it," Amanda replied. "But it's frightfully expensive."

"Walk on the wild side. It's Christmas."

Amanda laughed and ordered the item.

Two days later, when the ornate china arrived, Amanda gift-wrapped it in the office before starting dinner. When the meal was over, she returned to box the package for mailing. But the present had vanished. She looked everywhere, questioning her sanity. She'd left it by Jeb's computer monitor, hadn't she? She retraced her steps to the kitchen, thinking she might have set the package somewhere else. Jeb saw her wandering around and asked what she was looking for.

"My mom's Christmas gift. I thought sure I left it by your computer."

"I'm sorry, honey. I saw that you had it wrapped, so I already handed it off to Barney so he can send it out for us tomorrow."

Amanda hadn't heard the doorbell ring.

Jeb added, "You were busy cooking, and Barney didn't have time to come in and say hello. He's working the late shift tonight."

"But the present isn't boxed."

"At Pack and Mail, the owner takes care of that. I gave Barney your mother's address. Gerry will even make sure the bows don't get smashed." He started up the stairs. "I'm going to vanish for a while. I'll enjoy your company if you join me later."

Amanda frowned. "How did you get my mom's address?"

He paused with a broad, sun-bronzed hand on the banister. "She gave it to me so I could send her the laptop."

"What laptop?"

"The one she uses to Skype you. She had no computer, so I ordered her a cheap one."

Amanda's shoulders sank. "You shouldn't have done that. I already owe you so much. I'm in debt up to my eyebrows."

He winked at her. "Getting your mom set up with Skype is part of my Christmas gift to you and Chloe this year. The keyword in that sentence is *gift*. You don't owe me a dime for the laptop."

"But I—"

"And you have to admit it was a great gift," he went on. "Traveling to see your mom would be unsafe right now, but this way, Chloe can get to know her grandmother. And you can reconnect with Emma. I think that's special for all of you."

Amanda's throat went tight. "It's very special. I didn't know you made it happen by buying my mom a laptop." She shoved her hands into the pockets of her jeans. "Thank you."

Kate called Amanda the next morning to suggest that the family should celebrate Adriel's and Chloe's birthdays at the same time. "Adriel loves the idea, and she's happy to have the party on Chloe's birthday instead of her own."

Amanda was caught off guard. She couldn't recall mentioning to Kate that Chloe would turn seven on the twenty-second. Jeb must have said something. "I love the idea, Kate, but I've already invited Chloe's friend Molly to attend a party here."

Kate laughed. "That's fine, as long as you don't mind the entire Sterling family gathering at your house."

Amanda almost said this wasn't her house, but Kate moved ahead with plans. "I was thinking we could do the cake and open presents in the afternoon. Jeb says he's already booked a clown, which the little girls should enjoy. Then when all the folderol is over, we can have a casual dinner. Maybe the guys could grill some hot dogs and burgers. Jeb has that nice overhang over his barbecue, so the weather won't matter."

"Chloe loves hot dogs," Amanda replied. The child also loved Jeb's family. For the first time in her short life, she had doting grandparents and aunts and uncles. "I think she would love sharing her party with Adriel. They hit it off on Thanksgiving."

"It's a deal then! We'll keep it simple. I'll bring the cake and ice cream. I'll ring everyone else and tell them to bring chips and dip."

"I could make a potato salad," Amanda offered.

"Sounds good. What arrival time did you give Molly's mother?"

"Two." Amanda recalled Jeb's mentioning that he would hire a clown, but she hadn't known he'd actually made the arrangements. "I thought that would give the girls a couple of hours to have a good time and Molly could still get home for dinner."

"We'll be there at two then." Kate paused. "I might show up a little early to help you get set up. This will be so much fun. I haven't gotten to do a kid's birthday party in years."

After ending the call, Amanda stared blindly at the granite countertop with a smile curving her lips.

*   *   *

Chloe's birthday was upon them in no time. On the morning of the twenty-second, Amanda awakened feeling as excited as Chloe would be when her feet hit the floor. And Jeb had made it possible. Going over to the dresser, Amanda drew out her tablet to write him a note.

I'm standing on a boulder now instead of a cliff, and I know you'll catch me in your arms when I jump. I'm not only ready, but I need you to make love to me.

After dressing, Amanda took the slip of paper downstairs with her and laid it in front of the coffee machine. Jeb was already having his first cup of coffee at the table, but she knew he would refill his mug. When he did, he would find her message. Her heart skittered when she turned to meet his gaze. He grinned and winked at her.

As promised, Kate came early to help Amanda set up. Under her breath, she told Amanda that there were three deputies standing guard outdoors.

"Jeb arranged that," Amanda replied. "He's paying them to do it."

"I doubt it. They're all Barney's friends and probably told Jeb to keep his money."

Within seconds laughter filled the house. At two o'clock, Molly arrived, looking adorable in a light blue dress. For once, Amanda didn't feel that Chloe was outclassed, because she had ordered her daughter a pink birthday frock and matching patent leather shoes. The dress, sporting a deep rose sash, had a silk cap-sleeve bodice with a tea-length skirt of ruffled organza. With her dark curls tumbling around her shoulders, Chloe looked like the princess Jeb often called her.

Adriel and Sarah arrived shortly after Molly, and then Jeb's brothers and dad walked in. Jeb gave up on resetting the security system until the clown arrived. For some reason, Amanda had been expecting a man to fill the role, but Rocky Allen, a petite woman with wildly curly, bright red hair, turned out to be delightful. She wore billowing crimson pants, a garish polka-dot top, a conical hat, a bulbous red nose to complement her painted face, and floppy, oversize shoes. Apparently a gymnast who'd missed her calling, she utilized Jeb's roomy home to do cartwheels and backflips, executing the moves with graceful precision until she deliberately bungled one and sprawled on the floor. The seams of her britches were held together with Velcro, allowing her to split them during her falls, whereupon she would gasp, try to cover herself, and finally enlist the aid of Molly and Chloe to help her.

Enchanted, the girls insisted Rocky join everyone at the large dining room table for birthday cake. When the candles were lighted, the clown yelled, "Fire!" and hurried over to extinguish them. Jeb, going along with the game, explained that after making a wish, the birthday girl had to blow out all the candles with only one breath.

Face aglow, Chloe knelt on a chair in front of her cake and gave both Jeb and Amanda a long, wistful look before squeezing her eyes closed to make her wish. Amanda felt heat pool in her cheeks. Every adult in the room had to know what the child yearned for—not just a pretend family but a real one. The clown made a great show of trying to maneuver her fork past her gigantic nose, making the girls giggle even as they ate.

Amanda had planned games as the next activity, hoping to burn off the sugar both girls had consumed. To her surprise, the Sterling family joined in. The men looked silly playing ballet freeze. The back-to-back balloon pop elicited hysterical laughter. Then they played Pin the Tail on the Donkey.

Chloe grew so excited she trembled as she sat with Adriel to open gifts. Jeremiah and Kate got the child a play kitchen. Jeb's brothers gave Chloe fake foods and toy kitchen appliances. Adriel and Sarah went in together on a child-size table with two chairs and a tea set. Amanda's gift for Adriel was a basket filled with scented soaps, bath salts, a wineglass, fine dark chocolate, and a bottle of Merlot. She got her daughter a life-size baby doll complete with a receiving blanket, diapers, outfits, and a feeding bottle.

After the party ended, everyone helped with cleanup, and Jeb fired up the gas barbecue. The family gathered once again at the dining room table to share the evening meal. As Amanda helped Chloe add relish to her hot dog, she heard Jeremiah murmur to Jeb, "She's a keeper, son."

Kate overheard the comment and didn't bother to keep her voice down. "If he lets this one get away, he needs his head examined. Never have I seen two people more right for each other."

Once again, Amanda's cheeks went hot with embarrassment. Jeb noticed and winked at her.

That night after Chloe was tucked into bed with Frosty and Bozo, Amanda found Jeb waiting for her in the kitchen. The dollhouse was finished, and he'd recently resumed their nightly ritual of sharing a brandy. Two filled snifters sat on the round table, one on either side of a lighted candelabra. Startled by the formality, Amanda sought his gaze, and what she read in his eyes made her steps falter.

"What's the occasion?" she asked.

He motioned for her to sit beside him instead of taking her usual place across from him. After sliding one of the snifters toward her, he took a sip from his own. Amanda noticed a slip of pink paper lying near her snifter. With a fingertip, she drew it toward her.

Jeb had written, *I've made no secret of my feelings for you, Mandy, and at one point, you told me that you love me, too.*

An aching sensation spread through her chest. Looking up at him, she whispered, "It's true. I've come to love you with all my heart."

He looked deeply into her eyes and slid another note toward her that read, *Why are we stuck in this holding pattern? I know you're still legally bound to Mark, but I'm confident you'll be granted a dissolution of the marriage on January eleventh. There may be a brief waiting period for the divorce to be final, but then you'll be totally free.*

Amanda locked gazes with him. "Where are you going with this, Jeb? And why are you slipping me notes instead of just talking to me?"

He shrugged. "It's become a tradition."

She held his gaze. "I'm assuming you read my most recent message then?"

He smiled that wonderful smile that always made her feel as if the sun had broken through a cloud. "Yes. It was the invitation I've been waiting for, a sign from you that you're ready. But if I'm going to ask you to stay in my life, it seems to me I should hold with the tradition that brought us together in the first place, asking you in a message." Another pink slip rested beneath his fingertips. "There's no law against a woman being engaged to another man before the dissolution of her marriage is final, right?"

He slid the last piece of paper toward her. With trembling fingers, Amanda took it and read through a blur of tears, *Will you, Mandy Marie Lang, do me the great honor of becoming my wife?*

She blinked. Stared at the words. She was about to say, "Oh, yes," when he cut her off with, "You heard my parents today. We're perfect together. I don't want to push you into anything or make you feel trapped. But leaving so many words between us unspoken is—well, it makes me feel as if there's nothing solid that I can hang on to. You've said nothing to indicate that you plan to stay with me. You never speak of the future or say the word *forever*. And because you don't, I'm constantly curbing my tongue, afraid I'll scare you off if I say something wrong."

The last thing Amanda wanted was to make this wonderful man feel insecure.

He slid off the chair and went down on one knee beside her. Another rush of tears burned in Amanda's eyes as she swiveled to face him. Grasping both her hands, he said, "Mandy Lang, will you marry me?"

Amanda appreciated that he used her maiden name. It gave her a sense of identity that had been stripped from her.

She trailed her gaze over Jeb's sun-burnished countenance and said, "Under my clothing, I have scars all over me, Jeb. Wouldn't it be wiser on your part to see what you're getting before making a lifetime commitment to me?"

He released her hands to cup her face between his palms. "I know you have scars, Mandy. I saw all those photographs."

"So why—"

He cut her off. "I love you," he whispered. "All of you,

every inch of you, scars included. So I'll ask you again. Will you marry me?"

"Yes," she pushed out.

Jeb drew a small velvet box from his shirt pocket. Inside was the most gorgeous wedding set Amanda had ever seen. He slipped the engagement ring onto her left hand. A large center diamond surrounded by petal-shaped sapphires created a dazzling flower. "Oh, Jeb, this is so *beautiful*. It fits perfectly."

"Not nearly as beautiful as you are. And your mom told me your size. I ordered it from a fine-jewelry site online."

He set the closed box aside, cupped her face again, and kissed her, gentle and inquiring at first, his warm, silken mouth cajoling hers to open for him. Then he took, every caress of his lips and thrust of his tongue hungrier and more demanding than the last.

Grabbing for breath, Amanda drew back. "I've never really made love, Jeb. It wasn't this way with Mark. What if I—well, make a mess of it and disappoint you?"

He pushed to his feet and swept her up into his arms. As he carried her toward his bedroom, he said, "Nothing about you could ever disappoint me. You're the most perfect and beautiful woman I've ever known."

Chapter Eighteen

Over the last many months, Amanda had read numerous love stories featuring men who were tender, passionate, and romantic in bed, but she never believed she might find that with anyone. Jeb toed the door closed after they entered his bedroom and stood Amanda by his king-size bed. She tensed and closed her eyes when he began undressing her, for she truly did have scars, so many that she could no longer remember how she had received some of them. Her blouse slipped off her shoulders and down her arms. With the ease of long practice, Jeb unfastened the front clasp of her dingy bra, making her wish she'd thought to order herself at least one set of pretty underwear. Next, her jeans fell in a puddle around her ankles.

Her body jerked when she felt a hard, warm fingertip graze a mark on her right breast. "How did this happen?"

"I fell against a countertop corner," she replied, her voice quivery with nerves.

"Fell, or were you pushed?"

"Thrown, actually."

She heard him mutter a curse, and then she felt the

featherlight graze of his lips tracing the scar. "You're so lovely, Mandy."

He moved to yet another spot on her shoulder. Before he could ask, she said, "He worked at a mill then and kicked me with steel-toed boots."

And so it went, until he'd found and kissed every mark on her body. He even discovered the lump on her lower left rib and the protrusion at the tip of her sternum. "It never healed right," she whispered.

He nudged her to sit on the edge of his bed and knelt to remove her shoes, socks, and jeans. Opening her eyes, Amanda studied his carved features, his tawny brows, and the gleam of his toffee-colored hair. In her opinion, he was the beautiful one. When he'd finished divesting her of her clothing, he sat back on his heels and stripped off his shirt. She'd seen him naked from the waist up one night, but even so, the sight of his broad, powerfully muscled chest nearly took her breath away.

He pointed to a faded slash on his lower abdomen. "Table-saw mishap. I was ripping plywood, and the blade grabbed. A shard shot at me like a bullet." He stood, unbuckled his belt, and dropped his jeans. Indicating another scar on his work-hardened thigh, he said, "Chain saw. I was sixteen and ignored my dad's rule about wearing safety chaps." His endlessly deep gaze met hers. "I'm not a perfect package either. Are you still sure you want to keep me?"

Amanda couldn't help laughing. "You have the most gorgeous body I've ever seen."

"Same back at you. So what do you say we forget all about our imperfections and just love each other for who and what we are?"

She nodded, and that was all the answer he needed.

The next thing she knew, they were lying on the coverlet, skin to skin, one of his legs bent and pressed between her thighs. With one kiss, Amanda felt as if the world fell away and only they existed. With Mark, she'd only ever experienced pain. With Jeb, she discovered ecstasy.

When he skimmed a hand along her side and over her hip, he touched her as if she were made of fragile glass. She gloried in the steely feel of his back, marveled at how the muscles beneath his skin bunched against her palms when he moved. *Jeb*. The smell of him, a masculine blend of piney cologne, male musk, and fresh mountain air, permeated her senses. When he suckled her breasts, fiery tendrils of sensation spiraled through her, and she arched against him for more. Without abandoning her nipples, he slipped his hand between her legs and brought her to climax with only a fingertip.

Still trembling with the aftershocks, Amanda accepted the hard, silky length of him deep inside her. He established a rhythm, and she lifted her hips to meet each thrust, incredulous at the bursts of pleasure he ignited within her. As his passion increased, hers mounted as well, until they both reached a fever pitch, soared over the crest, and plunged into a dark yet sparkling void of exhaustion, clutched in each other's arms.

When their heartbeats slowed, Amanda snuggled against him, sighing with contentment. Jeb hugged her close. "That was amazing," he murmured.

"Beyond amazing. If I'd known it could be like this, I would have seduced you the first night."

He smiled against her hair. "We've only just begun, Mandy mine. Just always know that nothing that takes place between us will ever be anything less than wonderful."

Amanda believed him. Pillowing her head on the hollow of his shoulder, she toyed with his chest hair. "We used no protection."

"I know. I'm sorry. Being with you was so mind-blowing that I plumb forgot." He kissed her forehead. "I always practice safe sex, so there's no worry about STDs."

"I'm not thinking of that." She lifted her head to meet his gaze. "I think I'm one of those women who gets pregnant easily. After one time with Mark, I was in trouble."

Jeb arched a brow. "Will you be upset if that happens again?"

"I'd love to have another baby, but I'm not sure how you'd feel about it. I don't want—"

"Mandy, if you tell me we're pregnant, I'll be the happiest man alive. I'm one of six kids, and I always thought I'd have a family one day. When I found no woman I wanted to marry, I gave up on the idea, but now, with you and Chloe in my life, I'm excited about the possibility that we'll have more kids."

Amanda pushed up on an elbow to kiss him. When they were both breathless, she came up for air. "Let's see if we can get lucky, then."

He grinned, pushed her onto her back, and made love to her again. Afterward, Amanda's bones felt as if they'd melted. "Wow. That was quite a roll of the dice."

He chuckled and drew her into his arms. "We've got a little girl who'll be up with the chickens. In order to keep pace with her, we both need some rest."

Amanda wasn't sure she could walk if she tried. "I should go back upstairs so she doesn't find us here in the morning."

He toyed with the ring he'd put on her finger. "We're

engaged. Just stay put, and if she wakes up before we do, say we're going to get married."

Amanda stirred. "We should at least be wearing something."

He sat up. "Right. I'll take care of it."

Swinging out of bed, he entered the walk-in closet and returned a moment later with a T-shirt for her and a pair of fresh boxers for himself.

When Amanda awakened shortly before dawn in Jeb's arms, her body ached for more of him. He blinked when she kissed him. A smile curved his lips.

"If you're looking for trouble, lady, I think you've found it."

"Oh, good." She nibbled his neck. "I was afraid you'd be too tired."

Jeb rose on an elbow. "Not on your life," he whispered just before he settled his mouth over hers.

After they'd showered separately, Jeb got dressed and Amanda scurried upstairs wrapped in only a towel to get some clothes. When she entered the kitchen minutes later, Jeb presented her with a mug of hot coffee. As she took a sip, she opened the fridge and saw a slip of pink paper lying atop the eggs in the clear plastic storage container.

The note read, *I'm the happiest man alive. Thank you so much for last night. Perfect. Beautiful. Mind-blowing.*

Amanda grinned and turned into his arms to blow his mind again with a good-morning kiss. Before she knew it, his hands were under her top and cupping her breasts. She moaned as he teased her nipples erect and was disappointed when he suddenly stopped and kissed her forehead.

His voice thick with desire, he said, "We can't do this. Chloe may come downstairs and find us making love on the kitchen table."

Forced to agree, she said, "You're right. Let's focus on fixing food. For a minute, you made me forget that I'm *starving*."

"Sex burns calories."

"If I start to gain weight, I'll remember that."

"Trust me, if you ever go on a diet and come to me for a calorie-burning session, I'll never tell you to just have a sandwich and leave me alone."

She giggled. He stepped behind her to survey the possibilities for a meal. "Bacon and eggs sound good." He bent his head to nuzzle her nape. "Too bad I won't be able to have you for dessert."

Smiling, Amanda grabbed a pound of bacon, six farm-fresh eggs, and a sleeve of English muffins. "Eggs Benedict?" she suggested.

"Yummy."

As they worked together to prepare breakfast, Jeb gave her a mischievous sidelong look. "Please tell me you didn't agree to marry me to avoid having to pay back that loan. A wife can't very well repay her husband for money he gave her."

Amanda rolled her eyes. "I'd never be dumb enough to marry a man for money. Only for love."

"Music to my ears."

Sometime later, Chloe stumbled into the kitchen, her dark hair tousled from sleep, her small fists rubbing her eyes. Amanda gave the child a quick good-morning hug, fixed her a cup of hot chocolate, and settled her at the table while Jeb brought out platters of food.

After saying the blessing, Amanda dished up a plate of scrambled eggs for her daughter, who didn't care for eggs Benedict, and Chloe, though still bleary-eyed, caught a flash of the diamond on her mother's left hand. "Oh, Mommy, what a pretty ring!" She shot Jeb a questioning glance. "Did you buy it for Mommy for Christmas?"

Caught off guard, Jeb sent Amanda an imploring look.

"No, sweetie," Amanda inserted. "This is an engagement ring. Last night, Mr. Jeb asked me to marry him, and I said yes. He gave me this ring to make it official."

Chloe's eyes brightened, and she beamed a smile. "Does that mean Mr. Jeb will be my new daddy?"

Jeb spoke up. "Being your daddy would be one of the greatest honors of my life, princess. But only if that's what you want."

"It's what I want. Having you for my daddy was my birthday wish yesterday."

Jeb chucked the child under her pointy little chin. "Well, I guess this means your wish came true."

"Can I start calling you Daddy, then?"

Jeb nodded. "I'd like that."

Jeb originally planned to collect his ladies and drive to the Redmond airport to pick up Amanda's mother, but when Christmas Eve morning dawned, he got nervous and changed his mind. The divorce hearing was now only eighteen days away, and according to Clyde Johnson, Mark was undoubtedly stewing in his own juice, imagining ways to retaliate against Amanda.

Stepping into his office out of Amanda's earshot, Jeb called Barney and asked if he'd be free that afternoon.

"Hey, bro, it's Christmas! Why do you think I've worked

so many extra shifts? I was earning days of leave to take the holidays off. No work for me until the day after New Year's."

"Great. Mom can throw a birthday party for you since you worked on the actual date."

As Jeb expected, Barney groaned. "God save us. When is she going to realize we're all grown-up? Last Easter Sunday, I found a basket on my front porch. I liked the chocolate bunny, but those spongy yellow chicks are like eating flavored rubber."

Jeb barked with laughter. "I have to agree. They're awful. Kids seem to like them, but they're not my deal." Turning serious, he told Barney about Amanda's Christmas surprise and what time Emma would arrive at Roberts Field, the airport in Redmond. "I know I'm being overly cautious, but I get a tingle up my spine when I think about driving that far with Amanda and Chloe. On this ice, even my truck might spin out of control if Mark rammed me."

"How will her mother recognize me?"

"I'll tell her to look for a deputy wearing a tan uniform and a dark brown Stetson."

"Hello? I'm off duty. No uniform for me today. I'll shave before going over to the folks' house tonight, but otherwise I'm intent on being a slob for a change."

Jeb grinned. "Wave a sign that reads, 'I'm Jeb's brother, the slob.'"

Barney sighed. "Oh, all right, I'll shave. But I'm not waving a sign. What does this gal look like?"

"An older version of Amanda and Chloe. Her hair has gone partly gray, but she's slightly built, with delicate features and big brown eyes."

"Hmm." Barney sighed again, a little louder and longer this time. "I'll find her. You owe me one, though. I don't get days off very often."

"I really appreciate this, Barney."

"How often have I heard that? And then when I need a loan, you always say you're broke."

Jeb took umbrage. "You haven't asked me for a loan since your wild college days, and the only reason I said no back then was because Dad threatened to lop off my head if I gave you money. Your grades had gone to hell, and you were partying too much."

"Those were the days." Barney chuckled. "It's a good thing I had Dad to bring down the hammer. Studying the law is no walk in the park, especially with a blinding hangover." Silence. Then Barney added, "It's a great Christmas surprise for Mandy, bringing her mom down for a visit. But I gotta know, have you even made it to first base with her yet?"

Jeb preferred to keep the sexual aspects of his relationship with Amanda private. "She agreed to marry me night before last. I went the whole nine yards. Even got down on one knee when I proposed."

"Holy *hell*! You're engaged? Mom will be so excited she'll shit a brick."

"Don't tell her, Barney. I want to announce it officially at Christmas dinner tomorrow. We're all meeting here, four o'clock. Show up early to help in the kitchen."

"See there? I do you a huge favor, and in return I have to help cook. What's wrong with this picture?"

When Jeb returned to the kitchen, he found his counters powdered from one end to the other with flour. Amanda, fretting about her hostess duties the following day for a huge family dinner, had decided to make pies.

"I'm not very good with pies," she informed him. "Bread, fine. Cakes, no big deal. My brownies are to die for. But piecrust defeats me nearly every time."

Jeb watched her cut shortening into the flour with painstaking care. "Why are you doing that?"

"Because all recipes for crust say to do it."

"I just throw the whole works into my KitchenAid mixer. I do a killer meat pie. I don't see how fruit fillings would make any difference."

She handed him the mixing bowl. "Wave your magic wand, then." Jeb could tell by her expression that she felt edgy. "Otherwise we'll have patchwork pies."

"You've met my family. We're not fussy."

"It's different now! They're going to be my in-laws. I don't want to be the worst pie maker in the whole family."

Jeb stared into the bowl. "You know how to make the fillings, right?"

She gave him a look that said he had to be dumber than dirt to have asked the question. "In order to reach the filling stage, what do you have to make first?"

Jeb felt as if he'd just stepped onto thin ice. "Um, I guess the dough."

"Which has to be rolled out, and it all needs to stick together. And mine doesn't." She planted her gooey hands on her hips. "I never got to the filling."

"Well," Jeb replied, "I'll do the dough. In the meanwhile, get online and find some filling recipes."

"What kinds do your family like?"

"All kinds, but for Christmas we usually have pumpkin and apple."

"*Apple?*" Her eyes widened. "I've heard the filling's difficult to thicken. Oh, my stars, it's going to be a disaster."

*   *   *

The disasters were cooling on racks at two o'clock that afternoon when the front doorbell rang. Jeb glanced at the monitor. Amanda checked the camera views sporadically, but she wasn't diligent about it. He saw Barney standing on the porch holding a suitcase. Emma stood beside him, fussing with her coat and pushing at her hair.

"Who on earth can that be?" Amanda asked. "I didn't order anything. Did you?" She started toward the front door to peer out the peephole. Jeb stepped over to the security console to disable the alarm. Biting back a smile, he yelled, "Who is it?"

The only response he got was a shriek from Amanda. Then he heard her wrestling with the new dead bolt. More shrieks followed. He moseyed in that direction, grinning when Chloe, who'd been package-snooping again, dashed from the living room into the entry hall.

"Momma?" Amanda's voice rang with incredulity. "Momma!"

Jeb saw Barney step aside and switch the suitcase to his other hand as Amanda catapulted out onto the porch to hug her mother. "How did you get here? You said you couldn't afford—" Breaking off in midsentence, Amanda looked at Barney. Then, pulling from her mother's embrace, she turned to face Jeb, who approached the doorway with a wide grin plastered on his face. "You *didn't*."

"Merry Christmas, sweetheart. It was the best gift I could think to get you."

Amanda let loose another squeal and threw her arms around her mom again. "I can't *believe* it. You're *real*. You're *really* here? Oh, Momma." She burst into tears, her shoulders jerking with sobs. "Oh, God, oh, God, I am so blessed!"

Chloe moved in to hug her grandmother's hips. "Grammy!" the child cried. "Now I can see you for real!"

Emma untangled herself from Amanda's embrace and bent to wrap her arms around her granddaughter. "You are so beautiful!" she said. "Far prettier than on a computer screen."

When the initial excitement died down, Amanda raced back into the entry hall and catapulted into Jeb's arms. "Thank you! *Thank* you! This is the best gift *ever*."

Pivoting, he swung Amanda in a circle. When he drew to a stop, he bent to kiss her cheek and said, "Merry Christmas, honey."

As Jeb released his fiancée, he saw Emma limping toward him. When she stepped in close for a hug, Jeb enfolded her in his arms, taking care not to squeeze too hard for fear of hurting her.

Tears slipped down her cheeks when she tipped her head back to smile at him. "You'll never know how much it means to me to be here."

Jeb's first introduction to his future mother-in-law was as simple and wonderful as that. She was shorter than her daughter, but she so greatly resembled Amanda that he loved her on sight. He couldn't believe she worked at an assisted-living center, cleaning apartments and common areas when her hip clearly pained her with every step. No matter how he circled it, that seemed flat-out wrong.

It turned out to be the most wonderful Christmas Eve in Amanda's memory. Jeb seemed to like her mom and went out of his way to make her feel welcome in his home. He helped Amanda fix a simple but festive dinner, and in honor of the occasion, they dined at the formal table, using his fine china. Chloe was served apple juice in her wine goblet while the adults sipped a nice Merlot from theirs.

When it came time for kitchen cleanup, Jeb insisted that Emma relax with Chloe in the living room by the tree while he returned to help Amanda do the dishes.

She was surprised when he said in a low voice, "I don't want your mother to be climbing up and down those stairs. I think we should sleep in one of the guest rooms and let her have the master suite."

Amanda had noticed how her mother limped, putting as little weight on her right hip as possible, but she'd never expected Jeb to give up his sleeping quarters to make Emma more comfortable.

As if he read her mind, Jeb said, "All the rooms upstairs have adjoining baths, and the one at the end of the hall has a king bed. We'll be fine up there."

Over the last two days, Amanda had moved much of her clothing and toiletries into the master suite, and all of Jeb's stuff was in there. "I don't mind doing that, but it'll be a big inconvenience for you."

"No, it won't. I'll grab a few changes of clothes and my shaving gear. Going up and down those stairs will be hard on her."

Amanda nodded, and it was decided. When the kitchen was tidy, she helped Jeb collect their things, and then they hurried upstairs to get settled in the end bedroom. "I feel a little self-conscious about sleeping with you with my mom in the house."

Jeb grinned. "We're engaged. I think Emma will understand. Besides, after having you beside me for two nights, I'd be lost without you." Mischief danced in his eyes. "If you get all prissy on me, I'll move in with you, Chloe, Bozo, and Frosty."

Amanda laughed. "And I'd end up sleeping on the floor. No, thanks. We'll sleep in here, and Mom will just have to deal with it."

Before they left the room, Jeb pulled her close for a long hug, whispering to her of an idea he had to make the future easier for Emma. Amanda's heart caught when she heard his plan.

"Jeb, are you sure you want to do this?"

"I'm positive as long as you feel comfortable with it."

Amanda framed his face between her hands. "I think it's the most generous, wonderful idea *ever*, and I can't wait to see her face when you tell her."

They spent the remainder of the evening by the gorgeous spruce, aglow with multicolored lights and sparkling with decorations. Bozo and Frosty snuggled near the hearth, basking in the warmth that radiated from the burning logs. Jeb played holiday music at a low volume, and they visited long into the evening, Amanda and Emma catching up while Chloe admired all the presents.

"Grammy, there are presents for you, too," Chloe said.

Emma smiled at Jeb. "Being here is the only Christmas gift that I need."

Amanda studied the package in Chloe's hands and realized it was the teacup and saucer she'd wrapped. She narrowed an eye at Jeb. He chuckled. "Another white lie, Mandy. I didn't have it mailed because I knew your mom would be here."

"White lies are okay at Christmas!" Chloe announced. "That's so everyone can be surprised!"

Feeling happy in a way she hadn't for years, Amanda announced, "Speaking of surprises, sweetness, it's time for little girls to be in bed."

"But, Mommy, I want to stay up until midnight so I can put Baby Jesus in the manger."

Jeb saved the day by saying, "But then Santa can't come until after midnight, and that'll put him way behind on all his rounds. He has lots of boys and girls on his delivery list. So he wants little children in bed earlier."

Chloe pouted her bottom lip. "But I wanted to put the baby in tonight."

Jeb glanced at his watch. "It's almost Christmas in New York, so I guess we can do it now."

Jeb disappeared and was wearing the Glock on his hip when he returned. He went to the coat closet and dragged out Chloe's snow boots and parka. After bundling her up against the cold, he put boots on Bozo and fetched the manger piece.

Chloe's eyes sparkled with excitement. "I've never put Baby Jesus in his manger. Do I need to say a blessing?"

"We'll sing him the happy birthday song," Jeb told her.

Amanda knew the drill. The moment Jeb stepped outside, she closed the door behind them and reset the security system. Then she joined her mom at the living room window to watch man and child approach the life-size Nativity scene. Bozo circled the yard, exhibiting no sign that he sensed any danger, which eased Amanda's mind. Even so, she hoped Jeb didn't linger out there. As Chloe approached the manger with Baby Jesus in her arms, her small face glowed in the soft illumination of the icicle lights strung along the eaves.

"She's so darling." Emma sent Amanda a questioning look. "I've noticed that Jeb wore a gun outside, and you're both extremely diligent about keeping the alarm turned on. Is there a reason for that?"

Amanda had avoided giving her mom all the details

about Mark's break-in, so as not to worry her. "Mark is extremely dangerous, Mom. He was armed when he broke in last time, and if it hadn't been for Bozo's surprise intervention, he would have killed me. The divorce attorney Jeb hired says that violence by men like Mark can escalate as the hearing date approaches. That's scheduled for the eleventh."

Emma fixed a worried gaze on her daughter. "Do you think he can get in here again?"

"I think it's unlikely, but it would be a mistake to underestimate him. That's why we're so careful to always keep the system armed. Last time, he watched for an opportunity and got inside in a matter of seconds."

Emma rubbed her arms and shivered. Through the frosted glass, Amanda saw Jeb carrying Chloe back to the porch. She circled the tree to reach the hall and disarmed the system to let them back inside. After setting Chloe down, Jeb stepped over to the panel and hit Stay. Amanda took care of engaging the dead bolt.

Speaking of Mark's break-in had depressed Amanda's Christmas spirit, but Jeb helped her regain it as he assisted Chloe out of her jacket and boots. "You know what we almost forgot?"

"No, what?" Chloe asked.

"We haven't put out cookies and milk for Santa. He'll be up and down hundreds of chimneys tonight. At each stop, he needs a snack to keep his energy up."

Concern filled Chloe's expression. "But, Daddy Jeb, he can't come down our chimney without landing in the fire!"

Jeb grinned. "I'll put the fire out before I go to bed." He glanced at the hearth and then at Amanda. "Can you help Chloe put together a high-calorie snack for Santa,

Mandy? I have it on good authority that his favorite cookie is chocolate chip."

After Chloe had put a plate of cookies and a glass of milk on the hearth, Amanda led her upstairs for her customary bath and bedtime stories. When she reentered the living room later, Jeb and her mom were chatting like old friends.

Jeb glanced up. Every time his hazel gaze turned Amanda's way, she felt as if she'd received a physical caress. "Is she sound asleep?"

"Out like a light."

Jeb pushed to his feet. "Excuse me, Emma." He rubbed his hands together. "Now I get to play Santa Claus. It's my first time, so I'm really looking forward to it."

"Me, too." Amanda bent to kiss her mom's cheek. "I've had so much fun buying for her this year and I have presents hidden all over the place."

Emma smiled.

Jeb caught Amanda around the waist with one arm and twirled her in close for a deep kiss. When he drew his mouth from hers, she felt weak at the knees. "Merry Christmas, Mrs. Claus."

Mrs. Claus felt herself blushing. "We aren't standing under the mistletoe."

"Mr. and Mrs. Claus don't need mistletoe."

Moments later as Jeb returned with the dollhouse, Emma gasped in delight. When he pushed the plug into an outlet, the older woman clasped her hands and leaned forward on the cushioned chair.

"I've never seen anything to equal this," she said.

Amanda agreed. "It was gorgeous upstairs, but now, beneath the tree lights, it's truly amazing. Chloe will be over the moon!"

"It does look great," Jeb admitted with a wink at Amanda. "I had a lot of help."

"Gingerbread and fairy tales," Emma murmured. "It's a fantasy house."

Jeb stretched out on his belly to straighten the interior. Dishes had toppled during transport and furniture had shifted. Amanda joined him to help. Emma scooted an ottoman closer to watch them work.

When Amanda judged the house to be in perfect order, Jeb continued to fuss over this or that. "Jeb, it's after midnight. Chloe will probably wake us up before dawn."

"Get your mom settled in for the night and then go on up. I'll be along soon."

Amanda pushed erect. "Don't stay up too long. You'll be exhausted tomorrow."

He flashed a smile. "It's heck playing Santa Claus."

Emma chimed in, "Surely after all your hard work, you'll tell Chloe it's from you so she can thank you properly."

With a laugh, Jeb said, "She'll realize we made it for her someday. For now, it's more important that she believe in the magic of Christmas."

Emma protested about taking Jeb's bed, but while putting on fresh linens, Amanda convinced her that Jeb refused to have it any other way. Minutes later, when Amanda entered the upstairs bedroom she and Jeb would share during her mom's stay, she felt lonely. She was about to go back downstairs when the door opened and she briefly saw his large body silhouetted against the hall light before the room became blanketed in shadows again.

He moved to where she stood beside the bed and held one hand above her head. "We're legal now," he whispered.

"Legal for what?"

"Kissing. I stole a piece of mistletoe from downstairs."

Amanda giggled until his warm, hungry mouth claimed hers. Then she forgot everything but the man who held her in his arms. Later, as they lay naked with limbs intertwined, he whispered, "For a woman who once told me she detests sex, you seem to have developed a sudden taste for it."

"We don't have sex; we make love." She snuggled closer, loving the solid heat of him. "Thank you for everything. Having Mom here has made this Christmas perfect."

Chapter Nineteen

And the following day *was* perfect. Chloe awakened the household at five thirty in the morning, screaming at the top of her lungs, "Santa came! He really and truly came this time! Hurry! Hurry! You have to come see!"

After throwing on clothes, Jeb and Amanda got downstairs just in time to see Emma hobbling sleepily from the master suite. All three adults hurried to the living room. Chloe knelt in front of her dollhouse, her expression rapt. She didn't even glance up when Amanda said her name.

Jeb crouched beside the child. "Wow, that's quite some dollhouse. Is that what you told Santa you wanted?"

Chloe nodded, her eyes sparkling as she took in each room. "But I never meant for him to work so hard to give me one this nice!" She reached in to touch the tiny stove. Then she saw the dishes in the cupboard. "It's so pretty! If it wasn't so little, I'd live there."

The child's fascination with the dollhouse gave the adults some time to drink coffee around the tree and wake up. Then, with no little effort, Amanda distracted her daughter long enough for them all to unwrap their gifts. Emma loved her fancy teacup and saucer. Jeb liked the all-purpose knife that Amanda had ordered for him online. She was equally appreciative of the expensive wool slacks and sweater Jeb had ordered for her. Chloe was soon nearly eclipsed by piles of discarded wrapping paper and bows all around her.

Jeb brought in large black garbage bags for the used wrapping paper. While the adults adjourned to the kitchen to start breakfast, Chloe remained with her dollhouse, dressing the tiny dolls. After enjoying the light meal, Jeb announced that it was time for everyone to slick up for Christmas. Even though it wasn't safe for them to attend a church service, they dressed as if they were going to one. Amanda wore her new black slacks and the charcoal gray sweater Jeb had given her. Jeb complemented her attire with black trousers, a Christmas red dress shirt, and a gray sports jacket. Emma donned the only dress she'd packed, a lovely blue jersey, and Chloe wore her birthday outfit.

When they all gathered downstairs again, they sang some traditional hymns followed by Christmas carols. Afterward they spiffed up the house and prepared for the Sterling clan to arrive for gift giving and a huge meal. Emma expressed nervousness about meeting her daughter's future in-laws, but the moment Kate and Jeremiah arrived, her anxiety faded. Jeb's parents went out of their way to make Emma feel like part of the family, and all their kids followed suit. Amanda, who'd fretted for days about preparing a holiday meal to equal one of Kate's, soon relaxed as well. So many people went to work in Jeb's huge kitchen that no one could lay claim to any successes or failures. The meal became a group effort.

When everyone moved into the dining room, Jeb hurried to seat Amanda at the far end of the table from him, where a hostess would traditionally reign over a gathering. After herding everyone else to their places, he filled goblets with wine, and then, carrying his glass, he came to stand at Amanda's side. "I have an announcement to make."

Barney winked at Amanda, making her wonder if he already knew their secret. While cooking, she'd turned the ring so the diamond was toward her palm because she knew Jeb wanted to surprise everyone with the news.

"On the night of Chloe's birthday, I asked Amanda to marry me," Jeb said. Looking at his mother, he added, "Yes, Mom, I did it the old-fashioned way, on bent knee." Everyone laughed. "Anyway, she said yes." He captured Amanda's left hand to show off the beautiful diamond surrounded by sapphires that she now wore. "It's official. I'm no longer a free agent. We'll be married as soon as we can."

All the Sterling women vacated their chairs to look at the ring and gush over how gorgeous it was. Jeb accepted congratulatory handshakes from the men and hugs from the women. Amanda stood to receive embraces as well. The last came from her mom.

"You stinker. You didn't even tell *me*."

Amanda laughed. "You already knew. You told Jeb my ring size so he could order it, and I know you've seen it on my hand. *And* you were worried about meeting my future in-laws. So you're the stinker."

Emma smiled. "Okay, I confess. But I decided not to say anything until you were ready to share the news." She drew Amanda close for yet another hug. "Congratulations, darling. You picked a winner this time."

After the meal, the family gathered around the tree

for yet another round of gift opening. By evening, when the house emptied of guests, Amanda felt weary to the bone. The holiday had been a whirlwind of ceaseless activity. Leaving Jeb and Emma at the kitchen table, she took her snifter of brandy into the living room where Chloe was once again entranced by her dollhouse. Gazing at the tree, the child, and the dog snuggling happily with a kitten, Amanda couldn't help but think that this was every woman's dream come true.

Jeb came to find her. Slipping an arm around her shoulders, he said, "Deep thoughts?"

Amanda released a happy sigh and leaned her weight against his sturdy length. "I was just thinking that it took me a lifetime to get here, but I've finally come home." She smiled up at him. "*Home*. Isn't that a beautiful word?"

"For me, home is in your arms," he whispered, his voice gravelly with emotion.

Amanda went up on her tiptoes to kiss him. "And they'll always be open to you."

At bedtime, Amanda couldn't pry her daughter away from the dollhouse. She went back to join Jeb and her mom in the kitchen, allowing the child a few more minutes of playtime. After a quarter hour had passed, Jeb glanced at his watch.

"It's been a long day for her," he said, pushing to his feet. "Now that I'm Daddy Jeb, I think it's my turn to do her bath and bedtime stories." He leaned down to plant a kiss on Amanda's forehead. "Enjoy visiting with your mom. I'll take care of it tonight."

"Have you ever bathed a child?" Amanda asked.

He grinned. "I think I can figure it out, Mandy. Relax. I'll yell if she goes under for the third time."

Keeping an ear cocked, Amanda soon noticed that Jeb had encountered rough sailing. In a high-pitched voice, Chloe refused to stop playing.

Astounded, Amanda started up from her chair, but her mother's firm grip on her arm forestalled her. "Let Jeb handle it, Mandy. He isn't Mark. You needn't worry that he'll harm her."

"It's just—well, Chloe *never* argues. I mean *never*."

Emma smiled and swirled her brandy. "And now she has Daddy Jeb. It's good that she isn't afraid of him." She took a sip of the liquor. "If you interfere, it'll be a mistake. At some point, Jeb needs to step in and act like a parent."

Next Amanda heard her daughter start to cry. In fact, it sounded as if Chloe was pitching her first temper tantrum. A jolt of fear shot through her. But when she looked at her mom, Emma shook her head. To stop herself from leaping to her feet, Amanda made tight fists on the table's edge.

Jeb said in a firm voice, "You can put all your dolls to bed first. Tuck them in and pull the covers up to their chins. When you wake up in the morning, they can wake up with you. Then you can all play together some more."

Sniffling loudly, Chloe cried, "I don't want you to be my daddy anymore. You're bossy and mean!"

Amanda's heart caught. Emma snickered. Jeb replied, "Sorry, princess. It's a dad's job to be bossy and mean sometimes."

A moment later, Jeb strode to the kitchen table with a pouting little girl in his arms. Leaning over, he said, "Give Grammy a night-night kiss."

With begrudging obedience, Chloe gave Emma a peck on the cheek. Next, Amanda received a wet kiss from her daughter and a wink from Jeb. Then he headed toward the stairs. Over his shoulder, he called, "I'll be a while. Someone I know is wound up tighter than a Big Ben alarm clock."

Amanda couldn't focus on a conversation with her mother. Instead she listened to what was happening upstairs.

Emma patted Amanda's shoulder. "He's a good man, and he'll be a wonderful father, stern when he needs to be but never cruel. Your little girl is in good hands."

Amanda released a taut breath. "You're right. I know you are. It's just difficult to let go of the old and embrace the new."

Emma nodded her understanding. "Until you feel comfortable, fake it."

Amanda sent her a startled look.

"You can talk with Jeb about your feelings, Mandy, but you mustn't interfere between him and your daughter. Chloe should never feel that she can play the two of you against each other."

When Jeb reappeared in the kitchen, the sleeves of his red shirt were damp. Turning a chair, he straddled it and sat down, facing the table. "I have now memorized *'Twas the Night Before Christmas*. She went out like a light on the fourth reading." He sent Amanda a teasing look. "Our young miss finally told me that she guesses she'll keep me as her daddy, but she still wasn't happy about going to bed."

"She was up at five thirty, and she's been going full speed all day." Emma leaned forward to pour him a second measure of brandy. "Children grow cross and intractable when they get too tired."

Jeb accepted the snifter. "I'm not complaining. It felt good to see her act up, and even better, she did it with me. At first, she was afraid of me." He grinned and shrugged. "Now she isn't at all. That tells me I've done something right, although I know I still have a lot to learn."

"Did you scrub behind her ears?" Amanda couldn't resist asking.

"I followed a mental checklist, and all parts got washed, including her teeth. I let her do some of it herself. She is seven, after all, and starting to feel modest. She made me hold up a towel as she got out of the tub so I wouldn't see the same little bottom that she flashed at me when she climbed in."

Emma snorted with laughter. Amanda hid a smile.

Jeb stared into his brandy for a moment. Then he glanced up, his gaze holding Emma's. "Change of subject, and please don't start objecting before I've finished."

"All right," Emma agreed.

Jeb drew in a breath and released it slowly. "You may think we're crazy, Emma, so bear with me. As you know, I plan to marry your daughter soon, and I'll be Chloe's new dad. Even though Mandy and I can't make it official until her divorce from Mark is final, in my books, you're already part of my family, and Amanda and I are concerned about your trying to work when your hip is giving you so much pain. So, to get it said fast, would you consider leaving Washington and moving to Mystic Creek to be close to your daughter? You can live here with us. Mandy agrees that it's a great idea."

Emma shook her head. "Newly married couples need their privacy."

Jeb held up a hand. "Hear me out. I understand that Mandy and I will need our privacy, so I'm not suggesting that you live in this house indefinitely. Later, you may decide that you want your own place, but I'm thinking it would be more practical if I add on a mother-in-law apartment. I'm licensed as a builder, even though I mainly do finishing work and make furniture. It wouldn't cost much. Then you'd have your quarters but still be able to join us in the main part of the house whenever you wanted. Everyone would have their privacy that way. And without rent and utilities to pay, you could afford to miss work in order to have hip replacement surgery. Right after the operation, Amanda could care for you."

Emma gaped at him, apparently speechless.

"Until I can get a separate house built for you, Amanda and I will continue to use the larger bedroom upstairs. It'll be no hardship on us, and that way, you won't have to deal with the stairs. After you recover from the surgery, I can either add on to the house, or, if you prefer, I can help you find a residence here that's fairly close to us."

"At least think about it, Mom," Amanda inserted. "Your hip is pretty bad, and I worry about you trying to work. It has to be causing more and more wear on that joint."

Jeb added, "The financial picture for you would be advantageous as well. According to Mandy, you're sixty-four. That means you can start drawing on your deceased husband's Social Security in less than a year. And if you choose to live in a mother-in-law apartment here, you'd have so few expenses that that should give you plenty a month to live on."

Amanda waited with bated breath for her mother's answer. After a long moment, Emma replied, "I'd like nothing more than to live near my daughter and grand-daughter, but I'd need your word, Jeb, that you can afford to add onto the house. I don't want to be a financial drain."

"Trust me, we wouldn't offer if we couldn't afford it. All you really need is a living room, a bedroom with a bathroom, and a small kitchen. I'm not talking about adding on that much square footage."

Emma looked dazed. "I'm not even sure I can afford to move. I'd have to hire all the packing done and have a company transport my things. Then, until the apart-ment is finished, where would I store everything?"

Jeb chuckled. "I've got three brothers here in town over this holiday break. I'll recruit them to go with me to Washington, we'll pack, and we'll move all your stuff south in a U-Haul van. As for temporary storage, I've got a shop that's plenty big enough. I'll put tarps over every-thing so your things don't get covered with sawdust. While I'm away, you, Amanda, and Chloe can stay with my folks, where you'll all be safe. I'll ask Tony across the road to take care of my livestock for a couple of days. Bozo and Frosty can go to my parents' house as well. Bozo and their dog, Murphy, are pals, and both canines tolerate felines."

Emma downed the bit of brandy in her snifter and poured herself another modest measure. "Are you saying I'll never go back to Olympia? That I'll just stay here?"

"Is there a need for you to go?" Jeb asked. "You can call your place of employment and quit your job. My brothers and I can take care of all the details up north. Would you like to sell the house or rent it out?"

Emma's expression turned sad for a moment. "I raised my daughter there, and I have so many wonderful memories. But if I'm going to do this, it would be wisest to sell. Living so far away, I'd have to put the house with property management to rent it out, and that would end up being more trouble than it'd be worth. I need to just do it and not look back, because this is now where my family is."

Jeb shrugged. "It's your call. I won't rush you into making the decision. But I know that Mandy will be happier and have more peace of mind if you're close to her."

"Mom," Amanda said, "Jeb can sometimes seem impulsive and too generous for his own good. But he's discussed this with me. We have a lot of land here. If privacy is an issue for you, Jeb can build your apartment separate from the main residence to give us all a buffer zone. But honestly, I'd prefer to have your quarters attached, giving me the ability to just open a door off one of the downstairs rooms to say hi or check on you."

Emma smiled dreamily. "It would be wonderful to be close so I could see you often and watch Chloe grow up."

Jeb spoke up. "Then let's make it happen. You won't be without friends here. My mom is a social butterfly, and I think you ladies would enjoy each other. You're close to the same age." He winked at his future mother-in-law. "Just be warned, she'll convert you into being a bingo fanatic if you're not careful."

"Mom loves to garden," Amanda inserted.

Emma wore an excited grin now. "Well, I used to. With my hip, I can't do it anymore, but if I get it fixed, I'll have my hands in the dirt again."

The mention of gardening spurred Jeb to launch into details about his greenhouse and how he started his vegetables and kept them protected before in-ground planting. "I can even grow corn, doing it that way, and my tomatoes—oh, man, people who buy produce out of stores don't know what real tomatoes taste like."

The two exchanged gardening stories, and finally Emma said, "If you're sure you wouldn't mind having me around, I accept the offer. Living alone in Washington isn't how I thought it would be."

Jeb thrust his arm across the table, offering his hand. "Let's shake on it, then. My brothers and I will go up there, pack your stuff, and put the house on the market. Your only responsibility will be to schedule your hip surgery."

Emma's face glowed. "I've kept my insurance, which will cover most of the medical bills. I just couldn't afford to do it and miss work while I recovered."

Amanda clasped her mom's hand. "Now you won't be burdened with so many bills. You won't have to work. When you feel like it, you can garden or sew." She paused. "Jeb's right. It's going to be a lot of fun!"

Once snuggled close in the upstairs bedroom, Amanda nuzzled Jeb's neck, her lips curved in a contented smile. "Thank you so much for bringing my mom here to live. I can't begin to tell you how much it will mean to me, having her so close."

He rolled onto his back, taking her with him so she lay partly across his chest. "Brace yourself. If anything ever happens to my dad, I'll be asking if we can have my mom here, too."

Amanda giggled. "I adore your mom. When she's eighty, she'll still be going in high gear. There'll never be a dull moment."

Amanda settled against him, feeling so happy that she was almost afraid to believe it was real. "It's been a day of miracles. My daughter actually threw a fit. I still can't credit it. By the time she was only a few months old, she'd learned that Mark had zero tolerance for crying. When she needed something, she made soft grunting sounds to let me know, but she seldom cried. I was amazed tonight when she misbehaved."

Jeb chuckled. "I'll do my best to keep spoiling her so she'll be a brat more often."

Amanda smothered a laugh against his shoulder. "Spoiling her a little bit is okay, but we mustn't go overboard."

"I was kidding. Chloe is too sweet to ever become a brat. Emma had it right. It was a very exciting day, and Chloe was just wired. During her bath, she told me she was sorry."

He caught Amanda by surprise by suddenly rolling her onto her back. "Besides, I plan to be way too busy spoiling you to go overboard with Chloe."

Looping her arms around his neck, she smiled through the moon-silvered shadows. "And how do you plan to spoil me, Mr. Jeb?"

He trailed kisses down her cheek and whispered, "Let me show you."

The following day, Jeb called his brothers to recruit volunteers to help him move Emma from Washington. The suddenness of it took Amanda off guard, but after getting off the phone, Jeb explained his reason for putting the plan into action as fast as possible.

"Jonas is home from university, Barney took all this week off, and Ben isn't on the road delivering rodeo stock." He tweaked the tip of Amanda's nose. "Don't look so worried, honey. Dad has even installed security cameras at his place now, so you'll be as safe staying with him as you are with me. And it's not often that I have all three of my brothers in town and off work at the same time. We can leave early in the morning, knock it out in a snap, and be back here to celebrate New Year's Eve, no worries."

Amanda said nothing to stall Jeb's plans, but she *was* worried. It wasn't that long now before the divorce hearing, and knowing her husband as well as she did, she put nothing past him. What if Mark found a way to break into Jeremiah and Kate's home? What if they weren't as diligent about keeping the security system armed as she and Jeb were?

She wanted to throw her arms around Jeb and beg him not to leave her. He'd become her safe harbor. But when she started to talk with him about that, she felt foolish and clingy.

So instead of pleading with Jeb not to leave, she lectured herself. Mark no longer ruled her life. She was overreacting and letting herself fall back into the trap of feeling fearful. If she meant to move forward and have a wonderful future with Jeb, she had to put Mark and all the memories behind her.

That evening, Jeb moved all of them to his parents' house. Kate and Jeremiah had plenty of spare bedrooms, allowing Jeb and Amanda to share one their last night together. Frosty had a litter box in Kate's laundry room and another in the bedroom Chloe would share with Bozo. The Sterling house had a homey, well-used ambience that made all the guests feel relaxed—with the exception of Amanda, who felt as if invisible hands had permanently knotted her stomach. Though she said nothing of her concerns to Jeb, he seemed to sense how upset she was.

That night when everyone trailed off to bed and the house grew quiet, Jeb pulled her into his arms and drew the blankets over them, creating a cocoon of warmth. "Talk to me," he whispered.

She didn't want to talk, fearing that once she started, she'd burst into tears and cling to him like a three-year-old.

"Okay, if you won't talk, I will. You can't understand why I'd choose to leave you now when Mark may be in a dither and at his most dangerous."

Amanda made fists on the edge of his pillow. "It's the worst possible time! There's no rush to move my mom. You could at least wait until after the hearing."

He tightened his arms around her. "Your mom reminds me a lot of you, and I think she can equal you in stubbornness if I give her half a chance."

"Yes." She had to admit that; her mom could be stubborn.

"And she loves that house where she raised you and has so many memories. If I dillydally around and don't get her moved, she has a return flight out of here on January second. I'm afraid she'll start thinking about all her precious stuff and want to spend a few days up there by herself to sort through her treasures before my brothers and I start packing."

Amanda knew her mom. "Yes, she might want to do that. Then she could have special boxes packed and marked."

"And she'd be up there alone without any male protection or a security system."

The squeezing sensation moved to Amanda's chest. "Oh, God. You think Mark may go after my mom."

"Mark's upset right now. Intellectually, he has to know that you'll be granted a divorce. For him, that's a huge blow. He sees you as a possession, and you're about to be taken from him, so he's walking a treacherous edge. He sees himself as always in the right, all powerful, and entitled to keep what's his. And I've made it all but impossible for him to retaliate against you. So how can he hurt you, honey?"

Tears burned in Amanda's eyes. "By hurting my mom. He knows how much I love her and that it would break my heart."

Jeb smoothed her hair. "Your mom will be safe here with you and Chloe. My father understands that the security system must be set constantly, except for brief times while someone goes in or out. He's installed monitors, and he knows to watch them. He has loaded guns hidden all over the house. He'll have Bozo on duty to provide backup. Gowdy also helped him develop bulletproof passwords and installed two firewalls. Barney has asked his fellow deputies to take turns cruising the road to keep an eye on this house. If they see a car parked along the shoulder, they'll check it out. They'll also be patrolling adjacent roads, just in case Mark tries to slip onto this property on foot. He can't get past our defenses this time."

Amanda's body relaxed. "So you're doing this to protect my mother."

"Yes. I know she probably wonders why I'm in such a hurry to move her, and I haven't explained because if I mention that she may want to sort through her mementos, she may grab on to the idea. I don't think it's safe for her to be alone in Olympia even for one night."

Mark knew that town like the back of his hand. He'd grown to adulthood there. If he wanted to get revenge against Amanda by hurting Emma, he knew where to find her.

"Oh, Jeb, thank you. I never stopped to think about the danger to Mom."

He chuckled. "Am I forgiven now for haring off and leaving you with my dad?"

"Yes."

He leaned in to kiss her deeply. "Prove it. I'll be gone for three days. I need some loving to tide me over."

"What if someone hears us?"

"We'll be as quiet as two mice stealing the cheese."

Chapter Twenty

Over the next three days, Amanda battled to stay calm. Jeremiah kept the security system armed, except when he had to go in or out to care for livestock, which he minimized by hiring two teenage boys to help out. Given that the kids had no school over Christmas break, they were delighted to make some extra money. While indoors, Jeremiah frequently glanced at the monitors or checked the camera views on his cell phone. Rationally, Amanda knew that her future father-in-law followed all the same safety procedures that Jeb would have, that he was physically able to take Mark on, and that he had weapons handy, which he wouldn't hesitate to use if necessary.

But for Amanda, it wasn't the same as having Jeb there.

Kate and Emma kept Chloe entertained. Jeb had brought the child's dollhouse over, so the two older women spent one day making more outfits for the tiny figures that lived in Chloe's pretend world. Another day was spent baking in preparation for New Year's Day dinner, which was to be held at Jeb's home because he had more space.

When Amanda fished through her pillowcase for

clothing each morning, she found notes from Jeb written on pink slips. *I love you.* Another one that made her smile was, *Don't forget me. I'm coming home.* She laughed when she read, *If you and Chloe are bunking together, please let Bozo in bed with you. He'll keep you safe, and he won't be lonesome.* Amanda was tempted to tear through every stitch of her clothing to find all the notes at once, but she decided she preferred to get surprises. He'd put one message in a breast pocket, another in her jeans pocket. She cried when she read, *Thank you for loving me. You're a miracle in my life.* And again when a note said, *If you feel lonely, imagine that my arms are around you. I'm with you, in my heart.*

By the third afternoon, Amanda had moved from nervous to anxious and paced from room to room, rubbing her arms. Jeb had called that morning to let her know everything was packed, the U-Haul was loaded, they'd hired a property management company to clean, paint, and prep the house to be placed on the market, and they planned to meet with a Realtor before noon to list the property. Jeb felt the home would sell quickly and for enough money to give Emma a sizable profit.

"I doubt we'll head out today. We're all bushed. A hot meal, a shower, and a comfortable motel room bed sound pretty good to us right now."

As eager as Amanda was to have him back, she replied, "You need a good night's sleep before making that drive. I don't want any of you to get drowsy behind the wheel. Tell your brothers I appreciate all their work. They're the best."

"What am I, chopped liver?"

As tense as she felt, she couldn't help but smile. "You are my Mr. Wonderful, you and only you."

Now, many hours after that conversation, Amanda couldn't have smiled if her life depended on it. Her skin crawled, and dread mounted within her. Perhaps over the years, she'd become telepathically linked to Mark. *Ridiculous.* But she couldn't shake the feeling that he was gleefully preparing to do her great harm.

The easiest way for him to do that right now was to go after Jeb. The thought filled her with cold terror. *Oh, God, why didn't I think of that?* Jeb had protected the one person he knew Amanda loved, but he'd forgotten how dearly she loved him.

Palms slick with sweat, Amanda dialed Jeb's cell. Her call went straight to voice mail. Growing more panicky, she tried him again and again, all with the same result. Something had happened. She felt it in her bones.

Jeremiah found her in the living room, trying to place calls on her iPhone. When he saw that she was shaking, he grasped her by the shoulders. "Hey, hey," he said. "What has you so upset?"

He reminded her so much of Jeb. Even his voice had that same rich timbre. "I'm afraid for Jeb. He isn't answering his phone, Jeremiah. I've tried several times."

"It's Dad to you." Ignoring the cell phone clutched in her hands between them, he drew her into his arms. Stroking her hair just as his eldest son often did, he soothed her with words. "My boy is strong and fast as lightning with his fists. I know you haven't seen that side of him, but in his younger years, he was a scrapper. That puny little husband of yours doesn't stand a chance. Jeb will break him in half."

"You don't know Mark. He won't face Jeb. He'll catch him with his back turned."

Jeremiah passed a work-hardened palm over her hair

again. "Maybe he'll try, but Jeb is with his three younger brothers. Ben works the rodeo circuits. He's dealt with some rough buckaroos, and when he throws a punch, the guy he hits is lucky to have any teeth left. Barney is a police officer. Just because he's a small-town deputy, don't think for a minute he's small-town caliber. For a while, he was a state boy, and he loved the work, but in the end, he missed Mystic Creek and decided to kiss big-city crime good-bye. Jonas, our college boy, may look like a preppy, but he competes in wrestling, and in his weight class he placed third in the state last year. He also boxes. That punk Mark Banning won't get to Jeb when his brothers are with him."

"Mark carries guns!"

"And so do my boys. With the exception of Barney, they don't normally, but they're packing now. Jeb is fine, mark my words. He's probably in a dead zone right now. No reception. He'll call when he notices that you tried to reach him."

Amanda didn't know what the cell reception was like in her hometown of Olympia. At seventeen, when she got pregnant with Chloe, she'd just gotten her first cell phone, and she couldn't remember now if there had been dead zones in certain parts of town. "I can't live without him," she whispered. "I never told him that. Why didn't I think to say those words?"

Jeremiah chuckled and set her away from him. "Judging by the way he looks at you, I think he knows and the feeling is mutual. Trust in God, Mandy."

"I trusted in God for over six years," she blurted out.

Jeremiah bent to kiss her forehead. "Yep, and over time, as you came to a point where you could help him out a little by running, where did you land?" He grinned and shook his head. "In Mystic Creek of all places, with Jeb living one road over from you. Give God some credit. He not only helped you get out of there, but he guided you straight to the one man on earth who'd love you so much he'd die for you." He turned toward the back of the house. "Think about that."

"I am," she cried after him, "and I don't *want* him to die for me."

Jeremiah stopped, turned, and peered out the front window. "He looks pretty alive to me, honey."

Amanda whirled to follow his gaze and saw Jeb climbing out of his pickup. She shrieked and ran for the front door. Jeremiah trotted after her to disarm the security system just before she threw open the front door. She forgot about the icy surfaces. All she could see was Jeb striding toward her with that well-oiled shift of his hips that she'd come to love so much.

"Be careful!" he called. "It's slicker than greased owl—"

Amanda gained the front yard, sheeted with ice, and slipped, plummeting forward into a belly-first sprawl. Jeb cursed, ran forward, and reached down to help her up. The next instant, he let loose with "Son of a *bitch*!" as he went down beside her.

Amanda's cheek hurt, but she was so excited to see him that she didn't care. She tried to sit up and her hands went out from under her, sending her back to the ground. Jeb tried to help her, but he had no better luck. So instead of standing, they scooted toward each other, grabbed hold, and Amanda *finally* felt his arms around her again. They kissed like starving people who'd just stumbled upon a buffet.

Barney, wearing street clothes and a gun on his hip, moved gingerly toward them. He tipped back the bill of his off-duty ball cap to peer down at this display of undying devotion. "For heaven's sake, rent a room." He extended a hand to Jeb, who'd come up for air. Jeb clasped palms with his brother, Barney leaned back to lift, and his slick-soled boots went out from under him. He landed next to Jeb and grimaced as the blow to his hindquarters registered in his brain.

"Well, shit," he said. "If this is any example of how crazy people act when they fall in love, I want no part of it." He studied Amanda's face. "Double shit, bro. She's gonna have a shiner."

Just then, Jeremiah, who'd donned shoe chains, trudged out to stand near them, feet spread, arms akimbo. Kate had appeared on the porch, Emma, Chloe, and Bozo crowding behind her. "I raised idiots," he said. "In Mystic, after a plain old snowstorm, any fool knows to wear shoe chains."

"There wasn't any snow up north," Barney informed his dad. "Bust my ass and call me a three-year-old, but once you're finished, can you help us up?"

From the steps, Kate chortled with laughter. Jeremiah glanced over his shoulder. "Kate, get Emma and that child back in the house and set the damned security system. *Now.* I'll knock when I've got this crew on their feet and safe on the porch."

Kate, belatedly realizing that she'd left the entire house unprotected, hurried Chloe, Emma, and Bozo back inside and slammed the front door.

An hour later, Amanda sat at the Sterling kitchen bar with half of a raw potato, with shaved pulp at the center, pressed to her cheekbone. It was Jeremiah's cure for a black eye. Each time she got tired of holding the spud against her skin, someone ordered her to get back to business.

"It works," Kate informed her. "Having raised four boys, I know that for certain."

Kate served coffee and fresh cinnamon rolls to everyone. Over the refreshments, Barney said, "Remember that time, Jeb, when that senior kicked the snot out of you? You were only a freshman, I think, and half his size. He'd flunked senior year three times."

Jeb bristled. "I wasn't *that* little."

Amanda didn't care how big Jeb had been at the beginning of his high school career. All she cared about was that he stood well over six feet tall now, and every ounce of him adored her.

"Well, he did kick your ass," Barney insisted. "When you came home, you looked like you'd tangled with double-strand barbed wire and lost."

Kate interjected, "Watch your language."

Barney gave his mother a wondering look. "Hello, *ass* isn't a curse word. The Virgin Mary rode an ass into Bethlehem to give birth to Jesus in a manger."

Kate popped back, "She rode a donkey, poor darling, and if you read the word 'ass' in the Bible, fine. But in conversation, referring to the anatomy of humans, that is an inappropriate word." Barney cursed under his breath, and his mother said, "I heard that. If you'd like to trade out your cinnamon roll for a bar of soap, I'm ready at any moment."

Amanda had known from the start that she loved Jeb's family, but now, after a spill on the ice, she was seeing them without a polite veneer. She still loved all of them. When she glanced toward her mom, she saw Emma's glowing smile and knew she was equally impressed.

"So when are Ben and Jonas heading home?" Jeremiah asked.

"In the morning," Jeb replied. "On steep grades, that huge, loaded van will lug down." He glanced at Amanda. "I figured we could make better time in my truck and I could grab a good night's sleep here just as well as there."

A few minutes later, Jeb drove everyone home, along with their luggage and Chloe's dollhouse. Barney, who'd left his pickup behind at his parents' house while in Washington, followed them over to make sure all was clear at Jeb's place and that his brother got everyone inside safely.

After Barney left and Amanda had unpacked all their bags, she and Jeb started dinner. Working beside him, Amanda anticipated the coming night, when they'd be alone together in bed. Judging by the lingering looks he gave her, he was thinking along the same lines.

"Miss me?" he asked. "Did you find my messages?"

"More than you'll ever know, and yes, I found your notes. They kept me going. I only wish I'd sneaked some into your duffel." She paused. "I got scared when I couldn't reach you on the cell phone right before you got here."

"Just outside of town, on the old Mystic Highway, the road is really curvy and lined with rock cliffs. I had no reception."

"Why didn't you tell me you were coming home today?"

"We were tired. I wasn't sure we could make it the whole way without stopping, and I didn't want you to be expecting us only to be disappointed."

"Well, it was a nice surprise," she told him.

When the after-dinner routine had run its course, with both Chloe and Emma tucked in for the night, Amanda grabbed Jeb's hand and led him up the stairs to their room. She wanted—no, *needed*—to make love with him. She'd missed the pleasures of physical closeness that she could have only with him.

"I need a shower," he told her as he stripped off his shirt. At her look of disappointment, he grinned. "Join me?"

"In the shower? I've never done it in the shower."

"Then it's high time you experience it."

Moments later, standing with him under a hot spray of water, Amanda discovered the delight of soap-slick bodies while making love. By the time they'd toweled off and slipped into bed, she felt drained but happy in a way she'd never imagined possible.

Before drifting off, she whispered, "I can't live without you. I forgot to tell you that."

On New Year's Day, Amanda enjoyed entertaining Jeb's family again. The meal, bountiful and nearly perfect, was made even better by laughter and stimulating conversation. Emma and Kate seemed to have forged a fast friendship and sat next to each other. Jonas, seated to Amanda's right, celebrated getting high marks on his quarterly finals. Adriel, to Amanda's left, told funny stories about being a receptionist for Dr. Hamilton and Dr. Payne, an internist and a general practitioner, respectively. Ben, sitting next to Adriel, added spice to the volleys by tossing in tidbits about rodeo debacles, the most hilarious one about a notorious, much-feared bull that suddenly decided not to buck.

At the end of the day, Amanda stood near the beautiful spruce to peer out the living room window into the darkness. When Jeb found her and slipped his arms around her waist, she leaned back against him.

"Penny for them."

Amanda struggled to put her feelings into words. "Tomorrow is the second, and the hearing will be only nine days away."

"It's going to be a slam dunk. Johnson doesn't think Mark stands a chance."

Curling her hands over the backs of his wrists, she hugged his arms closer against her. "It isn't that I believe Mark can win in the courtroom. It's more a fear that he'll find some other way to win, some other way to destroy me." She fell silent for a moment. "For the first time since leaving home, I've found happiness, a wonderful man, a loving family, and I even have my mom with us. Everything is perfect, and I know I should just feel thankful, but instead I have an awful feeling of doom."

"Doom?"

"Yes. Don't you see, Jeb? It's all too good to be true. And Mark will stop at nothing, absolutely *nothing*, to ruin it for me."

"Aw, honey. Try to forget about Mark and just enjoy being happy."

Amanda wanted nothing more, but well aware of how cunning Mark was, she sensed, deep down where reason held no sway, that he had a plan. And when he made his strike, no one would be prepared.

Amanda wished she could stop the clock from moving forward, but the days passed like water through a sieve. Before she knew it, the morning of the hearing arrived. Amanda had ordered a lovely suit, a brown straight skirt with a matching jacket to be worn over an ecru silk blouse. She'd found some suede pumps of the same brown. After she dressed, she stood in front of a mirror, wondering where the raggedy Amanda had gone. She looked classy, but in an understated way, which, after conferring with Johnson, she knew was the perfect tone to set. The judge would see a capable, attractive, quietly elegant woman.

Amanda didn't feel elegant; she felt terrified. To reassure Jeb, she forced herself to eat breakfast, but the food didn't settle well, and she was soon in the bathroom purging her stomach. The hearing was set for one that afternoon.

Even though Clyde Johnson had chatted with Amanda several times over the phone, he wanted to meet with her at a restaurant near the courthouse at eleven thirty for a final briefing. She clung to Jeb's hand during the interview, wishing this whole day would speed by and be over. Johnson fired questions at her, some of which he would ask her in the courtroom and some that he guessed the other attorney would hammer her with. By the time the session ended, Amanda's head was swimming. Johnson patted her hand.

"You'll pull it off without a hitch," he said. "I know you're nervous and feeling confused, and while on the stand, you'll have moments when your mind goes blank. If that happens, politely ask for the question to be repeated. It's okay to say that you're feeling nervous. The judge will understand." He tightened his fingers over hers. "Just remember, the opposing attorney *can't* trip you up because you're telling the truth, so even if you get confused or don't catch a question, you'll come across well. Mark, if I'm guessing right, will be calm to a point. He'll smile at some of your answers, trying to convey that everything you're saying is untrue. Don't look at him. Pretend he isn't in the room."

Amanda's mouth and throat felt like cotton. "What if he brings a gun?"

Johnson shook his head. "Metal detectors. He can't get past court security with a weapon, and I've put a bug in the judge's ear that he has done you physical harm in the past and may try again. A court guard will frisk him before he goes through the screener."

Breath whooshed from Amanda's parted lips. "Thank goodness for that."

En route to the courthouse, Jeb talked incessantly, trying to allay Amanda's fears. She clung to his every word.

"I'll be in the spectator area right behind you. Because you're the plaintiff—the person who filed for the divorce—you'll sit on the right, facing the judge. Johnson will sit on your left between you and Mark, who will be seated on the far side of his attorney. So you'll have two lawyers as a buffer. The armed bailiff stands near the bench, where the judge presides over the hearing. The court clerk is also at the front of the courtroom near the judge's bench. So you're going to have quite a few bodies between you and Mark. He'd have to be totally off his rocker to try anything during the hearing."

Amanda took a bracing breath. "Mark *is* totally off his rocker when it comes to me. Always has been, always will be."

"But he also has a finely honed sense of self-preservation. He may get quarrelsome and say insulting things to you or about you, but I doubt he'll do anything more. And he'll pass through a metal detector, remember. In order to hurt you, he can only try a physical attack, and if he does, I'll be there to stop him if Johnson doesn't beat me to the punch. Johnson mentioned once that he was a football linebacker in college. He's gained weight over the years, but I can tell by looking that he still packs a lot of muscle, and I'd bet good money that he can still throw one hell of a punch."

Amanda knew they were drawing closer to the courthouse. She straightened her jacket and fussed with her blouse. "Do I look okay?"

He gave her a measuring look with those warm hazel eyes. "You look beautiful."

Amanda pushed at her hair. "So where will Chloe be? I forgot to ask."

"In a guarded cubicle outside the courtroom. If the judge wishes to speak with her in closed chambers, an armed guard will escort Chloe through an adjacent corridor directly there. She'll never enter the courtroom. Our moms are going to stay with her. There's a DVR, so they're taking some Disney flicks for Chloe to watch."

"Do you think the judge will ask to interview Chloe?"

"Johnson says he doubts it because of Chloe's age. More than likely, the judge will listen to the testimonies, look at the evidence, and make a judgment from the bench. When we leave the courthouse, it should all be over."

"Until Mark goes to trial for the abuse."

Jeb reached over to squeeze Amanda's shoulder. "One thing at a time, honey. Let's get through today. Then we'll worry about the trial."

The moment Amanda entered the courtroom, both her body and her brain went numb. Wood paneling, a low-profile judge's bench, curved seating and desks for the plaintiff and the respondent, mottled gray tile—everything blurred in her vision. Jeb escorted her up the center aisle to an opening in the bar, which divided the gallery from the court arena. Clyde Johnson met them and grasped Amanda's left arm to guide her to the plaintiff's table. Amanda sank into a well-cushioned and sturdily built wooden chair. Johnson sat to her immediate left.

Amanda kept her gaze fixed on the judge's bench, but in her peripheral vision she could see Mark sitting at the respondent's table with a thin, dark-haired man who she guessed was his lawyer. *Why is it that everything else seems hazy, but Mark's face is crystal clear?* She wanted to jump to her feet and flee, only she had nowhere to go. She'd run as far as her limited funds could take her, she'd tried to hide, and regardless of all her efforts, here she was, facing Mark again. He was *staring* at her. Against her will, she flicked a glance at him, and he smiled—that evil curve of his lips she'd learned to dread.

The court clerk called the hearing into session and said, "All rise." She said more, but her words rang like gibberish in Amanda's ears, announcing that the Honorable Somebody was presiding. For a moment Amanda thought, *Oh, no, I missed her last name.* But then she dimly recalled that Johnson had instructed her to call the judge Your Honor, no last name required.

The judge, a plump older woman with short blond hair and solemn gray eyes, took a seat behind the bench, and a rustle of movement followed as everyone sat down. Amanda knew she would be called to testify first, but she wasn't prepared for it to happen so quickly. As she walked on unsteady legs to the witness box, she wanted to scream at the armed bailiff, the court clerk, and the court reporter that this *wasn't* business as usual. A little girl's future hung in the balance, and they acted as if it was only another day.

Amanda took the stand. She thought maybe she was

sworn in, but if she was, she couldn't recall the details. Johnson rose from the plaintiff's table and stepped forward.

"Ms. Banning, would you like a glass of water before we proceed?" he asked.

Amanda tried to bring his broad face into focus. "Um, yes, please, if it isn't too much trouble."

A blurry someone brought Amanda a glass. She clutched it in both hands, thinking, *Don't spill it.*

Johnson asked her a question. Though she didn't quite register what it was, she heard herself replying. Her voice sounded as if it came from deep within a tunnel. *Please, God, help me get through this. Help me protect Chloe.* In a daze, Amanda fielded question after question, and then Johnson resumed his seat to let Mark's attorney cross-examine her.

Panic coursed through Amanda, for she knew this lawyer would come at her with his fangs bared. She searched frantically for tawny hair, a burnished face, and hazel eyes. *Jeb.* He sat two rows back from the petitioner's table, which hadn't been part of their plan. Prior to the judge taking the bench, Johnson had whispered to her why the courtroom was so crowded, saying that divorces were matters of public record and could be watched by anyone. *Divorce, a spectator sport.*

When Amanda locked gazes with Jeb, some of the tension eased from her body. *I can do this.* With Jeb's support, she could survive anything. Then, without meaning to, she locked gazes with Mark. His blue eyes glittered like ice chips, so cold, the hatred in them so venomous, she felt a chill touch her skin. He bared his teeth in that smile again and pursed his lips to blow her a kiss. *The kiss of death*, he'd often called it, just before pulling the trigger of a revolver he held to her temple.

Amanda started to shake. Her brain froze. Mark's attorney cried, "Ms. Banning, I've asked you the same question three times!"

Amanda jerked and forced her gaze to the lawyer, who reminded her of a nasty little weasel, and pushed out, "I'm sorry. Would you please repeat the question?"

He leaned closer to the witness stand. "Can you prove that Mark Banning inflicted any of the injuries you've documented in your photos?"

Amanda groped for an answer. Finally she said, "No."

"Louder, please!"

"No!" Amanda cried.

The attorney threw up his arms and smiled at the judge, as if Amanda's answer said it all. Water slopped from the glass she clenched. The coldness slid over her fingers and puddled on her lap. *My skirt,* she thought, and then realized how stupid it was to worry about her clothing. Chloe was all that mattered. Mark caught her gaze again and sneered. She searched again for Jeb, fixed her gaze on his face, and found the calm to answer the attorney's aggressive questions.

At some point, Mark's lawyer shoved a photograph of Chloe's burned hand under Amanda's nose. The curved wounds from the red-hot stove burner ran deep.

"You *claim* that your husband, Mark Banning, inflicted these burns on your daughter's palm. But you have no photographic evidence of that." He turned toward the judge. "Your Honor, may I suggest to you that children often accidentally burn themselves? There's no proof that Mr. Banning inflicted this injury on the child. In fact, this photographic evidence is so *weak*, I'm amazed that you've allowed it to be presented to the court."

Chapter Twenty-one

No! Amanda wanted to scream the word. Only Johnson's warnings that she should show no anger forestalled her. Mark's attorney sounded so reasonable that the judge might listen to his argument. There *was* no photographic evidence that Mark had inflicted any of the injuries on Chloe. How could anyone who saw those images think that Amanda could have taken snapshots while the incidents occurred? *Oh, God, oh, God, don't let Mark be alone with her.* Amanda had no doubt that he would kill Chloe if given half a chance.

Dizzy with fear, Amanda watched the judge. After studying the picture of Chloe's burned palm, she began flipping through others, her brows creasing in a deep frown. To Mark's attorney, she finally said, "If it were one instance of injury, I might consider your point valid, sir, but there are too many wounds documented in these photos for all of them to have been accidental." She folded her hands atop the stack of pictures. "I will also point out that Mr. Banning will stand trial to determine if he's innocent or guilty of inflicting these injuries. The court's duty today is to grant dissolution of the marriage to the plaintiff and to decide whether or not the minor child will be placed in possible jeopardy if the father is allowed to have unsupervised visitation."

"Yes, Your Honor, but the court's decision today will have bearing upon the outcome of that trial. If the father is granted only supervised visitation with his daughter now, there will be an implication of guilt, which may influence the decision of the Eureka judge."

The judge held up her hand. "The court repeats that the purpose of this hearing is to grant dissolution of the marriage and determine the probability of endangerment to the child if the father is allowed unsupervised visitation." Turning to Amanda, she said, "Ms. Banning, you are free to return to your seat." To Mark's lawyer, she said, "Do you wish to have the respondent testify?"

"I do," the attorney replied.

The court clerk called Mark to the stand. All went well for Mark as he responded to his attorney's questions. Amanda could tell that they had rehearsed his testimony several times. But then Johnson cross-examined. The older attorney went after Mark like a pit bull, tripping him up in his lies.

"My wife *always* had her own car!" Mark shot a blazing glare at Amanda. "She's lying in an attempt to make me look like some kind of monster. I always made sure she had a home phone line, too. What kind of husband would leave his wife stranded without a way to call for help if something happened?"

Johnson shot back, "Can you produce proof that you own a second vehicle and phone bills to document the home phone line?"

Mark lost his composure and nearly shouted, "Of

course. I don't have any paperwork with me, but I can produce it later."

Johnson turned and smiled at Amanda, pretended to check his notes, and then faced the bench again to drop a bomb. "That's peculiar, Mr. Banning, because I hired an investigator to check your phone records and vehicle registrations. According to his findings, you've never had a home phone line at any of your residences, and since your marriage to Ms. Banning, you've owned only one vehicle, an older-model gray Chevy sedan."

Johnson carried the investigative report to the bench for the judge's perusal. She skimmed the paperwork and then cast a questioning look at Mark, whose forehead had beaded with sweat. "How can you explain this, Mr. Banning? I've dealt with this investigator, and he's very thorough."

Mark waved a hand as if to flick away a bothersome gnat. "My credit went bad, so my father purchased the second vehicle and got us the home phone under his name."

An expression of pure delight played upon Johnson's face as he returned to the table to fetch another report. He pivoted to face the bench again. "I anticipated Mr. Banning claiming that, so I had my investigator check to see if any of this man's family members or friends had purchased a second car for Ms. Banning's use." He strode briskly toward the judge to hand her the report. "No car, no phone. Ms. Banning's testimony is the absolute truth. Her husband left her without transportation, telephone, or Internet services, and separated her from all her friends and family."

Mark started to speak, but the judge cut him off. "Need I remind you, Mr. Banning, that you may be charged with perjury if you give false testimony in my court?"

Mark yelled, "I'm not giving false testimony!" He pointed at Amanda. "She's the liar here! She abandoned me! She took my child away from me and kept her hidden from me for nearly six months!"

The judge brought down her gavel. "Order in the court! Lower your voice and remain in control, Mr. Banning, or the court will find you in contempt."

When Mark shouted a curse at the judge, she slammed the gavel down again. "The court rules in favor of the plaintiff, Ms. Amanda Banning. Dissolution of the marriage is granted and will be final in ninety days. Mr. Banning is granted court-supervised bimonthly visitation with his daughter, two hours per visit. Under no circumstances shall the child be alone with her father. If Mr. Banning is found to be innocent of the abuse charges in a Eureka court of law, the presiding judge can, and undoubtedly will, grant the father a more lenient visitation plan."

After releasing a pent-up breath, Amanda grabbed for more oxygen, her lungs burning. *We won!* The decision was in Chloe's favor. She'd be kept safe. Amanda couldn't think beyond that.

"But, Your Honor," Mark's attorney cried, "this is—"

The judge used her gavel again. "The court has ruled."

Amanda wanted to shout with joy, but instead she grasped the desk edge and clamped down with her fingers to stop from making a sound.

Mark leaped from the witness stand and rammed into the bailiff with such force that he sent the unprepared officer reeling off his feet. For Amanda everything went into freeze-frame mode. She saw Mark charging toward her, but time seemed to stop after each stride he took. Something white slipped from the right sleeve of his sport coat. "You lying, treacherous *bitch*! I'm a fit father, damn you! The breadwinner! My daughter has never gone without a single necessity!"

Amanda's gaze froze on the object in Mark's hand. With one terrified glance, she took in a serrated, heavy-duty plastic tool sharpened to a deadly point and less than a foot long—able to lie along Mark's forearm between his wrist and the bend of his elbow.

And he meant to kill her with it.

Clyde Johnson, standing before the judge's bench, had been only momentarily caught off guard, and he whirled to block Mark's path, but the assailant's momentum knocked the attorney back against the table.

"Order in the court!" the judge screamed. "Resume your seat, Mr. Banning!"

Amanda knew no one could stop Mark. She had to stop him herself. Shooting to her feet, she grabbed the arms of her chair and, with strength she never realized she possessed, swung the heavy piece of furniture up to shield herself just as Mark, now with only the table between them, slashed at her with the weapon. The chair lurched in her grasp as the hard, sharpened plastic dug into the underside of the leather-covered seat.

She heard a woman scream. Jeb's voice rang out. "Get out of my way, damn it! Out of my *way*!"

Amanda dimly realized that Jeb's path was blocked by people who'd sprung to their feet. *Alone, I'm all alone.* As that thought sank into her brain, anger exploded within her. In flashes, she saw a series of images, all of Mark coming after her. Always before, she'd been so scared that she couldn't think. *Not this time.* She swung the chair at Mark, nearly knocking him off balance. With a flurry of jabs, he came at her again with the blade. She met each thrust with the chair, knowing that if he got past the barrier it made, she'd be dead.

In a blur, she saw Johnson regain his footing. It didn't matter if Jeb could reach her or if Johnson could intervene. She'd learned over the last many months that she *could* stand on her own two feet. She'd learned that she *wasn't* stupid or ugly. But most important, she'd imagined herself taking Mark on, time after time, with nothing but a cast-iron skillet or a butcher knife. A heavy upholstered chair worked better. No matter how much force Mark put behind his thrusts, he couldn't penetrate wood and leather, and he couldn't knock her down as long as the sturdy table was between them.

She would defend herself this time—or die trying. She'd finally found happiness for both her and Chloe, and she would *not* allow Mark to steal that from either of them.

When Mark drew back to take another stab at her, Amanda saw an opening and swung the chair at him again. He staggered but didn't go down. He looked startled for an instant, and then pure murder returned to his blue eyes. Crazy, mindless, maniacal rage. Shouts rang out from behind her. She heard another woman scream. In her peripheral vision, she saw the bailiff regain his feet. From a side doorway, she glimpsed other officers bursting into the courtroom.

"I *told* you I'd see you dead if you ever ran from me!" Mark yelled. "Stupid cow!"

Amanda wished she had the strength to raise the chair high enough to bring it down on his head. But that would leave her body unprotected, and he would stab her. It was safer to let the wood and upholstery take the punishment. Somewhere in the din, she heard Jeb yell again, "Get the *hell* out of my way!" So she knew he was coming. She would hold Mark off until Jeb could tackle him.

Only it wasn't Jeb who body-slammed Mark. It was the big, burly Johnson, her cranky but kindhearted attorney. He lunged forward, body hunched, and launched himself into a tackle, colliding with Mark on his right and grabbing his legs. Mark hurtled sideways and hit the floor near the witness box like a felled tree.

Clearly prepared for a tussle, Johnson said in a voice gruff with anger, "Move, you miserable son of a bitch. Just try it."

Court deputies rushed forward, guns drawn. But Mark didn't move. Amanda, still holding the chair up with trembling arms, stared in mounting horror at her husband's still body. He lay with one arm flung outward. His other arm, the one that had been brandishing the knife, was tucked under his body. Stunned, her brain struggling to make sense of what she was seeing, she felt frozen in place.

Johnson rose to his knees. "Oh, God, did he hit his head? He's unconscious."

The stupefied bailiff collected his wits and went down on one knee to probe Mark's neck. "Call an ambulance!" he yelled. "No pulse! I've got no pulse!"

Amanda dropped the chair, her overstrained arms dangling uselessly at her sides. Her gaze fixed on the crimson pool of blood seeping out from under Mark's body, she blinked away black spots and struggled not to collapse. Suddenly strong arms encircled her torso to hold her erect. She *recognized* those arms.

"I tried to sit right behind you, but strangers took the first row. When he went after you, everybody panicked and left their seats. I couldn't get to you. I'm sorry, so sorry."

A big hand curled over the back of Amanda's head and turned her face against a chest that she had explored many times with her fingertips. "I think he's gone, sweetheart. Don't look."

Amanda registered Jeb's words and decided that she preferred to remember Mark this way. At least then maybe she wouldn't awaken from nightmares for the rest of her life, seeing him come after her or Chloe. She resisted the press of Jeb's palm and turned, still safe in his embrace, to stare at her dead husband. All she could think was that God had answered her prayer. Mark would never harm Chloe again.

Amanda had to answer only a few questions once the police descended upon the courtroom. Mark had made his last attempt on her life in front of too many witnesses, a judge included, for there to be any uncertainties about the cause of his injury. Amanda would always remember the judge's kindly gaze settling briefly upon her face before she told the police, "Leave the poor woman alone. He tried to kill her. I saw it, and his death was an accident. When Mr. Johnson tackled him to protect his client, Mr. Banning fell onto the lethal weapon in his hand and impaled himself."

The police officers seemed disinclined to badger a presiding judge with questions. The usual investigative procedures were disregarded. Paramedics removed Mark's body from the scene, and all that remained of him was a dark, quickly drying pool of blood on the mottled gray tile. Spectators lingered until the judge ordered everyone but the involved parties to leave her courtroom.

Still robed, she descended from her bench to approach Amanda, who remained in the safe circle of Jeb's arms. Jeb released her to stand alone to face the judge, but he kept a firm grip on her elbow in case her legs went out from under her.

The older woman grasped Amanda's icy hands. "I apologize for this. The metal detector couldn't pick up on a plastic weapon, and the officers obviously failed to check the forearms during their standard pat-down."

Amanda struggled to register what the judge said. Her voice seemed to ping off the walls of her mind like ricocheting BBs.

The judge went on to say, "That knife probably lay flat against his arm, not creating the usual bulge, so the court deputy might have missed it if he did pat the forearms. Mr. Banning filed the handle down to make it as streamlined as possible." She squeezed Amanda's hands, then glanced at the crimson evidence of Mark's sudden departure from this world. "It's clear to me that your husband knew that he would be prosecuted and serve a sentence for the horrible things he did to you and your little girl. Today's hearing and my judgment pushed him over the edge."

Amanda finally collected her wits. "He saw his life crumbling."

"I've had many men like Mark Banning come before my bench." The judge stepped back. Tipping her blond head, she studied Jeb's tanned countenance. With a smile at Amanda, she said, "I think you've found happiness now with someone else. You need to move forward and put the past behind you. I know it will be difficult, but try your best not to hate Mr. Banning. You'll heal more quickly and be better off in the long run if you simply accept that he couldn't help being what he was."

At that moment, Amanda was too shaken to consider how she was meant to move forward. So she said, "Thank you for your kindness, Your Honor."

The judge nodded. "Your little girl has already been removed from the building by her grandmothers. They waited until the emergency vehicles left so the child wouldn't be traumatized. One of the court deputies says that your daughter was complaining about missing the last part of her movie and was promised by her grandmothers that she could watch the rest at home."

Jeb sighed. "That sounds like our Chloe."

Smiling, the judge replied, "She is a happy, normal little girl. Think carefully before telling her how her father died. Children don't always need to hear the absolute truth. Sometimes they handle things better if they are told a different version of the truth, with some sort of happy ending. You can give her no greater gift than that."

Amanda sagged against Jeb as the judge turned away.

Once they were home—and Amanda had come to consider Jeb's house as her home—she felt like a bit of dandelion fluff floating along on the surface of a babbling brook, where the sound of water gurgling over stones surrounded her. Her mom and all of Jeb's family crowded the house, creating a drone of conversation that changed pitches. She noticed that Jeb was nowhere to be seen and wandered numbly from room to room in search of him.

Jeremiah caught her hand. "Hey, sweetheart, you look worried. What's wrong?"

Amanda struggled to speak. "I can't find Jeb." She felt as if she were emerging from a thick, blinding fog. "Mark—he's really dead, isn't he?"

"Yes. I'm sorry. At some point in your life, you must have loved him."

Amanda tried to remember when she'd loved Mark — or at least *believed* she had. Now that she had found true love with Jeb, her girlhood concepts of the emotion seemed foolish, and they'd turned out to be dangerous, too. "I need Jeb. I can't find him."

Jeremiah gathered her close in his strong arms. "Chloe overheard someone say that her daddy died today. Jeb took her upstairs to do some damage control."

After receiving strength and warmth from Jeremiah's embrace, Amanda went upstairs. *Damage control.* On the way home, she and Jeb had decided to stick as close to the truth as possible when they told Chloe about her father's death, saying that he'd been killed in a horrible accident. Amanda was thankful that Jeb had taken the initiative to talk with Chloe, because she couldn't think clearly right now, and her daughter needed honest but gentle answers to her questions.

Amanda opened the door to what had once been her and Chloe's barricaded sanctuary. Jeb lay on the bed with Chloe cuddled close against his chest, the slobbery Bozo and the tiny Frosty snuggling on the mattress beside them. Amanda took care, even in her dazed state, to enter and close the door without making a sound. She could trust Jeb to take care of her daughter.

Chloe said, "So my mean daddy fell on a knife?"

Jeb stroked her hair and drew her closer. "Yes. It was an awful accident. The ambulance came right away, but the paramedics couldn't help. Your daddy was already gone."

"Why did he have a knife?" Chloe asked.

Jeb smoothed her hair. "No one really knows, but lots

of men carry knives." He fished in his pocket for the utility knife that Amanda had gotten him for Christmas. "See mine? Ever since your mommy gave it to me, I've carried it almost constantly."

"Did they take my mean daddy to a place where they keep dead people in a great big refrigerator?"

Even in her fog, Amanda winced. How had Chloe learned about morgues? *Please, Jeb, don't leave her with that awful picture in her mind.*

Jeb gave the girl a gentle jostle. "Heck, no. The angels came and took your father straight to heaven, honey."

"But where's his earth body?"

Pain settled behind Amanda's eyes. Her daughter was too smart for her own good.

Jeb said, "It doesn't matter, Chloe. When people die and go to heaven to be with God, their bodies aren't part of them anymore."

"I don't know if God will want him," Chloe murmured.

"Of course He will. I'm not saying that your daddy was good. I know he was really, *really* mean to you and your mommy. But that was down here. In heaven, nobody's mean. Everyone loves each other."

"So he'll never be a mean daddy again?"

"Nope," Jeb replied.

"Not even if a puppy piddles on the floor? I had a puppy named Spots, and my mean daddy threw him against a wall and broke his neck."

Amanda leaned more heavily against the closed door, so exhausted that she could no longer trust her legs. She clung to Jeb's words just as much as her daughter did. As the judge had said, Mark hadn't been able to help being what he was. Surely God, in His Goodness, would bar nobody from heaven for being sick. And Mark had been so very sick.

"In heaven, puppies piddle on the clouds, and it doesn't make a mess," Jeb said. "And everyone loves them and takes good care of them. Now that your daddy is in heaven, he'll feel sorry that he hurt your puppy down here on earth, and from now on they'll be best pals, because your daddy won't ever be mean again."

"Will God be mad at me if I feel a little bit glad that my mean daddy fell on his knife?" Chloe asked.

Jeb planted a kiss on her forehead. "Not for a second. You were afraid of your father, and it's natural for you to feel a little bit glad that you'll never have to feel afraid again. It's not that you're glad your daddy died, honey. You're just relieved because now you and your mommy can feel safe."

"You make me feel very safe," Chloe said. "You and Bozo."

"That's nice. I'm happy we make you feel protected."

Chloe placed a tiny hand on Jeb's cheek. "I love you, Daddy Jeb."

"I love you, too, princess. You'll never know how much until you hold your own little girl in your arms."

Chloe grinned. "Will you love me even if I turn all your chickens loose again?"

Jeb chuckled. "I will, but can you wait until the ice melts? I fall a lot farther than you do, and hitting the ice hurt my bum."

She giggled. "It was so funny when you slid into the pigpen!"

Jeb grinned. "That's it. You get the ultimate punishment!" He wiggled his fingertips over Chloe's ribs, and she shrieked with laughter. "Tickle, tickle," Jeb said.

Chloe began tickling him back, and Jeb pretended to go weak. When the game ended, Chloe snuggled against him and closed her eyes. Amanda saw the beautiful gift of acceptance and closure in the expression on her daughter's face and slipped silently from the room. She moved toward the suite at the end of the hallway that she and Jeb shared, lay down on the bed, and held close what she'd heard Jeb tell her daughter.

It was over, finally over, and Amanda was able to bid Mark good-bye without any hatred. Perhaps he'd been born with something vital missing inside him. But it comforted Amanda to think that now, secure in heaven, Mark would be whole and filled only with love. It would be a good way for her to think of him from now on.

She closed her eyes, wishing that she could feel at least a trace of sadness. The father of her child was dead.

A moment later, the mattress sank under Jeb's weight, and she turned to seek the haven of his arms.

"You must feel as if you've been hit by a train," he murmured. "I'm so sorry, Mandy. It was a horrible way for his life to end."

"I can't feel sad," she whispered. "What kind of person can't feel sad when the father of her child dies?"

He tightened his arms around her. "Right now, you're in shock. He tried his damnedest to kill you. Even worse, he must have spent hours filing down that knife, which means it was premeditated. Go easy on yourself, okay? In time, sadness will come, if for no other reason than because Mark's life was such a waste."

"Thank you for talking with Chloe. I overheard a lot of it, and you did a fabulous job, ending the conversation with laughter."

He toyed with a tendril of hair at her temple. "I didn't

want it to be a talk that ended sadly, or for her to feel any trace of guilt. It's time for both of you to move on. She fell asleep, and I think she'll have sweet dreams."

Amanda locked her arms around his neck. "Make the numbness go away, Jeb. I don't want to sleep. I need you to make love to me. I need to feel *alive*."

"Now that's a request I can deliver on." He left her briefly to lock their bedroom door, and as he walked back toward her, he stripped off his shirt. In the fading sunlight that came through the window, every burnished line of his upper body glimmered like a carving of oiled teak. When he slipped under the covers, he asked, "Have I told you today how much I love you?"

Amanda shifted to trail kisses across his chest. "I'd rather you show me."

Epilogue

Eight months later . . .

Large with child, Amanda sat on a plastic lawn chair and sipped lemonade while watching Jeb put the finishing touches on two cradles, one smaller for Chloe's doll, the other larger for their baby boy, due to make his debut in a month. Chloe played nearby. A warm, mid-September breeze wafted through the cavernous shop, dissipating the fumes of the stain Jeb was applying to the well-sanded wood. Amanda wished she could help, but standing for any period of time made her back hurt, and Jeb had grown paranoid about protecting her and their unborn son. She wasn't allowed to reach up high to get anything off a shelf, because he'd been told that if a woman stretched, the umbilical cord could coil around the fetus's neck. *Old wives' tale.* She hadn't been allowed to help hang wallpaper in the nursery, either, because the fumes from the paste might be bad for her. Now, if she even wandered close to admire the cradles, Jeb shooed her away.

She'd tossed a crumpled pink message at his feet that

read, *I don't think a faint whiff of stain will hurt me or the baby*. With his stout woodworking pencil, he'd written back and dropped his answer on her lap because bending over was difficult for her now. *Humor me. I love both of you too much to take any chances*.

Their occasional use of pink slips of paper to communicate had become a tradition that Amanda hoped would last a lifetime. She anticipated their children finding romantic messages all over the house, and being appalled once they became teenagers. When Jeb had to work in the field and leave her for the day, she found notes from him tucked in places where she'd be sure to find them. By the coffee machine, where she now made herbal tea, she'd find, *Do you know how beautiful you are?* Or stuffed among her cosmetics, which she could now afford, *I didn't want to wake you. You and the baby need your rest. Just want you to know how very much I love you*.

They'd also started to settle squabbles with what Jeb called pink slips. *I'm sorry I was a witch,* she'd write. And on the same paper, he'd reply, *It's only hormone fluctuations, honey*. Or he'd jot, *I'm sorry I was cranky last night*. To Amanda, Jeb's definition of *cranky* didn't even rank on her charts. When he came home after a long workday, he liked to have a half hour of quiet time to read the daily news online, and Chloe, who adored him, often infringed upon his privacy and demanded attention. Sometimes he would be firm about her waiting until his thirty minutes was up; then later he'd feel guilty about it. *Cranky?* In Amanda's opinion, he was only setting boundaries that Chloe needed to respect.

She sighed now, holding a palm over her belly to feel their son move inside her. *A tiny miracle*. Jeb shared that sentiment, pressing his ear to her abdomen to hear his son's heartbeat and getting tears in his eyes when he felt the baby move. Life was good. In fact, life with Jeb, in and of itself, was also a miracle. She laughed often, and she felt cherished when he held her in his arms as they drifted off to sleep at night. How much better could it get?

Amanda was distracted from her musings by Chloe, who sat cross-legged on the floor, flanked by Bozo and Frosty, to play with Barbie and Ken. The dolls had been gifts from Chloe's aunts, Adriel and Sarah, for Chloe's big birthday party in May.

With a sharpened ear, Amanda listened to the pretend dialogue taking place between Ken and Barbie, all the words intoned by Chloe's high-pitched voice. "I, Jebediah Paul Sterling, take thee, Amanda Marie Lang, to be my wedded wife, to have and to hold from this day forward, for better and better, for richer and richer, in good health and better health, to love and to cherish until we both go to heaven." When the doll ceremony ended, Chloe threw pink slips of paper at Barbie and Ken before putting them in their car to go away on their honeymoon.

Amanda glanced at Jeb to see him grinning from ear to ear. This was one of his favorite doll enactments, re-creating their marriage on the Mystic Creek natural bridge. Jeb loved listening to Chloe's projection of their future, that they'd be either rich or even richer, never sick, and would love each other forever. The word *poor* had no place in the girl's predictions.

Listening to the child took Amanda back to that balmy day in early July when she and Jeb had exchanged their spiritual vows. Jeb had insisted that their marriage take place on the natural bridge, mostly to reassure Chloe that her mom and new daddy had found true and everlasting love. Nevertheless it had been beautiful, with Chloe giving away the bride. Already heavy with child and wearing a wedding dress that mostly hid her condition, Amanda had climbed to the apex of the rock archway from one side of the creek while Jeb approached from the other. They'd met in the middle to stand before Patrick Sully, the preacher from Praying Hands Community Church. After the nuptials, the reception had been held at Peck's Red Rooster Restaurant, with guests overflowing onto the deck above the creek. When Amanda and Jeb escaped to his truck to leave for their honeymoon, the crowd of well-wishers threw pink slips of paper at them instead of confetti or rice. Kate and her daughters had spent hours online, finding short quotations about true love and pasting them into a document, which they later printed out on pink paper and cut into individual strips. People who'd volunteered to clean up after the party had found the inspirational messages. *Love is a bridge over troubled water. True love waits. Love conquers all.*

Suddenly tiring of her pretend world, Chloe frowned and scratched Bozo behind the ears. Then she angled her gaze at Amanda. "Mommy, I've changed my mind about wanting a baby brother. My friend Molly has one, and he's a total brat who won't leave us alone to play with our dolls." Chloe made a face. "During our last playdate at her house, he pulled off her Barbie's arm and hid it. Then their dog found it and ate it."

Jeb flashed Amanda a look of alarm, a question in his eyes that couldn't have been clearer if he'd said it aloud. *What the hell do we say?*

Amanda giggled. Placing a cupped palm over her swollen middle, she told her daughter, "You'll just have to put your dolls away where they're safe from your brother, Chloe. It's a little too late to cancel our order for a baby. This little guy will arrive next month whether you still want him or not."

Chloe's frown turned into a scowl. Then her expression brightened. "Can I hold him sometimes?"

"Of course," Amanda replied. "In fact, I'll appreciate all the help I can get. I'll show you how to change his diaper and how to burp him after he eats."

Chloe scrambled to her feet and ran from the shop toward Emma's new mother-in-law apartment, yelling with each step, "Grammy, guess what! I'm going to get to hold my baby brother and maybe change his diaper!"

Jeb and Amanda shared a long look, both of them smiling. His diamond-studded wedding band twinkled in a shaft of sunlight. Amanda had used the money she'd gotten in a court settlement from her former landlord to buy the ring, and Jeb wore it with pride, refusing to take it off even while he worked.

"How's Chloe going to handle it when we reach our goal of having four kids?" he asked.

Amanda considered the question. She had lived her life as an only child and actually wanted six children, a secret yearning she'd share with Jeb at some point, possibly on a pink slip. "I suspect she'll try to cancel the next two orders at the eleventh hour. But as time wears on, she'll adjust."

Jeb gazed past her at the house. "Four kids," he mused aloud. "I designed every inch of that place for a big family, and now it'll be filled to the brim someday."

Amanda got pregnant so easily that *someday* might arrive quicker than he thought. "What if we end up with more than four?"

He gave her a long look. "A man who loves his wife— and I adore you—does something before she gets overloaded. Four kids will be a lot of work for you."

Oh, how Amanda loved him. "What if I decide I want six, though, so one day we'll have kids coming home for huge family dinners, just like your parents do?"

He shrugged, the looseness of his shoulders telling her he'd be fine with that. "We'll see how you feel as we go. Pregnancies can take a toll on a woman's health. If we end up with only Chloe and this baby, I'll be happy. But having grown up in a large family, I'm not averse to the idea of six, either. If God blesses us with that many, I can always add on to the house."

Amanda hugged his answer close. His first concern was for her welfare. How awesome was that? There had been a time in the recent past when Amanda had stopped believing that her dreams could ever come true. Now she knew for certain that they could, because she was living her dream with this man, who'd found his way to her by reading messages she'd sent flying away on the wind.

Life truly was a dance, and as the rhythm changed, she would learn the new steps, safe in Jeb Sterling's strong arms.

ALSO AVAILABLE FROM
NEW YORK TIMES BESTSELLING AUTHOR

Catherine Anderson

WALKING ON AIR
A Valance Family Novel

Random, Colorado, is just another stop on the road for solitary gunslinger Gabriel Valance. But when an upstart gunslinger catches Gabe off guard and shoots him down, he regrets his empty, lonely life with his last breath.

Golden-haired beauty Nancy Hoffman settled in Random after fleeing an abusive past. Caring for her younger sister and working in a hat shop help her to forge ahead, though she remains fearful and mistrustful of men—and marriage.

Their paths will cross when Gabe gets a second chance at life and a divine mission: to sweep Nancy off her feet, gain her trust, and convince her to believe in his love. And in doing so, the once-hardened cowboy may save himself....

"One of the finest writers of romance."
—#1 *New York Times* bestselling author Debbie Macomber

Available wherever books are sold or at
penguin.com

'JAN - - 2015   S0560